THE SORORITY

Mac leaned back in her chair and thought about Gavin and what he'd said, not just on the phone call in the middle of last night, not just at the hospital, but also his earlier call and at the cemetery parking lot.

Ethan was killed by The Sorority. One of them did it, or maybe more . . .

It was Kristl . . .

If not Kristl, one of the other of them. Maybe all of them . . .

They all had sex with him . . .

Was that true? *All* of them? Sounded like hyperbole to Mac, but she'd agreed to look into Ethan's death and she would . . .

Books by Nancy Bush

CANDY APPLE RED	YOU CAN'T ESCAPE
ELECTRIC BLUE	YOU DON'T KNOW ME
ULTRAVIOLET	THE KILLING GAME
WICKED GAME	DANGEROUS BEHAVIOR
WICKED LIES	OMINOUS
SOMETHING WICKED	NO TURNING BACK
WICKED WAYS	ONE LAST BREATH
WICKED DREAMS	JEALOUSY
UNSEEN	BAD THINGS
BLIND SPOT	THE BABYSITTER
HUSH	THE GOSSIP
NOWHERE TO RUN	THE NEIGHBORS
NOWHERE TO HIDE	THE CAMP
NOWHERE SAFE	THE SORORITY
SINISTER	THE PSYCHIC
I'LL FIND YOU	

Published by Kensington Publishing Corp.

THE SORORITY

NANCY BUSH

ZEBRA BOOKS
Kensington Publishing Corp.
kensingtonbooks.com

ZEBRA BOOKS are published by

Kensington Publishing Corp.
900 Third Avenue
New York, NY 10022

Copyright © 2024 by Nancy Bush

This book is a work of fiction. Names, characters, businesses, organizations, places, events, and incidents either are the product of the author's imagination or are used fictitiously. Any resemblance to actual persons, living or dead, events, or locales is entirely coincidental.

All rights reserved. No part of this book may be reproduced in any form or by any means without the prior written consent of the Publisher, excepting brief quotes used in reviews.

To the extent that the image or images on the cover of this book depict a person or persons, such person or persons are merely models and are not intended to portray any character or characters featured in the book.

If you purchased this book without a cover you should be aware that this book is stolen property. It was reported as "unsold and destroyed" to the Publisher, and neither the Author nor the Publisher has received any payment for this "stripped book."

All Kensington titles, imprints, and distributed lines are available at special quantity discounts for bulk purchases for sales promotion, premiums, fundraising, and educational or institutional use.

Special book excerpts or customized printings can also be created to fit specific needs. For details, write or phone the office of the Kensington Sales Manager: Kensington Publishing Corp., 900 Third Avenue, New York, NY 10022. Attn. Sales Department. Phone: 1-800-221-2647.

ZEBRA BOOKS and the Zebra logo Reg. U.S. Pat. & TM Off.

Zebra Books trade paperback printing: September 2024
Zebra Books mass market paperback printing: July 2025

ISBN-13: 978-1-4201-5729-1
ISBN-13: 978-1-4201-5571-6 (eBook)

10 9 8 7 6 5 4 3 2 1

Printed in the United States of America

The authorized representative in the EU for product safety and compliance is eucomply OU, Parnu mnt 139b-14, Apt 123
Tallinn, Berlin 11317, hello@eucompliancepartner.com

THE
SORORITY

PROLOGUE

The last day of Ethan Stanhope's life happened to be his last day at River Glen High School. Graduation day. Finally the end, finally, he thought as he swung into the school to pick up his cap and gown, having forgotten it every damn day this week even though his mother had been grinding her teeth each time she had to remind him.

But that was over, he thought, as he drove his black BMW into the lot and strode toward the school's front doors.

"Hi, Ethan!"

"Hey, Ethan!

"Yoo-hoo, *Ethan!*"

"ETHAN!"

A group of girls were waving frantically at him as he approached the high school's front steps. *Freshmen*, he smirked to himself. Almost sophomores but he wouldn't be around to see that happen. Nodding toward them with his usual half smile, he chuckled as they fell all over themselves in hysterical giggles. He was a graduating senior. And captain of the water polo team.

And king of the prom this year, although he'd taken off his crown as soon as the foil-and-glitter piece of junk was laid on his head and then he'd purposely placed it atop Katie Ergon-Smith's instead. From her wheelchair she gazed up at him in adoration, her cheeks turning pink. He didn't know why she was in the chair; some kind of birth defect he never knew the name of. Really sucked. He then bumped fists with Katie, smiled at her while ignoring his "queen," and the crowd had gone wild.

The queen was Mia Beckwith, his girlfriend. Ex-girlfriend now as she'd iced him out ever since he'd fooled around with Roxie Vernon at Gavin Knowles's parents' pool house during the senior barbeque. He'd told Mia that nothing had happened between him and Roxie, and really not much had. Roxie was a tease, which he could admit he kind of liked. It was just . . . well, there'd been less than a month of school left at the time and he'd wanted to do something else. Be with someone else before there was no more school, no more seeing everybody every day.

Sorry, Freshmen, he thought as he chirped his tires and raced his BMW out of the school parking lot. *I am fuckin' outta here.*

After this afternoon's graduation ceremony his classmates were once again gathering at Gavin's, once everyone took care of the "have-tos" with their own families. Gavin's parents had purposely left again, tacitly allowing Gavin to have the party for his class. But Ethan didn't really want to go if Roxie wasn't going to be there, and he'd asked her if she would be there and she'd simply shrugged. He didn't know what that meant. She'd been hard to pin down since the pool party. He just felt . . . unsatisfied. He'd kissed Roxie in the pool house, but she hadn't really kissed him back. She'd stood in front of him and intimated that he was too needy, which had really pissed him off. Needy? Who the hell was she to tell him what he was when everyone knew what a slut she was.

He'd opened his dumb mouth and said as much and she'd smiled and asked, "Who's the slut here?"

He'd pointed to himself in surprise. She couldn't mean him. "Guys aren't sluts," he'd said. "We're bees, sampling all the honey." He'd laughed, expecting her to, too. After all, she and that guy from Laurelton had been going at it for years.

"Is that right?" she'd challenged, pushing him onto the pool house cot. He'd tried to struggle upward but she'd leaned over and reached for the button of his pants and so he'd frozen in place, watching as she slowly pulled his jeans over his hips, then his boxers, then stared at his engorged cock. And when she'd bent over closer he'd groaned aloud in anticipation, but all she'd done was kiss his dick and then give it a friendly pat. "Not tonight," she said with a small smile.

"Fuck, no. You can't leave me like this!"

"Sometimes that's what we sluts do," was her dry response. "C'mon, Rox." He'd grabbed her hand and tried to yank it down to his dick, but she'd twisted away.

Through a haze of frustrated desire he'd heard, "Sorry, Ethan. No can do."

Then she'd sauntered out of the pool house and he'd had to wait a while to cool his blood before following after her. But then, of course, one of Mia's friends had seen him follow her out of the pool house and put two and two together. Everyone assumed he and Roxie had had sex and though Ethan halfheartedly stated that they hadn't, Gavin had thrown back his head and roared. "Sure. Wink, wink, Bro." He'd exaggeratedly closed and opened one eye a couple of times, grinning like an idiot. Ethan had let him think what he would.

Of course Roxie also maintained that nothing had happened between them, but no one had believed her. Mia had flat out called Roxie a slut, too, which had gotten more of a reaction from her than Ethan's comment had. Really pissed her off, even though, well, yeah, they all knew she was one. A real bitch, teaser, slut. Yet, Ethan wouldn't say so aloud because he still thought there was a chance they might get together at Gavin's, now that he and Mia were unofficially through. After that pool house meeting he'd gone home to learn Roxie had left red lipstick on his skin, and the realization had made him groan some more and engage in a little self-love.

He wanted more.

After collecting his cap and gown Ethan suffered through the graduation ceremonies at the school auditorium later that afternoon, watching as Roxie's long legs took her across the stage to receive her diploma. His parents were planning a full-on event at the country club for Sunday, but Ethan could only think about getting to Gavin's house tonight.

At five o'clock Ethan called Gavin to ascertain when to arrive. He didn't want to be the first one to show up, but if Roxie was already there . . .

"Nobody's here. Nobody good, anyway," Gavin informed him on a disgusted sigh. "All that graduation shit. I told my parents to just take my brother and get the hell out, and they were glad to leave."

"Who's there?"

"Well, the Sorority bitches."

"What about Mia?"

"Well, yeah, she's with 'em. Like always. You still into her? She's a bitch. They all are."

"Mia's good," Ethan had protested. "We don't hate each other."

"You sure about that?"

"Why? She say something?"

"No, but the rest of 'em. They're all standing around in judgment, man."

"Is Roxie there?" He tossed the question in lightly, but Gavin was all over it.

"Stop thinking about her, Bro. It's messing with your head, and we're done here. School's over. Graduation's over. Foxy Roxie's probably out screwing someone else. You know what she's like."

"Yeah, well, it wasn't like that between us."

"So you say, so you say . . . look, get over here and cheer these fucking 'sorority' bitches up like only you can do."

"What do you mean?"

"You know what I mean," Gavin said on a half laugh, half snort. "I'm gonna get hammered and maybe get laid, but not with any of them. They're all yours."

Ethan felt his hopes sink. If Roxie wasn't there, he really didn't want to go.

And he really didn't want to see Mia, and the rest of her posse. Leigh and Kristl and *Natalie*. God, she was one strange girl. And the other one, what the fuck was her name? The mousy one . . . Erin. That was it. Ethan was fully aware he could have any one of them at any time, no matter how much they professed to hate him, no matter how much they rallied around Mia. In fact, he'd had a few of them. . . .

Ethan shook himself all over. The heebie-jeebies. He hoped to God he would never see any of them ever again after tonight.

Gavin had actually tried to make it with Erin, at Ethan's encouragement. But she was needy and whiny and that hadn't worked out. None of them were worth anything but Mia, and even she had gotten on Ethan's nerves. It annoyed him no end that since the Roxie incident she'd stopped talking to him, but it was a relief, too. He could do whatever he wanted now.

And what he wanted was Roxie.

An hour and a half later he showed up at Gavin's. Maybe nothing had been happening earlier, but the party was in full swing now. Wasn't even seven and some of the guys were really wasted and loud, and so were some of the girls. Not Mia's group. They were all standing together and looking dead sober. Okay, maybe Erin Humbolt was staggering a bit, but the others were as grim as unsuspecting parents who'd stumbled upon a rager in their backyard. He noticed Mia's black hair, clipped back at her nape like always. She was talking to Jeremy Orsini, a total piece of shit.

Natalie lifted her chin in his direction, throwing him recognition. She'd zeroed in on him as soon as he'd entered through the back gate. She, too, had black hair, but unlike Mia, whose skin glowed with good health, Natalie's pallor was pale as death. Natalie Hofstetter was totally Goth, like she'd just climbed out of a coffin. And she was grim like that, too. Mia said she was the leader of their group. Kinda spoke for how much fun the lot of them were.

He watched as Natalie leaned toward Kristl Cuddahy, who was the tallest and heaviest of their group. Kristl was looking over at him, too. She wore a one-piece swimsuit instead of a bikini to probably contain the flab. The only attractive part of her was her reddish hair, and he momentarily pictured it in a soft blanket over his abdomen as her head bobbed up and down, her hot tongue and mouth on his shaft.

But she was nothing like Roxie. He imagined himself pumping away between Roxie's tan legs. He bet she was a wildcat, screaming and clawing. He thought about the red lips she'd left on his dick again, an indelible picture in his mind, and had to shake himself back to the moment.

He waved frantically at the lot of them, pretending to be crazily overjoyed to see them. Not one of them waved back, although Leigh surreptitiously lifted a few fingers. Leigh Denning had light brown hair and was sort of cute, but she was flat-chested and Mia said she was emotional. Mia, for all her proclaiming to love her "sisters," was full of shit.

Roxie was nowhere in sight. How she was even part of their group was a mystery. He'd learned they'd named themselves The Sorority. He snorted. More like The Coven. He laughed out loud. That was a good one. He was going to have to remember to tell Gavin.

He meandered over to a sweating metal tub full of ice, beer, and soft drinks and pulled out a tall one, but then another girl—an underclassman, he decided, since he didn't know her—talked him into a glass of punch. He accepted the pink drink and tossed back half of it, then set it down as some more people arrived. By this time it was finally getting dark and the air was starting to chill, so Ethan headed around the side of the house and to his car to retrieve his jacket.

He nearly ran into Mackenzie Laughlin on the way out to his BMW and had to stagger a bit to avoid her as she was standing in the driveway by one of the SUVs, eyeing the house, clearly thinking over whether to join the party. He'd recently seen her in the school play, *Oklahoma!*, that Mia had talked him into going to. Mackenzie hadn't been half bad. He couldn't remember the name of her character, but he could recall part of the song she'd sung.

"*I'm just a girl who can't say no,*" he warbled badly, chortling.

Mackenzie eyed him carefully, but didn't say anything. He started to feel a little foolish for making fun of her. As he shouldered past her toward the street she said, "Maybe you shouldn't drive in your condition."

His condition? "I've barely had anything to drink," he protested. Had his voice slurred? That was . . . weird. He'd purposely kept track of his alcohol consumption. His dad had caught him drunk one time and that one time was more than enough.

"You need a ride? I'm leaving." The words sounded dragged from her. She clearly didn't want to invite him but probably felt compelled to.

"You just got here."

"Yeah, well . . . I'm not staying."

"Yeah, well . . . I'm just getting my coat." He heard his voice and thought he'd said those words pretty clearly.

Mackenzie gave him a look he couldn't decipher before she headed back to an older model Ford Explorer that was parked on the opposite side of the street from Ethan's car.

He leaned into the BMW and half fell on the seat as he snagged his coat. Wow. What the hell was in the punch? Maybe he was a little drunker than he thought. Fine. He wasn't having any more.

He watched Mac drive away. In a way he was kinda sorry to see her go. She was pretty stand-up, as far as he could tell. And yeah, she was friends with Mia and her group, but she seemed like a bit of an outsider. They didn't allow many in their group. And there was something about her parents, too . . . hmmm . . . couldn't remember . . . oh, yeah . . . shit . . . her dad had died a few years back. That was too bad. Although the way his dad was on his ass all the time, sometimes he thought . . . oh, well. Fuck it. Dad was Dad. A lot of dads were like him.

Back at the party, Ethan forgot his own admonition and asked about the punch and was led to the kitchen by a girl from another school who knew Gavin; she told him as much as she showed him to the pitcher of pink refreshment still in the fridge. "Help yourself," she added, as she left him to pour his own drink. He filled the glass, then remembered he shouldn't drink it, then stood there a moment, thinking hard. He ended up carrying the drink back outside and sinking into one of the lounge chairs around the pool, which really pissed off Orsini, who'd been sitting there apparently and who made a big fucking fuss when he came back to find the chair taken, to which Ethan lifted his middle finger and muttered, "Your name wasn't on it, asshole."

The world was spinning and Ethan set the drink on the pool deck and fell asleep. When he came to, he realized most everyone had moved indoors. He thought about Roxie. She wasn't here so why was he? He noticed someone had put ice in his drink so he shrugged, picked it up, and swallowed about half of it down, glancing at the pool house whose windows were dark. However, the plate glass windows of the main house were brightly lit from within and he could see through the dining room to the kitchen. Mia was standing with the rest of her group. He felt a pang in his heart. Yeah, she was a bitch. She'd ditched him and he wasn't the kind of guy who should be ditched, but he wanted to get some loving this last night of high school.

Staggering up, he swayed a bit before walking back around the pool house through the gate and down the drive. When he got behind the wheel he saw that someone had left him some food on the passenger seat sealed between two paper plates and covered overall in plastic wrap. Mia, maybe? he thought hopefully.

He started the engine but sat there for a while. Maybe Mackenzie was right. He shouldn't drive. He certainly felt odd.

He didn't know how long he stayed that way before he shook his head. Fuck it. He didn't live that far away.

He pulled into the street and glanced in the rearview mirror. Someone was standing in the road behind him. Mia? Was she waving?

No. It wasn't Mia . . . he didn't think.

And they weren't waving. They were giving him the finger.

Well, shit. He threw the BMW into gear and roared away. He wanted to drive to the ends of the earth, but then remembered vaguely that there was some obligation he needed to do for his parents so he headed home.

He didn't know that he'd be dead before morning.

CHAPTER 1

Three weeks earlier...
River Glen High School
Class of 2013

The girls were flopped around the room in a haphazard circle, all in pajamas or lounge wear, all tousled and tired and settled down and quiet after an evening of pizza, pop music, and social media. There were six of them nearing the end of their senior year at River Glen High. Leigh sat on the floor, her back supported by a pillow, legs splayed along either side of Erin, who was sitting in the vee provided so that Leigh could braid her shoulder-length hair.

"Ouch!" muttered Erin.

"Shut up," said Leigh as she stretched Erin's thick, light brown strands into two elaborately twisted ropes, tying them off with tiny black leather thongs.

They were all spending the night at Kristl's house, like they had so many times during high school. They'd started out as gawky freshmen, members of a loose group of girls that had swelled and split and reformed a dozen times before the six of them coalesced into the unchallenged most popular girls in the whole class.

Kristl's house was their favorite hangout because Kristl's parents were at least ten years older than everyone else's and went to bed early and rarely checked on them. This had led to various nights of sneaking out, although last night had been Prom and their group had been up all night just hanging out together. Now, after a day of trying to catch up on sleep, they were still lazing around.

And they weren't getting along.

A rift had formed, a chasm, between Mia and Roxie, ever since Roxie had slept with Mia's boyfriend, Ethan. Well, duh, thought Leigh, yanking hard on Erin's hair.

"Oww!" Erin cried out again, twisting away from Leigh. "What are you doing? Trying to scalp me?"

Leigh couldn't exactly say what she'd been thinking. She was just pissed off. She cast a look toward Mia, whose parents always seemed on the edge of divorce. According to Mia, her mom was a "Tiger Mother on steroids," and felt her daughter was not living up to her potential. Mia's dad never intervened and spent a lot of time on business trips. Leigh kind of thought that was a blessing. Her own dad was constantly barking at her to get out of bed and clean her room and help her mother. A real tyrant whom she did her best to ignore.

Now Mia climbed to her feet, the near black ponytail at her nape swinging from side to side. She dusted the seat of her gray sweatpants and announced, "Let's do something. I feel like an invalid, the way the day's gone. I want to go for a walk, or something."

"God, no," moaned Kristl. She was tall with long,

mousy brown hair and about an extra thirty pounds on her frame. Kristl was half in, half out of a sleeping bag and looked like she was planted for the night. They'd all gone to Prom as each other's dates, eschewing the gown, corsage, killer shoes, and asshole or dorky guy for their group of friends. That had been Natalie's idea, their fearless leader. Maybe it was because she was a feminist, as she proclaimed, or maybe it was because she hadn't been asked to Prom herself. Natalie was tall, pretty, with dark hair and eyes and alabaster skin because she never went out in the sun. Unlike Roxie, the sixth member of their group, who was tan year-round and highlighted her hair with blond streaks, Natalie preferred black lace, boots, and eye makeup, Goth to Roxie's "California beach girl" looks. Still, it was Nat's militant attitude more than anything that put off the opposite sex. Not that she didn't have guys looking at her. She just didn't go there, as far as Leigh knew.

"I have no interest in exercise tonight." Natalie quashed Mia's suggestion before anyone else could even venture an opinion. She was seated cross-legged on Kristl's jumbo polar bear pillow. Now she gazed up at Mia, who looked about to argue, then apparently thought better of it and sank back down on the floor. Which left Roxie as the only one not seated on the bedroom carpet. She was lying on Kristl's twin bed and flipping lackadaisically through a magazine. Her hair lay loose around her shoulders and spilled across Kristl's blue-and-white quilt, the one made by her grandmother. Roxie had been disengaged ever since Mia had called her out in front of Ethan shortly after the two of them were seen coming out of Gavin's parents' pool house at the party Gavin had thrown while his parents were in Palm Desert. Gavin was always hosting parties and of course they always went; he was already planning another one for graduation. But the big scandal was that unaccounted-for hour that Ethan and Roxie had spent together in the pool house, though both of them swore nothing happened. However, they'd been high and giggling, which had infuriated Mia, who'd called Roxie a bitch in heat and worse, then stormed off. Ethan had half-heartedly tried to make amends, but so far Mia was having none of it.

Now, two weeks later, Mia and Roxie still hadn't spoken. They hadn't even looked at each other at Prom and if they'd exchanged any words tonight, Leigh hadn't heard them.

Leigh had been the one who'd first told Mia about Ethan and Roxie sneaking off to the pool house together. How they'd snapped the shutters closed and how rumpled and disheveled Roxie had looked in those first moments when she'd emerged before adjusting her bikini top and knotting a towel around her waist. Ethan, all muscles and longish sun-bleached brown hair that he shook like a dog whenever he got out of the pool, had pretended nothing had happened, too. But he and Roxie couldn't hide their smiles, even as they tried to act oh, so cool and disinterested around each other. It was pretty sickening, really. Mia had immediately broken up with Ethan, but Leigh could tell she regretted it. She was still mad at Roxie, but she wanted Ethan back even though she said she didn't. Leigh had asked Roxie point-blank what they'd been doing in the pool house, but Roxie hadn't answered. That piece-of-shit loser Jeremy Orsini had said Ethan had called Roxie a cock tease, but Jeremy thought Ethan was an asshole and vice versa, so you couldn't depend on him for accurate reporting.

Kristl hadn't really invited Roxie to the sleepover tonight, but she'd come anyway, like nothing had changed between her and the rest of The Sorority. Mia was trying to pretend Roxie was invisible but she kept sliding dagger looks her way when she thought no one was looking.

Now Roxie tossed down the magazine and looked over at them, her gaze fixing on Leigh, whose heart stuttered a bit under the scrutiny of those big green eyes. Foxy Roxie, the boys called her. That streaked hair, those big boobs. Fake boobs, they were all sure, but Roxie said no. She insisted the boobs were real, which maybe was the truth because how could she afford new boobs when she and her single mom could barely afford to pay for the dilapidated rental house owned by that lecherous Mr. Donnegal, who, according to Roxie, raised the rent every time you sneezed?

Leigh wondered if Roxie was having sex for money. She was poor and had no qualms about anything. Leigh tried to remember how she'd wangled her way into their group. In the beginning The Sorority had been just her and Natalie and Kristl and, well, Mackenzie Laughlin, but Mackenzie hadn't really fit in. She was just . . . not right. Didn't even try to fit in. Kind of a bitch, herself, actually, Leigh privately thought. Of course, Mac's dad had just died and so she should feel sorry for her. She had told Mac that she was praying for her, which Mackenzie hadn't seemed to know how to take.

Leigh finished braiding Erin's hair, but Erin didn't

move. She seemed content to lean against Leigh. Erin was like that. Always wanting human contact. Roxie said she was gay, but Erin just shook her head and said she just loved all of her friends. Leigh knew her parents were always fighting and Erin, an only child, was struggling with abandonment issues. Leigh had some of those herself.

Natalie, dark hair tied in a loose ponytail that ran down her back, said, "So, we're about to break out of this hellhole and go on to college. Aren't you sick of all the shitty fuckers at River Glen?"

"Absolutely," said Mia. She slid another look at Roxie.

Kristl said, "I'm sick of all kinds of shit."

"We all gotta stick together," said Nat. "We're coming up on the end of school as we know it. We need to make a pact to stay together, whatever happens. We're the women of our class, you know? The *women*."

Kristl glanced at the bowl of Hershey kisses but didn't take one, though she clearly wanted to. She was always on a diet, but Leigh had shared a locker with her a few years back and had seen lots of candy wrapper scraps scattered on the bottom that had fallen out of Kristl's backpack and coat pockets.

Kristl heaved a sigh that blew her bangs away from her forehead. "We should make sure we don't lose touch with others, too."

"Like who?" Nat frowned at her.

"Lots of people. We have other friends. We're graduating. How much are we going to see everybody? I almost invited Mackenzie over tonight." She wriggled further into her bag so just her face was showing.

Nat looked at her as if she'd lost her mind. "Why? We're good as we are."

"She wasn't even at Prom," said Mia, who'd purposely turned her back to Roxie.

"Mackenzie Laughlin's father was a cop," reminded Nat, staring Kristl down.

"Don't speak ill of the dead." Erin shivered and sat up away from Leigh. Leigh was kind of relieved as Erin had been getting heavy.

"I didn't speak *ill* of him, Erin. I just said he was a cop. I'm sorry for Mackenzie that he's dead, but he was a cop. She's not going to go along with us."

"Go along with us?" Erin repeated, frowning. "What does that mean?"

"She won't break rules."

"What rules?" Kristl pressed, peering from beneath her reddish bangs.

"You don't know that. How do you know that?" asked Leigh.

"Well, I like Mackenzie," Erin put in.

Mia said, "She's one of those drama geeks."

"I'm one of those drama geeks," Leigh retorted.

"Oh, for God's sake." Natalie was starting to get that pinched-lip look that came when she was frustrated. "We don't need *anybody* else. We're a sorority. *The* Sorority. Complete unto itself."

This had been Natalie's mantra from the time they were kids. They were a sorority, a sisterhood. Leigh had heard it and heard it and heard it. Once upon a time it had made her feel special. Now, she wasn't so sure.

"And speaking of our sorority, you two have gotta

make up." Natalie wagged a finger between Mia and Roxie.

Mia seemed hit by a freeze ray but Roxie unfolded herself from the bed and sauntered over to the window, looking at her own reflection in the glass. She wore a blue fuzzy sweatshirt and blue-and-pink plaid boxers for pajamas. She struck a pose, thrusting out a hip, and tried out the look.

"That's not going to work," she said. It seemed like she was talking to her reflection.

"Did you hear what I said?" demanded Nat.

"Yes. And I'm answering you. That's not going to work. Mia's not talking to me."

Mia stared at the floor, her jaw set.

"Right, Mia?" Roxie looked over at her, waiting for an answer. When there wasn't one, she gave Nat a *See?* look.

"Mia—" Nat began, but Roxie suddenly whipped around, a big grin on her face and said, "Hey, I've got a name for our sorority. We never call ourselves anything, but I've got this: *I ate a pie!*" She laughed and plunked herself down by Natalie and tried to snatch Kristl's polar bear pillow from underneath her. Natalie hung onto it with a hard grip and glared at her.

Reaching out from inside her sleeping bag, Kristl swept up another pillow and threw it at Roxie. It glanced off her head.

"Hey!" Roxie narrowed her eyes at Kristl.

"You deserved that," Kristl said, easing her words with a smile.

"And more," Mia put in.

Kristl reached around for another pillow, apparently planning to toss it at Roxie again until Natalie muttered. "Stop that."

"What did you say about eating a pie, Rox?" Erin cut in.

"Natalie just said we're a sorority and I said, 'I ate a pie.' *I*, like in iota. Then the Greek letters *Eta* and *Pi*. I ate a pie. That's our sorority. *I Eta Pi*."

"Oh, fuck," said Nat.

Kristl mumbled from inside the sleeping bag, "We're not really a sorority, Nat. My cousin's a Delta Gamma. *That's* a sorority. We won't be in one until college."

"I'm still waiting to see if I get into Stanford," said Mia. Roxie snorted.

"You have something you want to say?" Mia slowly swung her gaze toward Roxie.

Here we go, thought Leigh.

Roxie said, "You don't have the grades and you don't have the money. Neither do I. Sad but true."

"Maybe you don't have the grades, but I do!" Mia snapped back.

"Leigh's family has loads of money, but the rest of us don't," Roxie added, her green eyes sliding Leigh's way.

"Shut up and listen," Natalie cut in.

"Don't be a bitch," Roxie warned Mia.

"*I'm the bitch?*" Mia practically shrieked, looking around at the rest of them, hands splayed out as if asking, *Can you believe this?*

Kristl mumbled something again that could have been a snide repeat of "Don't be a bitch."

"Stop it! Just stop it. We *are* a sorority," Natalie insisted, jumping to her feet. "A group of sisters. The best kind because we've *chosen* each other. So this is our first serious meeting."

"The first meeting of *I Eta Pi*." Roxie smiled.

Natalie threw Roxie that ice-cold look only she could give. Leigh was kind of intimidated by her, but Roxie just looked at Natalie with a bland *I'm listening, bitch* expression and waited.

Kristl gave Nat the rolling wrist go-ahead gesture.

"We *are* a sorority. And we have a mission. We need to work together and make it happen."

"What mission?" asked Erin, frowning.

"We need to kill Ethan Stanhope. He's come between a couple of our sisters, so he needs to be taken out."

Leigh burst out laughing, but when no one else joined her, she grew quiet. They all looked at each other, assessing how serious Nat was, and just when the time felt like it was stretched to breaking, Kristl poked her head out and admitted, "Well, *I'd* like to kill him."

"No shit," Mia seconded.

The rest of them chorused their agreement except for Roxie, who crossed her arms over her chest.

"So, good. We all want him dead," said Nat. If she had made one of her famous to-do lists she would've crossed off Ethan's name right then and there. She glanced at Roxie. "Well, almost all of us."

"Ha, ha. We all want him dead," said Erin a bit nervously.

"I'm serious," Nat answered.

Erin's eyes showed her growing concern and Leigh felt it, too. Nat didn't joke around much.

"Ethan Stanhope needs to die," Natalie insisted.

"How do you feel about that, Rox?" Mia asked, chin up, turning to stare at her rival.

Roxie just lifted a shoulder. "Whatever."

"So, how are we going to do it?" Mia asked, still staring at Roxie.

"Don't look at me," warned Roxie.

"Look at *me*. I'm dead serious," said Natalie.

Mia finally shifted her gaze to Nat.

"You don't believe me," Natalie accused.

"I'm just asking for details." Mia cocked her head and added, as if this conversation was totally normal, "It's just that if I get caught, that'll really screw up things for my application to Stanford."

Everyone tittered at that, but when Nat remained silent, the tension in the room couldn't be denied. Even Roxie got a small frown on her face as she regarded their leader.

"I've got it all figured out. A car accident. This is why we can't have Mackenzie," Nat added, shooting Erin a swift glance. "She'd never go along with it."

"Like we're going along with it," said Roxie.

"If we're not, we're out of the sorority," Natalie stated firmly. "This is a first test. Like slicing our fingers and smearing our blood together."

"God," muttered Mia.

"What are you all talking about?" muttered Kristl. She was down in her bag again, just a thatch of reddish-brown hair and brown eyes visible.

"Don't we hate Ethan?" demanded Natalie.

"Not really," muttered Leigh.

"Well, you should. And Roxie, you should have never screwed around with him, but you did and now he has to die."

"I was drunk, okay? It wasn't like that."

"He said you had sex with him," accused Erin.

"Well, I didn't."

"Did you kiss him?" Erin pressed.

"No . . ." But it sounded like the lie it obviously was and Roxie seemed a bit flustered.

Erin flipped her new braid over her shoulder and shifted over toward her. "Yes, you did."

"Get away from me, you lesbo."

Stung, Erin slipped back toward Leigh. "I like guys."

"Maybe we should just kill Roxie," said Mia, examining her freshly painted fire-engine-red nails.

"Go blow yourself, Mia." Roxie's eyes were emerald ice. Natalie said, "Hey, get serious. We should blame the guy, not each other. Ethan's the one who broke the code of our sorority."

Erin murmured, "I don't like this talk."

"Me, neither," said Leigh.

Natalie gazed around the room, stopping to stare at each friend in turn.

They were all frozen, waiting for the punch line, but it never came. Slowly, they realized Nat meant what she was saying and Erin choked out, "I'm not killing anybody. I'm not hurting them, either. Why don't we just all shun him? He's such a spoiled jerk."

"Well, he lied about me," said Roxie. For the first time since she'd sneaked away to the pool house with

Ethan, her cool facade seemed broken. "So, yeah, let's kill him."

"One less asshole in the world," said Mia blandly.

They all looked at her. Agreeing with Roxie? Clearly she was just playing along. She still wanted Ethan. They all knew it. But, on the other hand, love and hate were opposite sides of the same coin.

"What about Stanford?" Kristl asked, sliding out of her sleeping bag, her face flushed. Leigh wondered if she'd been masturbating in there. She'd noticed some jerking movement that Kristl had tried to hide, like she thought she was being discreet.

"I'm going to get into Stanford whether we kill Ethan or not."

"Okay, everybody. Stand up. Hands in the center," ordered Natalie, stretching out her arm.

It was like a dream, Leigh thought later, or a drama sketch, as they all slowly stood as well, holding out their arms and placing their right hands on top of each other's. Mia even put her hand on top of Roxie's.

Natalie intoned, "Repeat after me: I solemnly swear, as a member of our sorority, that I will do my part to take the life of Ethan Stanhope."

They all echoed the words though Erin and Leigh spoke more slowly.

"Ethan Stanhope's selfish narcissism has created a rift between two of our members. For his crimes, he cannot live."

Again, they echoed Natalie's words but their faces reflected how uncomfortable the whole ritual made them feel.

"And now I pledge my own life and soul to The Sorority."

There was a slight hesitation, but they all complied. Afterward, Natalie dropped her hand and the rest followed.

Almost immediately Natalie doubled over from the waist and howled with laughter, pointing at them.

"You . . . you all bought it! You bought it! Like sure, we're going to kill Ethan." She dropped back onto the polar bear pillow and rolled onto her back, hooting with laughter.

"You're whacked," muttered Kristl, diving back into her sleeping bag.

The mood of the evening turned . . . well . . . weird, Leigh thought. They were all kind of annoyed with Natalie for toying with them, but it was so her.

Leigh slipped into her own sleeping bag and considered Ethan Stanhope. He was good-looking, arrogant, and had a swimmer's build. She'd slid him a covert look or two of admiration herself. They all had, she knew. He was great to look at, so chiseled and hard, and she'd had a nice moment with him she'd never told her friends about but that she thought about from time to time.

When they lined up for graduation three weeks later, Leigh's gaze lingered on Ethan as he accepted his diploma and shook hands with the principal. She watched him give a thumbs-up to his family as he stalked back to his seat, tassel on his mortarboard swinging. His mother, father, and sister cheered him on, none of them knowing that later that night he would pass out at the wheel, miss a turn, and plow straight into a tree.

But the further tragedy of the accident, the worst part of it, was that he took his little sister with him and she died, too.

CHAPTER 2

Now...

Mackenzie Laughlin hurried up the wet grass of the knoll that led to the graveyard, pelted by rain. She swiped the water off her face and wished she'd had the foresight to wear a hat. Her ponytail lay soaked and limp against her nape. She was going to look like the proverbial drowned rat and as this event was a fellow officer's death, she really wanted to reflect the solemnity of the afternoon. In fact she—

Movement on her right caught her attention and her black flats slipped. She went down hard, twisting her ankle. Pain shot up her leg. *Shit.* She glanced around but whatever, or whoever, she'd seen had disappeared. Rubbing her ankle hard, she staggered to her feet, glowering down at her shoes. If she'd had on her beat-up Nikes she wouldn't have fallen.

Brushing her hands against her black pants' damp knees, she worked her way up the rise and then hobbled toward the group gathering outside the open grave. Her ankle sent shivery bursts of pain up her leg, but she gritted her teeth and fought to ignore it. She imagined her foot swelling inside her shoe and had to struggle to get her mind off it. Seeing Detective Cooper Haynes standing on the near side of the grave, she forced herself not to limp as she moved over to join him, swearing inside her mind with each . . . damn . . . step.

She glanced around to see if someone else was joining the group late—maybe the someone she'd caught in her peripheral vision? She was fairly certain it was a person who'd split her attention, causing her fall, though maybe she was just making excuses for her own clumsiness.

People were shuffling in place on the far side of the grave site, near the blue-tarped tent where the funeral director stood, a solemn man whose gray hair was getting flattened and darkened by the rain. Umbrellas covered many of the mourners' faces, but she caught movement in a clutch of three women who, Mac realized, were her old classmates. They were huddled under a large black umbrella and they were turning and talking to a newcomer whom Mac couldn't see. As she watched, however, they turned back and lifted the brim of the oversized umbrella they shared so she could clearly see their faces. It had been over ten years since high school, but they looked the same: Natalie, tall, dark, and imperious; Erin, shorter, rounder, her face set in perpetual anxiety; Kristl, her freckles stark against her white skin, strands of dark red hair limp and sticking to her cheeks, her body slimmer now. She'd clearly shed a number of pounds. Mac didn't see Mia or Leigh . . . or Roxie Vernon, who'd disappeared directly after graduation, never to be heard from again, according to social media. Rumors were she'd been pregnant and Ethan Stanhope's parents had paid for *not* to have an abortion. Rumors were that she'd been pregnant and Ethan Stanhope's parents had paid her not to have an abortion, so they could raise their only grandchild as their own. Rumors were she and her mother had been forcefully evicted from their apartment by an ogreish landlord. Rumors were she and her mother had been given reduced rent by an ogreish landlord in exchange for sleeping with them both and when Roxie graduated, they ditched the arrangement. Rumors were Roxie had run off with a wealthy businessman and was now living on a privately owned island in the Caribbean. Rumors were she'd run off to Hollywood but was now working in the porn trade.

Yeah . . . rumors about Roxie waxed and waned but never seemed to really die.

Haynes was also standing hatless as Mackenzie moved up next to him. The rain was taking a momentary break, but beads of moisture glinted amidst his dark hair. He glanced down at her and said, "Hi."

"Hi. Wish we were meeting under different circumstances."

He nodded and looked grim.

Mac had worked with Detective Haynes during her stint with River Glen P.D. but the last few years she'd drifted into private investigation where she and Haynes had crossed paths during several cases. Some of those cases had involved his family and Mac had grown friendly with a number of them, specifically his sister-in-law, Emma Whelan, during one especially harrowing challenge.

Now, in the lull that had developed while latecomers appeared, Mac asked Cooper, "How are things going with Emma, Jamie, Harley, and everyone?" He'd gotten married earlier in the year to Jamie Woodward, whom Mac had also become friends with. She basically knew his whole family.

He drew a breath and something about it filled her with worry. Seeing her expression, he exhaled and assured her, "Everything's fine. I don't know if you know this, but Jamie and I are having a baby, actually two."

"Twins! Congratulations," she whispered.

"Actually, we're having one with a surrogate and . . . Jamie's pregnant, too."

Mac couldn't hide her surprise. "Wow."

"I know. Unexpected," he said. Finally, the faintest hint of a smile. "We didn't think it would happen . . . it was a challenge."

Though he appeared to be practically bursting with the good news, there was a shadow there as well. "Something wrong?"

"No, it's . . . Jamie's been ordered to keep her feet elevated. Basically bed rest. She's having to quit teaching."

"But everything's looking good?" Mac repeated.

"Yep. Just an abundance of caution." He hesitated, then added, "Emma's moved back to take care of her."

There was irony in his tone. Emma, though capable in her own right, wouldn't be anyone's first choice as a caretaker owing to a long-ago accident that had left her mentally handicapped. Still, that hadn't stopped her from helping save Mac herself from the hands of a killer. With Emma's unexpected aid, Mac was still on the planet.

"Glad everything's okay," she said, meaning it.

He nodded, but then his attention was diverted as the funeral director took a step forward and began to talk about the fallen officer, Tim Knowles. His voice droned a bit, and Mac found herself drifting off and thinking about Knowles herself. She'd already had a foot out the door when he joined the department, but she remembered Tim as being upbeat and ready to help others, a far cry from his older brother, Gavin, one of Mac's own classmates.

As the oak casket was lowered into the grave, it lurched a bit, the surrounding straps momentarily slipping, eliciting a round of gasps from the mourners. But then it steadied again and stayed put as it slowly disappeared into the yawning, waiting hole. A collective sigh from the mourners followed, echoed by the light wind that blew coldly across the near-frozen ground. Mac's ponytail lay cold and wet against the back of her neck as a bead of water ran down her temple. She'd purposely worn waterproof mascara and today she'd put on Think Pink lipstick—a nod to makeup she often had no time for—which she'd apparently gotten on the back of her hand as a small swath of skin sparkled pink in the gloomy sunlight from the shimmery transfer of color.

Tim Knowles had been with the department only a few years before being gunned down earlier this week, the first officer at the scene of a burglary. Gunfire had been exchanged and the burglar, a man with a long record of theft and violence, had raced away from the dying

Knowles. Other officers had chased him into a church where he'd turned the gun on himself, whispering, "Salvation," as he pulled the trigger.

Mackenzie shivered at the thought. She'd attended the indoor funeral service, but then had gotten in a tangle of traffic that had caused her to be late to this grave-site service. She glanced again at the knot of her high school friends, a small group within the student body of River Glen High who'd known Tim. Mac's class had just had their ten-year reunion, but Mac hadn't gone. For her and many others, high school was forever marked by the death of Ethan Stanhope and his little sister from a car accident graduation night, after their last senior party. It had shocked and hurt everyone at the school and it still had the power to make Mac want to steer clear of her classmates. She hadn't been that close to any of them anyway, and she hadn't been able to work up any enthusiasm for the reunion.

Maybe this is just a "you" problem.

The funeral director was extolling Tim's accomplishments. Mackenzie looked past him to the line of trees at the back of the graveyard, their naked limbs black fingers reaching against the gray November sky. Her ankle ached dully and she could feel the frigid cold seep up from the ground and inside her flats, numbing her toes. She realized she was counting down the seconds until she could gracefully leave and felt a bit guilty.

She was angry over Tim's murder. She might no longer be with the River Glen P.D. but she still wanted to bring criminals and miscreants to justice. That's how she'd wound up working with her mentor, P.I. Jesse James Taft, who would've been right beside her today as he was also an ex-RGPD officer except that he was at the reading of a friend's—frenemy's—will in which he was apparently named as a beneficiary. Taft hadn't actually worked with Officer Tim Knowles as his stint with the department had been long before Knowles's time with the force, long before Mac's two-year term as well.

The funeral director's every few sentences were lost to the wind, which was grabbing and tossing them beyond Mac's hearing. She had to step forward to hear, her ankle protesting, making her worry she'd hurt it more than she'd thought and would be paying the price later. She tugged her black coat closer but the fabric was thin and she looked forward to changing into jeans and a sweater.

Cooper ducked his head and whispered to Mac, "Something's off on this."

"What do you mean?"

"Tim Knowles shouldn't have been there."

"At the call to the burglary?"

Mac looked back at him but his eyes were fixed on the open grave. She wasn't sure he'd heard her. The director finished speaking shortly thereafter and he looked to the family. Tim's mother, Brighty Knowles, shook her head, and her husband, Leland, stood stoically and silent beside her as well. Tim's brother, Gavin, was a few steps away, along with his parents. As if feeling her eyes on him, Gavin met her gaze.

Gavin Knowles... Mac had been at the Knowles' house exactly once, the end of their senior year in that space of time when Gavin threw all those parties while his parents were in Palm Desert or New York or wherever his father's business or wealthy friends took them. It was graduation night, the night that Ethan Stanhope drove his car into a tree, killing both him and his sister, Ingrid. Mac remembered living through the next few weeks in a haze of disbelief and sorrow. She hadn't been close friends with Ethan, but she'd been his classmate all through elementary school, junior high, and high school, and it felt like part of her had been ripped away, a part she hadn't known existed until it was gone.

And now the terrible tragedy that had befallen Gavin's younger brother.

Gavin didn't drop his eyes from Mac's until his father bent his head and said something to him and he glanced back at the grave. Brighty, who'd been holding a tight fist of bloodred roses, stepped forward and threw them into the grave, the flowers fluttering in a fist of wind before dropping out of sight. All three of the Knowleses' expressions were the same: stern and frozen masks.

As the service ended, Mac wanted to ask Cooper what he'd meant again, but he was already striding toward the parking lot. Mac tried to do the same, forced to hobble and grit her teeth against the pain. Someone came up beside her and she turned to find Gavin at her elbow.

"Mackenzie," he said, his face drawn and pale.

"I'm so sorry about your brother," she said.

"Thanks."

Mac tried to hide her discomfort. She was sincere in offering her condolences, but it was hard to forget what an ass Gavin had been in high school. Maybe he'd changed over the years.

"I'm surprised to see you here," he said, stopping at the edge of the parking lot as Mac had turned toward her Toyota RAV. Apparently his ride wasn't near hers.

"I knew Tim from the department," she answered. Did he not know that she'd been with the River Glen P.D., too?

"Yeah . . . I just thought . . ."

He trailed off, apparently deciding there was no reason to pursue that discussion any longer. Like with Ethan, she'd traversed elementary school, junior high, and high school with Gavin as well, though they were never friends. Mac had mostly drifted around the periphery of her own group of girlfriends. She and those same girls had traded around who were "BFFs" throughout elementary school, but Mac had let it all kind of go during high school. She'd spent her upper-class years with the drama nerds who weren't really the cool kids of her original group, but who were accepting and fun and ironically made her social group drama-free. Gavin had been from one of the "rich" families around River Glen, as had Ethan.

"Would you come to my funeral if it was me?" asked Gavin now.

Mac gave him a long look. He was suffering, she could see that, and she felt for him, but he was just one of those guys who always brought the conversation back to himself.

She decided to answer honestly. "I probably would."

"Probably?"

"You asked."

"You're supposed to say, 'Of course I would Gavin. And I'm so sorry about your brother . . .'"

"I am sorry about Tim. He was—"

"Oh, forget it. Everybody liked Tim. He was a good guy. I'm just yankin' your chain."

There was always a pitfall, a trap, talking to Gavin. She couldn't think of an upside so she stayed silent.

"I feel like shit," he admitted.

She nodded.

Gavin was about six feet and though he'd been an athlete in high school he was starting to run a little bit to fat. His dark hair was thinning, but he still maintained the supercilious look she'd always associated with him.

This guy is *grieving*, she had to remind herself. Difficult, with his personality.

"Did you see the 'sisters'?" He jerked his head toward the far side of the parking lot where Natalie, Kristl, and Erin were huddled up. They seemed to be looking at someone or something over Mac's right shoulder, but when she turned around to catch what it was, all she saw were a few people talking to the funeral director, Gavin's parents among them.

"I saw them," Mac told him.

"None of them knew Tim. You, at least, worked with him."

"Maybe they're here for you, Gavin."

"That'd be the day. They hate me. Want nothing to do with me. Not since Ethan died. I never liked them anyway. Bunch of bitches. Still look good, though."

Mackenzie made a sound of agreement in her throat, trying to ignore Gavin's negative remarks. He was right about one thing, though. "The Sorority" did look pretty good, from what she could see. High school hadn't been all that long ago, she told herself, only ten years. She ran through a mental assessment of herself.

I'm okay. Still fit. Exercise regularly. Eat pretty good—well, except for that hot fudge milk shake yesterday from Café RG that Taft introduced me to . . . that wasn't well thought out. And that butter-soaked popcorn on his couch with the pugs afterward . . .

"Why are you smiling?" Gavin's ice blue eyes seemed to pierce right through her.

"No reason."

"Something to do with your friends?" He inclined his head toward the three "sisters" now walking across the parking lot tarmac.

Natalie pointed her key fob toward a grouping of vehicles and there was a flash of lights from a black Kia Sorento. Mac could see the rental car sticker in the window.

She almost said, "They're not my friends," but just shook her head.

"I'd like to smash their faces in."

She startled. "Wow. That was a hard turn."

"They thought they ran the school and they made Ethan's life hell the last few hours he had of it."

"Gavin, no one knew that he was going to—"

"You want to look at whose fault it is?" He hitched his chin in the direction of the three women.

"What I don't want to do is argue with you." She resumed walking toward her RAV.

"I'm not the bastard you think I am." She could hear his footsteps behind her.

"You didn't go to the reunion, did you?" he added.

"They were all talking about you. And me and everyone else."

"That's what people do at reunions," she muttered, opening her driver's door. He was right at her elbow. "Well, it was good seeing you, Gavin."

"When I see them, all together, it reminds me of everything . . ." He was still looking their way, but with the crowd of mourners flocking into the lot, the only one Mackenzie could get her eyes on was Natalie, the tallest. There were other River Glen alums in the crowd as well, but none that Mac really knew, though they all sent lingering sympathetic looks Gavin's way, looks he either ignored or didn't notice.

"Have you kept in contact with them?" asked Gavin.

"For someone who professes not to like The Sorority, you seem inordinately interested in them."

"Oh, I am. Because one of them killed Ethan. Spiked his drink and he ran off the road."

Was that what happened? Not as far as she knew. There'd never been a toxicology report made public, if there was one, unless the Stanhopes had gotten it suppressed. With their abundance of money and connections, that was entirely possible, she supposed. In any case, it was a long ago tragedy that she didn't feel like relitigating at Gavin's brother's funeral. She really just wanted to get in her RAV and leave. Her ankle was throbbing and though she thought she'd done a fairly credible job of walking normally to the car, she was about done.

On the other hand, sometimes you just needed to set the record straight.

"Ethan drove home and was there awhile before he

left with his sister. This has been debated and debated. He had some alcohol. I saw him come out and get his coat. But he wasn't wildly drunk when he left your party and then there were a few hours before he took off in the car."

"He was high at my place."

"His parents were home that night. They saw him. Even they say he was fine when he drove off with Ingrid. You don't think they would've stopped him if they'd seen evidence that he was high?"

"You're defending them," he muttered.

"I'm telling you what you already know." She slid into her seat.

"You're still friends with them? You see them all?"

"What are you looking for? No, I haven't seen them in a while."

"I see Orsini some," he offered. "But he's about it. He's still an asshole, though."

"Hmm."

"So, you're a private dick now, I heard."

"Working on it." He was standing outside her still open door. She grabbed the handle.

"What if I wanted to hire you? You're for hire, right? That's how you make money?"

"Yes." She was starting to shiver. Both of her feet now felt disconnected, not just her injured one.

"Don't you want to know why I'd hire you?"

"Sounds like you're going to tell me."

"It's really not for me."

"You're asking for a friend?"

He snorted. "I've been doing some talking to people. I'll let you know what I need. You got a cell number?"

Inwardly sighing, Mac gave him her information. She had a deep mistrust of Gavin Knowles, but who was she to turn down a job? His money was as good as anyone else's and probably better than most.

"I'll call you," he said.

"I am really sorry about Tim."

"Yeah, you said that." He exhaled heavily and Mac thought she caught a whiff of liquor. "He was the good one of the family."

"Well . . ." She lightly tugged on the door handle. She wanted to leave before things deteriorated, and this was not the time to let Gavin's entitlement get to her. He'd always been the guy who bragged about his parents' money.

"We're all just having a ball, aren't we?" he murmured and then wandered away toward where his parents, Brighty and Leland, were standing next to the funeral director.

She gave a last glance around and saw Natalie, Erin, and Kristl climb into the Sorento. Natalie folded the large umbrella, her dark blunt-cut hair blowing around her face as she slid into the driver's seat. Erin climbed in the back, her short skirt hiking up dangerously, and Kristl threw a glance Mac's way as she took the passenger seat. Her reddish hair was about shoulder length, mostly pulled back into a low ponytail, though escaping strands were still sticking to her cheeks. *She's really gotten her weight under control*, she thought. Then, *Is it wrong to think it somehow makes her look harder?*

Totally uncharitable thoughts.

Had there been accusation in the look Kristl had shot

her? Mac was pretty sure Kristl had sent her some kind of unspoken message, but she had no idea what it was.

Her gaze trailed from the Sorento back to where the three friends had stood for the grave-site service. Who was the fourth person they'd spoken to? The person who'd arrived late? The field of umbrellas covering the mourners' heads had kept her from seeing faces clearly.

Brighty and Leland walked across the parking lot toward the older couple standing near a Bentley. They looked familiar and Mac realized they were Ethan Stanhope's parents. She couldn't remember their names. It was a tragic reality that of the three Stanhope children, only one was still alive.

Shivering, she put her RAV in gear and headed out of the parking lot.

CHAPTER 3

Mac checked the time on her cell phone and headed out of the grave-site lot. She'd half expected a text from Taft, but there was nothing there. She wondered how the reading of Mitchell Mangella's will was going. Mitch had been a client and frenemy of Taft's, someone he'd worked for but whose criminality had manifested in a way he eventually couldn't abide. He'd quit working for him and there'd been bad blood all around. Taft had managed to put most of it behind him over the past months, but then recently Mitch had fallen off his roof and died, a shock wave that rippled through all of them. When Taft had gotten the notice that Mangella had left him something in his will, he'd sworn he wasn't going to take as much as one thin dime, even though he didn't know what it was. His break with Mangella had been permanent. Mac was the one who'd urged him to go to the meeting.

"At least find out what Prudence is up to," she'd counseled, and Taft had grudgingly agreed. They both knew how wily Mangella's wife was on a good day.

Mac drove to her mother's house. She'd promised

she would stop by and see her new kitchen, the result of a broken water pipe that had ruined the cabinets and flooring. For nearly a year it had been a wrangle with the insurance company and the contractors to get the place put back together, but now the final work was done and Mom had practically insisted Mac stop by after the funeral.

She pulled up in front of the house and took a look at herself in the rearview mirror. No running makeup. Good. Hair damp, though. She finger-combed her ponytail and stepped gingerly out of the car. Shit. That left ankle . . .

She hobbled up the walk, muttering, "Ow, ow, ow," all the way to the front door. Rapping loudly, she called, "Hey, Mom!" as she twisted the knob and let herself in.

"I'm in the kitchen!"

Mac tried to hide her limp as she followed her mother's voice. She was going to have to get her shoe off soon.

"What's wrong with you?" her mother asked.

So much for hiding her limp. "I slipped and twisted my ankle."

"Well, sit down. Take your shoe off. Let me look."

"If I take my shoe off, I won't get it back on."

Mom tsked and pulled out one of the oak kitchen chairs from around the table where a jigsaw puzzle of rows of seashells that looked impossible was half finished. She bent down to check her foot as Mac gazed across her dark hair, now faintly threaded with silver, to look around the kitchen.

"I really like the countertops," she said. She'd already seen the gleaming white-painted cabinets. The countertops were a light gray and crowned with a pearly farmhouse sink and gleaming chrome faucet and cabinet pulls. Before the water damage the cabinets had been yellowed pine from half a century earlier or more. "Don't take my shoe off. I'll never get it back on."

"You're going to have to elevate this foot," Mom predicted.

"Ya think?"

"I know I say it every time I see you, but I think you should get a different job."

"I didn't get this on the job. It was at the funeral." She went on to explain how she'd twisted her ankle as she'd hurried to Officer Tim Knowles's grave-site service. Mom asked who else was there and Mac gave her a rundown of the event.

"I always thought Gavin was such an unhappy little boy. I'm sorry for him. And the family."

Brighty and Leland Knowles had not been in her parents' circle of friends, but they'd known them. There had been talk, at one time, of sending Gavin to private school, but Gavin had pitched a fit and apparently they'd given up those ideas when Tim came along. Same for the Stanhopes. Mac knew for a fact that the Knowleses had detested their youngest son's choice of being a police officer because Tim had mentioned it once.

"They had a shit fit," he'd said with a shrug. "They wanted me to go to some Ivy League school, but I never had the grades. Gavin's the smart one, but he doesn't care."

"Don't sell yourself short," Mac had told him.

He'd shrugged again and said with a smile, "Truth is truth."

That had been the extent of their discussion about

his family and his life. Mac had been half out the door of the department by then, dealing with the unwanted advances of the then police chief who'd intimated he could take her job if she ratted him out. She'd quit before he could make good on his threat and eventually he'd lost his job.

"Dan stopped by," her mother revealed.

Dan the Man, as Mac thought of her stepfather, was a leech and an all-around asshole. Mac had never been happier than when her mother and Dan split up. It alarmed her that he'd made contact.

"Is he still at the condo?" He'd moved to one of the most expensive apartments in town, above the River Glen Grill, and Mac had marveled that he could afford the place.

"Oh, no. You know he moved." She peered at her. "I told you."

She did know, she supposed, but when it came to mention of Dan Gerber her mind shut down. She didn't actually hate him. That would take more emotion than she could credit. But she couldn't stand him. Couldn't abide being around him. He'd met her mother when she was in a vulnerable place after the death of Mac's father, and he'd wormed his way into their lives. Luckily, Mom had woken up before Dan went through all her money.

"He raved about the kitchen." Mom slid an ironic glance Mac's way.

"He's not moving back, is he?"

"Stop worrying. That's over." She walked to the refrigerator. "I think you could use some ice."

"No, I gotta get going."

"You need to put that leg up."

"I know. I know. I will. But don't let Dan worm his way back in."

"I'm sorry I said anything. He's not coming back here."

"Did he want money?"

"Mackenzie," she warned.

"He wanted money, didn't he?"

"If he did, he never got a chance to ask. Like you, I had somewhere to be, so I asked him to leave. Don't worry. I know who he is . . . now."

She could tell she was pissing her mother off, but her fear of Dan was too great to leave it like that. "He can be charming."

"Not anymore."

Mac forced herself not to say anything further. She wanted to believe her mother. She really did. It was just that Dan was that bad penny who kept turning up. She moved the conversation back to the remodel and got them back on solid ground before she left.

At the door, Mom said, "Oh, I forgot. One of the people from Parker Flooring knows you. She looked familiar. I took her card."

"Who?" Mac asked as her mother walked back toward the kitchen. She returned holding a small white card that she handed to Mac.

PARKER FLOORING

Elayne Sommers, Design Specialist

"I don't know her."

"She knew I was your mother, so she dropped by here. She asked where you lived."

"You didn't tell her, did you?"

"She works at the company." She pointed at the card. "Her cell phone's on there, you can call her."

"You told her? Mom!"

"She's someone you know!" She threw up her hands. "I just gave her the name of your apartment building."

Mac controlled herself with an effort. Except for her disagreement over Dan she and her mother had always gotten along. But sometimes, even though she worried about Mac's safety, her mother inadvertently assumed certain people were safe, like old friends who may or may not be old friends.

"Okay," said Mac.

"I'm sorry, honey. But she really is someone you know. I swear I almost remember her."

Twenty minutes later, Mac was working her way up the outdoor stairs to her second-floor apartment when her cell phone rang. It was a number she didn't recognize and she almost let it go to voice mail, but then answered it just before.

"You sound so official," Gavin Knowles's voice drawled into her ear.

She sighed aloud and didn't care if he heard her. *That didn't take long.* "Hi, Gavin."

Ignoring her dispirited tone, he said, "I want to set something up."

"I told you I'm not officially a private investigator. If you really want to hire someone you should check with my boss, Jesse Taft."

"I've just got some questions. I don't even know if you're the right person. Maybe you're not. But I want to work this out."

He sounded like he was having a debate with himself. Mac thrust the key into the lock of her apartment door and twisted it open. "I just got home. I need a few minutes. Is this more about Ethan? His death was ruled an accident."

She stepped inside and turned to shut the door. A breath of air swooped over the back of her neck, and she quickly glanced around to see if there was an open window. There wasn't. In fact, the apartment's air was still. She touched her hand to her nape and felt the now dry ponytail. The hairs on her arms lifted. Was someone in her apartment? This Elayne person?

On high alert, she ignored the pain in her ankle, which was getting worse, not better, limped rapidly to her bedroom and threw open the door. The closet doors were ajar and she threw them back, searching inside. There was no one there. She next went to the bathroom and peered in. Holding her breath, she threw back the shower curtain. No one.

"Ethan was killed by The Sorority," Gavin insisted. "One of them did it, or maybe more."

"Okay, look, I'll have to call you back." Mac headed toward her living room and the one and only easy chair. Her ankle was throbbing and already turning a lovely shade of purple. There was no one in her apartment. Nothing had been disturbed. If she was a superstitious person she would say just the mention of Ethan

Stanhope's name had caused her skin to react. There'd been no swooping wind. No change of air pressure.

"Wait. Wait. Don't you want to know who drugged him?"

"Drugged him? I thought it was established that Ethan was drinking at your house. I don't think—"

"It was Kristl."

Mackenzie pulled the black flat off her good foot, then eased off the other shoe with the bare toes of her opposite foot. She felt almost as cold now as she had at the graveyard.

"Did you hear me? She drugged him at my party."

She didn't want to talk to him. She was close to hitting the off button. "We already discussed this. There was a lot of time between your party and when he drove into that tree."

"A couple of hours. So what. It was a slow-acting drug."

"His parents said he was sober when he got home."

"Okay, it didn't happen at my party. I told the police that at the time. He told me how shitty it was that he couldn't get wasted at graduation because of fucking water polo. But he was dead sober when he left the party."

"You know this for a fact?"

"Yee . . . es."

She heard the lie. "This is what's bullshit, Gavin."

"It's the truth!"

"I saw him that night and he wasn't dead sober. Just because you tell yourself something over and over again doesn't make it true."

"Goddammit, listen to me. I want you to find out who killed Ethan. I think it's Kristl. Something happened between them and she got her revenge. I'll pay you. Tell me what your rate is and I'll double it."

"Oh, come on." She couldn't believe she was rehashing high school with Gavin Knowles *on the day of his brother's funeral*!

"I'll meet you tomorrow and you can name your price."

"Gavin, I'm happy to take your money, but it's likely I will never uncover whatever it is you're looking for. Ethan didn't date Kristl in high school, he dated Mia. And then there was Roxie. I can hear in your voice that you think it's some grand conspiracy. I just don't want you screaming for your money back when you don't get the results you want."

"I won't. Just do some digging. I bet you find who killed them. Kristl blamed Ethan for cheating on Mia, so she drugged him."

Mac shook her head and looked out her living room window. There was a line of maples that separated the back of her apartment building to the next property, which was an access road behind several other commercial buildings. The maples were dancing furiously beneath a sharp wind. She wondered if outside weather had entered her apartment, but the air remained still.

"Mac?"

"I've got your number now, Gavin. I'll talk to Taft, see what he says."

"He'll blow me off, just like you are. I'm serious about this."

"Okay."

"We have a deal?

"I—"

"Just say you'll look into it. Prove me wrong," he challenged. "If not Kristl, one or the other of them. Maybe all of them."

"If I say I'll look into it, will you let me do it my way?"

"Sure. I'll need to pay you, so we'll get together."

"Hell, no. I'll send you a bill."

"You're such a bitch. I like that."

"Goodbye, Gavin." She clicked off before he could say another word.

She was just working her way toward the kitchen, planning to get that ice her mother had suggested, when her doorbell rang.

Now what? Had he followed her here?

Maybe it was Taft.

She hobbled over to the door and peered through the peephole. A blond woman stood outside. It took a brief moment to recognize her and when she did she drew a deep breath. It was old home week for sure as another member of The Sorority was standing on her doorstep. Leigh Denning.

Mac took a moment before answering the bell. Leigh hadn't been at the funeral today, so what was this about?

Standing on her good leg, Mac opened the door with, "Well, this is a surprise. Hi, Leigh."

"Hi. Mackenzie. I . . . saw you at the funeral."

"So you were there."

"Just for a minute. May I come in?"

Mac swung the door wider, then tentatively half-hopped into the kitchen and pulled out the freezer drawer at the bottom of her refrigerator, picking up an ice cube tray. She had a drawer of plastic grocery bags and pulled one out as Leigh shut the door and stood at the entry of Mac's tiny kitchen, watching as she twisted the ice cube tray and popped several ice cubes into the double-baggie.

The penny dropped.

"You were the one who stopped by Mom's place and got my address."

Leigh nodded. "What happened to you?" she asked, eyeing Mac's bare foot.

"Twisted my ankle at the funeral. I'm going to seat myself in that chair." She pointed to the easy chair, worked her way to it, and then settled the baggie of ice on her colorful ankle.

"That looks painful."

"It is." Mac regarded her expectantly. "You're Elayne Sommers. Mom gave me your card, but I didn't put the name together till now."

"I stopped using Leigh after high school and went back to my real name. And then I got married to Parker Sommers and so . . . sort of a new identity, I guess."

At least Mac could stop worrying about Mom's loose tongue. She understood why Leigh had looked so familiar to her. Once upon a time, when they were in elementary school, they'd been pretty close.

Leigh perched herself on the small love seat Mac had gotten from her mother. She was an ash blond with blue eyes. Like Kristl, she was more fit than she'd been in high school, where she'd carried a few extra pounds and had seemed softer. Her hair was blonder now, though her manner was still slightly diffident. She'd vied for the lead of Laurey in *Oklahoma!* and had lost out to a girl with a stronger voice and personality, and had been forced to settle for the ensemble without a serious speaking part. It echoed her role within The Sorority as well, Mac realized. A member but not a leader.

"What can I do for you, Leigh, er . . . Elayne?" asked Mac.

"Leigh's fine. I went to the funeral mostly to see you. But it just didn't feel like the right place, and Natalie, Erin, and Kristl had gone together and I felt . . . I don't know . . ." She lifted a hand and waved whatever she was going to say away. "It was all so sad. I'm just worried, I guess. And God, I know it's ridiculous, but it feels like they were all freezing me out a little. So much for 'The Sorority.'" She smiled faintly. "But that's not why I'm here . . . exactly. I want you to find someone for me. Mia. She's been missing for months. A really long time. I told the others but they say Mia's just living her life. I don't think so. Natalie said Mia was not M-I-A. Ha, ha. Funny. She's missing and no one's doing anything about it."

First Gavin, now Leigh? The timing seemed more than coincidental that they were both requesting her services at the same moment. Parroting herself, she said, "The person you should talk to is my boss, Jesse Taft."

"Oh, no. No, no, no, no. I want this to stay between us. I don't want Parker to know about it. He thinks I'm hysterical already, but I just know something's wrong.

Mia always kept in contact with me until about four months ago. I've tried to reach her and I've failed. She's in that marijuana business with her boyfriend. I just know something's happened."

Vaguely Mac recalled hearing that Mia had been living in Northern California, growing legal cannabis. She'd headed to Stanford after graduation but had apparently dropped out. Mac set that aside for a moment, deciding instead to ask her own questions. "Did you know Tim Knowles well?"

Leigh blinked. "Tim? I—no. I went to the funeral to support the family."

"Gavin?"

"Well, sure. We were all friends. I saw you talking to him." A frown creased her brow. "What were you talking about?"

"Well, his brother, of course."

"Yes . . . yes . . . It just seemed like, something else, too . . . maybe?"

Mac wondered how close Leigh had been to the Knowles family. She hadn't seen her at the grave site, but a lot of people had been exiting about that same time and Mac's and Gavin's attention had mostly been on Natalie, Kristl, and Erin. "I didn't see you at all."

"Well, I wasn't there long."

Mac wasn't about to tell her about Gavin Knowles's request that she look into Ethan Stanhope's death. It would be a breach of business ethics and it didn't have anything to with Mia Beckwith's supposed disappearance.

"I can do some searching for you about Mia's whereabouts, but I'm not an independent investigator. I work for Jesse Taft. He wouldn't do anything to betray you."

Leigh gave a pained smile. "I don't want to involve anyone else. Can't you just try? I've got money."

She opened her purse and pulled out a roll of bills that she thrust at Mackenzie. "If you have to tell your boss, make sure he doesn't tell anyone else. You've got my card. Call me but don't leave a message if you don't reach me. And don't text, please. I just don't want my husband to know."

"What about Mia's parents . . . and her brother? Have you talked to them?"

"Ye . . . ess," she said slowly. "They didn't have much to offer. I talked to Mason, too. He blew me off and said Mia was fine."

"Maybe she *is* fine."

"Okay, look, I wasn't going to give you this . . . I thought, I don't know, that you would just help me. But she left this note on my windshield." Leigh reached into her purse and pulled out a tiny, yellow sticky note with the words *Help me* written in cursive. "That's Mia's handwriting." She held the note up to Mac.

Mac squinted at the words. She thought the tiny, squished together letters could be anyone's, but then she was no expert. "Why didn't you give me this right away?"

"Because I wanted to hire you first. I don't want everyone to see this. If you're not going to go find her, I don't want this floating around. It could be dangerous for her!"

"Okay." Mac held up her hands.

Leigh's cheeks pinkened. "I'm sorry. I'm just so worried."

"I thought she was in California."

"She was. I don't know where she is now."

"She's not in the cannabis business?"

"Her boyfriend's family is. Mia didn't talk about it a lot. I think they kind of keep it on the down-low because there's a lot of rivalry and theft because the marijuana business isn't federally regulated. It's why I'm so worried about her."

"Do you know the name of her boyfriend?"

"Ben . . . something? I think she told me. I can't remember. I never paid that much attention. Then she just went off the radar, and then I got the note." She exhaled heavily and looked at Mac from beneath her bangs, silently pleading with Mac in a move she recognized from high school.

"I'll talk to her parents," Mac conceded.

Leigh sighed with relief. "Thank you!"

"I can't promise anything."

"I know you'll find her. You were always so capable. Remember when we were in *Oklahoma*? You were so great as Ado Annie."

"Thanks. That was a long time ago."

"I should've been Laurey, but Summer was really good." Her quick smile was brittle. "She's still in New York."

"I heard she's been in a few productions," said Mac. Summer Cochran had won the lead of Laurey Williams in their senior year production and her voice had been so pure and lovely that the crowd had been transfixed during her solos.

"Ensemble. No main parts."

"But still, that's pretty impressive," Mac acknowledged, adding, "I thought you would go on in drama."

"Well, I met Parker at summer camp and that was it. How did you get into the P.I. business?"

"I was with River Glen P.D. first, then moved to this."

"Why didn't you stick with acting?"

Mac snorted, then realized Leigh was completely serious. "It was fun in high school. It just . . ." *Didn't seem like a viable career path.*

"Everything kind of changed after Ethan's death, didn't it?" Leigh said soberly.

"Well, yeah." Although Mac's choice of career had been more of a "look in the mirror and know what you're good at" moment.

"*You* don't think anything's . . . weird about Ethan's accident, do you? I know that Gavin thinks it was some kind of setup. He blames The Sorority, doesn't he?"

"I've always thought it was an accident, nothing more," Mac offered.

"But it's what you two were talking about, wasn't it? I saw Gavin last weekend and he was drunk and ranting and we all felt sorry for him because of Tim, but I guess his brother's death sort of set him off. He's never thought Ethan's car accident was just a car accident, and now this has brought it all up again."

"Who's 'we'?"

She flicked her wrist. "Just people at the Waystation."

"You were at the Waystation?" Mac was surprised to think that Leigh would ever set foot inside what could only be construed as a dive bar. Leigh just had that well-tended look about her, and an inner snootiness that couldn't quite be disguised, no matter how she gushed about the accomplishments of others.

"I went with Parker." She rolled her eyes. "He likes

beer and he knew Gavin would be there, and I felt bad about Tim, too, so we went. What did Gavin want you to do?"

Mac realized she was subtly being pumped for information, so she told the truth, as much as was prudent. "I told Gavin what I told you. I'm not the investigator. Jesse Taft is."

"But you *will* look into Mia's disappearance," she quickly reiterated.

The money she'd thrust at Mac was still in her hand and she tried to hand it back but Leigh wouldn't hear of it.

She folded Mac's hand over the bills. "Keep it. Please. You're going to look into Mia's disappearance, right?"

"I'll do some checking," said Mac. This was twice in one day she was agreeing to work without coordinating with Taft first. Ah, well. He wasn't one to turn down work, either, unless it appeared to be blatantly illegal.

"Call me on my cell, but don't involve Parker, okay? Don't call the business," warned Leigh.

"I won't."

"Good."

Once Leigh was gone Mackenzie checked the time, wondering about Taft's meeting with the estate lawyers. Dumping out the baggie of melting ice, she replenished it and went back to her chair in the living room.

CHAPTER 4

It was a scene straight out of a movie: the reading of the will with all the suspects seated in the wood-paneled den. Taft was somewhat amused at being part of the scenario, but the image of Mitch Mangella falling off his roof to his death kept the smile from growing on his lips. He just couldn't picture Mangella on the roof in the first place. Mangella had people who did tasks for him; he never did them himself. Taft didn't believe for a minute that Mangella had been actually fixing something on the roof. So, what was he doing up there? It was a mystery worth pursuing, although the police seemed to be satisfied. For them, it was the end of a thorny problem. Mitch Mangella, River Glen's most successful and famous citizen, who'd tiptoed the line between legality and criminality before taking the plunge into pure criminality, had died before the D.A. had enough to prosecute him. *Arrivederci* delicate and messy problem.

The estate lawyer and an assistant introduced as Veronica Quick had arranged for the reading to be at the Mangellas' palatial home and now all of the potential beneficiaries were seated in the den, or more aptly, bar. There were bookshelves with ladders on three sides of the room, a bar on the fourth wall, low, comfy chairs scattered around the room.

Taft was standing against one wall of books. He had too much energy to take one of the chairs. Mitch's widow, Prudence Mangella, was seated directly in front of the table where the estate lawyer, Martin Calgheny, sat tall and straight in a dark blue suit, Quick beside him in a prim, long-sleeved gray dress.

Prudence's tan and shapely legs were crossed beneath a very short, black skirt. She wore a white shell beneath a black jacket that matched the skirt.

I want a girl with a short skirt and a loooonnnng jacket.

The words to a song by Cake ran through his mind. Prudence had her hair pulled into a French twist. She looked like an icy blonde out of an Alfred Hitchcock movie. She and Mitch had been in a complicated relationship where they played games on each other, serious games that sometimes involved the police, each accusing the other of theft of their personal property or abuse, emotional or physical or both. Several times Prudence had tested the waters to see if Taft was up for an affair, which he'd made sure she knew was a no go, but she would then only smile as if the whole thing tickled her. It was all part and parcel of their twisted marital relationship, but at some level Taft had understood that this was how they added spice to their union. Strangely, he'd always believed that underneath it all, the marriage was solid. Now he wasn't so sure. Now he wondered if there was more behind Mitch's death than what Prudence was telling. He could even believe it was one of their pranks gone wrong. Maybe.

"Very sorry I'm late," Mr. Calgheny said for about the fourth time. Quick darted a glance from him to Taft to Prudence, then down at her notes.

Calgheny was a tall, thin man with clipped gray hair and wire-rimmed glasses. They'd all assembled at the correct time, but then he and Quick hadn't shown up. A fatal traffic accident had stopped traffic on the freeway and Calgheny had been trapped for nearly an hour.

Prudence re-crossed her legs and smiled at him. "It couldn't be helped."

Taft slid his gaze from Prudence to the woman seated next to her, Anna DeMarcos, who was as elegant as her good friend, but her hair was dark whereas Prudence was a silvery blond. Taft had history with Anna DeMarcos as well. He'd been responsible for the death of her lover, Keith Silva, and though Taft had been lucky to survive that encounter—Silva had been attacking him, not the other way around—Anna seemed to blame him entirely. Taft hadn't seen either of them for some time, ever since his association with Mitch had ended, and the two women's friendship seemed stronger than ever. As he watched, Anna reached over and clasped Prudence's hand and squeezed it for a brief moment. Prudence looked at her, her smile brave. Anna nodded sympathetically.

There were several other people in the room. Business associates, Taft guessed. The Mangellas had no children and Taft knew Mitch had cut ties with his family long ago. He wasn't even sure there were any other Mangellas left. Prudence, as his wife, was bound to inherit the bulk of his estate anyway.

Maybe he's left me his hundred-year-old bottle of scotch.

Taft smiled faintly to himself. He'd told Mackenzie he'd commented on Mangella's prized bottle of Macallan once, and Mitch had facetiously told him he'd leave it to him in his will.

"Maybe that's coming true," Taft had told her.

Ever practical, Mac responded, "Drink it. What good is it holding onto a bottle of liquor?"

"Some people would call it an investment."

"Then sell it. Seriously. I see a dust collector." They'd been at his condo and she'd pointed to the tops of his kitchen cabinets where, yes, he'd set a fondue pot and where it had sat ever since. The fondue pot had been his sister's and after her death he'd been hard-pressed to donate any of her belongings, even though he knew Helene, who was his muse to this day, would roll her eyes and tell him to move on. He could almost see her now, outside the window on the Mangellas' front yard, smiling and shaking her head at him.

Maybe he would drink that scotch in honor of both Mitch and Helene.

Calgheny cleared his throat and started reading from the will. Prudence slid a look Taft's way, her expression hard to read. Since he'd left Mangella's employ her demeanor had shifted from kittenish to cold and stony mistrust. The only hint he saw that she was truly feeling sorrow over her husband's death was her pallor. Anna, however, looked in the pink of health and there was a glitter in her eyes, and a kind of repressed energy, like a cobra coiling to strike.

He glanced back through the window to his vision of

Helene, but she wasn't there. He was disappointed, wanting her to shake her head at him some more, letting him know that her little brother's suspicions were unfounded.

"'... and to my wife, I leave all the jewelry I have ever given her. Even the pieces she stole from me that I gave her back again.'"

There was an uncomfortable titter from the assembly. No one knew what Mangella was talking about except Taft and maybe Anna. Prudence had once pretended that jewelry Mitch had bought her was stolen when in actuality she'd taken the gems herself and placed them in a pawnshop. Then when the truth came out she just shrugged it off, and so did Mangella.

"'She may also have the three cars that are in both of our names. Pru, remember that long drive through the Tetons? Do with the cars what you will. I don't give a sh—'" Calgheny cleared his throat. "I'm sorry, Mrs. Mangella."

"It's all right." Her lower lip quivered. "It's how Mitch and I talked. There was no drive through the Tetons." She half-laughed.

The lawyer and Quick both regarded her soberly. After a pause, Calgheny said, "I so rarely read the contents of a deceased's will. But your husband requested this formality."

"I understand."

"'The rest of my estate, all financial considerations, the house, all my personal effects, I leave to Mr. Jesse James Taft.'"

The room went dead silent.

After a charged moment, Calgheny read on: "'Mr.

Taft is the only person who never lied to me. Taft, do what you will with my money, just don't give any of it to my loving wife.'"

It was Anna who erupted first. She turned to glare at Taft with pure venom. "What did you do?" she hissed. Yes, definitely a cobra.

Taft's head was reeling. Wouldn't you know it. He didn't want anything from Mangella in any way. No more jobs. No more money. Nothing. He'd made that perfectly clear to the man and Mangella, with his warped sense of contrariness, had purposely dumped it all in Taft's lap.

He opened his mouth to say that it was another of Mangella's games, but he didn't get anything out before Prudence slowly swiveled in her chair to face him, then pushed herself up from her seat. "You knew," she said, moving toward him.

Other guests, Mangella's business associates, stood up awkwardly, sensing some kind of standoff, but it was Quick who stepped between them.

"It's all right," Taft told the young woman.

Ruffled, Calgheny also stood. "There's a bit more. 'If anything should happen to Mr. Taft, some unfortunate accident to himself or any of his friends, contact Detective Cooper Haynes of the River Glen Police Department or anyone else who works there and tell them that the culprit will be my loving wife, Prudence Mangella. Taft, keep an eye on her. You know what she's like.'"

"What a fucker," Anna DeMarco said, faintly appreciative.

Prudence just kept staring at Taft, her head tilted, her eyes filled with a kind of curiosity. "This won't stand."

"We're going to contest," agreed Anna.

"Of course we will," said Prudence.

Taft kept quiet, processing. He hadn't wanted Mangella's money. He still didn't want it. What he wanted was to let Prudence know that he didn't want it. But Mangella had warned him. From the grave he'd let Taft know that he didn't trust his wife and that this time it was no joke.

Maybe she did kill him . . .

"Mr. Taft, if you could come to my office early next week, we'll finalize everything." Calgheny gathered his briefcase and papers.

"There'll be no finalizing!" Anna declared.

Prudence had regained her seat and now swivelled back around, putting a hand on Anna's elbow. Unlike her friend, she was cool and collected. She was good at game playing. "Of course there won't." She tilted her head slightly for Taft's benefit. "I think it's time you left my house."

My house, Taft mentally corrected, but knew that was just begging for a scene as he headed for the door.

He felt a stab of cold between his shoulder blades and could imagine Prudence's and Anna's twin frigid glares. He kept walking to his Rubicon, half believing he'd be struck down as he crossed the street. Even when he was safely inside and pulling away from the curb, he braced himself for something cataclysmic to happen to him.

Only when he was pulling into his condominium complex and saw his neighbor, Tommy Carnahan, walking his two pugs in the waning light of the chilly November evening did he breathe a sigh of relief. He got out of the car and joined them, then pulled out his cell phone and called Mackenzie.

"Did you get the scotch?" she asked.

"Uh . . . yeah . . . in a manner of speaking."

"What's so funny?" she asked because Taft had started laughing and thought he might not be able to stop.

"Holy shit," Mac said into the phone for about the fiftieth time since Taft finally managed to tell her the terms of the will. "Holy shit, holy shit . . ."

"Holy shit." She could hear the smile in his voice. "I gotta go. Plaid and Blackie need attention."

The pugs were snuffling in the background. She could envision their comical black faces and suddenly longed to be with Taft at his condo. He took care of the pugs about half the time as their owner was away a lot. In his early eighties, Tommy Carnahan was still lithe and vibrant and spent a lot of time traveling with various female companions, which put Taft at the top of the dog-sitter list.

"What are you going to do with all that money?" she asked.

"A trip around the world. Wanna go?"

"Ha, ha. Seriously."

"I was thinking of—"

"Don't give it all back," Mac interrupted. "He wanted you to have it, keep at least some of it!"

"—donating it to charity."

"Oh, please. Not all of it. Don't go all noble on me. Mangella had some legit businesses. He wasn't a total crook."

"He left it to me to knife Prudence. That's all. Who knows how many wills he wrote? Probably dozens. He never expected to die and have this be the last one."

"You don't know that."

"Doesn't matter. I'm not going to keep it. I have enough money to be comfortable, any more than that can play with your psyche. Look at Mitch and Prudence. They abused each other with money, played those dangerous, vicious games."

Mac's brows lifted. He wasn't usually so philosophical. "You going to tell Prudence and Anna that?"

"Maybe."

"Ooh, boy," she murmured. "You'll be in their crosshairs."

She could hear the faint smile in his voice as he said, "I'm sure I already am. But the estate's bound to be tied up in court for years, the way these things go. So, what are you doing for dinner?" he asked, changing the subject. She was pretty sure he didn't really care what she was doing, he just wanted to stop talking about Mangella. But she wasn't above holding him to the invitation.

"DoorDash. I'm not really mobile at the moment. Twisted my ankle at the service today."

"Want me to bring food to your place?"

"Yes. Goldie burgers. I've got a few things to tell you, too."

"See you in half an hour."

"Okay."

Mackenzie had an ongoing argument with herself about her feelings for Jesse James Taft. She'd been working with him for a couple of years now and had grown to think of him as a mentor and partner, at least in the private investigation business, but she also had other feelings as well. They surfaced at night, when she was alone and thinking about her life and the people in it, and sometimes an ache would suddenly envelop her so deep that she would drag her pillow over her face and scream into it. During the day, she didn't feel that way . . . much. Sure, she would look at him sometimes and marvel at how much she loved the dimples that peeked out from his close-cut beard, or what exact color of blue his eyes were, somewhere between cerulean and sky, or look at the brown hair at his nape, sometimes a bit shaggy, and think about its texture. She wasn't in love with him. She'd never been in love with anyone and wasn't sure she ever would be, or that it even existed. She was intrigued and infatuated. Definitely horny. But more than any of that she wanted to keep working with him, and she didn't believe a quick fling, or a short romance, or whatever you want to call it, was going to do anything but harm that relationship. In her experience, indulging in romance and sex and wild swings of joy and exuberance to despair and sadness wasn't a healthy way to live. Her last relationship hadn't been quite so up and down, which was good, she supposed, but it hadn't lasted either. If she was missing the highs and lows of so-called love, so be it. She knew she couldn't have both her career with Taft and a relationship. One or the other, and she'd chosen the long-term one.

Didn't mean she had to look like a hag when he came over. With that in mind, she hobbled to the bathroom and checked the remnants of her makeup. Yeah, she could use a little help. Mascara, eyeliner, some blush. God, was that a zit trying to develop beside her eyebrow? She swore beneath her breath and added some concealer.

"Connect with some high school friends and watch your face break out," she muttered. She shot a black look at herself, then limped back for more ice, unlocking the front door on the way and leaving it ajar. She then eased herself back into her chair, plopping the ice on her ankle.

It wasn't that there hadn't been awareness between her and Taft. More than once she'd contemplated kissing him and sensed that he'd felt the same way on other occasions. But Taft had a reputation as a serial dater, or maybe just a player, as he never stuck with one woman long and yet always seemed to have women circling around him. Mac had run into several already onetime lovers, or "friends," as he liked to call them, in the course of working with him. She wondered if Prudence Mangella, now that she was a widow, would reconsider her animosity toward Taft and decide to use a new tack. Mac could easily picture her wrapping herself around him. She winced at the thought.

"Door's open," she called a few minutes later when she heard Taft's footsteps on the outside stairs.

He appeared in the doorway carrying a white, green, and yellow Goldie's bag. Taking one look at her in the chair with her leg up on the ottoman, he frowned. "What happened?"

"I told you. I twisted it when I was going up this little, grassy hill at the grave-site service. I looked over at someone and lost my footing."

"You're gonna need it taped."

"Okay." She wasn't going to argue with him.

"Who'd you look over at?" He began pulling the burgers from the bag and the hot, salty scent of the French fries caused Mac's mouth to water. She hadn't eaten since a banana and orange for breakfast and she was starving.

"I don't know. I just saw movement. Everybody was already there but us. Maybe it was Leigh. I sure didn't see her, but she apparently was skulking around."

"Who's Leigh?"

Taft grabbed several plates and placed the burgers and helpings of fries on each one. He carried Mac's to her, then sat down on the edge of the chair and looked at her Technicolor ankle.

"Where's your burger?" she asked.

"Over there." He hitched his head toward the other plate still sitting on the counter, never taking his eyes off her foot. The bag of ice had shifted some and Mac reached down to readjust it, but he stopped her by picking up the bag himself and setting it aside. She opened her mouth to protest, then sucked in a breath as he gently rotated her ankle a bit to get an all-over look at it.

"That hurt?" He looked up, his blue eyes intent on hers.

"No, no, not really . . . I'm just . . . worried."

Actually, she was totally distracted by that intent look. Taft was a guy who went from clean-shaven to a three-day beard and back again with regularity. She knew he just got tired of shaving but also didn't want a full beard. This habit only increased his attractiveness in her opinion. Clean-shaven was nice. He almost looked like a businessman, but the raffish beard was even better.

She swallowed as she felt every one of his fingers against her skin.

"You really did it. That's gonna be pretty for a while," he proclaimed, replacing the ice pack.

"Yep."

"So what was it you said you had to tell me?"

"Go get your burger and let's eat." She was struggling a little with having him so intimately check out her injury.

He obediently got up to oblige and Mac let out a pent-up breath. She concentrated on her food and ten minutes later they were both making short work of their fries. She wiped her fingers on her napkin and proceeded to tell him about Gavin approaching her at the funeral and then Leigh surprising her at her apartment. She finished with, "Which had nothing to do with Tim Knowles's funeral. It was like they were both lying in wait for me. Detective Haynes was the only one I spoke to who seemed focused on Tim's murder."

"What did Haynes say?"

"Nothing, really. He seemed to feel there was something off about the circumstances of Tim's death. I don't know. I wanted to ask him what he meant, but I didn't get the chance."

"Beer?" he asked.

"Water, please."

Taft picked up her empty plate and took it into the kitchen, then returned with a water bottle for her and a beer for himself. He handed her the water and said,

"So, you have a couple of potential jobs, and something hinky about the burglary/homicide of Tim Knowles."

"I told both Gavin and Leigh they should talk to you."

"And they said, no way. They want you," he guessed.

"How'd you know?"

"Classmates."

"Huh," she agreed. "They don't really see me as a professional, but they want to use me."

"Have 'em write up a contract."

"Leigh gave me a fistful of cash and I put it in the drawer." She pointed toward her kitchen junk drawer. "I wanted to give it back, but I'm not moving fast enough." She'd already told him that Leigh was hiding her payment to Mackenzie from her husband. "And Gavin wants to get together and convince me to look into the death of Ethan Stanhope, which is his white whale. Ethan's death was an accident." She lifted her hands and dropped them.

"Any good reason to think it wasn't?"

She slowly shook her head. "I don't know. He and his sister died in a car accident. High speed around a tight corner, which Ethan didn't make." She thought about it a moment. "I never heard about toxicology. Maybe I can check on that. I went to the funeral to pay my respects. I don't know what it says about Gavin that Tim's death wasn't top of mind for him. Or maybe it was, and Ethan's death is a distraction? Something else to think about? Either way, the result is he talked to me about Ethan at the grave site, then he called me and started pushing for me to open an investigation. He's serious."

Taft picked up the ice pack, which was half melted,

and took it back to the kitchen. "So, what do you think Haynes meant about Tim's death?"

She heard him open the freezer and rattle the ice tray. "He wasn't satisfied. He was talking more to himself than to me. He seemed angry."

Taft returned with a new bag of ice. "An officer shooting . . . Bet he wants to dig into it further."

"Maybe." She sucked air through her teeth as he settled the cold pack on her ankle again. "Why? What are you thinking?"

"Maybe I'll do some digging myself."

"You think there's something there?"

"If Haynes thinks something's there, I wouldn't be surprised if he's right. But the department's closed the books on it, so he'll be hampered looking into it. I won't."

"I want to help." Mackenzie regarded him earnestly.

He pointedly looked down at her ankle. "This is going to take a while to heal."

"Not that long," she argued.

"And what're your plans for Gavin Knowles and your friend Leigh?"

"Elayne," she corrected, aware that she was lucky Leigh didn't object to being called by her high school name because Mac wouldn't be able to call her anything but Leigh at this late date. "She's not really a friend . . . more of an acquaintance. I don't know what I'm going to do with either of them. Make a few phone calls." She carefully turned her ankle a bit, and the cold pack slipped off. Taft picked it up again and held it aloft for a moment as they both looked at her stretched and swollen blue-and-purple skin—skin that had already swallowed up her ankle bone.

Taft said, "If you need me, I'll help. You've been the legs for me before. Guess it's my turn now."

"I'm not going to like being incapacitated."

"Your patience is legendary."

"Ha," she groused.

"Well, let me know what you want and I'll be there."

She met his gaze. For reasons she couldn't explain—maybe just her overall weakness right now?—her inner core felt molten and her emotions were too close to the surface. Her nose was hot. Swallowing, she nodded.

He left a few minutes later and she blew out her breath. She felt unsettled that he was making enemies of Prudence and Anna, and though Taft was certainly capable of handling his own life, she had a prickling sense of danger waiting in the wings.

CHAPTER 5

Natalie Hofstetter looked around Kristl's mother's house with an inward sniff. The tired kitchen sported dated and scarred maple cabinets, the floor was linoleum in a godawful pattern of orange, brown, and yellow pinwheels, and the jewelry of the room, the chrome fixtures, had been dulled by years of use, the finish failing. Yes, this was the house where The Sorority had spent so many high school sleepovers, but it hadn't aged well, and Natalie, being in the renovation business, started mentally ticking off all the things she would change if she lived here. Not that she ever would. It wasn't the kind of property her company looked for. It was too . . . well, cheap.

But it wasn't for sale anyway. It was owned by Kristl's mom and Natalie knew Kristl had no say in the matter. Her father had died about six years earlier and Natalie guessed that's when things really went to shit. Now, it was just beyond hope and though Kristl had made a few remarks that maybe Natalie's company could do some minor renovations and get her mother's house on HGTV and they could possibly get a stipend from the network or Nat's company itself... there was not an ice cube's chance in hell that this ratty house with its moss-covered roof and dilapidated garage could ever be considered. Natalie was in Portland looking for that special property to get herself back on TV, and there was a condo in Portland's Pearl District that was just perfect. Good bones, bad decorating, just crying for her help.

If Phillip would ever make a fucking decision in his life it would help.

She inwardly fumed. She'd dragged her husband through the last few renovations. He owned half the company but he didn't do jack shit. His one saving grace? He looked good on camera and so the producers were reluctant to go with just Natalie who, she could admit, was a bit tense on camera. But she was the one who did all the work!

Isn't that always the case? Having to haul the dead wood around?

She looked around at Kristl and Erin, checked her Apple watch and demanded, "Okay, so where is Leigh?"

"I don't know." Kristl's lips were pursed. Natalie wondered if choking out a laugh when Kristl mentioned her mother's house instead of taking her seriously had been the smart thing to do.

"Didn't you say she was coming right over?"

Resentment crossed Kristl's face. At least she'd lost weight and learned to put on some makeup over the years, Natalie thought. She'd been a real dog in high school, though all of the sisters had lied and told her she looked great. Maybe that was a mistake. That brassy red hair was now darker, an improvement. When

Natalie had asked her if she dyed it Kristl had glared and snapped, "NO!" Touchy, touchy. It was just an innocent question.

You should be nicer. She spends every day taking care of her mom, who's spiraling down deeper into dementia every day.

"I don't know exactly when she's coming. She didn't give me a time," Kristl muttered.

Natalie cleared her throat and vowed to be more patient. "Well, let's call her. Find out where she is."

"Why don't you call her, Natalie?" Kristl expelled. "I mean, why do I have to?"

"You're the one who told Leigh to come late and spy on Mackenzie Laughlin."

"I did not!" Her face turned red. "I just said Mackenzie would be there and I hoped she didn't talk to Gavin."

"You told Leigh to follow her in and she did," Natalie reminded. "Caused her to trip. Isn't she supposed to be this private investigator or something? Well, if she is, she's the clumsiest one around."

"She *is* a private investigator," Erin clarified.

Natalie eyed her. Now, here was someone who had definitely changed for the worst, picking up the pounds Kristl and Leigh had shed. Erin also still had that little girl look Natalie found so unbearable. Round cheeks, mousy brown hair and wide eyes, and *boring* conversation about details no one cared about. Natalie had felt like slapping her since the minute she got back to River Glen, just to wake her up.

Kristl said, "I know we didn't do anything wrong. It's just that Gavin's been saying all this shit, like it's my fault Ethan died. Well, I did nothing to hurt him.

I even . . . I was nice to him even when he was so mean to Mia with Roxie . . . and . . ." Her voice was getting smaller and smaller. Natalie had to lean in to hear her. "Well, we didn't kill his little sister," she suddenly burst out, startling Natalie. "He did it all by himself."

"Hmmm . . ." murmured Natalie.

There was an uncomfortable pause and Kristl looked like she was fighting tears.

Erin said, "Hey, it's okay. We all know you didn't do anything. None of us did anything. Gavin's just having a hard time over his brother's death, and I mean, that's why we're all here today. Because of Tim's death."

"Yeah," said Natalie shortly.

"Yeah," agreed Kristl on a deep sigh.

Another pause ensued and Natalie's bid for patience ended. "Can we be real for a minute? I know we're all tense and yes, we went to Tim's funeral, but we're really here to do damage control. I've got a TV career, and I don't want these dumb leftover rumors from high school turning up on *TMZ*."

"What's *TMZ*?" asked Erin.

"Seriously?" Kristl swung her head at her. "Celebrity gossip show? Oh, c'mon. You've seen it. You have to have seen it."

"All I'm saying," Natalie broke in, "is that we're all here to put this *chatter* . . . these rumors, to bed. And if Gavin's the source, then we need to deal with him, and that's why I want to know where the fuck Leigh is!"

"Could you stop saying . . . the F word," Erin said, bunching her shoulders.

"Fuck, fuck, *fuck*."

"Natalie," Kristl muttered on a sigh.

"Well, c'mon. Let's stick on the hot issue here. Leigh was supposed to let us know what Mackenzie knows, about Gavin or whoever. What he's saying, what other people are saying. Is this a hot button, or is it just really old news? That's all I want to know. I've got things to do. We all do. We just need to move on."

Kristl's face darkened. "Gavin's been blaming me for a while. He's centered on me right now and it sucks."

"Who's he been talking to?" Natalie demanded.

"Everybody!"

"Is he on social media? Is he telling friends? Classmates?"

"Well, he told Tim, and Tim told me what he'd been saying!" Kristl's lips tightened. "And now Tim's dead . . ."

"None of this is our fault," reminded Natalie, once again.

Erin pulled her shoulders in and said, "Maybe it would be better to leave Gavin alone."

"There's an idea," agreed Natalie.

"It was Tim's funeral today and it just feels like we don't care enough," Erin added, a bit timidly. You never quite knew which way Natalie would jump.

Natalie sucked in a calming breath. "Look, it's terrible. I would never be a police officer. Too dangerous. I'm sorry Tim's gone. I didn't know him that well, but he always seemed like a nice guy. Big smile. Big heart, too, I guess. But let's be honest, we went to the funeral to see what Gavin was up to. He's the real reason we went."

"Krissy . . ." a feeble female voice sounded from down the hall. "Krissy?" And all three of them turned to look in that direction.

"Mom," Kristl explained unnecessarily, heading toward the hallway.

Natalie watched her go and asked Erin, "Is it Alzheimer's?"

"I'm not sure. Maybe. Some kind of dementia, anyway. She's gotten a lot worse since Kristl's dad died."

"Hmmm . . ."

"It's hard. It's really hard when your parents start to fail," said Erin.

She was looking at Natalie as if she had something more to say. Taking the cue, Natalie asked politely, "What about your parents?" Her own had divorced long ago and were happily living separate lives in separate states. They'd both congratulated their daughter on her one television season, but neither had they been as impressed as Natalie thought they should be. She bet they didn't even know she'd been put on hiatus, a nicey-nice term for *cancellation*.

"They're doing okay. They sold the house and bought a smaller one in Laurelton. Dad plays golf."

Natalie couldn't have cared less. Being alone with Erin made her want to pace the room and work off nervous energy. She wished Kristl would get back here and *Leigh*, for shit's sake. Where was she? She, at least, had money and could possibly make some kind of deal with Natalie, or maybe just put money into renovating another property. That would be just fine. A good start. Everything was just too damn expensive in San Diego and Phillip could just *rot* there. Natalie had decided to come back to the Greater Portland Area where she grew up and start a new show. *Rose City Renovations*, or maybe just *Rose City Ren-o*.

THE SORORITY

"But what if it does comes out?" Erin asked suddenly.

"What?"

"That you had us all pledge to kill Ethan by a car accident and that's exactly what happened to him."

"C'mon, Erin. It was a joke! A fucking joke! How could we engineer that? We were all just mad at him for Mia's sake."

"But it's weird, and the way things happen on TikTok and Insta . . . ? I mean. I can just see this going viral. One of those *Datelines* that asks . . . *Were they all in it together?* You know what I mean. And you, the television star? Don't you see it?" She threw out her arm like she was revealing a breathtaking vista. "'Natalie Hofstetter orders a murder.' No. 'Natalie Hofstetter and The Sorority pledge to kill high school classmate . . . and *do*.'"

Natalie gazed on Erin's cherubic face with distaste. "You're giving me a stomachache with all this bullshit. I don't know how many times I have to say it, it was a joke. Okay, a bad joke, but it was a joke. A JOKE. And you put your hands in, too. You pledged."

"Do you think Gavin could know that?"

"Who cares? It was a JOKE!!"

"I care. And you care."

Natalie held onto her temper with an effort. "Who would tell him?" she snapped. "No one knew but us."

She nodded, then said in a small voice, "Maybe Roxie?"

Roxie. Roxie Vernon. Natalie thought about the rogue member of The Sorority with mixed feelings.

"For fuck's sake, I need a drink. You think there's any wine around here?" She walked over to the refrigerator and peeked in. A moment later she slammed the door shut and moved to the cabinets, flinging open and throwing closed doors one by one.

"I'll get you a glass of water," Kristl told her mother, fighting back the huge sigh that wanted to overtake her. Her gaze turned to the window. She could draw a straight line from here across all the residential houses and commercial buildings to that bar on Eighth Street. That's where she wanted to be. Not here with her mother, who grew more addled every day, and not with the Sorority, who'd never really been her friends though at one time in her life she'd thought she'd die without them. She'd been fat and freckled and dying for a boyfriend and it still made her shudder to think of how pathetic she'd been. Now she looked better, lots better. She'd worked out and found a healthy diet and kept snacking to a minimum and shed the pounds. Makeup tamed the freckles and she'd started dyeing her hair a less brassy shade of red. At the bar, which was frequented by mostly men, a lot of cops, she could slide onto a stool and get all kinds of looks and offers of free drinks. Sometimes she'd tune into a guy, let him run his hand down her leg, maybe wrap his fingers around her inner thigh, maybe go to his place. Sometimes she'd be aloof. Sometimes she'd hit on the bartender, Rob Something, and end up fucking in the storeroom behind the bar. Rob always zeroed in on her when she came in, and she could read the jealousy on his face, the tightening of his jaw, whenever she flirted heavily with someone else.

But the bar was off-limits now . . . now that Gavin Knowles had decided she was to blame for Ethan

THE SORORITY

Stanhope's death. It was insane! She'd become friends with Tim at the bar and though they hadn't had sex, they'd been working up to it. She really liked Tim, even thought she could fall for him. Things were looking good. But when Tim mentioned to Gavin that he knew her, and then Gavin just started spouting all those old rumors from high school about Ethan's death, Tim had carefully moved away from her. The last few times at the bar he'd lifted a beer in acknowledgment from across the room. And then he started acting like he didn't even know her. Like maybe she was poison . . . like maybe she was a killer.

It burned right down to her soul.

"Where are you going?" her mother asked in that whiny voice that made Kristl want to climb the wall.

"To get you water. I just told you that."

She walked back to the kitchen to find Natalie throwing open drawers. A bottle of red wine, her best bottle, was on the counter. "You want an opener?" Kristl asked, a little miffed.

"Yeah. Where is it?"

Kristl walked to the other side of the room, threw open a drawer, and collected it for her, irked at Natalie's highhandedness, but then when had she been anything else?

She took her mother the water, though Mom had closed her eyes now and was breathing shallowly. Kristl looked down at her, wondering if she might die. She set the glass on a cardboard coaster she'd brought back from Lacey's, the cop bar. A flutter of regret filled her chest. She was sorry Tim was gone.

Back in the living room, Natalie was pouring glasses

of wine and Erin was looking anxious, as always. Kristl took a moment to study them both. There was no need to be intimidated by Natalie anymore, Kristl told herself. She'd toned down her black hair a bit and she'd traded her alternative lifestyle for commercial success as a home renovator with her husband. They lived in San Diego and had done a season on HGTV, with mediocre results, according to Erin, who kept up on those things—but not *TMZ*, God!—but she was now living in Portland, at least temporarily, trying to reignite that career.

Natalie's dark eyes swept toward Kristl, who then said to Erin, "Maybe try Leigh again."

Erin sighed heavily. "I have. I've texted her, too. I don't know what else I can do."

"Just try."

Natalie handed both Kristl and Erin a glass of red wine. She then glanced at Kristl and said, "You've got some house maintenance ahead of you." She was facing the sliding glass doors that led to the backyard wooden deck, currently slick with rain and greenish alga gunk.

"I know." Kristl was short.

Erin set her glass down, tucked in her chin, and angrily punched numbers into her phone. She put it on speaker and let it ring on and on until Leigh's voicemail kicked in. Holding up the phone to them, she shot them both a *See there?* look, as Leigh's tinny voice asked them to leave a message, then disconnected the call.

"I think we're all overreacting to Gavin and Mackenzie Laughlin talking," said Natalie.

Kristl swirled her glass and watched the red fingers of wine travel down the inside of the glass. Were they?

"You're the one who got upset," reminded Erin, carefully.

"Gavin just watched his brother lowered into the ground. He's processing. People grieve all kinds of ways. It's not some big conspiracy between the two of them."

Erin looked doubtful at Natalie's rationalization.

"They were commiserating with each other," agreed Kristl. She took a long swallow of her best wine, the bottle Natalie had so carelessly opened. She didn't have a lot of good wine.

She could have asked.

"But . . ." Erin began.

Both Kristl and Natalie swung their heads her way.

"But what?" Natalie's staccato question hung in the air.

"It's just that Leigh said that Gavin's been talking a lot about Ethan again—"

Kristl groaned. "We know that."

Natalie gave an unintelligible growl and tipped back her glass.

"You just said yourself, that's why we're here," Erin reminded her unhappily.

"Call Leigh again! I want to talk to her," Natalie demanded. "No, give me her number. I don't have it in my phone. I'll call her."

Erin reluctantly told Natalie the digits for Leigh's cell, and both Natalie and Kristl entered them into their phones. Natalie stabbed the numbers onto the screen, then held the cell to her ear with her left hand and threw her right arm across her waist, waiting.

Once more Kristl could hear Leigh's recorded voice mail greeting. Natalie said in a brittle voice. "Hi, Leigh, it's Natalie. We're all here. Where are you? Call me back as soon as you can . . . please." She rattled off her number and ended the call. She shook her head and muttered angrily, "Why are we even still talking about Ethan?"

Because you told us how he was going to die, Kristl thought. She looked at Erin, who was clearly thinking the same thing. Erin swallowed hard and tried to avoid eye contact. Kristl inwardly sighed. Erin was weak. She still didn't want to go against Natalie and well, Natalie was tough.

"Leigh didn't say she overheard them talking about Ethan," reminded Erin.

"Well, good. Would it affect my show, my business, if it came out that we *jokingly* pledged to kill him? It wouldn't be good. And we didn't kill him. But I don't love the idea of having to explain it."

Natalie finished the last swallow of her wine and set the glass down on the counter with more force than necessary. Kristl started, worried she'd break the stem. They weren't expensive but they were all she had—*all Mom has*, she corrected herself.

"God, I just don't need this," muttered Natalie. She looked down at her nails. They were a glossy, dull red, but the pinky finger on her right hand was chipping. She worried it a little with her opposite thumbnail. "Anybody want another glass?"

"No, thanks," Kristl said dryly, since her glass was still half full and, well, it wasn't Natalie's wine. But

Natalie, being Natalie, didn't pick up on her tone as she moved to pour herself another.

"Shit!" Nat yelled suddenly. She'd spilled on her black dress.

"It doesn't show," said Erin as Natalie refilled her glass, emptying the bottle.

"I paid a fortune for it," Natalie muttered, swiping at her dress with a paper towel.

They were all dressed in black, but Natalie's dress fit her like a second skin and was severely cut. Something about the red nails and red wine reminded Erin of Nat's Goth days even though now she looked more like a cutthroat executive. Her dark hair was swept into a tight bun and her eyes were outlined in black with thick, sweeping lashes. Her mouth was a slash of dark red. And of course she'd worn smooth black Louboutins with their bright red soles winking to the crowd whenever she moved, even though the heels had partially sunk into the mud. Natalie had kicked them off and rinsed them in Kristl's kitchen sink without asking. Her gall still amazed Erin, but then in high school she'd made them all promise to kill Ethan and they'd agreed, which was mind-boggling in itself.

But who was she kidding? This was the question that kept Erin awake at night. Ethan Stanhope had died just the way Nat had described. Nat had been so furious with him, blaming him for breaking up their sisterhood, it had really seemed like she'd wanted him dead, even though Roxie was as much to blame as Ethan was. And what about Mia? In one of her rare visits home, Mia had met with Erin and Leigh and confessed that she'd been a little relieved Roxie had helped her break up with Ethan that spring. "I didn't love him," she'd told them to their collective surprise. "I wasn't even sure I liked him. He was so full of shit. So full of himself. And then he died, and I couldn't say anything bad about him. I'm not a monster. I'm just being honest here. Let's face it, I especially didn't want to bring up anything and put attention on us."

"It wasn't our fault he died," Leigh had quickly corrected her.

"He died in a car accident," Erin said.

Mia had given them both a look that said they all knew better, which was not the truth! Both she and Leigh had been disturbed, and afterward Erin had gone home to her apartment and gathered her cat, Chili, close, feeling vulnerable.

Now, here they were discussing Ethan and Ingrid Stanhope's deaths again and feeling responsible somehow, though none of them had forced his car off the road. Sure, they'd agreed on it, but that was meaningless. Ethan had taken a corner too fast and lost control. That's what killed him . . . and Ingrid.

"We can't be blamed for wishing Ethan dead," Erin said, echoing what Leigh had pointed out to Mia that day. Mia hadn't answered her, and Erin had gotten the impression she might not feel the same way. Leigh had doubled down on their being innocent, but Mia had remained silent.

Now, Kristl said, "Of course we can't. Life's full of tragedies that are no one's fault."

"Optics, ladies." Natalie glanced over her shoulder at

them. "We all agreed to kill him and that's what people will remember, if it should ever come out."

You were the one who posed the car accident, Nat!

Erin felt a small spurt of anger. She barely managed not to blurt out what she was thinking.

"Wishing someone dead isn't a crime," said Kristl, impatiently.

They all grew silent, sipping their wine, none of them really relieved by their attempts to minimize the odd and eerie way Ethan had died.

Erin sent Natalie and Kristl a sideways look, not wanting to appear that she was staring, sizing up, cataloguing. She was a little envious of Kristl's new svelte figure. She looked absolutely great. She'd mentioned there was a workout room at the back of the garage now, and she apparently used it regularly while Erin sat home with Chili and a bowl of ice cream or popcorn. She'd picked up some of those pounds that Kristl had shed. Just looking at Kristl and Nat, Erin resolved to cut down on the calories.

"Should we open another bottle?" asked Natalie, already pulling one from the cupboard. "Uh-oh. It's your last one. Unless you have more somewhere?"

"No. That's it." Kristl was curt.

Erin could tell she was sort of pissed but that didn't deter Nat in the least. She opened the bottle, filled her glass and Kristl's, then looked at Erin. Erin tipped her goblet and swallowed the last bit, holding out her glass, too. *The diet starts tomorrow*, she thought, watching as Natalie poured the pinot noir into her glass, the red wine catching the light, emitting a dark carmine glow.

"I don't have any appetizers except cheese and crackers," Kristl said.

"That would be great," said Erin, her resolve fully crumbled.

Kristl shot a glance at Natalie, who seemed completely disinterested in food. She then went to the refrigerator and cut pieces of cheddar cheese into small orange squares and ringed them with Triscuits on a plate. Erin reached in and placed the cheese atop the cracker and took a bite. She didn't care that they weren't super special hors d'oeuvres. She understood that, like her, Kristl was not floating in money like Natalie and, well, Leigh, she thought as she munched away.

Natalie was just finishing off her latest glass of wine when they heard tires crunch on the gravel drive. Erin hurried to the front window. "She's here!" she said in relief.

Leigh entered a few moments later. Like Erin, she'd always been a bit soft and round, maybe not as round as Kristl had been, but now, like both Kristl and Natalie, she was slim and trim, having shed the doughy pounds. Her hair was blonder and seemed to make her eyes bluer. Erin felt like a failure among her friends. If not for Leigh, she wouldn't even have a job.

"Well, there you are," said Natalie.

"Sorry. I didn't really know we were having a meeting." Leigh eyed the wine bottle as she set down her large black purse on the counter, but she didn't pick up one of the empty glasses. "I thought you were all trying to get rid of me at the funeral."

They all chorused a "No, that's not true" on that,

then Natalie said, "You almost blew it when Mackenzie tripped."

"I didn't trip her. I just tried to duck out of sight, like you all told me to."

"We didn't tell you that." Kristl frowned.

"Then why was I the one chosen to hide from her like a criminal?"

"We just needed intel, Leigh . . . *Elayne*," Natalie exaggerated. "So, what did you learn?"

"I don't know why you're all so worried about Mackenzie. She's a private investigator, I guess? She doesn't know anything, and there's nothing to know anyway."

"It was an accident," said Kristl in a singsong voice, echoing Nat.

Natalie waved that away. "She was talking to Gavin at the grave site."

"Gavin doesn't know anything," said Leigh, shaking her head as Kristl held the bottle above her glass.

"I'm sick of Gavin accusing us all of stuff he knows isn't true," Natalie said firmly.

"I'm just sick of him blaming *me*," added Kristl.

Leigh shook her head. "It doesn't matter. He tried to hire Mac, but I think she thinks he's a nut job." She shrugged out of her black coat and laid it over the edge of the couch. Beneath was a black dress with a white collar that Erin had seen in a magazine and knew cost a small fortune.

"He tried to hire Mac?" Natalie repeated.

Erin just wanted them all to quit talking about that damn pledge. "It was a nice service," she said, trying to steer the conversation in another direction, though actually it had been a very sad affair. She would be haunted by the looks on Mr. and Mrs. Knowles's faces for days.

"Well, what did Gavin say about Ethan?" persisted Natalie.

"*Nothing*." Leigh looked exasperated.

Erin glanced away from them, knowing that she was bad at holding her thoughts to herself. Her expression always gave her away. That wasn't what Leigh had been saying before. She'd worried to Erin that Gavin's continued probing about Ethan's car accident was like a tongue obsessively searching the hole left from a missing tooth.

"After the service, I went to see her," Leigh admitted, not meeting anyone's eyes.

"Mackenzie?" Natalie snapped, her eyes wide.

Kristl asked quickly, "You went to see her? Why? Where?"

"I went to her apartment because a) she's a friend and b) I couldn't hear everything she and Gavin were saying, so I thought I'd just ask her." Leigh then shook her head and grabbed a glass and the wine bottle, delivering a healthy pour to herself. "You all act so scared."

"Concerned," corrected Kristl.

"Very concerned," echoed Natalie. "Did you ask her point blank what she was talking about with Gavin?"

"Yeah, I did, as a matter of fact. They were apparently discussing his brother's death, which makes sense. We *were* at Tim's funeral. I did press her, but she didn't say anything more." Leigh sighed. "It was really sad today. I felt really bad for the Knowleses."

"The Stanhopes were there," said Natalie.

They all looked at her, but no one was surprised. Gavin and Ethan had been good friends.

"The Stanhopes have become really religious," revealed Leigh. "They lost two of their children graduation night."

No one said anything for a while after that. Finally, Leigh put in, "Have any of you heard from Mia lately?" They all shook their heads and she added, "Me neither." She then ran a finger over her lower lip and said, "I was going to keep this a secret, but I can trust you guys to keep it from Parker. I asked Mackenzie to find out what happened to her."

"You hired Mackenzie?" Natalie looked appalled.

"Just to find Mia. What's wrong with that? If you're all so concerned about her, at least I'll be in contact with her. I don't know if she's going to do it, though. She's thinking it over."

They all plied Leigh with more questions after that revelation, but she didn't have much more to add other than that she and Mia had kept in fairly close contact until recently, and that suddenly there was no communication between them at all.

"What about Roxie? Anybody heard from her?" Natalie asked after they exhausted the subject of Mia.

"She was never part of our group," remarked Leigh, her mouth turning down.

"Well, yes, she was," Kristl disagreed. "Until the Ethan thing."

"Mia said Roxie maybe did her a favor. She said she didn't even like Ethan that well," revealed Erin.

Nat snorted. "Easy for her to say that now. Like that's going to absolve her of agreeing to kill him."

"You said it was all a joke," Erin reminded her anxiously.

"Relax, Erin. Once again, I'm joking." Natalie rolled her eyes.

"Well, Mia sure cared about Ethan when Roxie went after him," reminded Leigh. "None of it matters anyway. Ethan's gone, and now Tim Knowles is gone, too . . ."

"And Ingrid," Kristl said quietly.

"And Ingrid," Natalie repeated after a moment.

Ethan's little sister's death was the real tragedy.

Natalie was the first to seem to shake herself back to the present. "Well, as long as no one's trying to blame us for anything, fine. I just don't want to hear that Gavin's suddenly going all in again on Ethan's accident. He did that when it first happened, and it was grief talking. We were all upset. But now again after his brother's death . . . this blame game is not okay."

"It was before his brother's death," said Erin. They all looked at her. "Well, that's what you said," she reminded Kristl.

"I don't know when he started blaming me, he just did." Kristl pressed her lips together.

The conversation moved off Ethan Stanhope's death to catching up on their current lives: Natalie's TV aspirations; Leigh's job with her husband's company, Parker Flooring; Kristl's care-giving for her mother and her mulling over a career; and Erin's dud of a love life. Erin would have preferred not to talk about it, but Leigh nudged her and she admitted that she'd been sporadically dating but every guy she met was a loser.

Kristl asked, "Are you on dating apps? That can be really rough."

"How'd you meet your guy?" Erin asked Kristl, who straightened as if goosed.

"I'm not dating anyone."

"I thought I heard you were."

"How? I've got Mom," Kristl reminded her.

Leigh slid her a look from beneath her lashes. "I heard you were seeing the friend of someone else you were dating."

Kristl flushed. "That was before. It just kind of happened and then it was over."

"Sounds a lot like Roxie and Mia . . ." Natalie smirked.

"It wasn't like that at all. Mike and I were already through. We were just kind of friends and so we were open to meeting other people. It just happened to be Stu."

"You and Mike still friends now that you're with Stu?" asked Natalie.

Kristl pursed her lips. "I'm not with Stu. I'm not with either of them."

"Still, it was poaching," said Nat.

"Jesus," Kristl muttered. "They were just guys at a bar."

Natalie pointed her finger at her in the shape of a gun. "That's what I'm saying."

Erin thought that was no excuse for bad behavior. "Roxie went after Ethan when he was still with Mia. Maybe Mia didn't like him anymore, but Roxie didn't know that. She just went after him."

Leigh said, "Mia liked Ethan a lot. She just said that to us to cover up that he basically dumped her for Roxie."

Erin thought of their friend with her shaggy blond hair and fresh-faced look. Her big smile. What a lie Roxie

Vernon had been. She wasn't sorry they didn't see her anymore.

"Where *is* Roxie?" asked Natalie, as if reading Erin's thoughts.

"Don't know. I only care about Mia," said Leigh. She kind of sounded like a sourpuss, which warmed Erin's heart. She liked Leigh and wished they hung out more together. She and Kristl lived in town and Leigh was in the neighboring city of Laurelton, and now Natalie was in Portland, at least for a while, drumming up business. They could restart The Sorority. She said as much and everyone kind of went silent and didn't look at each other.

"So, I guess that's a no," Erin said, disappointed.

"We're all still kind of in it whether we like it or not," remarked Kristl, not sounding like she enjoyed it all that much.

"Is your husband joining you?" Erin asked Natalie now.

"Doubtful," she said through a smile. "I may just stay here and leave Phillip in San Diego."

"Seriously?" Leigh looked a bit scandalized, but then Leigh was married to Parker, who was kind of a bastard himself, according to her. According to others, his business ran on Leigh's family's money, but Erin had recently gotten a job at Pickwick Lighting on Leigh's recommendation, as Pickwick and Parker Flooring did a lot of business together, and Leigh being half owner of Parker Flooring had some sway. Erin felt indebted to her and didn't want to look a gift horse in the mouth. Leigh had apparently had to pull some strings with Parker to make it happen.

"I'm just exploring options," said Natalie. "It's kind of good to see all of you guys again."

Did Nat really feel that way? Erin wasn't sure.

"Wish Mia was here," said Leigh.

"And Roxie?" asked Kristl with a devilish smile.

"None of us want to see Roxie again," said Erin.

Natalie's smirk returned. "Maybe we should make a pact to kill *her*. It worked last time."

Erin laughed uneasily, but Leigh and Kristl chortled as if they found that really funny.

"Once again, I'm kidding, Erin. Kidding." Natalie looked exasperated.

"I know," said Erin quietly.

"Can no one take a joke around here?" Natalie clutched her empty glass and looked a bit sadly at the finished bottle of wine.

"I have some cheap stuff in the garage," Kristl said after a long moment. She didn't sound all that excited about sharing another bottle.

"Fine. Let's get drunk." Natalie shrugged. "The sisterhood's back together again."

Kristl left, her shoulders tight, and returned with a bottle of Chardonnay, the label Erin knew well as it was within her price range.

Natalie made a moue with her lips, then took her glass to the sink, where she rinsed it out. Erin thought she was done, but when Kristl opened the bottle of white, Nat filled her drink halfway and said, "To the Sorority," lifting the glass high.

Leigh raised her own glass and looked at Erin, who shrugged and tentatively lifted her empty one. She had a job she was settling into and still had to put in an appearance later today. Even though she was with Leigh, her friend wasn't her boss. Seth Halliday was, and he wouldn't appreciate Erin coming to the office half drunk.

As if reading her mind, Leigh said, "I'll text Seth and tell him you're out for the day. It'll be fine. Don't worry."

"You sure?"

"Yeah."

"Okay," Erin said gratefully. She didn't want to go back. It felt a bit dangerous to be back with her friends, friends she knew had always been more popular than she was, but she wanted to ride it out. She'd considered herself lucky to be part of their group back then, and would have done anything to stay there . . . even when she'd half believed they were going to kill Ethan.

"To The Sorority," they all chanted, clinking their glasses together, though with less enthusiasm than in their younger days.

"So, we all agree we're going to kill Roxie, right?" asked Natalie.

"Shut up," groaned Kristl.

"You *have* run that into the ground," agreed Leigh.

Kristl then reversed what she'd just said, by announcing, "I'd kill her. Gavin already thinks I killed Ethan, so what's another one?"

Natalie started laughing, nearly spitting out some wine. "I love you guys!"

"Me, too!" Erin declared.

She meant it. They added color to a pretty drab life. And she wanted to be with them, to be one of them. It was important. Nevertheless, she could feel anxiety building in her chest. Their toasts to the death of another always made her squirm. Like they were tempting fate or something.

It was only much later when she was back in her apartment, in bed in her pajamas with Chili wrapped in her arms and purring in her ear, that she could feel that knot of anxiety loosen.

Mac's cell rang in the middle of the night and she dragged herself up from the depths of sleep, surprised by the noise as she generally turned her phone off when she retired for the night unless she was actively working a case. She realized dully that she'd fallen asleep in the chair, having not wanted to move after Taft left. Now she fumbled around in the dark for her cell, twisting her ankle further in the process. She yelped in pain, swore, then swept up the phone, catching it on its third ring.

Gavin Knowles.

Shit. Damn. This wasn't going to work out. She should've never given him her number. Her finger hovered over the button to disconnect, then clicked on.

"Gavin," she answered coolly, calling herself an idiot. *Do you know what time it is?* She almost went with the cliché but didn't have a chance as he yelled into the phone, "Mac, I'm being followed! They know I talked to you!"

"Gavin . . . who? I don't think—"

"I know I'm being followed!"

His voice sounded a bit slurred. "Have you been drinking?"

"Was with my folks, but they're—Shit, those brights! Those brights in my mirror! I can't see!"

"Gavin, if you're driving, pull over."

"WHAT THE FUCK!"

"Pull over! Right now. Stop!" She tried to throw off the blanket she'd tossed over her legs and got caught up in it somehow. His terror ran through the phone line to electrify her. She was wide awake. She half fell out of the chair, bit back another cry of pain that infuriated her as her ankle screeched at her.

"Oh, shit . . . Oh, shit . . . ahhh . . . they went around me," he said.

Mac snorted, annoyed, settling herself back in the chair. "Good. Now, listen. Stop. I don't think you should be driving. Pull over. Where are your folks now? Can you catch a ride? Uber or Lyft? Or is there someone you can call?"

"I called you."

"I realize that," she said patiently, "but I mean, is there someone else? Someone who could come pick you up?"

"They know I talked to you. They're afraid you'll find out who killed 'im. They wanna get rid of me 'cause I keep bringing it up."

"Ethan . . . ? Gavin, you don't want a DUI on top of everything else. Park the car."

"I didn't drink that much. We were just talking. Tim's

death was wrong place, wrong time. But Ethan was *killed* . . . maybe Tim was, too . . . I doan know . . ."

"Gavin."

"I know you doan believe me, but I'm right. I'm always right. Oh, holy mother . . . oh, fuck, oh . . . fuck . . . They're coming back! THEY'RE COMING BACK!"

She heard the rev of an engine. "Gavin . . . Gavin?"

"I'm going, I'm going! *THEY'RE COMING BACK!*"

"Don't drive! *Gavin!*"

"AAAARRRHHHHHH!"

"GAVIN!"

CRASH!

The sound was horrendous, even through the phone. "Gavin! Gavin? Can you hear me? Gavin? Are you there?"

The line was dead.

CHAPTER 6

Mac immediately swiped to her favorites list and called Taft. She looked at her bedside clock. 12:33 a.m. The line rang a couple of times and then he answered, "What is it?", sounding solidly awake.

"I just got a call from Gavin Knowles." Quickly, she brought him up to speed.

"Did you call nine-one-one?"

"No. I don't know where he is and I don't know what happened. I don't even know if it's real. Knowles isn't entirely trustworthy. But it sounded real. I think it's real."

"You said he was with his parents? Do you know where they live?"

"Yes. If they're at the same place as when we were in high school."

"Do you want me to come get you?"

She thought about the urgency in Gavin's voice. He'd been frightened. It wasn't a trick . . . was it? "Yes," she said firmly.

He was at her place in twenty minutes. "Some traffic," he told her as she hobbled down the stairs in a rain jacket, the sweats she'd fallen asleep in, and a slipper on her injured foot. Taft was in the same jeans, gray T-shirt, and black jacket he'd worn to her place. The rain was lightly falling as he helped her into the car.

"You need that taped," he said again, shooting a look at her ankle as he started the engine.

"I know. Stillwell Hill. Toward the East Glen," she answered.

The East Glen River ran southward, defining River Glen's eastern perimeter. There was new housing construction, a large development on the southeastern end of the city that butted up to the city of Laurelton, and a strip of unincorporated county land where Mac had once had an incident with a killer and been run off the road. She couldn't drive by the area without thinking of it, as she did now, though the thought was fleeting as her attention was on Gavin's call.

The Knowleses lived on the exclusive ridge where older, sprawling estate homes had held reign for decades until recently, when large parcels of land had been lopped off and divided into lots sold to home builders. But there still remained a number of untouched estates, and Leland and Brighty Knowles owned one of them, Art and Coral Stanhope another.

They were flying up Stillwell Hill and Mackenzie kept her eyes on the underbrush on the passenger side. Maybe the crash had been here? Somewhere near here? She'd heard it through her cell phone; that was a fact. Something had happened to Gavin, but was it here?

They reached the Knowleses' property without seeing any evidence of an accident and Taft slowed down and looked over at her.

"I don't know," she said.

Her cell phone rang at that moment and she yanked it out of her pocket and answered the unrecognized number with an anxious, "Hello? Gavin?"

"Hello. This is Officer Marks with the Laurelton Police Department. Is this Mackenzie Laughlin?"

Mac's heart plummeted. "Is this about Gavin Knowles? Is he all right?"

"Ma'am, you spoke to Mr. Knowles this evening?"

"Where is he?" Taft whispered to her. They were idling in front of the Knowles estate.

She shook her head and said into the phone, "Yes. Did he tell you that? Are you with him? Was there an accident?"

He hesitated. "Yes, ma'am. A witness said he was on the phone when it happened and we have his last number as yours."

"A witness? Someone called it in. Is Gavin okay? Where are you?"

"Ms. Laughlin, it sounds like you're in a car?"

"Yes, I'm . . . a passenger and I just came up Stillwell Hill. We're looking for him." She knew a lot of the River Glen officers, but they'd crossed into Laurelton territory here, and she'd never heard of Officer Marks. "Did someone call in the accident? Is Gavin okay?"

The officer hesitated again. Initially relieved that someone had alerted 911, she didn't misinterpret the unspoken messages Marks was giving out.

"Officer Marks, is Gavin Knowles alive?" she asked, swallowing.

"Someone from the department will be calling you back."

As soon as Marks clicked off, Taft, who'd heard

Mac's side of the conversation, said, "Musta happened on the downside of the ridge," and hit the accelerator again.

"Someone said that Gavin was on the phone. They got the number and called me."

Taft nodded. He'd gleaned that. "He's dead?" he asked grimly.

"I don't know."

A half mile later, they saw the rhythmic red-and-blue flash of a police car light bar emanating from around a corner. Taft slowed as they made the turn. They'd traveled the crest of the ridge and were just starting its downward slope. In front of them was a patrol car with an officer standing outside, talking to three people in varying states of dress, coats over pajamas and hurriedly thrown-on clothes. Over the cliff edge on the right side Mackenzie could just see the glint of metal from the back left fender of a silver Mercedes sedan that was tipped forward and jammed into several trees. The wink of red taillights moving down the road proved to be the back of an ambulance.

"They've already got Gavin inside," she said.

Another car was parked on the road. A dark green Lexus. A man in business clothes was leaning against the back of the vehicle, looking spent and bedraggled in the continuing drizzle. The witness, Mac guessed.

Taft pulled over and Mac got out and stood by the front fender, her left hand on the hood for balance. "Officer Marks? Mackenzie Laughlin. I used to be with the River Glen P.D." She saw then that there was a phone in a plastic evidence bag. They'd gotten her number and bagged the phone.

Taft got out and came around to her side of the car to stand by her. Both of them looked at Officer Marks, who was somewhere in his thirties and regarded Mackenzie through hard eyes, as if the accident were somehow her fault. The three people in haphazard dress appeared to be from the house across the street whose wrought iron gates were swung wide. Mac figured they'd been awakened by the crash and had come out to see what had happened. This proved true as Officer Marks requested they return to their home. The group reluctantly complied, at least as far as the gate at the end of their long drive, where they remained, shivering in the rain.

"EMTs got here pretty quickly. That your witness?" Taft asked, pointing to the man in the business suit.

Officer Marks ignored him and asked Mackenzie, "Were you meeting with Mr. Knowles?"

"No, we were just on the phone. Are they taking him to Laurelton General?" *And not the morgue . . . ?*

"What were you discussing?" he asked.

Mac looked at him. He was the responding officer, not a detective. She didn't owe him that information, especially since his attitude was somewhat hostile. She said evenly, "Gavin Knowles's brother, Officer Tim Knowles with River Glen P.D., was killed in the line of duty last week. I was with Gavin at the funeral today."

The officer's eyes widened and he inhaled a sharp breath. They stared at each other in the rain for a few moments and then Mac swiped her damp forehead and said, "I'm going to the hospital."

Taft helped her back in his Rubicon, Mac putting her arm around his neck to aid her hop to the passenger door. She looked down at her wet and muddy slipper, feeling Taft's sturdy arm holding her close. She thought of the whole day—the ankle sprain, the dreary weather, the meetings with Gavin and Leigh and her feelings about them both—and was swept by a wave of emotion that left her drained.

"Wait," Marks demanded, but Mackenzie didn't look at him.

Taft moved back to the driver's side. He glanced toward the bedraggled witness, who seemed to be unaware of the rain and cold. "What happened here?" he called to the man.

The man lifted his head to look at Taft and then straightened. Caught in Taft's headlights and dashed with blue and red flashes from Officer Marks's light bar, his face was ghastly pale.

Marks ordered, "Sir, would you mind waiting by your car?"

Ignoring him, the man said to Taft, "I didn't see the car go off the road. I heard the crash and I came around the corner and he was over the edge. The car was bouncing like it might just break right through the limbs. I thought it was going to go right down, but it just hit that one—"

"Sir!"

"—tree and stopped cold. I called nine-one-one and pulled over. They were here fast. They got him out but—"

"SIR!"

"—I think he was already dead. He looked dead. They did CPR, but—"

"That's enough!" Officer Marks's voice was the crack of doom. He looked around wildly, as if expecting a raging riot. "We'll wait for Detective Rafferty!" he declared.

"September Rafferty?" asked Taft.

The officer turned slowly to look closely at Taft. Mac recognized that Marks felt he'd been challenged by Taft, by both of them. She sensed the young cop bristle and said, "We both worked for River Glen P.D. for a while and have worked with officers from Laurelton."

If she'd hoped to defuse the situation, she quickly learned that was not the case when Marks snapped, "You both need to get back in your vehicle. Stay there until the detective arrives."

"Rafferty can meet us at the hospital," said Taft.

"Gavin's parents live just down the road," added Mac. She hooked a thumb behind her as she and Taft got back into the Rubicon and said to Marks, "Leland and Brighty Knowles."

"We have the information," he snapped out as she slammed her door shut. Taft pulled away.

Mac shook her head. "What was that all about?"

"He doesn't know where his authority begins and ends," said Taft as he navigated the curves down the hill and into Laurelton.

"Marks had no authority to keep me there."

"He can complain to Rafferty when she gets to the scene."

They reached Laurelton General fifteen minutes later. The hospital had been built on a hill, so the first floor on one side was the third floor on the other. They pulled into the parking lot off Emergency on the downward side of the building. The ambulance was still there, but Gavin had already been rushed inside.

Mac got out and tried to hurry toward the entrance, damning the sudden clutch of pain that shot up her leg and caused her ankle to give way. She stumbled and ducked her head against the light drizzle.

"Wait," Taft ordered, remote locking the car as he came around to her once more. He wrapped his arm around her, beneath her breasts. Her attention was divided between the pain and annoyance of her ankle, and the awareness and warmth of being cradled by Taft.

"You need that ankle looked at as long as we're here," he said.

"Are you kidding? I'm not paying ER prices. I just want to know about Gavin."

"You can do both."

"I don't think so."

They worked their way into the Emergency Room waiting area. Mackenzie shifted away from Taft as soon as they were out of the weather. She swiped at her damp, lank hair. He suggested she sit in one of the faux leather gray chairs arranged around the periphery of the room, but if he was getting information, she wanted to be with him.

The place was dead quiet except for the muffled noises, maybe shouts, they could hear behind the double doors that led to the examining cubicles. There was one nurse seated behind a counter in a booth-like area surrounded by plexiglass. Her eyes dropped to Mackenzie's wet and muddy slipper as she and Taft approached.

"We're here about Gavin Knowles," Taft alerted her. "An ambulance just brought him in. He was in an accident up above Stillwell Hill."

"Are you a relative?" she asked, looking from one to the other of them.

Mackenzie put in, "No, but his parents have probably been alerted. I'm a friend. I was talking to him on the phone when he crashed." She could hear the tension in her voice but it wasn't penetrating the nurse's stolid demeanor.

"You'll have to wait, ma'am."

Mac was ready to keep pushing, but Taft told the woman, "Thanks," and pulled Mackenzie away to one of the chairs.

"He's alive," Mac said.

"Yeah. She didn't deny that they brought him here."

"He's behind those doors, not at the morgue."

Taft nodded.

Mac thought back to the conversation with Gavin in the cemetery parking lot, her annoyance with him. Maybe she should have listened harder. She'd thought his ranting about The Sorority was part of his grief. Rage before acceptance. But now she wasn't so sure. "What do you think? He was positive someone was after him and then I heard screeching, braking, and his screaming and the crash. The phone went dead on his scream. He wasn't paranoid, as far as I know."

"You're second-guessing yourself."

"Maybe. I feel kind of guilty. All I was thinking about was that I didn't like him and didn't trust him, and I still don't."

He nodded.

"You don't have to stay. I can Uber home."

"I'm staying."

"Taft, thank you, but—"

"I'm staying," he repeated and Mac subsided, grateful.

Twenty minutes later, Brighty and Leland pushed through the door into Emergency. Brighty wore dark gray slacks and a white shirt beneath a long black coat, tied at the waist. She'd slapped on lipstick and her mouth was a gash of red against her white pallor. Leland's face was haggard and slack. He was in wrinkled gray slacks, a cream shirt open at the throat, and a navy jacket. Mac had seen them earlier in the day and they'd both been put together, solemn but calm. Now, with this second tragedy, they were rumpled and spent.

Both Brighty and Leland were taken through the hydraulic doors that led to the inner sanctum. Mac caught a glimpse of a green curtain around a cubicle and the stockinged foot of whoever was behind the curtain. The noise she'd heard earlier had subsided, though there were two ER personnel—nurses, maybe—standing beside whoever was on the gurney inside the cubicle. Brighty and Leland stopped and looked at the occupant who was obviously Gavin.

The hydraulic doors hissed shut.

Half an hour later, the doors opened again and the Knowleses walked out, Leland's arm around his wife's waist much as Taft's had held Mackenzie. Brighty was struggling to walk, fighting emotion. She looked on the verge of collapse, like she wouldn't be able to make it to a gray chair before she fell. Mackenzie automatically straightened as if to help her and Taft did the same, moving in front of Mac to offer aid. Brighty ignored

Taft, her eyes on Mackenzie. She pulled herself together with an effort. Leland squeezed her hand hard and said, "No, Brighty," but she brushed him off and stepped in front of Mackenzie, bristling with anger.

Mac wanted to shrink back into her chair, but managed not to.

"His last words were for you," Brighty told her in a voice sharp enough to cut through steel. "'Tell her it was Kristl.' That's what he said. 'Tell her it was Kristl.' I don't care what he says, it was all of you high school girls who ruined his life. All of you girls who tormented him and Ethan Stanhope. And then Tim . . ."

"Brighty," Leland murmured.

She swept on, "Your dad was a cop and he and you influenced Tim to join the force. If it weren't for you . . ."

Taft stiffened beside her, but Mac held up her hands. "Last words?" she repeated. Her heart had seized on *his last words were for you*.

"He's not dead," Leland put in quickly, shooting his wife a glance. "They're taking him to ICU."

Brighty rounded on Leland. "He's in a coma and I can tell they think he won't come out of it!" She turned back to Mackenzie. "And it's your fault. All of you!"

With that she marched blindly toward the doors, stopping at the last moment and heading down the hallway toward the hospital elevators, where she slapped her palm down furiously on the button about twenty times. Leland worked his way to her, moving like a condemned man.

***

It wasn't Detective September Rafferty who showed up at Laurelton General twenty minutes later. It was a slim woman with dark curly hair and slanted blue cat's eyes who looked around the room and saw Mac and Taft. Her gaze sharpened on Taft, and Mackenzie knew she recognized him, had likely heard about his reputation for being a thorn in the department's side. His two stints on the force had been contentious, and he fit far more easily in private investigation.

"Sandler," he said, recognizing her as well.

"Well, well, well," she responded, eyeing him up and down.

"Hi, Gretchen. Didn't know you were back."

"Jesse," she acknowledged. "L.A. didn't work out."

Mac guessed they were about the same age, approximately six years older than she was. The look Gretchen Sandler gave him was one of cautious appreciation. Mac had seen that look before from women who were intrigued by him.

One more reason he was off-limits.

"What happened to Rafferty?" he asked.

"Busy on another call. It's been kind of a wild night." She gave Mac a cursory look before asking, "Why were you at the crash site?"

"You spoke to Officer Marks?" asked Mac.

"He told me you were following the ambulance to Laurelton General. Fill me in."

"I was on the phone with the victim, Gavin Knowles, when he crashed. He thought he was being followed. I don't know if that's true. I heard the crash. I just wanted to make sure he was okay. Officer Marks seems to think it was something more than a single car accident."

"I just want to hear facts, Ms. . . . ?"

"Laughlin. Mackenzie Laughlin."

"You look familiar," she acknowledged.

Taft said, "Like me, she used to be with RGPD."

"Like you? Let's hope not." Her smile was faintly ironic. She turned her attention back to Mac. "Marks seems to think this could be more than an accident. The victim's parents feel the same way. I'd like to know what you know."

"Only what Gavin believed," she responded honestly. "He thought someone was following him. He was panicked. And then I heard the crash. Is there evidence it was a two-car accident?"

"Haven't got the report yet." Then she allowed, "Possibly. Was that the gist of your whole conversation? He called you because he thought you could help?"

"We'd had a conversation earlier. At the grave-site service of his brother, Officer Tim Knowles."

She gave a deep nod. "I understand he was a good man. I'm sorry about losing him. You think this had anything to do with that?"

"I . . . don't know."

Her blue eyes narrowed on Mac, who could feel Taft tensing beside her. He knew as much as she did about all that had transpired since this morning—no, yesterday morning as they were approaching three a.m. Maybe it was time to lay her cards on the table. Who was she protecting anyway?

"Gavin blames classmates of ours from high school for the death of a high school friend and he's been pretty vocal about it lately, I understand. His brother's death seemed to exacerbate that some. I don't know for certain, but when he called, he blamed them."

"Classmates? Plural?"

"Yes, well, currently one of them specifically, Kristl Cuddahy, but all of them—us—over the years." She then explained about Brighty and Leland saying much the same thing to Mac.

"These were your friends that he blamed, but he called you?"

"I wasn't really a friend. It wasn't . . . I was on the periphery. It was high school," she added, as if that explained it all. "Gavin mentioned Kristl, but it felt like he was pulling a name out of a hat. Kristl's part of the group, but I don't think she has any more enmity toward Gavin than the rest of them."

"Who are these people?" Sandler repeated. She'd pulled out a small booklet and a pen.

They call themselves The Sorority.

"Girls from high school. A clique. There have been bad feelings between Gavin and them ever since his friend, Ethan Stanhope, died on graduation night." Mac then explained about Ethan's car accident not long after attending the party at Gavin's parents' house that a lot of their classmates had attended.

"And these girls were there. This clique."

"Yeah."

"And you?"

Mac could feel her skin heat up under the questions and she sensed Taft's interest in her answers as well. "I went to the party but couldn't make myself go in. I saw Ethan Stanhope in the driveway and he teased me about being in the school's spring play. He died later that night. From what I've heard, Gavin never got over it and has blamed The Sorority ever since. That's what they called themselves."

"These friends of yours."

"Friends . . . classmates . . ." Mac's ankle was throbbing and she could feel exhaustion creeping in around the edges of her subconscious. "Gavin asked me to look into Ethan's death. He was upset at his brother's death, but Tim Knowles's murderer was shot and killed, so there's no mystery there. I don't know what Gavin really wants from me. Some sort of resolution."

"And this accident?"

"I heard the crash. Was it two cars hitting, or him going off the road? He said someone was following him."

"One of this 'sorority'?"

Mac spread her hands. "He was good at blaming them but he never came up with any evidence."

Taft said, "Maybe he can answer your questions himself."

"Maybe." Sandler glanced away, looking around the ER as if searching for someone. "All right. Give me your information and we may be calling you."

Mac gave her all her pertinent contact information. It seemed like Sandler thought she might be going down a rabbit hole on this one and Mac didn't blame her. A lot of Gavin's theories came from his desire for a justice that might be unattainable. Still, his voice had been filled with panic. Either his conspiracy theories about The Sorority had made him paranoid, or someone had pushed his car off the cliff. Examination of the vehicle should clear that up.

Mac hobbled on her own back to Taft's SUV. She didn't want any further closeness with him when she was feeling so strangely vulnerable. She leaned her neck against the headrest and closed her eyes as he drove them through the dark wee hours of the morning back to her apartment. She felt tired to the bone and wasn't as convinced as the detective appeared to be that there was no case. And now that she'd had time to think it bothered her that Brighty had blamed her for being part of The Sorority, which she wasn't, and maybe even that her father had been an officer and therefore she was complicit in Tim's decision to join the force. Where had that all come from? Her father was gone long before Tim had even graduated high school.

"What are you thinking?" asked Taft.

"Brighty Knowles mentioned my dad being a cop, like he'd influenced Tim somehow. She was throwing blame all over the place." She opened her eyes and pressed her lips together. "It's a little thing among everything else, but the more I think about it, the more it bugs me."

"People do strange things when they're grieving. No social handcuffs. It can be really raw."

"I'd like to think that way, but it pissed me off. I should be feeling sorry for her, but I'm just sitting here, pissed. Guess that makes me the bitch."

"She was out of line."

"Thanks, but I'm still the bitch, right?"

His brows lifted. "I'm not touching that one."

"Smart man," she said, her soul feeling a little lighter.

After a few moments of companionable silence, he said, "I remember your father."

Mac blinked. "You do?"

"Met him once when I was with Portland P.D."

She straightened and half turned in her seat to look at his profile directly in the lights from the dash. She saw him flick her a look. She realized the scent of rain was on him and it smelled good. "How did you meet him?" she asked.

"Random. I was off duty in River Glen. There was a domestic dispute at a barbecue at the house next door to where I was. Little girl was in the street, crying, so I went over to see what all the screaming was about. Your dad and Cooper Haynes came and brought things under control."

"How come you never told me?"

"You don't talk about your father. I never interfaced with him again, and he was gone by the time of my short-lived stint on the River Glen force."

"My dad died when I was in high school but he seems so present all of a sudden, with all my classmates contacting me and Tim Knowles's death. I don't know. It's weird." She purposefully changed the subject. "Sandler seems to think it might all be in Gavin's head, another expression of grief."

He grunted in agreement.

"But Gavin said someone was following him, and there was a crash. He said, 'They're following me,' actually. I thought he meant The Sorority, but maybe not."

"Tell me about this sorority."

"It's just what that group of girls called themselves." Mac filled him in on Natalie, Kristl, Erin, Leigh, Mia, and Roxie.

By the time Taft dropped her off, and insisted on

once again helping her up the stairs, the rain had finally stopped, though Mac felt chilled to the bone, made worse when Taft deposited her at her door, taking his warmth with him. She crawled back into bed, expecting to have trouble falling asleep, but she drifted off instantly, dreaming of rain and car taillights and the rhythm of lovemaking.

I wake from sleep, but my mind spins like a hamster in a wheel as I review over and over again how much care I've taken to cover my tracks. I parked the van and walked around it, examining the front fender. It was crushed, but then it already had been. Yes, if Forensics gets hold of it, it will likely have some paint chips from Knowles's Mercedes, but detectives will have to connect this particular vehicle to the crash and I'm going to make sure that doesn't happen.

I walked away from the van to where I'd hidden my car, parked down an alley from the empty lot with the for-sale signs inside the windows of the rows of pathetic looking vehicles for sale by owner. I chose the site because I knew the owner of the nearly abandoned property with its weeds pushing through the cracks in the concrete: an old and feeble man with major hearing loss. He also doesn't give a shit about the vehicles parked for sale on his property. He doesn't give a shit about anything, really, except the news station he keeps on twenty-four/seven. That he rails on about to whoever's within hearing, usually no one, as he's too slow to catch anyone who's left their car parked on his lot, victim to the elements.

I then drove home . . . home . . . there is no home. There's just a place to be for the hours that I need to sleep. But tired as I am, I'm also exhilarated. I've stopped the harassment. My plan wasn't as carefully thought out as I'd hoped, but maybe sometimes, not often, but maybe sometimes that's for the best.

And on the unlikely chance anyone comes sniffing around about the accident that had to have killed Gavin, they'll find I was home at the time. My phone was home and I was asleep. I did it. I killed someone who deserved to die. Again.

CHAPTER 7

Cooper Haynes breathed in the scent of his wife's hair and neck as he snuggled up against her in bed. He had about a minute this morning before the alarm went off, but he didn't want to leave this nest until the absolute last second. He splayed his hand over her abdomen where their baby was growing. Incredible. First Mary Jo Kirshner, their surrogate, had discovered she was pregnant and they'd barely gotten used to that wonderful news when Jamie herself learned she was going to have a baby. An abundance of riches, Jamie had said, shocked, as she'd looked up from the pregnancy test she'd taken. Now they were getting ready for two children.

Jamie murmured and half turned toward him. He kissed her jawline and the alarm began its annoying *beep, beep, beep, beep* until Jamie slapped her hand down on it and said, "I hate you," as it cut off.

Cooper took no offense as this was Jamie's relationship with the alarm clock. "Don't go," she said, reaching for his hand as he slipped from beneath the covers. "This is the most excitement I'm going to get all day."

"You don't have to spend every moment in bed," he said.

"Did you hear something different than I did?" She gave him a look.

Jamie was about six months along and suffering from preeclampsia. There was worry that she was going to lose the baby. Bed rest had been ordered by her doctor, but it was a controversial stance amongst the medical community these days. Some doctors felt it didn't really help. Others believed in it entirely. Jamie had endured some early bleeding and was terrified she would miscarry. She'd started the school year teaching second grade but had had to give that up several weeks ago. Now the question of whether she should spend the next three months—*three months!*—in bed was up for debate, and Jamie was trying to comply by limiting the time on her feet. Cooper knew that if the pregnancy failed Jamie would blame herself, but he couldn't imagine her staying sane after that much time confined to a bed. He knew he wouldn't.

"Moderation," was all he said as he headed for the shower.

Twenty minutes later, he was shoving his arms in his sport coat and heading out of the room. Detectives at River Glen P.D. weren't required to wear a tie any longer, so his white shirt was unbuttoned at the throat. However, RGPD's chief of police, Marcus Duncan—nicknamed Humph for his long, world-weary, Humphrey Bogart face—still wore a tie.

Cooper started to open the door and Jamie said, "Don't let the cat in," at the same moment Twink streaked into the room and hopped up on the bed, turning its black-and-white face to Cooper as Jamie growled and pulled the pillow over her head. Twink, short for Twinkletoes, was a black-and-white tuxedo cat who'd recently become part of their family when Jamie's sister, Emma, had brought it over from Ridge Pointe Independent and Assisted Living, where Emma lived. The cat had become persona non grata with the administration at the retirement home because of its uncanny ability to sneak into residents' rooms and settle next to them in bed right before they died.

Emma had been on a mission to rescue Twink from Ridge Pointe over the past months and had finally gotten her wish. With only a few beds in their home, the house Jamie had been bequeathed by her deceased mother, and with Jamie in bed most of the day, the cat had apparently decided there was only one place to be: the master bedroom. It didn't help that Twink loathed Emma's dog, Duchess, who traveled with Emma every time she visited, which was more and more often now that Jamie was incapacitated.

"I'm no match for the cat," apologized Cooper as he watched Twink chew at and lick one of her front paws.

"None of us are."

With a sigh Jamie propped herself against the pillows and reached above her head, desultorily petting the cat. Twink immediately pushed her head into Jamie's hand, reveling in the attention and purring. "Can you knock on Harley's door?" Jamie asked. "I'd do it myself but . . ." She threw out an arm to encompass the bed, the baby, the whole situation.

"I'll get her up." He came back to kiss Jamie on the top of the head and she groaned. Twink took a playful swipe at him and he muttered, "Cat thinks she owns you."

"She probably does," Jamie said on a heavy sigh. "And you make me feel like an invalid. Okay, I am an invalid, but you don't have to make me feel like one."

"You're not an invalid. You're a hot babe in a flannel nightgown."

She looked down at herself. "It's not flannel, it's Pima cotton."

"What's the difference?"

"Do you even know what flannel is?"

Twink worked up a yawn, her pink tongue stretching between sharp white teeth.

"We're boring the cat. Goodbye. See you tonight."

"I'm not a hot babe, I'm boring . . . What will I be like by the end of this prison term . . . ?"

"Still hot!" he called after her as he left the room, walking down the short hallway to rap on Harley's door.

"I'm sleeping!" she yelled at him through the panels. "I don't have to be in school till eleven."

"What about your mom's breakfast?" Harley made a sound in her throat but Cooper heard the thump of her heels on the carpet. "Will you pick up Emma before dinner?" he asked.

"On it," she called back.

Harley was Jamie's daughter from her first marriage . . . and a college freshman at Portland State University. The gap between Harley and her soon-to-be two half siblings was a pretty big one and they were all a little boggled, but the excitement was growing. Even Emma, who rarely showed any emotion—the result of a terrible attack her senior year in high school that had forever mentally altered her—showed how agog she was as well by all the plans she was continually making to get ready. She'd even announced she was moving back to the house to take care of Jamie, but that was still up in the air, as Emma's help, though well meant, sometimes interfered with the actual running of the household, and with Jamie incapacitated Cooper wasn't sure how well he and Harley would bridge the gap with or without Emma.

He headed downstairs and out of the house, grabbing a banana on the way. Better than the perpetual donuts in the break room. He'd managed to ignore them most of his years at River Glen P.D., but he could already see his eating habits were going to deteriorate.

As he entered the department, his partner, Elena Verbena, said, "Gavin Knowles is at Laurelton General. He was involved in a car accident early this morning." She was just sitting down at her own desk, which butted up to and faced his.

Cooper stared at her. "How bad is it?"

"Don't know yet. We heard from Laurelton P.D. Detective Sandler, who was called to the scene and now techs are checking if it was a one-car or two-car."

Cooper had met and exchanged information with Detective Gretchen Sandler a time or two as the cities of Laurelton and River Glen were next to each other. "He was forced off the road?"

"That's what they're checking."

The good feelings Cooper had carried into work from

his family dynamics faded into the background. "Any indication alcohol was a factor?" he asked.

She shrugged and shook her head. They'd both been to yesterday's funeral, though Verbena had taken a call and missed the grave-site service because of a family matter. It wouldn't surprise either of them if the Knowles family, gutted by Tim's death, downed a few drinks after the stressful events of the past week. In fact, it would be more than likely.

Verbena added, "You could ask Mackenzie Laughlin. She and Jesse Taft were at the scene last night as well. Knowles was apparently on the phone with Laughlin at the time of the accident."

Cooper felt a jolt of surprise. He'd mentioned to Mackenzie that he felt something was off about Tim's death. Had that had anything to do with her being on the phone with him? "What time was the accident?"

"Around three a.m., I think. Thereabouts. Check with Sandler . . . or Laughlin."

Or Taft . . .

Cooper knew the private investigator as someone who cut to the truth. Some of his colleagues in law enforcement thought the ex-policeman had sold out, gone to the side of the enemy, and Cooper had half shared that opinion because Taft had been linked with Mitch Mangella, whose own reputation of stepping across the legal line was well deserved. But Taft had always shown himself to be a canny investigator and Cooper knew his recent split from working with Mangella was his own choice. Now Mangella was dead, having fallen off the roof of his own home, which had raised a few eyebrows itself, though no one currently at River Glen P.D.

was overly anxious to dispute that his death was an accident. The department had no love for the likes of Mitch Mangella, even though at one time he'd been such a rising star in the business world that the mayor and others in the city's public office had touted knowing him. Not so anymore.

"How's your mom?" he asked Verbena, as he took his seat at the desk and looked across at her. The squad room accommodated about twelve desks, though they were the only ones around at the moment.

"Home again. Low on salt this time." She splayed her hands and shook her head, meaning she had no idea what was coming next. Her mother had been having a series of medical events that led to ambulance trips to the hospital. She'd just stepped outside of the funeral home yesterday when she got the message that her mother was in an ambulance after being found unconscious on the bedroom floor.

"Anything for today yet?" Cooper asked her.

"Not so far."

They both looked toward the door to the chief's office. The blinds were drawn and the room was dark. It was early yet, but Chief Duncan was notoriously slow to get to the office, though he often stayed later than most of his staff.

Cooper thought about Gavin Knowles, lying in a hospital bed. He wasn't sure if his accident had anything to do with what had happened to his brother, apart from the result of grief and bad luck, but he knew he wanted to reexamine the facts surrounding Tim's death and Gavin seemed like a good place to start. But Gavin Knowles's accident had taken place in Laurelton and was therefore under their jurisdiction, so there wasn't a lot he could do until he knew what the techs uncovered to even decide if his crash was purely an accident.

But if it was discovered another car was involved, then he was going to do his damnedest to shoulder his way into that investigation as well. He could feel in his bones something wasn't right about Tim's death; the reported circumstances leading to it were woefully incomplete, in his opinion. He picked up his phone and searched his contact list for Jesse James Taft's number.

Bzzzzz . . . bzzzzzz . . .

Mackenzie stepped out of the shower, awkwardly leaning on the sliding door handle to hold her weight, swearing a blue streak, before managing to grab a towel and hobble to her bed where her cell phone was still ringing. She didn't recognize the number, so she took a moment to tuck the towel around her torso before sinking onto the bed and answering. Being dressed, such as it was, made it feel like she could concentrate more.

"Hello?"

"Mac? Mackenzie?"

Ah, yes. Leigh. She recognized her voice and made a mental note to add her to her contact list. That thought was immediately followed by the realization that Leigh likely knew about Gavin.

This theory was proved right when Leigh asked in a tremulous voice, "Have you heard what happened to Gavin?"

"Hi, Leigh. Yes, I do know about the accident . . ."

She wasn't sure how much she wanted to reveal about her involvement at the scene yet.

"Do you think it was a suicide attempt?"

Now that surprised her. "No. That really hadn't occurred to me."

"He's just been so . . . morose. Living in the past and all. It's been hard on everyone." She sounded like she was barely holding back tears. "He's been obsessed with Ethan's death. Well, you know, he talked to you about it."

Mackenzie blinked. She hadn't told Leigh anything about what she and Gavin had discussed upon leaving the grave site. "How do you know what he talked about with me?"

Now she was sniffling. "Well, I just assumed. He's been talking about it for weeks. You don't think it was a suicide attempt?"

"No . . ."

"What do you think happened?"

Mackenzie really didn't want to go into it all. "I'm half dressed. Can I call you back?" She needed some time to think things through.

"I guess. Will you call me right back?"

"Sure."

Mac clicked off, put on underwear and eased her injured foot through the leg of her jeans. She pulled the jeans up and hobbled to her dresser where she grabbed a blue V-neck sweater. Her ankle wasn't too bad if she stayed in one place, but any movement of her foot and leg caused her to clench her teeth. *How long is this going to take to heal?*

She brushed out her hair while standing on one foot

and balancing herself with her free hand on the counter. Sighing, she made her way to her chair. It was going to be far more difficult than usual for her to conduct any investigation, either for Leigh or Gavin or anyone else.

She sank into the chair, feeling tired to the bone. Not enough sleep, by a long shot.

She really didn't want to return Leigh's call, but she'd said she would and she'd agreed to work for her.

As she pressed Leigh's number she thought back to Gavin's panicked call: . . . *They're coming back! THEY'RE COMING BACK!*

He'd believed he was being targeted and maybe he was. She wondered what chance she might have to see him at the hospital today. Maybe he'd awakened from his coma and she could find out exactly what he remembered, although with his mother out for blood and Gavin's condition unclear at this time, it was hard to know what was real and what wasn't. He'd certainly been scared last night.

"I just want to know if you're going to look for Mia," Leigh said after she answered, getting right to the meat of what she wanted.

Mac looked down at her bare, injured foot, rotating it a bit, wincing from both the pain and the expectation of the pain. Leigh had already given her a hefty retainer and there was nothing holding her back except for her swollen and colorful ankle, which she was not going to let stop her from doing what she wanted. And though she'd tried to dismiss Gavin's words about Ethan Stanhope's death, he'd stoked her curiosity, which had been further ignited by last night's accident. Maybe it was worth delving into the past after all. And looking for Mia gave her a legitimate reason to ask questions.

"Yes," she said determinedly, to which Leigh sighed in relief.

"Good. Thanks. Just one thing, though? Don't talk to anyone else about her when you learn her whereabouts, come directly to me first, if and when you find her, which I know you will."

"I'll do my best," Mac answered.

"So, no one else. Just me. I'm the only one you talk to."

"That's what you're paying me for."

"Good. I'm just so . . . flustered and sad. I just don't want to advertise the fact that I'm worried."

"Well, I will be asking questions."

"Okay . . . I did tell my friends about your investigation."

Mac blinked. "Yesterday you were adamant that no one should know."

"I know. I still don't want Parker to know. I just don't want the grief, but The Sorority . . . I don't care."

"Okay. I'll probably start with Mia's family." Mackenzie vaguely knew the Beckwiths. Couldn't remember the parents' names, but knew Mia's brother, Mason, was a few years older than Mia.

"Let me know as soon as you've got anything."

"Will do."

She'd just managed to get herself back from a trip to the bathroom when she heard the loud rap at her front door. Sweeping up her phone from the side table, she checked the time as she made her way carefully toward the door. Almost ten. Her tiredness was still persisting and probably would all day.

"Hey," she said, opening the door to Taft.

He held up a small sack for her to see.

"What's that?"

"Ace bandage. I'm here to help."

"Great. Thanks. How do you look so wide awake?" she grumbled, moving back into the living room.

"Have you had breakfast?"

She snorted.

"I should've brought you something."

"What is this? You don't have to take care of me." She eyed him suspiciously as she propped her foot on the rather worn ottoman she'd taken from her mother, and Taft pulled out the elastic bandage and started wrapping it around her ankle.

"Tell me if it's too tight."

"It's too tight," she said. In actuality she was having trouble concentrating again as his fingers moved gently and smoothly around her tender skin as he began wrapping her ankle.

He stopped short. "Is it?" His blue eyes regarded her intently.

"No, maybe not. I don't know. I don't really . . . think I need all this. I'm good, really."

He sat back and regarded her with a faint smile. "No, you're not. What's going on? Just let me finish and we'll see where we are."

She braced herself as he kept winding the elastic band around her foot and across her ankle. She was propped on the heels of her hands, shoulders at her ears, by the time he was finished.

"How's that?" he asked, smoothing the elastic, testing its tightness. He looked up from his work, saw how she was braced, and said in surprise, "Does it hurt? I can unwind it," and bent to do just that.

"No, no. It's fine. Really. I think it's going to be good."

"Then why do you look like you're about to leap out of your skin?"

"Because . . ." *You're touching me.* She wriggled her toes. "Actually, if feels pretty good. Thanks. I mean it."

"It's got to be tight enough to give you support."

"I get it. Good." She closed her eyes to block out his face so close to hers. But his face seemed imprinted on her retinas. She could still see the blue and green striations in those eyes, the light raffish beard that she wanted to feel against her skin, the hidden dimples, the curvature of his jaw . . . She blinked open immediately.

"You thought of something?" he asked.

A great excuse . . . one she could use rather than feeling like she was going to groan with desire if he didn't get away from her. "Yes, I . . . uh . . . want to see Gavin Knowles today. Think I can get past Brighty?"

"Depends on how he's doing," he answered. "I called the hospital but they wouldn't give out any information. Maybe we'll have to go there and see for ourselves."

"Yeah, we? Okay? You done wrapping?" she asked a little breathlessly.

"Let me check." He smoothed the bandage with his hands once more, checking for creases that could irritate, running his hand under her arch, brushing against the ball of her foot, which was still bare skin.

So help me God . . . She slowly inhaled, hoping to calm her suddenly galloping heart. It wasn't hard to imagine his body atop hers.

"I think you're good. How does it feel?"

Like I want to melt into the cushions right here. "Not bad." Did her voice crack? It felt like it cracked.

"So, what do you want to do?" he asked, watching her.

"I . . . think I'll . . . go to the Beckwiths. And ask them about Mia."

"This is the job your friend, Leigh, asked you to do?"

"Mmm-hmm."

"So, you decided to take it." He got to his feet and leaned his head in the direction of her ankle. "That slipper you had on last night . . ."

"Yeah, it's toast."

"You got a shoe that'll work?"

"I got some clogs with a back strap," she said dubiously. About a hundred years old, brown, and ugly as sin.

"Put a tennis shoe on the good foot for support. You might need crutches."

It was better now that he'd put a little space between them. She'd worked with him long enough to be over this. What the hell was wrong with her?

You must be in a really weak state.

"Want to try putting some weight on it?"

"Sure."

She started to lift herself up, but Taft reached for her hands. She held them out and he closed his over them and pulled her up from her chair. It put her in close proximity and she waggled a bit, placing a hand on his chest for support. She felt the heat beneath his shirt and snatched her hand back, nearly overbalancing.

"Whoa!" He quickly grabbed her arm, steadying her. "You gotta put some weight on that foot."

"Sorry. Yep. You're right."

It was clear he wasn't feeling anything that she was. *For the best,* she told herself. *For the best.*

Taft's cell buzzed and he pulled it from his pocket, his brows lifting. "Cooper Haynes," he said.

"Really?" That caught Mac's interest. Though Taft knew the police detective, their respective jobs often kept them on opposite sides of an investigation with the police considering PIs a nuisance and sometimes even an impediment.

"Taft," he answered, taking a few steps away.

There was a very long pause while Mackenzie had a chance to view Taft's profile, his strong chin and dark brows, the faint curl of his hair at his nape, his jeans and gray, long-sleeved collarless shirt. The outline of the taut muscles of his upper arms. He'd tossed his jacket over the back of Mac's love seat when he'd come inside and now he picked it up, listening hard.

"When do you want to meet and where?" he asked. A pause, and then he said, "Come to my place. I'll be back there in twenty, thirty minutes." Another pause, and then, "Okay," and he hung up.

"Well?" asked Mac.

"He wants me to work the Tim Knowles case. The department's closed it, but he thinks there's something there."

"It must be really eating at him to go behind the department." Now it was her brows that were lifting.

Taft smiled faintly. "A little like rejoining the River Glen P.D. again, without all the restrictions."

"Don't get Cooper in trouble over this."

Taft moved his hands toward his chest in an innocent *Who, me?* gesture.

"Yeah, right," she muttered, glad that her crazy sexual pique was a little more under control . . . at least as long as he stayed *over there*.

"I'm not going to get anybody in trouble. I'm just going to do the job."

"Legally."

"Of course." He gave her a quizzical look. She knew it wasn't like her to caution him about how to conduct himself. It wasn't her place and she wasn't one to give advice anyway. But she also knew Taft had a tendency to step outside the lines, which was a) why he'd failed at being a police officer in the first place, and b) that walking the knife's edge seemed to be his favored modus operandi.

"Now that you're digging into Tim's death, am I on my own to try and see Gavin?" she asked.

"No, I want to talk to Gavin about both his accident and his brother's homicide. Hopefully they'll let us see him. I'm not meeting Haynes until he's off work, so I'm at your disposal this afternoon. You might need to lean on me to get around."

"I might be going to the Beckwiths . . ."

"If you think it would be better to interview them alone, I'll stay in the car. Or walk you to the door, if you want." He smiled, getting a kick out of this reversal of roles as he was generally their lead investigator. "I'll get a driving cap and you can call me Jeeves."

"Okay. Sure."

But all she could think about was a day of leaning against Taft's strong frame, his arm under hers for support.

CHAPTER 8

Natalie sat in a chair in front of the floor-to-ceiling windows of the Portland condo, staring across the city skyline. She'd watched Portland wake up while she'd sipped the Chai Tea Latte she'd gotten from the Starbucks outside the condo building's front doors. The sun had skimmed the horizon, chasing away the clouds and rain of the day before and filtering across the downtown buildings, turning them the faintest of pink, and she'd stood for a good hour or more, taking a few pictures with her phone, soaking it all in. Then she'd sat down in one of the two club chairs by the windows, yawning, as she pulled out her cell phone and caught up on the emails and texts that had come in over the last couple of days. Every once in a while she would close her eyes and lean back in the chair, then she would open them again to look at the skyline. It was an unusually beautiful November day, yesterday's rain a memory. She whiled away the morning this way, hoping the anxious knot in her stomach would subside a little, but it never did.

And then it was afternoon and time to get some real food, but she didn't feel hungry. She felt . . . she searched around inside herself, trying to focus. Angry, maybe. And impatient. And—

Scared.

Her cell rang, startling her. She drew a breath, then realized it was just Phillip. She had to get over these nerves, be the hard ass she'd projected to Erin, Kristl, and Leigh. She *was* that hard ass . . . mostly.

"Hello, Phillip, darling," she answered sardonically.

"Oh, you're already in a bad mood."

"I was just thinking how pretty it is here. This condo is nice. Fifth floor is a little high for stairs and the elevator's kind of small, but the view makes up for a lot of it."

"You know we're not going to Portland, Nat. And that's what I want to talk about. They're asking for too big a commitment. I don't have the time and it's not good for me."

"The deal with Cottage Industries? It's not good for you? We've signed to make a pilot, actually three shows," she snapped at him. "They're ready to go with us and Portland would be a great place. I'll talk to Beatrix, send her some photos, but you can pitch it to them when you meet with them tomorrow."

"I can't do it right now."

Natalie counted to five before reminding him again, "It's a signed contract."

He sighed. Phillip was good at sighing. "You're just going to have to tell them the deal's off. I need some time right now. It's not good for my soul."

She wanted to laugh. She had so many things to worry about and her husband—the one who looked so good on camera that every production company always made sure he would be the one in front of the lens, not her—was worried about his beige soul. And it wasn't the first time! Hell, no. He and his fucking beige soul—not black, not white, just beige, nothing particularly bad about it, but nothing good, either—were top of mind for him, at least when he wasn't thinking about his other favorite part, his dick. They both occupied way too much of his time and while his beige soul apparently needed some time off, the dick part had been rumored to be following around every production assistant in a short skirt.

"Phillip, are you going to make me fly back and drag you to that meeting?"

"Why do you always have to make everything so hard?" He sighed.

"I'm the one making it hard?"

"Sorry. I'm going to Sedona for a retreat and I'm not sure when I'm going to be back."

"You're going to *Arizona*? And you can't meet with them before you go?"

"That's what I said." She heard the creeping belligerence in his tone she'd grown to hate so much.

"Who's this 'we'?" she asked.

"My group."

Phillip always had a group. Discontents, malcontents, broken people, gurus, lost souls, beige or otherwise . . . God, she was sick of it.

THE SORORITY

"If you don't make the meeting with Cottage Industries, we don't have a television deal," she said evenly.

"You're threatening me. I can hear it in your tone. If you want this deal so bad, *you* meet with them tomorrow."

"It pains me to admit, my love, but they want you, not me. They want the 'face,' and unfortunately that 'face' is your face."

"Well, I'm sorry, Nat. I'm really sorry."

No, he wasn't. He never was. She thought of the gnawing worry she'd felt over the pledge she and The Sorority made to kill Ethan by making it look like a car accident; how bad, if that ever got out, it would look for her, and all of them, especially since that's exactly how Ethan . . . and Ingrid . . . died. She thought coming back to River Glen would put that to bed somehow, but everything was just worse. The producers of Cottage Industries would run away from her, if they knew. She, and all of The Sorority, would more likely end up on *Dateline*, like Erin said, or worse: KILLER HIGH SCHOOL CLIQUE PLOTS DEATH OF POPULAR CLASSMATE.

Except now, even if she somehow managed to keep that under wraps, there was no deal anyway because the producers wanted Ethan, not her.

She emitted a soft gasp at her own mental faux pas. She meant the producers wanted *Phillip*, not her.

"Fine," she clipped out.

"What does that mean?"

"I don't know. You figure it out. I'll handle this like I handle everything. You go ahead and take psilocybin and mescaline and weed and whatever else you need to enhance your mind, and visit all the natural wonders of Arizona and Utah, and commune with the earth and the groupies that hang on your every word and believe in the same beautiful bullshit you do while they suck your dick and tell you how great you are and help you find deep inner peace. And while you're at it, go look for some tent or yurt or bed of fucking leaves to sleep in, because if and when you come back to San Diego, I will have sold our house."

She clicked off and fought the urge to throw her phone across the room. Instead she laid it on the small glass table between the two club chairs, avoiding the rings left by the Chai Tea Latte, then pressed her fingers to her temple. It was unfortunate, but she had a bit of a wine headache from yesterday. And now she was going to have to book a return flight home and do her best to talk Beatrix and Cottage Industries into forging ahead without Phillip Wernstad, who just happened to look a hell of a lot like Ethan Stanhope.

The Beckwiths' home was a sprawling one-story house set back from the road, the lot defined by two lines of trimmed maples, a brushed-concrete walkway curving toward the front door, which was at the same level. The roof was clean, bright blue tiles in neat rows ending at eaves that sloped upward at the ends, adding an Asian feel to what might otherwise look like your basic ranch. The house was set back from the road in an older River Glen neighborhood where many lots were overtaken by landscaping run amok. It was at the bottom of Stillwell Hill rather than the crest.

Taft pulled his Rubicon over on the street in front of the house and looked at the winding pathway. Before he could say anything, Mac said, "I got this," and let herself out of the car before he could try and help her. "I'll call the hospital," he said just before the door slammed shut behind her.

Mac trundled up the walkway in her clogs. She'd phoned the Beckwiths for this interview on their listed land line and had let it ring a number of times, preparing for the voice mail when the call was suddenly picked up by a male voice, answering, "Hello?" in a careful tone.

The voice sounded younger than what she expected from the Beckwiths and Mac said, "I'm trying to reach Charles and Lynda Beckwith? Is this the correct number?"

"Who's calling?"

"I'm Mackenzie Laughlin, a classmate of Mia's."

"Hmm. Who are you looking for—Mia, or my parents?"

"Mason?" she'd asked.

"Got it in one. Who is this again?"

So she'd introduced herself and explained that she and Mia had known each other since elementary school and into high school, but hadn't kept in touch once they'd graduated, and that she was in the process of looking up old friends.

"Mackenzie Laughlin," he'd said, repeating her name

as if testing it out. "You just want to connect out of the blue?"

"That's how it works sometimes."

He hadn't bought it, for reasons Mac couldn't quite decipher. Mason had been a senior when they were incoming freshmen and the little she recalled of him was that he was brilliant but a complete slacker in school. She remembered Mia saying once that he drove their mother "abso-friggin'-lutely insane."

"Well, Ms. Laughlin, you're not going to get anything out of my mother. My father's hard of hearing. Maybe he'd talk to you, if my mother would ever let him talk."

"Would it possible to see them?" she'd pushed, and he'd finally agreed to tell them she was stopping by, as long as it was within the next hour or so because he would have to be there or they wouldn't answer the door.

So, here she was on their front porch. She rang the bell and it was Mason who answered. His hair was shoulder length and black with a few silver hairs catching the overhead light. He sized her up and then showed her down the hall to a sitting room off the kitchen where Charles Beckwith sat in a chair with an iPad on his lap. She caught a glimpse of what looked like a financial report of some kind and realized he was looking at a stock portfolio.

He turned to look at her and said loudly, "Took early retirement last year," as if they were in a middle of a conversation. "Charles." He half stood and offered a hand, looking down at her wrapped foot. "Looks like you had some trouble there."

"I sure did," said Mackenzie, slipping into her "friendly person" persona that she thought might work with him. "Slipped on my way to a funeral, if you can believe that."

"Eh?"

"SLIPPED ON MY WAY TO A FUNERAL," she repeated.

"Mother, this is Mackenzie Laughlin," Mason said smoothly, directing Mac's attention to Lynda Beckwith, who didn't so much as move one facial muscle as she observed Mac's jeans and sweater. She was petite and in a straight peach-colored dress that looked as if had been freshly ironed. She wore black flats and her hair and makeup were immaculate. She said something that Mac thought might be Mandarin, but Mason rolled his eyes and said loudly, "She's only here for a little while. Try to act like a human." Then he stomped off down another hall and a door slammed hard, a punctuation mark to his annoyance.

"You have to talk to me," Charles half yelled. "She doesn't talk about Mia!"

Mac shifted her attention back to him. He was gray-haired but still had a thick mane that swept across the back of his neck. He wore a Polo shirt and slacks and brown mule slippers.

Mac moved closer to him in order not to shout and he gestured her to sit down.

"Mia doesn't live here anymore," Charles said loudly. "She went off to school and then dropped out. She stopped coming home. We haven't heard from her in years." His smile was sad. "As far as we know, she's still in California."

"She could be anywhere."

Mac turned to look at Lynda, whose tone of voice could cut through glass. Mia's mother harbored a deep and dangerous anger. "Do you mind me asking how long it's been?" asked Mac.

"Were you a classmate of hers?" Lynda's dark eyes glittered.

"Yes."

"She was valedictorian of your class. She was an accomplished pianist. She attended Stanford." Lynda's voice chopped off the words as if she were cutting them in half.

"Lynda . . ." Charles admonished. Mac wasn't sure he could actually hear her, but he seemed to know exactly what she was saying.

"She is worse than Mason," said Lynda, ignoring him.

To say Mac was beginning to feel uncomfortable was an understatement. In the course of her work, she'd learned to soldier through some tough interviews, but it was never easy. She was already questioning why she was helping Leigh find Mia. She had no good reason for looking for her.

"She accused us of terrible things," Lynda burst out after a moment of silence. "Said we didn't love her. Said we *abused* her. I told her friend Leigh this already. But now she's sent you here."

For someone who didn't want her husband to know

what she was doing, Leigh was blabbing all over the place. "Leigh is worried about Mia," said Mac.

"Eh?" Charles cupped his ear.

"Get your hearing aids, foolish man." Lynda sniffed. "Tell Leigh, we *still* don't know where Mia is. We have disowned her."

Mason came out of his room and leaned a shoulder against the wall, listening to the end of their conversation. He lifted his eyebrows at Mac as his father said, "Speak up, Lynda."

"I SAID WE DISOWNED MIA." Lynda closed her eyes and turned her head away. For all her bitter fury, she was hurting over the terrible split in their family.

Charles looked at her and then at Mac. "Wish we could help more," he half shouted.

Mac nodded and thanked him. Apparently that's all they had to say, so when Mason moved toward the door and gestured for her to follow, that's what she did.

He revealed, "Mia dropped out of Stanford about her junior year and got into some kind of psycho-pseudo therapy that made her believe she'd been abused by our parents. She was not abused by our parents," he added firmly, as if she'd questioned it. "Our parents were tough, especially our mother, but you just had to shine it on and not get so wound up. Mia could never do that. She was always so *tight*. So, she comes back and spreads all this bullshit blame around. In high school she was driven and straight-laced and a *fucking bitch* when she wanted to be, but this was low, even for her. I told my parents to disown her. They didn't need a big push. They just were done with her."

"I didn't intend to stir it all up," said Mac.

"You didn't. And my father's deafness? Might be partially an act. He's just sick of listening to my mother. Ask me why I'm still here. Go ahead."

"Why are you still here?" Mac complied.

"Because unless someone keeps them on opposite sides of the room, it'll be a murder/suicide, or maybe a murder/murder. I can see them stabbing each other to death and cracking each other's skull open. They've always had trouble getting along but Mia's declaration made them go to their corners, plan their attacks. My father pretty much ignores her, but sometimes she flies at him. Someone's going to end up dead, I just hope it's not me."

"Wow."

"I know. It's a lot. I was just thinking somebody needed to know and here you are." He paused, then asked, "You have a number? Just in case . . ."

"In case you hear from her?"

"Just in case," he repeated and Mac verbally recounted her number, which Mason didn't mark down.

Mac moved carefully back to Taft's vehicle. He saw her coming and came around and opened her door. When he was back in the driver's seat, he queried, "How'd it go?" as he turned the ignition.

"Wonderful. Really, really good."

"That bad, huh?" he asked, catching her tone.

"No leads."

He hitched his chin in understanding. "I say we go to Laurelton General and see if we can get in to see Gavin. He woke up this morning—so not really much of a 'coma,' I guess—but hasn't been allowed visitors, as yet, although one of his nurses called me back and whispered maybe we could see him if we headed over there."

Mac nodded and after they were on the road, he asked, "You all right?"

"They knew I was asking about Mia for Leigh. Leigh said she'd talked to them, but they wouldn't tell her anything. What she didn't tell me about were the . . . dynamics of that marriage."

"Meaning?"

"I was just thinking about Prudence and Mitch Mangella. You think she might have killed him."

"I have trouble believing he was fixing something on his roof. That just wasn't him."

"The Beckwiths' son, Mason, said he allowed me to see his parents because he wanted someone to know what they're like, in case they kill each other. And he blames Mia for bringing them to this point."

"Be careful," he said.

"Me?" Mac pointed to herself.

"In case he's planning to kill them himself."

"*What?*"

"Maybe he's telling you this because he's the one who wants them dead. Maybe he's already been planning it and you presented yourself as a perfect character witness. He's already let you know they would kill each other given half a chance, so that's what you'll believe."

"That's a hard turn. You're really that suspicious of people?" Mac gave him a long look.

"Well . . . yeah . . ."

He clearly had Prudence Mangella and Anna DeMarco top of mind, and she took a moment to look at

Mason from another angle. It didn't hurt to be extra careful, even if Taft did seem a little paranoid.

As if following her reasoning, he shrugged and backtracked, "Maybe it's just what he said: a long-term marriage that's devolved into hate. Those're dangerous in their own way. You never know what's really going on in other people's lives."

"No, you don't," she agreed.

"Kristl? Krissy? . . . Krissy?"

Kristl braced herself at the bathroom sink, staring at her eyes in the mirror, eyes that looked bruised from lack of sleep. She glanced over at the black shirt and short skirt she'd tossed on her bed. She knew if she went and picked them up they would smell like sex. She'd kicked her silver heels across the room and winced now, worried that she might have scraped the heel when a shoe hit the wall, and those weren't cheap.

"Krissy?"

"Just a minute, Mom!" she called back.

Just a minute, Mom . . . how many times did she say that a day? Just a minute, Mom . . . Just a minute, Mom . . . Just a minute, Mom! How had her life devolved to this?

The health care worker had cautioned that her mother couldn't be left alone because she could wander and hurt herself. Kristl had pointed out that her mother was in a wheelchair and couldn't even seem to push it on her own any longer, so she wasn't worried about wandering. Once Mom was in bed, she stayed there. That's what the adult diapers were for in case she couldn't make it through the night. The health care worker, whose name was Sammy, simply reiterated that Mom couldn't stay alone.

Kristl sighed. Even if she sold the house, there still wouldn't be enough money to cover the cost of the kind of facility her mother needed, not once the mortgage was paid off. Kristl had been forced to stop teaching and had taken a job as a student career counselor that was totally online. It was hellish trying to coax students into thinking about what their next step in life might be, especially if they were the ones who thought they might go to college, or maybe not, just live at home and figure things out . . . It was lucky she was on Zoom because she wanted to grab them and shake them hard enough that their heads wobbled and then scream in their entitled faces, "Make a plan! Do something! Make your own way! And whatever you do, don't fall in love with someone who is fucking unattainable!"

She took a shower, letting the hot water run over her skin, so hot that it almost burned. She thought of Tim Knowles and the way he'd pulled away from her.

"Hey, no offense," he'd said, "but I'm not the guy you want."

"I think I know the guy I want," she'd returned, smiling. She knew how good she looked these days.

He'd just shaken his head and moved away. She'd learned later, from one of the other cops drinking at Lacey's, that Tim had mentioned that his brother, Gavin, had said something about Kristl. "Whad'ya do to Tim's brother?" Karl Bradley had panted as he'd been fucking her at his piece-of-shit apartment. She'd only gone with him to get information and to pretend he was someone else.

"Nothing!" she'd assured. It hurt her that Gavin was still telling everyone she was responsible for Ethan Stanhope's death.

Last night, she'd been with Karl again. Another trip to the piece-of-shit apartment, another night of sex in his king-size bed that barely squeezed into the bedroom, another grand fantasy in her head where she dreamed of someone else pushing into her and making her moan and scream. Karl thought he was this amazing lover and he wasn't half bad, but he wasn't anyone she really wanted. He was a placeholder until she found someone better. That someone was supposed to be Tim Knowles . . . She swallowed. If she could have just gotten him in bed. If he would've just *looked* at her! And now it was too late . . . and all because of Gavin! It totally sucked.

And now Tim was dead, too.

She clenched her teeth, then went out to see what her mother wanted. Mom was stuck in the hallway, unable to move her wheelchair either forward or backward. She was in the process of trying to get out of the chair.

"Whoa, whoa, whoa, Mom. What are you doing? Sit down! I'll get you free."

"I called you," she mewled. "But you didn't come."

"I'm here now."

Kristl helped her mother to settle back in the chair and wheeled her back to the bedroom where she banged her hands on the arms in frustration. "I want something to eat! I want to go to the kitchen!"

"All right, I'm sorry. I've got it." She turned the wheelchair around with a little more force than necessary and banged into the door.

"Ow!" her mother cried.

"It didn't touch you! It was the side of the foot rest!"

"You're mean to me. You're always so mean to me."

Kristl swallowed back her frustration. Her mother and father had been inseparable; she knew because they always told her how in love they were and how much their lives changed when they had her, this colicky baby who upended their lives. Oh, but they loved her, too, they both assured her. It had taken a long time to realize they actually didn't, not in any meaningful way. When Kristl bonded with her friends they were relieved. That's how it looked anyway. Her mother had been slipping into dementia before her father died and Kristl had tried to tell him what was happening, but he wouldn't hear of it. Or maybe he did, because he died of a heart attack soon after Kristl began appealing to him for help. And then she'd been faced with her parents' financial affairs, how little they'd planned for the future. They had the house nearly free and clear but there were other expenses and no income. Her mother was years away from social security and the small nest egg they'd accumulated was gone. Kristl had applied to the state for help, but there were a lot of hoops to jump through and she could tell she was being looked at as an ungrateful child who was trying to put her mother in a facility and still keep the house, as per the state regulations, and . . . well, yeah, that's exactly what she was trying to do. If only things would happen faster.

She couldn't be her mother's keeper. She wasn't made that way.

And neither were the rest of them, she thought resentfully, thinking of The Sorority. Natalie with her big TV job, Leigh with all her money and a loving husband, even Erin with her new job and her mangy cat. None of them had the responsibilities that she did. It wasn't fair.

She pictured Mia with some brilliant Stanford guy who was making a fortune in the marijuana business. Mia was brilliant, too, undoubtedly, but Kristl had always thought she wanted to be a slacker, like her brother, a kind of "fuck you" to her overachieving parents. Kristl could understand that completely. How many times had she wanted to give her own folks both middle fingers?

And Roxie . . .

No question she's slept her way to whatever she's doing.

"Krissy?"

She'd left her mother at the kitchen table and was currently staring blankly at the inside of the refrigerator. She pulled herself back to the moment and grabbed a package of thin, packaged ham slices that still looked edible, though they wouldn't be for long, and the mustard and mayo. "I'm getting you a sandwich."

"I want oatmeal."

"It's lunchtime." Really past lunchtime, but Kristl wasn't going to raise that issue because she might hear about it the rest of the day.

"I want oatmeal for lunchtime."

You get what you get and you don't have a fit. How many times had she heard that growing up?

Kristl slapped together the sandwich and went back to the refrigerator for some weak-looking iceberg lettuce and served her mother. She then checked the cabinet where she'd kept the wine. Natalie had opened three bottles. There was only one left. She'd recklessly spent money on all four of them, then had squirreled them away with the vague thought of sharing them with someone over candlelight. Mom would be asleep, or maybe even gone, and Kristl would be on the back patio on a summer night with a guy she wanted to take to bed and they would share the wine and move to the bedroom. She would wrap her legs around his waist and he would carry her in, both of them laughing about not spilling the wine, managing to get their glasses on the nightstand before falling on the bed together and making love like there was no tomorrow.

Her throat tightened. It wasn't so much a wish as a memory. Her one night with Ethan before Roxie stepped in and whisked Kristl straight out of his head. Mia had been over him, no matter what she said after his death. She'd been focused on college and Kristl had been focused on Ethan, but so had Roxie, apparently, though she'd blithely told them all, "Nothing happened," which was such *bullshit*. Ethan had practically had his tongue hanging out, following after Roxie those last few weeks of school.

When Natalie had urged them all to pledge to kill him, Kristl had agreed. She was mad at him. And *Roxie*! She could've killed her with her bare hands! That last overnight at her house, prom night, Kristl had ducked inside her sleeping bag and tried not to grab Roxie by the shoulders and bang her head against the wall until she was bloody and senseless. She'd pulled off hiding her antipathy enough to make them all think she didn't mind Roxie crashing their party, acting like she was one of their group when she'd *cheated*. Kristl's skin had crawled when Roxie's palm covered hers as they all spoke the words to seal Ethan's fate. Of course, Kristl had been envisioning Roxie broken and bloodied in a pile of wreckage, not Ethan. Well, not exactly Ethan. She'd concentrated on Roxie, but she was mad enough at Ethan for being such a stupid jerk that she wanted him dead, too.

But he'd been gone for a lot of years now . . . still, she could feel the burn of tears whenever she thought of him, like now, and those tears starred her lashes and made her nose run so she had to sniffle.

Her mother tsk-tsked. "You cry too much," she said.

Did she? Kristl blinked a few times, getting herself under control. She thought of her last conversation with Tim.

"You slept with Ethan before Roxie did," he'd accused her. "Who told you that?" she demanded. "Your brother? Gavin's always, always blaming me, and Ethan's death isn't my fault!" And she'd broken into tears.

But Tim, though not an absolute ass, said softly, "Gavin says you always cry because you secretly loved him."

That had sent her into gulping sobs. It was true! It was true! And Tim knew it. He could read it in her eyes. She'd wanted him to hold her and kiss her and tell her it was all going to be okay, that she was safe from now on, that he understood and from here on out he was going to stand up to Gavin and protect her because she was his and he was hers.

And she was so much better now. She'd lost the weight and pulled herself together. Ethan hadn't been able to see her inner beauty but now Tim could. He would. She was beautiful on the outside and the inside.

But instead he'd pulled away. *He'd believed Gavin.*

And then things had gotten out of control a bit. She'd been so hurt and she'd wanted to hurt back.

If you were really a good person, you would tell what you know to . . . not to the police . . . to Mackenzie . . .

"Oatmeal," Mom stated firmly, pushing the sandwich aside.

Chapter 9

The hospital smelled like antiseptic, and Mac sneezed as they entered through the main reception doors, causing an elderly couple who were wearing masks and moving at the speed of snail to look back at her in terror. "Sorry," she said. "The chemicals in the air . . . I'm just . . . here to see someone."

They tried to hustle away from her as best as they could.

"Don't think you filled them with confidence," Taft observed drily.

Taft had proffered her his arm as they'd headed up the walk from the parking lot and she'd brushed it away. "I'm not an invalid," she told him coolly. He'd responded with, "How about a wheelchair?" to which she'd tried to hobble faster. She knew she wasn't acting like herself, but she didn't want him to recognize that she'd been overtaken by madness where he was concerned. She couldn't seem to get a clamp on her emotions. Had something jarred loose in her brain or nervous system when she fell? Some gush of endorphins, or serotonin, or whatever the hell those "feel good" hormones were called?

This was coming on before you fell.

Well, shit.

Taft moved up to the reception desk and began. "We're here to see—" but the woman lifted a finger and winked at him, silently asking him to wait as she spoke into a headset, "Dr. Clemmons is still at the hospital, but he's currently unavailable. Would you like his voice mail?" A pause. "I'm sorry, what was that last name? Does that start with an *N* or a *K*?" She turned to her computer screen and pushed several keys.

Taft and Mackenzie looked at each other. *N or K? Did she mean Knowles . . . ?*

Taft eased forward and looked over the desk.

"He's out of surgery and recovery and been taken to his room." She seemed to sense Taft's interest, closing her screen. "I'm not sure," she added into the headset. "That's up to the doctor." One more pause, then, "You're welcome," and she clicked off, throwing a glance toward the elderly couple, who had finally made it to the bank of elevators.

Mac said, "I'm here to see Dr. Clemmons."

The woman half stood up in her chair and said loudly to the couple at the elevators, "You're on the correct floor. This is the third floor at this level. The hospital is on a hill. Just go down to the nurses' station." She motioned for them to turn away from the elevators.

She shot Mackenzie a look, noticing her taped ankle as she glanced over the top of the counter. "Dr. Clemmons is not an orthopedic surgeon."

"I'm not seeing him for myself. I'm here about Gavin Knowles . . . with a *K*."

"I'll just give them some help," said Taft, moving toward the couple, who were still dithering about where to go. He gestured with an open arm to direct them down the hallway.

The receptionist frowned, watching him for a moment, but Taft was gracious and when he blasted you with that smile . . . The elderly couple were putty in his hands as he asked if he could get them a wheelchair. They dithered some more but eventually the three of them walked slowly down the hallway.

The receptionist said briskly to Mac, "Mr. Knowles is not receiving visitors right now. Are you family?"

"Yes, well, I'm a cousin. I know Brighty was here earlier, his mother. And Leland. I just couldn't get here till now. Is there somewhere I can wait for Dr. Clemmons?"

"Post-op waiting room is on four," she said grudgingly.

"One floor up?" Mac gave her her most earnest smile.

She nodded curtly as her phone lightly buzzed again.

Mac moved to the elevator. She looked down the hall and saw Taft engaging one of the nurses on behalf of the couple. He glanced back and she hitched her head toward the elevators. He walked back toward her with ground-eating strides and Mac pressed the up button.

"Fourth floor is post-op," she told him as the doors to the elevator opened. They waited as three people exited, then had the car to themselves for the brief ride up. "She said I could wait for Dr. Clemmons on four.

I'm Gavin's cousin, by the way, but he's not receiving visitors."

"That's what they kept telling me, too." Taft had been rebuffed by the hospital each time he'd called, so they'd finally decided to just show up in person and see what they could learn. "But I think I saw his room is 617."

"Oh, okay. Good. We'll go up." When the doors opened on four, Mac pressed the button for six, and the doors slowly closed once again. "If he really shouldn't have visitors, let the nurses on six tell us."

Taft nodded.

"You really don't have to babysit me."

"It's not babysitting. I'm working."

"Okay, sure. When you meet with Haynes, could you ask him for something?"

He keyed in on her. "Such as?"

"The toxicology on Ethan Stanhope. It was never released, as far as I can tell. I want to know what it is."

"You think somebody got to somebody and quashed it."

"If I'm going to follow through with Gavin's request, I think I need to start there."

"I'll see what Haynes says," Taft agreed.

Mac was still looking at him when the elevator doors opened on six, and she faced forward to gaze directly into Brighty Knowles's face.

"You!" Brighty declared, her face turning red.

Leland was also there, and grabbed her arm to hold her back as Mac and Taft stepped out of the elevator.

Leland said soothingly, "It's okay. Gavin wants to see her. It's okay."

"Dr. Clemmons said he needed rest!" she spurted. "He needs rest . . . ! You stay away from him!" she snarled at Mac.

"I'm sorry," said Mac.

Taft waded in. "Gavin wants to see Mackenzie?"

Leland answered, "Yes . . . the doctor wants him to rest, but he keeps calling your name." He looked imploringly at Mac, but she wasn't sure if he wanted her to see Gavin or not.

"He shouldn't have called you!" Brighty pulled herself together. "I told him not to call you!"

Mac tried to correct her. "Dr. Clemmons didn't call me. I came—"

"I told him you would kill my son. I told him about all of you, but he wouldn't listen. No one listens to me!"

Leland put his arm around her, and said, "C'mon." He pushed the button to call the elevator car back.

Mac felt Taft's hand on her upper arm, gently pulling her away from them. "He's been asking for you," Taft said in her ear as Mac couldn't take her eyes off Brighty and Leland. Her stomach felt leaden.

A nurse was just coming out of 617. She stopped when Mac and Taft tried to enter. "Who are you here to see?" she demanded, blocking the way.

Mac cleared her throat. "Gavin Knowles. I'm Mackenzie . . . he's been asking for me."

She frowned and Taft said, "She's his cousin. Was on the phone to him at the time of the accident."

"You're . . . Mac?" the nurse queried.

"Yes," said Mac, a little surprised that Gavin had verbalized her name so clearly.

"Dr. Clemmons requested no visitors, but . . . he's in distress." She looked at Taft and ordered, "You need to stay out here."

He lifted his hands and nodded, and Mac took the nurse's words as permission and pushed open the door. She walked in and stopped short at Gavin's hospital bed. He lay gray-faced against a white pillow. His head was wrapped with white gauze and the wrap came down over one eye. The other eye was open but seemed to be looking dully at the blank television screen mounted on the wall. His mouth was slack, his breathing shallow.

The difference between this Gavin and the one that she had spoken to in the parking lot of the cemetery just *yesterday* was breathtaking.

"Gavin," Mac said quietly. Now that she was here she felt like a fraud. Her pulse raced and her stomach was tense. Her thoughts about him had been less than kind up till now.

He didn't respond and she wasn't exactly sure what to do. Maybe the brief coma had deteriorated his condition so much that he couldn't talk. The car accident, if it was an accident, had inflicted terrible damage.

"Gavin, it's Mackenzie Laughlin. I'm sorry about what happened to you. I heard you last night. You told me that you were being chased by another car last night. Do you remember? I think that's why you wanted to see me."

She waited about ten seconds. No response.

"You asked me to look into Ethan Stanhope's death.

You also intimated that you thought your brother's death was . . . also worth investigating?" She wasn't sure that was exactly right, but Cooper Haynes thought it was and Gavin had seemed to conflate the two deaths in some way.

His one eyelid fluttered and she thought he was going to close the eye, but he held it open, shifting his gaze a little to the right of the television. She moved into his range of vision so he could possibly see her properly.

She could hear voices in the hallway. "I don't know how much time I'll have. I think your doctor and your family want you to rest." Was that shouting? Was Taft involved? "I can maybe come back tomorrow. I just wanted to see you. Your call scared me. I went to find you."

The eye focused on her. His lips moved.

"I can't hear you," she said urgently, leaning closer.

"She killed them. Tim told me. I told him . . . to be careful . . ."

"Did you see who was in the vehicle that smashed into you?"

"White van. She . . . at the wheel."

"She?"

"They did it . . . Mac!" he said in louder voice.

Mac jumped at the change in tone. "I'm right here, Gavin."

"They all had sex with him!" he almost yelled.

The voices in the hallway were getting louder. Not Taft's voice. Someone else's.

"A woman was at the wheel of a white van that ran into you?" asked Mac, her eyes on the door, expecting it to be shoved open at any moment and her ass kicked out.

His eye closed and his head lopped to one side.

At the same moment, a man in a white lab coat pushed back the door that had half shut and brushed past Mac to look down at Gavin, checking his chart. He shot a hard look at Mackenzie. "You're the Mac he's been asking for?" His voice was cool and stern.

"Are you Dr. Clemmons?" she asked, though his name was right there on the tag clipped to his white coat.

"I'm afraid you're going to have to leave. This room is off-limits. No visitors."

Mac spared a glance at Gavin, who was clearly unconscious now. She nodded.

"That's on order of the police," Clemmons added, as if he expected her to come up with some reason to stay.

So, Gavin was likely telling the truth and the police had found evidence that suggested he'd been deliberately run off the road.

"I understand," she told him as she pushed out in the hall. Brighty and Leland had reappeared and it was Brighty's strident voice that Mac had heard. She apparently had turned her vituperative tongue on Taft, who was regarding her patiently. She turned as Mac reentered the corridor.

"What did he say to you?" she demanded through tight lips. "What did my boy say?"

Mac hesitated, and her hesitation fueled Brighty's fury. She actually swooped at Mac and only Taft's faster reflexes as he stepped in front of her shielded her from whatever Brighty had in mind. Leland moved a second or two too late.

Taft said in a firm tone to Brighty, "Mackenzie didn't

put your son in this hospital," as Dr. Clemmons came out of Gavin's room and asked, "What's going on?"

"Oh, Doctor," Brighty's eyes filled with tears and she swayed on her feet. Dr. Clemmons put a hand on her back and helped her down the hall away from Mac and Taft. Leland followed forlornly after them.

"Thank you," Mac said to Taft.

"Did you get to talk to him?"

"A little bit. He blames The Sorority. 'They did it,' he said."

"Okay." He nodded. "Think I'll take a trip down to Lacey's, the cop bar in the neighborhood where the burglary occurred. Tim was hanging out there."

"I should go with you. Find out what made Gavin tell his brother to be careful."

"Then you need to get crutches, a wheelchair, a knee scooter, or lean on me."

Mac visualized herself in the bar, sitting on a barstool or a small table, unable to get around easily, dependent on Taft. Nope. "Okay, I'll go home . . . for now."

He lifted up his elbow and this time she put her hand in the crook of his arm and let him help her back to his Rubicon.

"Nat?" the teary voice on the phone asked.

Natalie was still staring out the floor-to-ceiling windows at the condo, watching clouds gather, unwilling to make the airline reservation to take her back to San Diego even though the sun was past its zenith, only half visible behind the growing cloud cover. She'd glanced at her phone as soon as it rang, so she already knew who was calling even before they spoke because she'd inputted Leigh's number into her Favorites List . . . at least for now. She drew a deep breath and said, "Hi, Leigh."

Leigh just started bawling, which made Natalie sit up a little straighter, her heart suddenly pounding. "What's happened?"

"It's Gavin. I'm sure you've heard about Gavin!"

"No. What about him? I've just been in the condo."

"It's on the afternoon news. There was an accident. He was in a car accident last night! His car ran off the road and there are investigators, apparently. Like maybe it wasn't an accident. Turn on the news!"

Natalie picked up the remote from the glass table. "What channel?"

"I don't know . . . oh, God . . . what am I on? An NBC affiliate? I think?"

"The *number* of the station, Leigh," Natalie ground out with forced patience, clicking on. The condo's owners were renting out their unit through Airbnb, but the television was certainly not a Smart TV.

"I don't know! Um . . . oh, yeah . . ." She hesitantly mentioned a number and Natalie pressed the buttons. Up came the tail end of the report about the accident on the Laurelton side of Stillwell Hill complete with a bright, emergency lit video of the vehicle being slowly swung from where it had landed in towering firs, whose trunks disappeared into a ravine far below. Nat drew a breath and held it, then was distracted by that annoying woman reporter who was still on the air, Pauline Kirby, though she was getting a little long in the tooth.

"... possibly more than a one-car accident. Police are continuing to investigate."

The news show then switched to a segment on Christmas decoration pop-up stores flooding the area and Natalie snapped off the remote. "I didn't see much. What happened?"

Leigh was still blubbering, trying to get hold of herself. "I don't know! That's just it. They're not saying. What do you think happened? Should I call Kristl, and Erin? God, I wish I could get hold of Mia."

"No! Wait for more information." She shook her head, her mind racing. Leigh was really pouring on the grief. "I didn't know you cared so much about Gavin Knowles."

"I'm scared! It's *another* accident. How many of us are going to die?"

"We're not going to die! What are you talking about?"

"I went to bed last night feeling calm. You helped make me feel calm, Nat. But this . . . His brother just died a week ago!"

"None of it had anything to do with us. C'mon, Leigh. You're not like Erin, or even Kristl. You don't fall apart and say crazy things. You and I are the sane ones, the practical ones."

"I'd like to think so."

She still sounded upset, so Natalie poured it on. "When everything came down about Ethan's accident, they all wanted to freak out. Even Roxie. You and I held everybody together, remember?"

"Yes . . ." Leigh inhaled and exhaled several times. "When I learned about Gavin, it just felt like . . . someone was out to get us."

"No one's after us. We, of The Sorority, are all still fine."

"I don't know about Mia," she fretted. "I haven't heard from her in so long and she used to keep up with me all the time."

"We haven't heard from Roxie, either, but I'm sure she's fine," Natalie said with a trace of disgust. People like Roxie were always fine.

"I don't care about Roxie." Leigh's voice was flat.

"Well, none of us do, really. But she was one of us once. I don't know about now."

"Maybe she's the one doing this."

"Doing what, exactly?" Natalie asked carefully.

"Maybe she's the one who killed Ethan and Ingrid . . . and somehow took out Tim Knowles and then Gavin."

"Leigh, come on. You're not the conspiracy theorist! Tim Knowles was killed by a burglar he caught coming out of a house. That's a fact. And Ethan's accident was an accident, no other car involved. I'm not going to say it again. No, I *am* going to say it again," she reversed herself. "Ethan's accident was Not. Our. Fault. Let's not argue about this anymore. I don't know what happened to Gavin, and I don't want to think about it. I've got a whole lot of other shit to get through. I'm sorry for him, but it's no big conspiracy."

"I'm not a conspiracy theorist . . ." she agreed. "I don't know. It's just eerie, but maybe you're right."

"I *am* right."

"Okay," she said a bit reluctantly.

"Good. Now, let it go. If the police are involved, we don't want to be. We can't be. We just need to keep our mouths shut and see what happens next."

"I just keep thinking we should be doing something."

"That's because you feel guilty. You shouldn't. There is nothing to feel guilty about. Hopefully Gavin will recover quickly and stop blaming Kristl and the rest of us for . . . I don't know. Perceived crimes we committed."

"What if he dies?"

"Then it will be a tragic accident. Nothing more." She hesitated, then added, "Is anybody saying that?"

"No . . . they're not saying anything . . . I'm just worried." She sighed. "I thought about calling his parents like I did the Stanhopes after Ethan . . . and Ingrid died."

"You called the Stanhopes? When did you do that? Holy shit, Leigh . . ." Natalie shot her gaze back to the skyline, seeking relief from all the shit that constantly rained down on her, but more dark clouds were rolling in once again, spoiling her peace of mind. "I have to go back to San Diego."

"What? *Now?*"

"I have to take care of some things with Philip. But I'll come right back. I promise. We need to clean this up."

"Oh, my God. This is a nightmare. I don't want Parker to know any of this."

"I don't want *anyone* to know any of this! Send Gavin a get-well card. Express sympathy for me, too, if you see his family, but don't engage unless you have to."

"Should I call Mackenzie?"

"NO. Oh, my God. Are you not listening? And get her to stop looking for Mia. Call her off. Just stay away from her."

Leigh didn't answer, which didn't bode well.

Natalie shook her head to clear it. She never would

have credited Leigh with falling apart so completely. She hadn't been this bad after Ethan's death . . . had she? All of them had walked around like automatons for months. Nothing had seemed real, but Leigh, like Natalie, had snapped back to reality quicker than the others.

Natalie ended the call, done trying to jolly Leigh from her outsized fears. She then clicked on to her Alaska Airlines app and booked a flight for eight p.m., growling at the exorbitant price of a ticket at this late date. Then she stood for a moment, thinking hard. She had to almost physically shake off the heebie-jeebies that seemed to blossom every time she brushed against the past.

And Leigh . . . and Gavin . . . and Ethan.

It always comes back to Ethan, doesn't it?

Natalie slowly walked back to the windows, her arms crossed over her torso. As if following her mood, the skies suddenly opened up, pouring wild sheets of rain over the already misty skyline, covering the whole area with gloom.

She hadn't been honest with The Sorority members yesterday about her relationship with Phillip. There really was no relationship with her husband outside of any potential job Natalie might bring in. She'd called him dead weight, but he was worse than that. He needed to work on his beige soul when he wasn't fucking around, but the fucking around in turn made him want to work on his beige soul. It really chafed her that he looked so good on camera, that he possessed that *je ne sais quoi* that the camera loved. How had she ever fallen for him? What had she been thinking?

The ugly, little truthful part of herself answered: He looks like Ethan Stanhope. Same golden brown hair, same sexy blue eyes, same ironic smile. Maybe Phillip never had the muscular torso or strength of Ethan's swimmer's body from all those hours of water polo, but Natalie had overlooked that, at least in the beginning, so enamored with the man that she'd practically chased him down and offered herself up for whatever he wanted. What he wanted was to be adored, and in that way he and Ethan were also alike. Natalie had always thought she and Ethan had a special under-the-radar bond. While he professed his love for Mia, his eyes roved over all the other girls. Natalie had kept her gaze from his, though she'd watched him from beneath her lashes, until the day she calmly caught those blue eyes and held them. They'd passed over her, but with her continued focus, had returned back as if pulled by a string.

"What?" he'd asked, about a week before he'd taken that fateful trip to the pool house with Roxie. They were at school, outside the gym where she was waiting for Mia and Leigh, who were both in dance class. Ethan had just come from the pool and he'd slipped a shirt over his damp chest that was sticking to him like a second skin. His trunks were still wet, as was his hair, and she found herself curiously studying him as his team members pushed against the bars of the exit doors, clunking their way past them, some throwing Natalie a look or two. She wasn't any of their type. She'd made certain of that. She was the unapproachable Goth girl, which was just fine. Kept her looking sexy and mysterious, but too scary for the milquetoast sports guys at River Glen.

"I was just wondering what Mia sees in you," she said.

"You're weird, Nat," he said, but he was smiling. "You like being weird."

"I like being weird?" she scoffed.

"Yeah. Ya do." He then drawled, "There's always somebody like you around. The kind that wants to be seen, but not seen like everybody else. Cooler, better, smarter." He pointed a finger at her. "That's you."

She'd been shocked and incensed. He didn't know her. He was just the dumb jock on the water polo team. "Who knew you were a student of psychology," she said sarcastically.

"You always have to run the show." And then he'd laughed and slammed against the exit bar himself, leaving her in the echoing hallway.

As soon as she was alone Natalie had looked down at her black voile skirt with its layers of netting, her black blouse with its plunging neckline, the rows of black beads around her neck, the fingerless black lace gloves. She knew her face was ghastly white, having dabbed on the white powder herself. And the black-rimmed eyes. Getting that eyeliner right was painstaking, but she was good at it now.

Leigh and Mia appeared from dance class and climbed in Natalie's car. She was the one with the car so it seemed she was ferrying her car-less friends wherever they needed to go. She took them directly home even though they protested that they'd like to go to Starbucks and get an iced drink, but Natalie was in no mood. Ethan's words kept circling her mind and she was . . . mad at him.

She went home and looked at herself in the mirror

and her chest hurt. It wasn't that she looked bad. She liked the Goth look. It was that he'd pierced her armor and pricked her heart. She couldn't let him know how much he'd wounded her.

She knew Ethan was on a club water polo team that used the school pool, and she went to the next event, but stood outside in the hall, smelling the chlorine, feeling her hair wilt under the dense air anytime someone opened the door and walked through. She didn't let her friends know what she was doing, especially Mia, who thought she and Ethan were Prom King and Queen but never seemed to really feel comfortable with him. Mia had smooth skin and black, straight hair and just faintly slanted eyes and a body that was thin and tight in all the right places. And she aced all her tests and turned in exceptional work, and Ethan liked that she was so incredibly perfect. What he didn't know, but Natalie did, was that Mia was untouchable where it counted. Good sex was out because Mia was too driven. But no one could really drill down to Mia's real self, maybe not even Mia. Both Ethan and Mia seemed to like the "idea" of their relationship, but not the relationship itself.

At least that's what Natalie scribbled down in her notes. At one point she wrote that she wanted to have sex with Ethan. Then she crossed it out, blacking it over with big ink circles so no one could ever read it. After that she wrote a short story about a girl who was obsessed with a boy and just wanted him to fuck her all the time. She read it over when she was done and felt herself flush, but then was embarrassed and quickly scribbled out "fuck" and changed it to "screw" and then rewrote it again with "make love" and then laughed hysterically, tore the story into tiny bits, and ate the little pieces of confetti.

Afterward she lay on her bed and pretended Ethan was on top of her, groaning and grinding against her, telling her how beautiful she was, that he couldn't get enough of her, that all he wanted to do was slide into her and stay there forever . . . well, slide in and out, and then stay there forever. Natalie's experience with sex wasn't that great even though she told her friends she'd been screwing since she was fourteen, fifteen, okay, sixteen. She had to keep refashioning her story, when in reality she hadn't actually done it till she was *eighteen*, long after the obsession with Ethan, when she'd gone off to college and purposely had sex with enough guys to give her an idea about what the whole thing was all about.

But during her Ethan period she could hardly think of anything but him. She watched him from the sides of her eyes. She catalogued what he wore. The green shirt Tuesday, Wednesday the blue, Thursday that black one—God, that one was good— Friday a different blue. She thought about retaking the SATs and ACTs, but it was really too late and she was never going to reach Mia's stellar numbers, but then, though she wanted to beat Mia with all her jealous heart, Ethan wasn't looking for a brainiac, so it didn't matter anyway. She thought he was looking for a *look*, so she thought about Mia's short plaid skirts and white blouses, the knee highs, the Mary Jane–type shoes and decided to emulate her. Her friends remarked on her change of style and she bit back that she was just trying things out and went back to all black. Ethan never noticed anyway. He really was a dumb jock and she was loads smarter than he was, but she didn't care.

One night at the Knowleses' before the weather improved and the pool was open—a night that Gavin's parents were gone, again, and some of her friends and classmates had wandered over to hang out—she had her moment alone with Ethan. He wasn't much of a drinker. Was too into water polo to risk getting "mipped"—a Minor In Possession—by the police and thrown off the team. She caught him alone after he'd had a minor spat with Mia over the phone. He explained that Mia hadn't been able to come to the party because she was studying, and he snapped back that she was always studying and she told him maybe he should study more if he wanted any chance to be with her, and he said he wouldn't get into Stanford no matter what he did, which was just fine, and she said, "Fine," and they hung up and he fumed about it to anyone who would listen.

Then he said to Natalie, "Can you give me a ride? I need to get home, finish up some shit, and my car's at my house."

Natalie had looked around, wondering where his bros were, half expecting one of them to come out and say he'd take him, but that didn't happen, so she said, "Sure," and then they left together and she didn't tell Kristl and Erin, who were still at the house, that she was leaving. Like Mia, Leigh and Roxie hadn't been there, either. Natalie had almost skipped the party herself. She was tired of her obsession, tired of herself, tired of school, but she'd changed her mind at the last minute.

THE SORORITY

She'd only been there about a half hour when Ethan asked for the ride.

They barely spoke as she drove to the Stanhopes' sprawling home. She'd never been to his house before and had immediately realized there must be quite a view from the back, west, toward Laurelton.

"Nice house," she said as they pulled up.

"Yeah?" He'd been lost in thought or was just tired, hard to tell. "Thanks," he told her, unbuckling from the passenger seat.

She couldn't tell if his parents were home. All three doors of the triple-car garage were closed and the house was dark except for one light on in an upstairs room, a bedroom by the looks of it. She stepped out of her car and he looked at her in surprise.

She caught up to him as he was walking toward the back, along a sidewalk that circled the house.

"What are you doing?" he asked, stopping short.

"I don't know. I kind of want to see the view."

"The view?"

"From your backyard."

"Okay," he said dubiously.

She followed him as the sidewalk was too narrow to walk side by side. He kept going right to the end of the property where the land sloped off an abrupt edge. A carpet of lights glittered below—the city of Laurelton. They were facing west, toward the Coast Range, the mountains blocking out the stars. A crescent moon hung low in the sky.

Ethan stood beside her and said, "You've been following me."

She'd been lost in the view, envious of the Stanhopes' house and grounds. Her lust for real estate had been building for a while, but that view, that house, that night made it all coalesce. His words brought her back to the moment. "What are you talking about?" she'd snapped.

"My friend saw you at the pool. He said you were watching me."

"Watching you?" she repeated on a laugh, her heart in her throat at being found out. "I was the ride for Kent Deruso. Our parents are friends," she said dismissively. A lie. A big, fat lie. She barely knew Kent Deruso apart from his name and he mostly kept to himself. She hoped to God she wasn't throwing herself on a grenade.

"I told him he was a dumbass." He accepted her answer without question. "You don't talk to me."

"I talk to you. What do you mean? Of course I do. Mia's my good friend."

"Uh-huh. You're all a bunch of bitches."

He said it without rancor, like it was just a fact, then yawned. "G'night."

When he headed for the house, she stepped in his way. She didn't plan it. She just did it. He had to stutter-step to keep from running into her. He stared at her, his expression hooded in the moonlight. He didn't say anything and neither did she. She couldn't believe she was doing what she was doing, but well, she was doing it! Her heart was trying to leap from her body. Every muscle tensed.

He drew a breath and then put his hands on her waist. "My friend was right," he said, drawing her hips closer to his. She let herself be pulled. He fit himself between her hips; they were almost the same height. He was hard and she felt him against her in a way that made her knees tremble. She laid her hands on his hips, feeling the flange of bone, wanting to reach down and touch his dick but afraid to break contact.

A light came on the back porch. "Ethan?" a girl's voice called. His sister. Ingrid.

"Yeah, I'm coming in." He stepped back and walked away from Natalie as if it had never happened.

Later, she could almost believe it had never happened. Mia never said anything and apparently neither did Ethan. Except Gavin started looking at her funny and one day Gavin put his arm around her and let his fingers slip down the side of her breast. She jerked away from him and elbowed him in the chest. He stumbled and half fell, moaning and rolling his eyes, exaggerating his pain. He really was an ass.

After that, whatever bubble of romantic fantasy she'd lived in for those mind-numbingly stupid weeks burst. She watched Ethan snuggle up to Mia, putting his chin on her shoulder, kissing her hair while she swatted at him and laughed. Natalie was pretty sure her laughter was forced. She was also pretty sure Ethan was putting on the act with Mia for her.

And then he and *Roxie* . . . in the pool house. Roxie with her pink smile and shaggy hair and delicious bouncing breasts.

That last night after graduation, Natalie had been standing with the rest of The Sorority and Ethan had blown them all a kiss, his insouciance sending a tidal wave of disgust through all of them. A few weeks earlier she'd made them all pledge to murder Ethan, then had laughed at them when they'd gone along with her. She'd said it was a joke. Over and over again. A JOKE! A FUCKING JOKE!

And it was . . . it was meant to be a joke . . . only she'd wanted him dead in that moment. She'd pledged to kill him and had meant it. They'd all pledged.

And she'd wanted him dead graduation night, too.

Sometimes she still heard Ingrid's voice in her head, querying, "Ethan?" through the darkness while she pressed Ethan up against her and her mind planned how she was going to get him to fuck her without anyone knowing.

Now her cell phone rang, the ring tone a soft trill of bells she'd picked because of its pleasing tone.

It was a number she didn't recognize. "Natalie Hofstetter," she said briskly. She'd never taken Phillip's last name, though they'd been married for six years. Six years! It still shocked her when she thought about how much time had passed in the blink of an eye. Long past the time she should've instigated a divorce to cut out the dead weight.

"Hi, Natalie. It's Beatrix. Got a minute?"

Well, of course. Natalie sucked in air and put a smile on her face. It always went through the line if you weren't smiling, and by God she was going to smile through a rigor mask and show them just how personable she could be if it killed her. "Got a minute" was Beatrix's stock phrase that warned of bad things to come.

"Sure. What's up?"

"Well, we can't reach Phillip and wanted to know if you could remind him of tomorrow's meeting."

The meeting Phillip would miss because the beige-souled cocksucker was going to the red cliffs of Sedona.

Beatrix was co-owner of Cottage Industries, which had produced Natalie's first show, the show Natalie designed down to a gnat's eyelash. She was tall and rangy and with eyes all over Phillip, though Natalie knew her assessment had nothing to do with sex. Beatrix had plots and devices rolling around in her head all the time as she sized up the potential for a show, what the pros and cons were. She knew Phillip was on the plus side, but Natalie didn't have to be told that Beatrix thought she was the dispensable one.

"I'm so sorry, Beatrix, I'm still in Portland. Just wrapping some things up after yesterday's funeral. I'm not sure Phillip can make it." *Ever.* "But I'll be there."

"I didn't know you were at a funeral," she said.

Of course you didn't, you cow. You don't pay any attention to what I'm doing, only Phillip. "Yes, really sad and unfortunate. A good friend, a policeman, shot in the line of duty."

"Oh . . ." She sounded nonplused.

You don't know what to do with that one, do you?

"Well, sure, tomorrow. We'll see . . . Tell Phillip to call me," she said after a moment or two.

Will do, Fuckface. "I'll sure let him know."

"I told him we're mulling the deal over—that is, if you actually purchase that house. He wasn't sure, but I guess I'm asking you. Are you making that deal on the Dover Road house? Phillip said it was only a matter of time."

That *deal* was purchasing a piece-of-shit house in an older piece-of-shit neighborhood that, yes, might be having a resurgence . . . in maybe *twenty-plus years*. Natalie had nixed it as their next project but Phillip liked to dig his toes in whenever she objected, whether it was a good deal or not. Phillip had actually plunked down some of their joint money this time, but she thought she could get it back. It would cost too much to reno it. She'd redone three older houses in spectacular neighborhoods and gotten some interest from HGTV and other networks, and had earned that one full season of *Natalie's San Diego*—the name changed for season two to *Phillip's San Diego*, where she made "guest appearances." They'd made decent money and gained a lot of recognition, and she wanted more of it, but without Phillip . . . well . . .

"The Dover House deal is still in negotiation," Natalie lied. "We're actually working on a project in Portland. I'll send you some photos of a couple of houses and high-end condos, properties just begging for our kind of love and attention."

"Mmm . . . have Phillip call. I'm not sure Portland is right. Let's talk about it later."

"Sure."

Natalie hung up in a blue funk. *Phillip* . . .

Signing on the dotted line for that property was throwing money down a rat hole. It made her *crazy* to think of the Dover House. And that's the one Beatrix now wanted? Phillip must've really put on his best song and dance for her. Maybe she was wrong. Maybe Beatrix and Phillip had joined together—in more ways than one—and they were freezing her out.

But then Phillip was out finding himself now and that didn't seem to include his career.

She put a call through to him. When it went straight to voice mail, she said, "Get out of the Dover House deal, whatever it takes. You should've never signed that contract. My signature isn't on it, because I didn't want to do it, so the contract's null and void. I talked to Beatrix. We're good to go in Portland . . . without you."

She stalked to the bathroom and looked at herself in the mirror. Her agent, Jenn, had told her to lighten her hair a little. "Stop dyeing it black. It's where light goes to die. Nobody wants Morticia rehabbing their house."

She leaned closer, recognizing how pale her pallor was. She'd never thought much about it since her ill-fated attempt to look like Mia. Mostly she liked the black-and-white contrast of her hair and her skin, but at twenty-nine maybe it was too much of a contrast. She'd started dyeing her hair when the first silvery threads had appeared. She was one of those people who was going to gray early, so she'd decided to take care of that herself. Unfortunately, the flat black hadn't played well on camera, so she'd lightened it up some, added a bit of chestnut color into it, and that had actually really done the trick on warming up her image—not that Beatrix would care, she thought darkly.

She was going to make this work. She was. In Portland,

where she could keep a close eye on her "sisters." One way or another.

And make sure they didn't do something to explode her image . . . like admit to being the cause of Ethan Stanhope's death.

CHAPTER 10

Cooper grabbed his coat from the open closet in the break room and headed for the department's back door. He needed to get out from under Humph's watchful eye. The chief was a good guy, a solid investigator, and he had your back most times. He wasn't the political animal the last chief had been. In the short time Humph—Chief Duncan—had had the job, there'd been only one other time Cooper had disagreed with the man, and that time Cooper had let it go.

But this time . . . no.

"Haynes."

He was already pushing through the back door, ready to duck against the rain and hopefully dodge the flowing skin of water that was still spreading across the concrete lot even though the rain was taking a break.

He looked back. Verbena stood in the doorway. She said, "Chief wants to see you before you go."

Cooper held in his sigh of annoyance and headed back in. He texted Taft on the way. *Will be late.* Damn. He wasn't one who believed in inexplicable feelings or messages from beyond, even though his wife had experienced something very like that when her mother died, but he couldn't shake the powerful sense that time was of the essence on the Tim Knowles case. The feeling defied explanation. Tim's death was cut-and-dried and he should accept the outcome of the very obvious investigation and move on.

The chief sat at his desk, his hangdog gaze focused through his office windows at the rest of the squad room, which had thinned out appreciably by five thirty. Verbena was slinging the strap of her messenger bag over her shoulder. She shot a look toward the glass office, but didn't meet Cooper's eyes.

"How was the service?" Humph turned his gaze back to Cooper. Like Verbena, he'd only been able to attend the funeral.

"Fine. Raining some."

"Tim's brother was in an accident last night."

"I know."

"Techs came back with white paint on the rear of that silver Mercedes. Someone pushed him off the road."

Cooper took that in. He hadn't heard.

"Public already is trying to make it out to be some kind of conspiracy. Two brothers, dead within a week."

Cooper's mouth was dry. "Gavin Knowles is dead?"

A pained expression came into his eyes. "He's still alive. I should've said two brothers *attacked* within a week."

But you think he's as good as dead. You didn't mean to, but you spoke the quiet part out loud.

"I want you to be the voice for us. Keep those conspiracy theorists from making it more than it is. Can you do that?"

"Yes." Cooper straightened under Humph's deep frown.

"Because I know you don't like the way Tim Knowles's death was decided. You think there's something more. Do you think the department is covering up?"

"No." Cooper was positive. "Dale Kingman killed Tim and was killed himself. It's on camera."

"But . . ."

Cooper wasn't certain who had told the chief of his reservations. Or maybe he hadn't been as careful as he'd thought in hiding his intentions. "I have a few questions about what led up to it. How it happened."

"Meaning?"

The chief's tone was neutral but Cooper sensed the pitfalls of answering directly. The department was chafing to put Tim Knowles's death to bed, and by all accounts, it should be. Even Cooper sometimes wondered at his own obsession.

"I'd just like to do some follow-up checking," he said.

"If you need a cold case, there are a lot of unsolved ones that could be looked at. Don't waste your time on a cut-and-dried homicide. I want you to make it a point to speak with the press and squelch all of the recent speculation that Knowles was shot from the 'grassy knoll,'" he said in his gravelly voice, referring to conspiracies that still circled the Kennedy assassination. "Put that one to bed. For the department, and for yourself."

"Yes, sir," said Cooper, though he rarely was so formal with Humph.

Minutes later, he drove away from the station in his

Explorer, punched in Taft's number, and put him on speaker.

"Change of plans," he said, as soon as Taft answered. "I'll tell what I've got over the phone, but I can't be seen with you." He then told Taft about the new directive he'd been given to quash the rumble of conspiracy theories that were rising in volume concerning Tim's death and Gavin's accident. "Call if you need something, but you're basically on your own."

"Give me what you've got so far," said Taft.

Cooper came home to the scent of basil, tomato sauce, and garlic. As he entered from the back door he heard a sharp bark from Duchess, whose toenails scurried down the hall to find him, and a chorus of hellos from Harley and Emma.

Emma was standing by the stove, gazing very seriously at Harley, who was pushing some recalcitrant spaghetti noodles into boiling water, trying to hook the strands with the prongs of a pasta spoon and get them to settle down.

Emma looked at Cooper and said, "Harley is not good at this."

"Yes, I am," Harley protested. "You have to get them wet and then they get all noodle-y and you can push them down. See?"

Emma did not appear convinced and Duchess gave another bark as if seconding her opinion.

"Your mom in bed?" he asked, looking at the marinara

sauce bubbling furiously in its pan. "Maybe turn down the heat on that."

"Harley is not good at that, either," remarked Emma.

"Emma . . ." Harley mock-threatened her with the spaghetti spoon, which still had a noodle drooped over its side.

Emma ignored her and looked at Cooper. "Jamie is in bed where she's supposed to be. Twink is guarding her and the baby."

Harley snorted like she was going to lose it. "That's giving Twink a lot more credit than she deserves. We all know what she's good at."

"Jamie and the baby are not going to die." Emma grew very serious.

"Of course not! Jesus. That's not what I meant. The cat predicts that about *old* people, the ones on death's door." Though she vehemently seconded this opinion, Harley looked slightly alarmed.

"She's just a cat," reminded Cooper. "I'm going to go upstairs."

He took the steps two at a time and knocked lightly on their bedroom door, peeking in to see Jamie sitting up in bed with a cranky look on her face while Twink lay curled in the covered chair and deigned to open one eye as he entered.

"I'm going crazy," said Jamie.

"Going to be a long few months," Cooper agreed.

"I can't stay in bed. I can't."

"You don't have to all the time. The doctor said—"

"The doctor said I should be careful. Really careful.

What if I start walking around and miscarry and it's my fault? I just couldn't live with that."

"Then you're on the road to crazy and there's no detour." He sank on the bed beside her, propping himself on one elbow.

"It's an expressway."

He chuckled and she bonked him with a pillow. "It's not funny," she said, half laughing herself. "Oh, God. What am I going to do? You know what I did today? I said goodbye to my class by Zoom. Some of the second graders were crying." Tears immediately filled her own eyes.

"Maybe you should have stuck to substituting at the high school. Bet they wouldn't be crying."

"They'd be telling me how cool it would be to never get out of bed, or want to know if I peed in a bedpan, or . . . I don't know . . . if I'm checking the internet to see the healthiest way to give birth with or without marijuana brownies as a meal of choice."

He started laughing. He couldn't help it. Jamie had always been great with teenagers, his stepdaughters Marissa and Harley two good examples of how she'd help them positively navigate their high school experience. She'd moved to teaching the lower grades when a full-time job had opened up at River Glen Elementary.

"It's not funny," she said again, flinging the pillow at him. He caught the pillow and threw it over the edge of the bed, scooting closer to her, grinning as he snaked an arm around her, his hand sliding alongside her hip.

"What do you think's happening here?" she asked him, mock serious. "With Harley and Emma downstairs and Duchess? Every time the dog walks by the door Twink rears and arches her back like a Halloween cat. If Duchess whines, Twink gives that low cat growl and Duchess always whines. So, I don't think we'll ever have sex again."

Cooper nuzzled her neck. "Okay." His hand slid up to just beneath her breast.

"Bullshit on 'okay.' I see where your mind is."

"Do you mind where my mind is?"

"No . . ." She grabbed his hand and helped it atop her breast. "That's another question the high schoolers would ask: How do you 'do it' when you're really, really pregnant?"

"Sounds like they need sex ed," he murmured against her throat. "There's no really, really pregnant. There's only pregnant and not pregnant."

"Yeah, as you well know they would be referencing my shape, which is getting into that pear zone."

"I like the pear zone." He moved his hand from his wife's breast to the bulge at her abdomen.

"So do I," she admitted.

Cooper smiled and pressed his forehead to her temple for a moment before collapsing onto his back and staring at the ceiling. "How're you really feeling, besides bored?"

She sighed. "Fine. Don't worry. I can do this." She was still sitting up and turned to look down on him. "Harley took Emma back to Ridge Pointe to get more of her things and now they're making dinner. What more could I ask for?"

None of them knew exactly how this was going to

work when two babies entered the household, especially as Emma required extra care herself. Not that she wasn't helpful. She just didn't process the world the way most adults could and sometimes it came with interesting consequences.

"I haven't told Mary Jo yet. Not sure I want to, somehow."

Mary Jo was the surrogate who was carrying their first child together. She was due about two months ahead of Jamie. Even though they'd embarked on the surrogacy together, it had taken Jamie a long time to warm up to Mary Jo and vice versa, and since then Jamie had been reluctant to tell her about her unexpected pregnancy.

"Take your time with Mary Jo," he advised, like he had from the beginning.

"I don't know why I'm so worried. She loves babies. She's been a surrogate before. My being pregnant shouldn't change any of that." A frown creased her forehead. "What's going on with you?"

"Gavin Knowles, Tim Knowles's brother, was in a car accident last night. He's in the hospital. Serious, maybe critical, condition. Looks like there was another car involved that didn't stick around to help."

"Oh, no. Hit-and-run?" She sucked in air between her teeth. "What about the parents?"

He shook his head. "I don't know."

"You told me you think there's something more going on with Tim's death. Does this have something to do with that?"

"I don't know," he said again. "I've been warned not

to investigate." At her look of concern, he brought her up to speed on his meeting with Humph, finishing with, "I'm the one who's supposed to tamp down any and all conspiracies."

"So Humph chose you because he wants you to stop investigating."

"That's what I'm thinking, but . . . I have someone looking into it."

"Really? Who?"

"Better you don't know." He smiled wanly.

"Okay."

She squinched down in the bed beside him and pressed her nose lightly to his. "So, you're a double agent? I could get into that."

"How into it?" he asked.

"I think I could 'do it.' Maybe later, after dinner? When they've all gone to bed."

"I thought we were supposed to stop. Being careful and all."

"Nobody said that . . . exactly." Her brow furrowed.

"Well, if we can't 'do it,' we can try some other things."

"Like what?"

He spread his hands and arms to encompass his whole body. "You could certainly have your way with me."

"If I had another pillow I'd smother you with it," she muttered.

He leaned forward and gave her a big sloppy kiss. She started laughing and so did he and suddenly Duchess was barking at their door, which made them laugh even more and sent Twink into full-on Halloween cat mode with arched back and furious hissing, which only added to their mirth.

Duchess actually leapt at the door and the latch hadn't quite caught so the door burst open with the rushing dog. Twink leapt from her chair onto the bed, swarming up to the headboard, where she deemed the safest place, so both Jamie and Cooper immediately covered their heads with their arms.

"Oh, God!" Jamie laughed.

"Emma!" Cooper bellowed.

"Duchess!" Emma snapped from the stairway and the dog, shivering beside the bed at the still hissing cat, looked back at the door and whined. Duchess was a great dog, really a great dog, who generally listened to her mistress's commands, but the black-and-white tuxedo cat was almost too much for her.

"That cat has got to go back to Ridge Pointe," Cooper growled.

"She only hisses or spits when it's Duchess," Jamie defended Twink.

The brown-and-black midsized mutt seemed to understand they were talking about the cat and barked twice more at Twink, her tail wagging. Duchess was torn between wanting to scare the cat away or play with it, unaware that Twink was completely disdainful of her.

Emma appeared in the doorway. Her blue eyes were stern as she took in the scene.

Upon seeing Emma, Duchess padded slowly toward her, head down. Twink slowly lowered her back but that low growl continued.

"Twink can't go back," reminded Emma.

The cat being a prognosticator of death was a little bad for business at Ridge Pointe. But having her at the house, and now with Emma and Duchess moving back . . . Jamie's prescribed peace and quiet was going to be hard to achieve.

"This might be more excitement than you need," said Cooper, getting up from the bed. He stood between Twink and the dog, whom Emma had firmly by the collar and was half walking, half dragging out of the room.

"It's entertaining," said Jamie, lifting her chin to look at the cat behind her head. Twink was still on alert, every hair on end.

"Dinner's ready," Emma said, as she closed the door behind them. From the hallway Duchess gave a bark of disapproval at being so summarily removed.

Twink stopped growling, then stepped delicately around Jamie's head to curl into a ball where Cooper had just been, one eye still on Cooper as if challenging him. Cooper picked up the thrown pillow and handed it back to Jamie, shooting Twink a mock glare at her high-handed way of taking over. At the door, he said, "Don't think that feline has pride of place in my bed."

"Never."

"I'll bring you up some spaghetti."

She rolled her eyes. "I am not eating spaghetti in bed."

"I'll bring a tray with a small vase and flower."

"Yeah, right."

"And we can talk about what you can do for me

later." She freed her pillow and it hit the door just as he closed it.

Mackenzie sat in her chair and slowly unwrapped her ankle, wrinkling her nose at the purple and slightly green swelling. She gently started to rotate her foot and then instantly stopped as pain shot through her. Okay, no serious rotating yet.

"Ouch," she muttered through her teeth.

She leaned back in the chair and thought about Gavin. It had shaken her to see him brought so low. Sure, he was an ass and she'd thought a *lot* of unkind things about him . . . a lot of unkind things . . . but man, she hoped he was going to be all right.

Which brought her back to what he'd said, not just on the phone call in the middle of last night, not just at the hospital, but also on his earlier call and at the cemetery parking lot.

. . . Ethan was killed by The Sorority. One of them did it, or maybe more . . .

. . . It was Kristl . . .

. . . If not Kristl, one or the other of them. Maybe all of them . . .

. . . They all had sex with him . . .

Was that true? *All* of them? Sounded like hyperbole to Mac, but she'd agreed to look into Ethan's death and so, okay, she would. And also, was there any correlation between Tim's death and Gavin's accident?

Mackenzie shook her head, chasing out the cobwebs. One thing at a time. She wanted to review what she'd learned from the Beckwiths about Mia, which wasn't much. They had information on their daughter that they were withholding because they had effectively disowned her. She would bet that Mason had an inkling of Mia's whereabouts as well. They all knew where she'd been living before she disappeared, but were unwilling to share.

If she disappeared, she reminded herself.

The person to talk to again was also Leigh . . . Elayne. She'd basically dumped the job of finding Mia in Mackenzie's lap and rushed away. Mac glanced toward the drawer where she'd stuffed the money Leigh had thrust into her hands. It was a large enough amount that she should really put it in the bank, but the thought of making a deposit with her sprained ankle made her feel weary.

Mac picked up her cell and called Leigh's number. It rang and rang and went to voice mail. Well, okay. She would leave a message.

"Hi, Leigh, it's Mackenzie. I've run into a brick wall with the Beckwiths. They're unwilling to give me any information about Mia. I need some actual dates: when Mia stopped contacting you, where she was at that point, that kind of thing. Call me." She left her number again, though Leigh already had it, and clicked off.

It was entirely possible Leigh would give up on the idea of hiring Mac. She'd assumed the Beckwiths would have more recent information on Mia and would be willing to share it with Mackenzie, which had turned out to be false. In that regard, Mac had fewer "ins" to information than Leigh did herself.

She limped to the kitchen and rooted around in her refrigerator. Nothing even remotely worth eating. Everything inside was too close to rendezvousing with the garbage disposal or waste bin.

She settled for peanut butter on crackers and a glass of Syrah from a bottle that hadn't turned sour just yet. She stared out the kitchen window and let her thoughts wander to Taft. She seemed to have gotten over the worst of her utter madness about him, at least during the past few hours. She'd tolerated holding his arm as he'd led her to his car without *swooning*. If she got involved with him, and then inevitably the relationship ended . . . then what? Could they still work together? Maybe? Possibly?

She made a sound of disgust in her throat. Who was she kidding? *She* wouldn't be able to make it work.

"Future tripping," she warned herself.

You can't let it happen. You know you can't let it happen.

Why not? her head argued. *Why the hell not? Take a risk, Mackenzie.*

The restlessness inside her core seemed to be growing. Even recognizing getting involved with Taft as the bad idea it was couldn't quite quell it. The kind of bad idea that made you exchange dinner for a bottle of red wine and a sixteen-ounce bar of chocolate.

She wanted to rip her thoughts out of her head.

Back in her chair she put in a call to her stepsister, who was more sister than step-, needing to hear a sane and friendly voice. Stephanie was in the first year of motherhood and she and her husband, Nolan, were over the moon about their baby daughter, Jessica. Mac felt a lot the same way. In her downtime she tried to spend as much time with the Redfields as possible.

As Mac waited for her to pick up, it occurred to her that none of The Sorority had any children yet. Yes, they were still young, but Leigh and Natalie had both been married a few years. It wasn't unusual, it was just . . . a point to consider.

The call went straight to voice mail, so Mac left a message telling Stephanie to kiss the baby for her, that there was nothing urgent, and to call when she had a chance.

Her thoughts drifted back to Taft and the anxious feeling she had in her gut, which she examined and realized was less about her feelings for him, and more about her concern for his wellbeing since the reading of Mitch Mangella's will. He'd simply brushed her worries away, but he had to know, as she did, that Prudence Mangella and Anna DeMarcos were not the kind of women who would wade lackadaisically through a potential lawsuit that could string out for months or years. They were more likely to act. And they weren't going to forgive and forget in any case, no matter what the outcome was. That was the kind of women they were. Deadly. Vindictive. Grudge holders and worse. Gavin Knowles thought the members of The Sorority were the same, but Mac didn't necessarily believe that, though she couldn't say she would trust them, based on past experience.

Her cell buzzed and she saw that Leigh was calling her back. Well, good. She was sick of her own company. "Hi, Leigh, I was—"

"I'm just about to be seated for *SIX*, so I don't have a lot of time. Did you talk to the Beckwiths?"

"I did . . . I didn't learn anything, though. They wouldn't talk about Mia, and neither would Mason."

"Shit. Okay . . . Goddammit," she muttered. "I can't talk now. I've got to go in."

"You want me to keep trying to locate Mia?"

"Of course. You're not giving up, are you?"

She sounded almost put out that Mac could even think that way. "Nope."

"Let's talk tomorrow. I've got to go."

"Okay, enjoy *SIX*. I hear it's really good."

"You haven't seen it?" asked Leigh. "I've seen it four times, this is my fifth."

"Wow. Okay. No, I haven't seen it yet." *SIX* was a one-act rock opera/musical where each role depicted one of Henry VIII's six wives through mostly song.

"Don't you go to the theater anymore?"

"Well . . . not a lot."

"It could've been a career choice, for both of us. In fact, I just went to an audition for *Chicago*. Trying out for the role of Roxie Hart."

"Ah. Well. Good luck," Mac said lamely.

That didn't seem to be the answer Leigh sought. Tersely, she said, "I gotta go. Bye."

Mac clicked off, remembering how destroyed Leigh had been when the part of Laurey Williams had gone to Summer. She sure hoped she'd found some balance in rejection, now that she was older, because it was always difficult to get the main role if you weren't a name. While Leigh's passion for the theater apparently still burned bright, Mac's had been pushed aside as soon as she graduated. Ethan's death graduation night had brought reality home with a bang.

We're all just having fun, aren't we?

Gavin's words came back to her.

She wondered if Taft had connected with Cooper Haynes yet.

CHAPTER 11

Lacey's was the kind of bar that wanted to be nicer than it was but couldn't quite seem to get there. The fir walls and floor were coated with Varathane till they were practically plasticized and there had been an attempt at one point to upholster some of the chairs around the groupings of tables, but the fabric was stained and ragged now and many wooden chairs had replaced the upholstered ones. There was a poolroom in the back, currently empty with a hanging faux Tiffany shade, the green felt glowing beneath the light. Strategically placed televisions hung near the ceiling, football players running silently as the sound was off, a nod to keeping things classy. Even with its failed attempts to rise to the level it seemed to want to be, Lacey's was several tiers above the Waystation.

Taft took a seat at the U-shaped bar. His stool was covered in faux black leather that looked fairly new. Above his head hung upside-down wineglasses in a matching U-shaped cabinet that echoed the layout of the counter below. The bartender was talking with a nice-looking woman at the other end of the bar and barely glanced at Taft.

The place was about half full. Taft was probably a bit early for the main crowd. It was Friday night, so he expected it would fill up. He knew it was a cop bar. He'd gone a time or two when he was with the department. Not a lot. Like the job itself, it hadn't quite fit him.

Another bartender came from the back—a tough-looking woman wearing a black T-shirt with white letters that read: I DON'T THINK SO, F**CKER.

So much for classy.

She took his order of a Stella, pulled the beer tap, then dropped the glass in front of him, leveling a narrow-eyed look at the other bartender as she headed to the back again.

Cooper Haynes had given him the rundown on Tim Knowles's homicide. Taft knew the basics, but he'd gained a window into the inside from Haynes's account over the phone . . .

"Tim was a regular at Lacey's," Cooper told him. "Couple nights a week. Not a big drinker. Just liked hanging out with other cops. Sometimes he might leave with a woman, most times not. He lived alone in an apartment about a mile from the bar, toward Gresham. We did a cursory search of his place after he was killed, but there was nothing that would suggest the kiling was anything more than what it was: a burglary that turned into a homicide that took Tim's life.

"He was at Lacey's when the call came in, a couple

minutes before he was off duty, so he felt compelled to take it. He'd been at the place about ten minutes before then. Hadn't even gotten a beer yet. Told them he'd be right back and then headed out.

"The caller was Gena Colville, fourteen, calling from her bedroom closet, saying someone had broken into their home. She was alone. Her mother and boyfriend were on a date. Body cam shows Knowles went straight to the door. It was just getting dark. No lights on in the house. He rapped loudly on the door, called out, "Police," and shots were fired through the door, hitting him in the chest. He went down and a man, a penny-ante thief named Dale Kingman, burst through, knocking Knowles off the small concrete porch and pitching him into the yard. Kingman ran to a nearby church. He was in the vestibule and looking up at the ceiling as officers arrived on scene. He said one word, 'Salvation,' before he shot and killed himself."

Taft had known most of that, but it was chilling to hear Haynes's objective reporting. "Pretty clear set of circumstances."

"It is," Haynes agreed. "Chief Duncan and the department see it as an arrest gone wrong. Kingman was high. Had just broken into the house for cash. Probably thought there was no one home. Panicked when he heard Knowles on the porch. Knowles's death is a reminder of how an arrest can go awry with deadly consequences."

"But . . ." Taft had encouraged when Haynes fell silent for a moment.

"Why that house? Kingman was a burglar, but not in that neighborhood.

"Gena's mother, Sally Colville, was called by Gena, after she called nine-one-one. Sally was nearly hysterical to find an ambulance and officers at her house and Knowles dead in her front yard. When she had time to look around, she said nothing was taken except for about four dollars in change. Gena had heard Kingman in the house, had seen the bobbing light from his flashlight. He'd seemed to be looking for something, muttering, 'Where is it?,' or something like that. He'd stopped searching and was grabbing up the change when Knowles arrived and called out. Gena said Kingman yelled something back and just started shooting. When asked what he yelled, Gena said she couldn't hear. She'd covered her ears and it was just noise. She didn't know Kingman ran out of the house until much later. She was still hiding in the closet.

"Kingman usually burgled homes in Portland, where he lived. Never in River Glen. It's possible he stepped outside of his usual area to avoid police."

"You're not convinced of that," said Taft, listening to his skeptical tone.

"Kingman was a creature of habit. He didn't venture far from home. He kept buying old cars that were nearly ready for the junkyard. Undependable. He had a long list of petty crimes behind him, some jail time, some homelessness. Recently, he'd found God, and his friends and acquaintances had fervently declared he was a changed man. Then the Colville break-in."

"What do you think happened?"

"It feels like a setup. I don't know how." He exhaled heavily. "Kingman was never caught in possession of a gun before. Maybe I'm wrong, maybe this is my way of mourning Tim's death, like the chief thinks, maybe I just need further justice for Tim. In any case, I can't let it go."

Taft knew the feeling. He'd felt that way himself more than once. "Where do you want me to start?"

"With Tim . . . what was going on with him right before. Everything's been focused on Dale Kingman. I ordered a look into Tim's background and barely got started when I was shut down. Not that there was anything to find. What you saw is what you got with Tim. I wasn't trying to pin anything on Tim, but that's the way it was taken by his family."

"I've met some of the family recently," Taft admitted, Brighty Knowles's angry face glaring at Mackenzie still alive in his mind. "I'm in," he'd added.

"This is a nonpaying job," Haynes had reminded him.

"Understood." There could be no trace of Cooper Haynes's involvement if he wanted to keep his job in good standing. "I have my own reasons for wanting to get to the truth."

"Good. Thanks."

"Maybe you could do a favor for me, actually for Mackenzie Laughlin," Taft had rejoined.

"What would that be?"

"Gavin Knowles asked Mackenzie to look into Ethan Stanhope's car accident and she agreed. She said she's never seen the toxicology on Stanhope. She's heard conflicting reports about his sobriety that night and wondered what was in his system. You know the accident?"

"I remember it. You want the report?"

"Just to know what's in it."

"Stanhope wasn't the only victim. Both he and his sister died in that accident," Haynes reminded him.

"I wasn't around when it happened, but I remember hearing about it some. Maybe check a tox screen on her, too?"

"She was young. Nine or ten, I think," Haynes said carefully.

"I don't expect there's anything there. But if you're checking one, you might check both."

He'd waited while Haynes apparently turned that over in his mind. Finally, the detective answered, "I'll see what I can do."

Taft had then made plans to go to Lacey's and now here he was. The female bartender in the T-shirt had disappeared, but the guy had finished his conversation with the young woman at the end of the bar and was back at the beer tap, filling an order. He felt Taft's eyes on him and came over. "Never seen you here before," the guy said. "But you're one of 'em."

"I look like a cop?" Taft was a bit surprised. He was dressed more like the current crop of tech CEOs in a collarless shirt and casual jacket to ward off the rain.

"You have the eyes of a cop. Looking around, assessing."

"Maybe I'm looking for love."

The bartender swallowed a chuckle. "What do you want, man?"

"I want to know about Tim Knowles."

That got his attention. He was lanky and scruffy,

with longish brown hair and a beard that needed trimming. He wore a T-shirt with a plaid shirt over it, a throwback to '90s grunge. "What do you want to know?"

"Who he saw. What he was doing. Anything."

"He was a good guy," the man said testily.

"That's not in question. He *was* a good guy," Taft agreed. "And good guys need good justice."

He frowned, still holding the pulled beer, looking at Taft.

"Hey, Jerry!" a guy down the bar yelled. "I'm dying of thirst down here!"

He turned away from Taft, handed the customer his drink, then came back to Taft. "Another?" he asked, indicating Taft's empty glass.

"Sure."

"You don't think Tim got good justice?"

"I want to make sure he did."

Jerry left to take care of several other orders. When he came back, he was looking thoughtful. "Tim was a chick magnet. Just one of those guys that didn't have to do anything and women were all over him. Hard to explain. Wasn't the best looking, wasn't the most ripped. Just a decent guy." He paused. "Not like his brother. He's an ass. Heard he's in the hospital, though. Sorry. Just the truth."

"Jerry! Jesus!" A different customer spread his hands. "Stop runnin' your mouth and get us some drinks. The lady here wants a mojito."

"Excuse me," Jerry said.

Taft thought about Gavin Knowles as he sat there. What would it be like to have everyone like your younger brother and no one like you? Would it make you become less of an ass or more? *Guess we know the answer to that,* he thought.

When Jerry returned, Taft said, "What about that night? Tim got the call and left. Anything unusual?"

"Only that it was right in the neighborhood. We don't have tons of crime around here and it was a surprise. Even Tim seemed surprised. Said he'd be right back. He only went because he felt guilty about leaving work early. That was kind of his M.O. The only slightly shady thing about him. He would leave his shift early if nothing was going on."

"So he took the call because he felt a little guilty and the crime was near here."

"Yeah, I know Sally Colville. Her house is only a couple of blocks over. She and Ham come in here sometimes. Ham's her boyfriend." He made a face.

"You don't like Ham?"

"He's not a cop, but thinks he is. Ask any of your brothers." He hitched his chin to include the other patrons. The place was beginning to fill up and the female bartender was back and taking orders, shooting Jerry resentful looks.

"I'm not a cop," said Taft.

"Sure."

"Was. Not anymore."

"What are you, then? Private dick?"

"Got it in one," said Taft with a faint smile.

He left Lacey's shortly thereafter as the place grew crowded and the music swelled, and headed back to his condominium through a dark night with a faint damp breeze. He thought about turning around and heading to Mackenzie's, but held himself back. She was fairly prickly since her sprained ankle and he wasn't sure exactly what was going on with her. Sometimes it felt like . . .

He shook his head. Didn't allow himself to finish the thought. Theirs was a working relationship. She'd made that clear and he'd agreed with her wholeheartedly. It was just sometimes he felt the air charge between them. If she felt it, she did an epic job of acting like she didn't.

He turned into his lot, parked the Rubicon, then walked rapidly toward his front door. He heard the pugs next door, Blackie and Plaid, barking at something Tommy was doing, their muffled yipping sounding through the front door.

He smiled as he let himself into his unit. He enjoyed being the pugs' unofficial godfather of sorts, remembering Tommy had tapped him for dog-sitting sometime this week.

Dropping his keys on the console table by the door, Taft headed for the cupboard above his microwave where he kept his liquor. He pulled out an unopened bottle of scotch, thinking of the bottle that was supposedly his from Mitch Mangella. No matter what Mackenzie thought, if it came into his possession, he would be loath to open it.

"Mangella," Taft muttered regretfully.

He opened the bottle, splashed several fingers into an old-fashioned glass before putting the bottle back on the shelf.

He sank onto his couch and lay his head back. What had he learned, if anything, at Lacey's? Tim was a nice guy with a less likeable brother, said brother currently fighting for his life at Laurelton General. Tim was a

THE SORORITY 211

good man and a good cop who took seriously the "to protect and serve" credo. He also seemed to be a "chick magnet" without putting in any effort. Tim's parents were grieving and his mother was—and this was an opinion on Taft's part—a real piece of work.

Taft picked up his cell phone, holding it lightly in his palm. He wanted to call Mackenzie but for reasons he couldn't quite explain, it didn't seem like a good idea. He set the phone down and frowned at it, picked it up, then set it down again.

He turned on the television with the remote and forced himself into a mindless program that couldn't keep his attention no matter how hard he tried.

Mac jerked awake, gray morning light streaming through the half-open blinds in her bedroom. She looked at the bedside clock. Seven a.m. She did an internal check and realized she still felt tired, but better. And she was in her bedroom, which was a lot better than sleeping in her chair.

Throwing back the covers, she examined her foot. Yeah, well, still Technicolor, but if she got it wrapped again she should be able to move around better. Maybe even make it to the store for some groceries. Wouldn't that be a good idea.

And she felt less directionless. Ready to grab onto both of the investigations she'd been so lackluster on. She was going to check Mia Beckwith's online social media profile, find out if she was a regular user or more like Mac, with an account on several platforms that she rarely looked at. When Leigh called her back, she was going to ask questions she should've asked from the onset, although Mac hadn't been certain she was even going to take the case and the pain of her swollen ankle had derailed her a bit from work . . . and apparently made her more susceptible to fantasies about Jesse James Taft.

"Not today," she muttered, getting to her feet, testing her ankle. Still hurt, but she was going to power through.

She took a shower and dressed in jeans and a black turtleneck, then headed to her chair. She messed with the length of Ace bandage that wanted to maddeningly stick to itself and got her foot wrapped, sort of. Not nearly as good as what Taft had done.

The memory of his fingers on her flesh caused an internal thrill she could really do without. She clamped her mind down on anything but the present, put on her clogs, and headed down the outdoor stairway to her RAV. A sharp wind slapped rain at her face and she realized she'd left without a rain jacket. Too bad. She wasn't going back for it. Like a true Oregonian she didn't need an umbrella. She just walked through the shivering rain and slid herself behind the wheel.

Forty minutes later, she was home again with supplies. She'd also picked up a breakfast burrito from a food cart outside the Safeway parking lot. Fantastic. She ate standing up at the kitchen sink again, looking out her front window, watching as the clouds opened and poured rain down in wavery silver sheets. There was something about being inside and warm while everything beyond her window was drenched and cold.

Grabbing her cell, she sank back into her chair, went

to the Notes folder on her phone, and starting typing in questions to ask Leigh. Did Mia join a real sorority at Stanford? Mac remembered hearing that was one of her goals. How long did she attend school there? Did she graduate? When exactly was the last time Leigh saw her, or talked to her on the phone? What did they talk about? Did she know what Mia's long-term goals were? Who were the people important to her in college, and who are they now?

After a moment she opened another folder in Notes and typed in: *Get Stanhopes' phone number . . . or knock on their door.*

Mac considered that. Just showing up at the Stanhopes and asking them all about their son's death . . . and their young daughter's. Bad idea. Leigh had said they'd become very religious since Ethan's death and she'd heard that somewhere before as well . . . ?

She thought about it hard, trying to recall where she'd heard that comment. It took a while but she remembered it was someone from the reunion committee, trying to get Mac to attend the ten-year, which she hadn't. It was Tawny Price, who'd spent her high school years riding horses and performing in rodeos and, like Leigh, her keen interest in her avocation had carried into adulthood as she lived on a ranch with her husband. Tawny had mentioned Ethan Stanhope and his parents as her family attended the same church, Riversong, a Christian church near the East Glen River, not all that far from Ridge Pointe Independent and Assisted Living, where Cooper Haynes's sister-in-law, Emma Whelan, resided.

Tomorrow was Sunday. The Stanhopes would likely

be at Riversong. As would Tawny Price, maybe, though she was married and her new name escaped Mac at the moment.

With her sprained ankle, she tried to imagine how she might slip into a pew unnoticed. Maybe she could keep from limping. Still, meeting the Stanhopes at church was a way to introduce herself as a classmate of Ethan's, ease into an introduction before she started asking questions and came off like Sergeant Joe Friday from *Dragnet*.

She shook her head and stared into space for a moment. *Are you really going to do this? Is it worth the intrusion into these people's lives? Does Gavin really know what he's talking about?*

She could picture how betrayed and hurt the Stanhopes would likely be when they learned Mac had an ulterior motive for meeting them.

... *It was Kristl* ...

... *If not Kristl, one or the other of them. Maybe all of them* ...

... *They all had sex with him* ...

Even Leigh? Even Erin?

Mac firmly set her misgivings aside and picked up her cell to call the hospital to check on Gavin's status again.

Tomorrow she was going to church.

Leigh walked through the showroom looking for her husband. All around her were samples of flooring—tile, hardwood, carpet—all in removable squares with handles to lay out on the tables for prospective home buyers and remodelers to pore over. The business had been her idea, originally, conceived when she got fed up with waiting and waiting and waiting to redo her own kitchen. Parker had seized on the idea and somehow named it after himself, Parker Flooring, which was a better name than his original choice, Parker Flooring and Hardwood, a dumb name because hardwood *was* flooring, but as ever, he hadn't listened to any good ideas from his wife. It took Leigh's father to point out what she'd been trying to tell him before he smartened up.

Ray was helping another customer who couldn't decide on the color of her hardwood planks. Leigh itched to pick it for her. She could have designed the woman's home in half an hour. Natalie might be the television house renovator but Leigh knew without a doubt that she would be better at it. The few times she'd watched one of Natalie's shows—two, possibly three, out of that first season—she'd felt anxious and envious, and fully aware that Phillip, who was the host, was a know-nothing but did look good on camera. She'd watched Natalie's husband with fascination. There was something about him that drew her eye and it wasn't until the end of the last episode that she realized it was his mannerisms and resemblance to Ethan Stanhope. She'd switched off the TV with a dry mouth.

Because of Phillip, Leigh had been cautious around Natalie when they met after the funeral. She'd tried hard not to let her know that she was following her with her eyes, totally attuned. She was pretty sure Natalie hadn't noticed. She was too into being in charge and her bullish, take-charge ways were as evident now as they'd been when they were in high school.

High school. The only really great friend Leigh had made was Mia. She was the only one in The Sorority that Leigh really cared about. The only one she could really talk to, to really trust. She suddenly yearned for that Mia, the one she'd grown up with and shared secrets with. That Mia had pretty much disappeared when she hooked up with Ethan. Leigh had been bereft and then that terrible debacle when Leigh had been relegated to the ensemble while Summer Cochran stole the lead in *Oklahoma!* . . . Leigh could still feel the pain. She remembered how hard it hurt. How the only thing that got her through her misery was when an underclassman told her she should have won the part. Leigh could have kissed the girl, but she was a nobody so it really didn't count.

But Mia, her friend who *did* count, had been wrapped up in Ethan and getting into Stanford . . . and Mackenzie had been Ado Annie but was as independent and unreachable as ever . . . and Erin had just been too wishy-washy . . . Leigh's hurt had been bone deep and even now, when her mind touched on those last weeks of school, she felt anxious and miserable and wanted to cry or scream or do something self-destructive.

And that's where Ethan had come in.

It was the night she didn't get a callback. She checked her cell phone over and over again, waiting for a call or an email or something from the drama department. Nothing. When six p.m. came and went, she knew that Summer had won the part. Of course she had. She had that *voice*. Leigh knew that she was the better actor, but Summer could really sing. Even with all her voice lessons, piano lessons and choir and dance and special acting coach Leigh had spent so many hours on, she had been relegated to ensemble. Brenna DeSalt was Aunt Eller, but Leigh thought Brenna was built for the part. Big chest, squatty body, booming voice. Leigh hadn't wanted that part anyway. And she hadn't wanted Ado Annie, either. She'd wanted the lead.

The guys in the ensemble were drama geeks, like her. They were nice enough but they were basically talentless. Even the guy who played Curly wasn't much. It was a miserable time. So, so miserable.

She'd left the house in tears and driven around blindly. Driven like a maniac at times, pouring on the gas as she flew down Stillwell Hill, barely making the corner where so many accidents had occurred over the years. She'd stomped on the brakes and flipped around the curve, turning a U-ey without meaning to, lucky no car was coming the other way. She'd driven cautiously back up the hill with a hammering heart then down again into Laurelton, pulling into the parking lot of a 7-Eleven where she leaned over the steering wheel and cried her eyes out.

She didn't know how long she'd been there—an hour, maybe?—before she'd looked at her bleary, tear-stained face in the mirror and wanted to cry some more. But then she'd slowly grown mad. Everybody got everything they ever wanted, but not her. Poor little rich girl, they all thought because her parents had money that her life was perfect. If she ever complained, The Sorority generally dismissed her, even Mia!

She was still sitting in that parking lot when there was a tap on her driver's window that made her startle. She hadn't heard or seen Ethan approach. But seeing his handsome face, all she could think about was that she looked like a mess. She waved at him and gave him a sick smile. She just wanted him to go away, but he made the motion for her to roll her window down and so she turned on the vehicle and pushed the button.

"Hi, Ethan," she said. She didn't like him. He'd taken Mia from her. He was too charming and sure of himself and sometimes she wanted to just punch him out.

But that was when she had her armor on, her makeup, her Elayne persona. At this moment, though, she'd just felt small and broken.

"What's wrong?" he asked her.

"Nothing!"

"You were crying. What happened?"

"Go away, Ethan." Her nose grew hot and she knew she was going to cry some more.

"Hey, you want a Slurpee?" He hitched a thumb back toward the 7-Eleven.

"No . . ."

"You sure? I'm buying."

Why was he being nice to her? He was never nice to her, or any of The Sorority, for that matter. He only wanted Mia.

"What are you doing here?" she asked.

"Oh, you know . . ." He half laughed. "Got too many

speeding tickets and lost my wheels. Dad'll relent but I'm in that place right now where I have to wait for my parents to forgive me. I was with Gavin, but he ditched me."

"So you need a ride?" she asked unenthusiastically.

"Nah, I can wait."

Leigh felt like a heel because it was obvious she didn't really want to drive him home. She said into the awkward gap, "Maybe I will have that Slurpee. But you'll have to bring it to me. I'm not going to be seen like this."

He snorted. "You look fine."

"No, I don't." But she was glad he said so.

He shrugged and left without asking her what flavor she wanted and when he came back he brought two slushies, one for her and one for himself, both red. He climbed in the passenger seat without being invited. She wasn't sure how she felt about that, but she didn't say anything.

"Wild cherry," he said as she tasted her drink.

"Mmm." They drank their Slurpees in relative silence. He drained his and she drank about half of hers.

When he looked at her his lips were red. Seeing her looking at him, he stuck out his red tongue. She stuck hers out back at him. He laughed, rolled his window down and tossed his empty cup outside. Driven by some craziness she couldn't credit to this day, she did the same with her half-full one. They started laughing like hyenas. When the laughter finally died down they were both looking at each other, and when he reached for her arm and pulled her closer she didn't resist. In fact, she leaned in and they were kissing and sucking on each other's tongues, laughing some more, but then it got serious and they broke apart only to climb into the back seat, and before she knew it she was lying beneath him and he was humping against her and she was grabbing at the button on his jeans and pulling them down, and then she was sucking his dick like she'd done it all her life.

Just thinking about it now made her place her hand on her forehead and close her eyes. She'd never told anyone. It had been on the tip of her tongue to tell Mia, after she'd confessed she wanted to break up with Ethan. He was gone by then, taking Leigh's secret to his grave, but even so she'd almost let her best friend know what she'd done in a moment of madness. Luckily, she hadn't said anything because she suspected what she'd done was irredeemable. But Mia had cooled off to her anyway.

Ethan may have told Gavin and maybe *he* blabbed? But nothing had come of it at the time, so maybe not.

Only now, years later, Gavin chose to get all weird about Ethan and the accident.

And now Gavin was currently in the hospital, fighting for his life. She'd called Laurelton General this morning, but no one would tell her anything.

"Elayne?"

Parker's impatient voice cut into her reverie.

"What?" she asked him.

"What are you doing? Standing there?"

"Thinking. Is that okay?"

"Maybe you could think somewhere else. You're

standing in the middle of the room and we, that are working, have to walk around you."

"Well, I'll let you, that are working, get back to it." She strode out of the front door and into the parking lot, walking through a misting rain to her black Tesla, pressing the keyfob and watching the gull wing rise. She climbed behind the wheel and drove to their home, pressing the button to open the wrought iron gates with the large *S* in the filigree. At least Parker had used the initial for Sommers instead of a *P* for Parker. He was fucking obsessed with his first name.

And she had been, too, when she met him. Parker Sommers. He was *the* name at musical theater camp. He had the most amazing baritone voice. He sucked at dance and wasn't much of an actor, but he could really sing. Leigh had a real weakness for someone who could sing, as her own voice was merely adequate.

Parker's parents had sent their son to the same summer camp year after year and he was a counselor by the time Leigh learned of it and signed herself up. She'd just finished her second year at the University of Washington and wasn't going back. Her own parents were beside themselves. She'd bombed her classes, even drama, and was home with nothing and no plans. They threatened to cut her off, but she knew they wouldn't. She was just so . . . miserable.

She had to squeeze money out of her stingy parents for the summer camp. Her father wanted her to work for the family business, which was investments, venture capitalism. She wanted to become a working actress. She asked for a five-year plan. She would go to Los Angeles and if she didn't make it within five years, she would come home. Her father denied her and her mother followed along with him, but they allowed her to go to the monthlong musical theater camp while they decided what to do with her. She was their only heir and unless they wanted to give all their money to charity, which Leigh knew they would never do, then she was it.

So she pushed everything out of her head and went off to camp. Her parents would come around. They always did. They would give her the five-year plan. They would support her.

She met Parker on the first day. How they'd never crossed paths when he was a student at Sunset West in Laurelton, a rival school to River Glen High, she couldn't imagine. But then Parker was more of a sports guy than an actor, and he'd just fallen into singing because he had a great voice.

Most of the other campers were younger than she was, still in high school. It was kind of embarrassing, but no one knew her exact age and she didn't tell them. Parker flirted with her, but he flirted with all the girls. He was cute and self-important and used to adoration and Leigh just Fell. For. Him. She told him about her family's money. He didn't seem that interested, which only made her double-down on trying to impress him with potential inherited wealth. Leigh didn't care that she was trying to "buy" him. Whatever leg up she could use, she would.

It wasn't till almost the end of camp that he seemed to finally show some interest in her. To her surprise, he told her that her wealth intimidated him, otherwise he would have made a move sooner. Leigh was so relieved and delighted that she didn't object when he invited her to his cabin and they both stripped naked and got down to business without much of a word spoken. When he was sliding in and out of her she thought of Ethan's red tongue probing her mouth and couldn't get the image out of her head. Sometimes even now, when she and Parker made love, she thought about Ethan. If things weren't going all that well, it helped bring her to a climax.

Now she pulled into her quadruple car garage. Parker's black Humvee and his Harley took up two of the spaces. Leigh's father had died of a heart attack shortly after the wedding and her mom had crumbled and let Leigh take over the finances. Parker helped. Parker Flooring began with seed money from Leigh's family. Both she and Parker were interested in residential building, so they worked hard to get their business off the ground. And it was a success! Sure, she'd had to inject more cash here and there, when there were temporary slowdowns, but overall the business was doing well. Leigh could have started paying her mother back for the "loan" she'd given them, but Mom didn't care so Leigh let that money just be absorbed in their flooring business. Parker had pushed for years to take over Mom's finances as well as Parker Flooring and, well, Leigh had ceded over a lot of control.

In hindsight, maybe that hadn't been the thing to do.

She walked into the kitchen and looked at the gleaming Wolf stove, microwave and steamer oven, the Sub-Zero refrigerator, the dull gold kitchen faucet and pot filler, the light gray ceramic tiles and quartzite countertop, white with its faint gold veining, the black pendants with their gleaming gold interiors . . . and thought she would give up everything—every bit of it—for the part of Roxie Hart in *Chicago*.

Chapter 12

". . . I tried telling them I was his cousin again, but it didn't work beyond them mentioning I should talk to Dr. Clemmons. I'm taking that as no change in Gavin's status," Mac told Taft, who'd brought a pizza from Pizza Joe's for a late lunch. "I did get groceries today. I'm getting up and around quite well," she said, biting into a piece thick with curling slices of pepperoni. God, it was good.

"Groceries. Good for you."

"Really stepped outside of myself today."

He smiled around a big bite. They were both standing in Mackenzie's kitchen, in front of the window, though Taft held a paper plate under his piece as he moved to Mac's tiny table. Mac had taken a bite as soon as she picked up her slice and glanced out the window as she reached for a paper plate from the stack she'd set on the counter. In the parking lot one floor below, she saw her Toyota RAV in its designated spot and now there was Taft's Rubicon taking up a visitor's space. A blue car she didn't recognize—it looked like a Honda Accord—was turning around and leaving the way it had entered and Mac's neighbor was climbing out of his Ford Escape and squinting up at the sky. No rain was currently falling but the dark gray clouds were threatening.

"I'm going to text Haynes in a minute. Maybe he'll give us an update on Knowles's accident and condition." Taft finished his slice and she watched him press his lips together, checking for leftover oil. Seeing him, she slid her tongue over her lips.

His gaze dropped to her mouth for a moment and she felt that pull. "How was Lacey's?" she asked quickly. He'd told her that Haynes had suggested that's where he should start in checking into Tim's homicide.

"Have you been?" he questioned.

"You'd think I would've when I was on the force, but I never did."

"I'll call it Waystation Plus. Not a full grade up. Just a plus."

"Our kind of place." Her eyes had traveled back to the pizza while she considered another slice; she brought them forward again, looking at Taft. His hair was slightly mussed from the wind, she guessed, and it gave him an appealing raffish look.

"I got some background from Jerry, one of the bartenders. Sally Colville, the woman whose house was burglarized by Dale Kingman, is a semi-regular at Lacey's. According to Jerry, she's good people, but her boyfriend, Ham, is not. He acts like a cop, but isn't one."

"You gonna talk to him?" She forewent another piece and took the wooden chair across from him.

"Them, I hope, but they've had a lot of cops over the

last week or so. Don't know how receptive they'll be. Also, with Tim's brother in the hospital now, they might be rolling down the blinds and closing their doors, wanting to shut out all of it."

"I would," Mac admitted.

"I'd really like to talk to the daughter, Gena, but I think that's going to be a hard sell."

"I'm going to Riversong Church tomorrow to see the Stanhopes."

His brows lifted. "Church, huh?"

She then filled him in on what she'd learned about the Stanhopes turning deeper into their faith after the deaths of their son and daughter. She finished with, "I've got a call into Leigh. I wasn't sure I was going to help her, so I didn't dig deep enough at first."

"I'm going back to Lacey's tonight, check some more on what people thought about Tim. I've got a call into a couple of family members for some background on Kingman."

"Good."

He left a few moments later and Mac was lost in thought about Ethan Stanhope and Gavin's comments about The Sorority when Leigh finally called back.

"Sorry," she said. "The morning got away from me. What do you need?"

To Mac's ears, she sounded kind of down. "Can you remember exactly the last time you heard from Mia?"

"A few months ago. She changed her cell phone number, so I went to her parents. I was hoping you'd get further with 'Tiger Mom' than I did. She told me to stop calling. Ordered me, actually."

"Do you have anything on Ben? What's his last name?"

"I asked her and asked, but she never told me. I don't think she wanted me to know."

Mac had checked Mia's social media accounts but though they were still up, they were clearly fallow. No recent posts. And no pictures. "Got any idea why she'd want to keep him a secret? She's not posting anymore."

"I know. And no, I don't know why she kept him a secret, but I can guess. I mean his family's in the marijuana business. It might be legal now, but it's all cash and there's probably more to it. Mia's parents were not happy about it."

"They said she accused them of . . . abuse, of some kind."

"I don't know what that's about. If anyone's being abused, it's her. That note I gave you? That was a direct call for help."

Mac had dismissed the note. Something about it hadn't rung true, but maybe she was wrong about that. "You're sure the note was from Mia?" she asked.

Leigh's voice tightened. "You think I'm lying?"

"No."

"What, then?" she demanded.

"Maybe mistaken?"

She asked coolly, "Why don't you believe me?"

"If the note's from her, why did she leave it on your car? Why not just call you? Or text you? If she doesn't have a phone, why not wait by your car for you to show up?"

"Maybe she couldn't," she argued. "Maybe she was hiding it from someone who was scaring her."

"If that's the case, maybe this is a task for the police."

"Fuck, Mackenzie. You just don't want to help me!"

Mac didn't answer. She couldn't rightly say why she was resisting, but there was something so . . . *contrived* . . . about the note. "All right. If the note's real, you think she's here in River Glen and in trouble."

"I didn't say that."

"The *note*, left on your car, here in River Glen says, *Help me*. Where was your car?"

"I was . . . um . . . Jesus, you've got me so flustered!" She heaved a frustrated sigh. "I was by the arts center. I take classes there. I just finished. It was about seven at night. I looked around for her, but she wasn't anywhere that I could see."

"You knew it was her writing right away."

"Yes."

"What day did this happen?"

"Um . . . Thursday . . . two weeks ago?"

"You think she followed you to the art center and left the note?"

"She must have," Leigh said. "Why are you interrogating me?"

"I'm not interrogating you. You want me to find Mia, I need to know where to start. You don't think she's in River Glen? You think she just dropped the note off and left."

"I think he took her away."

"The boyfriend. Ben."

"Yes," she stated flatly.

"When you got the note, what did you do?" Mac asked, switching gears.

"I came to you!" Her voice was tight.

"I'm not trying to piss you off, Leigh."

"Well, you're doing a bang-up job!"

"I meant, what did you do immediately? Once you found the note," Mac clarified.

She inhaled and exhaled, as if trying to pull herself back from the brink of fury. "Like I said, I looked around to see if she was still in the area, but I didn't see her, so I just went home and . . . I didn't tell Parker. I just don't want him to know any of this."

"I'm clear on that," Mac assured her.

"I just want you to find her. Her parents were really strict and she just got sick of dealing with them, and that's why she went to Stanford anyway. To get away from them. But they love her. She's their shining star, no matter what they say about disowning her. Mason's the disappointment. And I don't know who this Ben is, but I think he made her disappear."

"Was she in California the last time you talked?"

"Yes. With Ben. She said they were just hanging out but she was tense. I think he was right there listening. I don't think he lets her out of his sight."

"You think he brought her to River Glen, then? That's how she left the note, maybe visiting her parents? They didn't act like they'd seen her for a while."

"That's why I want you to find her! Are you going to do it? It doesn't sound like it."

"I'm trying," Mac said a bit testily. She, too, was holding onto her patience with an effort.

"Sorry," muttered Leigh.

THE SORORITY

"Did she join a sorority at Stanford? I remember she wanted to."

"No. She changed her mind. After Ethan died, everything just kind of changed. You know that."

"I do," admitted Mac. "Do you have the names of any other friends from Stanford?"

"No. Are you giving up? Or are you still going to try to find her?"

"Getting background is the first step," Mac tried to explain, but Leigh cut her off.

"Oh, I know. I'm just . . . pissed that Mia's gone dark."

Mac switched gears. "How did The Sorority act when you mentioned that I was looking for Mia?"

"Oh. Well, they weren't happy about it. They . . . don't trust anybody but themselves." She paused. "You know, I really wanted you to be a part of our group back in high school. You were in drama with me, and so I asked Natalie, but she kind of brushed me off. I'm sorry, I—"

"It's okay," Mac cut in dryly.

"—just wanted you to know."

"Well . . . thanks." Mac shook her head, momentarily derailed that Leigh would still worry about that. "I have a question for you. It's off point, but I'm curious. What exactly happened between Mia and Ethan Stanhope back in high school? Do you know?"

"Ethan and Mia?" Her voice rose. "What does that have to do—" She broke off and stated firmly, "Well, *Roxie* happened. That ended everything for Mia. And by the way, Roxie's not in The Sorority anymore. We haven't seen her since high school and that's just fine."

"But Mia and Ethan didn't immediately break up after the supposed Roxie incident. They still were together."

"Supposed?"

"There were a lot of rumors at the time. But, as I recall, people talked about how Mia was still with Ethan even after he and Roxie were seen coming out of the pool house together."

"Mia wanted to break up with him. She just didn't!"

"How long was it before Mia got with Ben?"

"Couple years. Why?"

"Do you know anyone besides yourself who's had contact with her?"

"No. Mia and I were besties. Nobody else."

"Okay. I'm just trying to find a place to begin," she explained. "Mia left Stanford about eight years ago, apparently with Ben. You've never heard his last name, but I imagine her parents have, or Mason. I have to find a way to shake that information loose."

"I thought you might go to California, or something."

"California's a pretty big state to start looking when I don't know what area to search," Mac pointed out.

"It sounds like you're starting to believe Gavin. And he's such a liar! Don't listen to him."

"Well, he's in the hospital, fighting for his life," Mac reminded her carefully.

"I'm just saying, he's got that all wrong. His brother's death has really messed him up and he wasn't good before that."

Noted.

They hung up a few minutes later and Mac got the

distinct impression Leigh was rethinking hiring her. She wanted immediate results, yet didn't seem to want to help much in giving Mac information. Maybe she thought investigative work was more glamorous than it really was. In any case, Mac recognized her most efficient way to proceed would be to get Mason on her side, a task that was going to take some doing.

Also, she didn't think Gavin Knowles was lying about The Sorority. He might be mistaken, but she wasn't going to stop asking questions.

". . . well, you were right. White paint on Knowles's car was transferred from another vehicle," said Verbena on the phone to Cooper.

Cooper was standing on the back porch and looking over the flattened, wet grass from the light rain that kept coming in fits and starts. Humph had already told him about the white paint, but he appreciated Verbena keeping him informed. Knowles's accident was a confirmed two-car accident, and from what Cooper had learned from Taft, Knowles felt he'd been run off the road on purpose.

"Thanks," said Cooper.

"*De nada.*" Verbena was working this weekend while Cooper was off. "This is Laurelton's case," she reminded him.

"I know." Being outside River Glen P.D.'s jurisdiction, Gavin Knowles's hit-and-run wasn't his case.

"Oh, and a copy of that tox report you ordered came in. I can pull it up, or you want to wait till Monday?"

"Give it to me now." She did and Cooper's brow furrowed.

"Take care of that wife of yours and check in with me on Monday," Verbena signed off.

He pushed through the back door and into the warm interior of the house, walking down the hall, drawn to the kitchen by the scent of pumpkin spice. Harley was really taking this "taking care of Mom" thing to heart. She'd become the self-appointed household cook.

Duchess looked over at his approach and gave him a big doggy smile and wag of her plumed tail. Emma stood to one side of Harley, who was mixing up batter in a bowl. Emma glanced at Cooper and said, "Pumpkin spice is the flavor of the month."

"The flavor of last month," Harley corrected. Her phone dinged at her and she glanced down at the screen. "I'm making Greer cookies," she said. "He's on his way."

Harley's high school boyfriend, Greer Douglas, had transferred from another college and enrolled in Portland State this fall to be near her. They'd reconnected this past July at a summer camp that had turned into a nightmare of multiple injuries and deaths. Cooper's stepdaughter, Marissa, had been there as well, as had Jamie and Emma at a parent/alumni weekend. It had all come to a violent conclusion that Cooper hadn't learned about until it was basically over.

Another case outside your jurisdiction, Cooper thought, a cold finger of remembrance tracking down his spine. Feelings of anger, guilt, and impotence still reared up whenever he thought about how his whole family had suffered near life-ending trauma. All of them were lucky to have all escaped mostly unharmed.

"We're having ravioli for dinner later," pronounced Emma, and Duchess seconded this with a short *arf*.

Spaghetti last night, ravioli tonight. With Emma around, pasta was almost a nightly meal, though she tried to enjoy other dishes. It was just a quirk of her mental state that she rarely considered anything else.

"No bats and pumpkins this time," Harley added, setting the bowl aside and starting to spoon dough into little mounds on a greased baking sheet. She was referring to the ravioli they'd had before Halloween, black bats and orange pumpkins. "Guess they don't make turkey pasta."

"How many minutes till the cookies are done?" he asked. He'd been sitting around watching football before Verbena's call had taken him outside for privacy. Now he headed for the stairs. "I'll come back for some to take to Jamie."

"None for yourself?" Harley questioned with a smirk in her voice.

"I don't want to ruin my girlish figure," he responded.

Harley snorted and Emma said, "Jamie is eating for two."

"Where's the cat?" he asked as he looked down at them from the upper hallway.

"Around," said Harley, but Cooper knew Duchess would not be so sanguine if Twink was lurking outside the bedroom.

He tapped on the bedroom door, waited, then opened it a crack when he got no response. Twink was once again wrapped around the pillow above Jamie's head and turned bright amber eyes on Cooper, who lifted his arms as if he were a perp caught in a searchlight. Jamie was dozing, a book lying open beside her on the bed.

He still marveled that she was pregnant. The doctors had labeled her uterus inhospitable, had said that becoming pregnant was almost out of the question, but she'd conceived anyway and the baby was apparently growing without any problems.

Jamie stretched and turned half-lidded eyes Cooper's way. "I called Mary Jo," she said.

"You did? What did she say?" asked Cooper.

"I didn't get her. I was going to leave a message for her to call me, but I haven't yet. I don't know. It's all good news, but I don't want to rock the boat." She shook her head. "So, they're making cookies down there?"

"Smells great, doesn't it?"

"Really great," she said enthusiastically, but he could see the little line of anxiety drawn between her brows. "How's your spy doing?" she asked, purposely changing the subject.

"Haven't heard from him today." He thought about the proposed ravioli and suggested, "How about I make dinner tonight?"

"Hardy-har-har."

"You malign my cooking skills?"

"I can't malign them if they're nonexistent."

"Then be prepared for more pasta."

"Okay," she sighed. She glanced at her cell, which was sitting on the nightstand, as if willing it to ring. He saw her tighten her lips in determination as she reached for it. "I think I'll call her again."

"I'll go see about a change of menu," he said.

She nodded, her mind already on the task at hand. Cooper walked downstairs, texting as he went.

Taft stared at his phone, ignoring the rise and fall of voices in the bar around him, thinking hard. He debated on calling Mac but didn't want to be overheard so he just forwarded her the text he'd just received from Haynes.

He nursed his beer as he sat in the same seat at the bar he'd occupied the night before. Lacey's was growing crowded faster tonight. There were a number of off-duty cops, one Taft recognized from Portland P.D. He'd lasted a few years there, about the same amount of time as he'd lasted at River Glen P.D. He'd been gone from both of them long enough that only the longtimers would recognize him. This cop didn't give him much of a look, but then he was busy telling some long, involved story to a couple of guys whose eyes wandered around, lighting occasionally on some of the women who arrived in twos and threes, mostly. Bradley, Taft remembered. Officer Karl Bradley. Taft had been an officer as well, but had been on track for detective on a rapid course, which had pissed Bradley off as he'd been with the department longer. Taft had left before the promotion had happened and had bounced to River Glen, where Cooper Haynes was already one of the department's detectives.

The male bartender was younger than last night's Jerry. He had dark hair combed back and a thick black mustache that almost looked fake. He got Taft a beer without glancing at him directly. His focus was on the woman in the tight black dress and dark red hair who was studiously avoiding his gaze. Taft figured there was something between them, though she didn't seem to care about his attention, at least right now. He only caught a few words of her conversation but then he heard "Thursday's funeral" and his ears pricked up. She was talking about Tim Knowles.

The bartender could hardly turn his eyes Taft's way, so engrossed was he in overhearing the redhead who was talking to a couple other guys. The woman with the I DON'T THINK SO, F**CKER T-shirt appeared from the back, clearly annoyed that she had to come out front again. Tonight she was wearing a plain white shirt with a button-down collar that stretched a little around her middle. She shrugged past the bartender, who someone called "Rob," pointed to Taft's glass, and asked, "Another?"

"Yep."

She walked over to the tap, gave it a tug while scowling at Rob. When she brought Taft his beer, she stayed at his end of the bar. "What are they talking about?" Taft asked, hitching his head toward the redhead and guys.

"Tim Knowles. You know him?"

"Some."

"That why you're here . . . Taft?"

"You know me," Taft said, brows lifting. He looked at her hard again, but didn't recognize her.

"Heard some of what you were talking about with Jerry last night."

"I didn't give my name."

A faint smile touched her lips. "Some of the other guys knew who you were. Said you were Mitch Mangella's fixer. No one's mourning your boss, by the way."

"Not my boss," Taft said. "But I do kind of mourn him."

"What do you want to know about Tim?"

Taft almost reiterated what Jerry had told him about Tim knowing Stacey Colville and her boyfriend, Ham, but decided on a different tactic. "Tim spent a lot of time at Lacey's?"

"Off and on." Her eyes drifted to the redhead.

"With her?" Taft guessed.

"She wishes. Looked like it was gonna happen, then no. Something about his brother, Rob said, but then Rob isn't reliable."

She was looking at the other bartender, not bothering to keep her voice down, but Rob was too focused on the redhead.

"His brother, Gavin," said Taft.

"Rob was banging her hard against the wall of the supply room a while back," she said, "so he was glad the brother said or did whatever it was that turned Tim off her. She comes in now and again, but she really wanted Tim. And it looked like he was going there, which drove Rob and a couple other guys crazy, but then Tim just wasn't interested anymore. Would slide away if she came in, find a booth, fill it with other friends. I think it really pissed her off, but she was crying her eyes out last week about him. Boo-hooing over everybody that he was gone."

"Who is she?" asked Taft.

"Kristl somebody. Seems to have a thing for cops." She shrugged. "Some do."

Kristl . . . Taft's gaze sharpened on her. Mac had said Gavin blamed someone named Kristl for Ethan Stanhope's death, one of the high school group that called themselves The Sorority.

He pulled out his phone, thinking of texting her, when Kristl stepped out of the group of men she was talking to and wiped the tears off her cheeks. "Thanks, guys," she said. "You made me feel better and that's hard to do right now." She gave them a watery smile and then she grabbed up her coat from where she'd hung it on a hook. A black slicker with red lining. Slipping it on, her gaze met Taft's. He tucked his phone away and gave her a smile.

Her eyes assessed him and she must've liked what she saw because she came over to him as she shrugged into her coat.

"I haven't seen you here before."

"Last night was my first night," said Taft.

"You aren't a cop . . . I know most of 'em. Why'd you pick Lacey's?"

"I knew Tim. I was a cop, a while ago."

She momentarily stilled, as if he'd said something momentous that needed processing. But then she shrugged it off. "I was a friend of Tim's," she said. "I miss him."

Taft could feel the female bartender's eyes practically boring holes into him, she was staring so hard. "He was a good guy," said Taft.

"He *was* a good guy," she repeated her lips quivering. She pressed them together.

"You're leaving? I could buy you a drink, if you feel like staying," he said.

She hesitated, looking at his beer. "I should go." He nodded understandingly but still she hesitated. "Maybe . . . wine, or a Cadillac Margarita . . . ?"

He signaled the female bartender, who said dryly, "I heard," before Taft even opened his mouth.

"I'm Kristl Cuddahy," the redhead introduced herself. "Who are you?" She perched one butt cheek on the stool next to him, apparently deciding whether to stay or run.

"Jesse Taft."

"That name's familiar. Why is it familiar?"

"I've been around."

"How did you know Tim?"

"I know his brother, Gavin. Did you know he's in the hospital?"

Her expression froze. "I heard that." The female bartender slid the drink across the bar and then Rob was hovering nearby, watching Taft and Kristl like the proverbial hawk.

"He says someone ran him off the road," said Taft, picking up his beer and taking a few swallows.

"*He* says. I thought . . . he was in a coma or something." She looked a bit panicked.

"He might be. I don't know. That's just what I heard."

"I feel bad for him. I really do. But honestly . . . well, never mind. You don't want to hear."

"No, go ahead." He spread out his palm to encourage her.

"Okay, well, he said some things about me that just weren't true and he made Tim believe them. It was really uncalled for. I just feel so bad and I never got a chance to explain it all to Tim. All of a sudden, he was just gone." More tears surfaced.

Taft didn't have anything to give her except for an extra cocktail napkin, which he handed to her.

"I was in love with Tim," she said in a tight voice, dabbing at her eyes, to which Rob made a disparaging sound and stomped to the other end of the bar.

"Were you with him the night he took the call?" asked Taft.

"No . . . no . . . I was here at the bar, if that's what you mean, but the damage was done by Gavin. Tim wasn't talking to me anymore."

"What did Gavin say about you? If you don't want to tell me, that's fine," he added, giving her an out.

She shook her head, then looked unseeingly across the room. "He said I killed one of his friends. Like I was a mastermind or something that made his friend go off the road! I can't believe Tim listened to him. And then Tim said he was a cop and couldn't be with me. Maybe he was right—if he believed in those kind of rumors, I couldn't be with him, either."

"That sounds like quite a leap," agreed Taft.

"Yeah . . . it was." Her expression grew stony, remembering, as she slid her whole butt onto the stool and picked up the margarita. "I don't know why I'm telling you this, Gavin being your friend."

"More like an acquaintance."

She slid her gaze over him, really looking at him. Taft was aware of female appraisals. He'd been looked at a lot over the years. And he sensed a sharklike intensity in Kristl that reminded him of Prudence Mangella and Anna DeMarcos.

The female bartender emitted a short bark of laughter and shook her finger at him. Taft knew it was because Kristl was examining him as if he were her next meal.

CHAPTER 13

" . . . didn't make any other friends at the bar after that," Taft admitted. "Kristl was hinting about going to my place, but I said I had to catch an early flight and we left it at that. She gave me her number and I told her I'd call her when I got back."

Mac was listening to him on her cell's speaker as she drove to Riversong Church. She flexed her hands on the wheel. She'd felt a flare of emotion at his first words about Kristl that she'd pushed aside.

"I said I would call her Monday, after my 'trip' to Phoenix, where I have family. She said she's taking care of her mother, which has precluded any other kind of job. Meantime, still waiting to hear from Kingman's family, his mother, mainly, and I've changed my mind. I'm going to go ahead and contact Sally Colville and Ham. Let me know how church goes."

"Sure thing."

"How's the foot?"

"I'm not as good at wrapping it as you are, but it's passable. I think I can hobble in without support."

"Let me know if you need my expert touch again."

"I will." Taft had started this conversation with the fact that Detective Haynes had called him with the information that there was white paint scraped along Gavin's vehicle and now the department was treating his accident as a potential crime.

But the big news was the results of the tox report on Ethan Stanhope. Fentanyl.

He and Ingrid had both died of fentanyl poisoning.

"What?" she'd gasped after Taft gave her the grim news. Taft's sister, Helene, had died of a drug overdose and Taft was a bulldog when it came to bringing drug dealers and their ilk to justice. The whiff of Mangella dabbling in that market is what had ended Taft's relationship with the man, and though Mangella swore up and down he wasn't involved in drugs, Taft didn't believe him.

"Yeah," Taft said grimly. "It's likely the accident was caused by loss of control from the drugs."

Taft then went on to tell Mac that the tox report hadn't been made public at Coral and Art Stanhope's request, which gave Mac the uneasy realization that Gavin's insistence there was more to Ethan's accident was correct. She'd absorbed that news slowly, but concluded that was what he'd tasked her to find out, so she was going to do it. Was Gavin also right about The Sorority being involved? And did his own accident have any correlation to Ethan's? Someone wanting him to stop telling everyone and anyone that Kristl, or some other Sorority member, was to blame for Ethan's death?

And what about his brother, Tim?

Taft swore under his breath, bringing Mac back to the present. "Prudence is calling again. I've put her off too many times. Let me know how church goes," he said again. And he was gone.

Mac stared at the road ahead of her. She needed to shake herself all over like a dog, throwing off all the unwanted feelings. Maybe engage in scream therapy or go for a jog . . . if she only could.

She exhaled and forced herself to consider this disturbing twist. Gavin blamed Kristl for Ethan's death. He'd flat out said so to Mac, before veering off and blaming all of The Sorority. *They all had sex with him.* And Kristl had complained to Taft that Tim Knowles had turned away from her because of Gavin's warning that Kristl was responsible for Ethan's death. So, why was Gavin so sure Kristl had something to do with Ethan's accident? Mac hadn't really listened to him when he'd accused her before. She had firmly believed Ethan Stanhope's death was an accident, but if it wasn't . . . why did Gavin blame Kristl? When had he started blaming her? From the beginning, or had he focused on her as the supposed killer because she and Tim were getting together?

And how had fentanyl ended up in Ethan's and Ingrid's systems? Ethan could have taken the fentanyl himself, but Ingrid? How had she come in contact with it?

She pulled into the parking lot of the church. If Gavin was right and some or all of The Sorority had been involved with Ethan, might one or two of them wish to shut him up? And if that was true, would they really resort to murder? And if so, how did they do it? They didn't spike his drink at the party. Too much time passed between the party and the accident, and also, Ingrid wasn't with Ethan earlier that night.

Mac headed for the church steps. She was wearing black slacks and a white sweater and had a thin black trench coat thrown on, unbelted. No rain at the moment, but she was forced to carefully dodge shallow puddles in the shiny wet asphalt.

She'd arrived in time to meld with other members. As she moved forward she got lucky. Tawny Price was just climbing the front steps. Mac tried to not limp, though that was impossible, and her awkward gait drew Tawny's eyes. Her brows lifted as she recognized Mac, and no wonder. Apart from Tim's funeral, Mac couldn't remember the last time she'd been inside a church.

"Mackenzie," Tawny greeted her in surprise. "What are you doing here?"

Tawny, despite her name, had dark hair that she wore in a no-nonsense short bob. She fit perfectly in Mac's mental image of a rodeo rider with a rangy build. Her nails were clipped short, and she wore flared black pants with the toes of her cowboy boots peeking out from beneath.

"Truthfully? Gavin Knowles asked me to look into Ethan Stanhope's accident just before he was in an accident himself. I wanted to talk to the Stanhopes so I came to church."

"Really." Tawny eyed her carefully. "Coral and Art don't talk to many people. They're pretty closed off. And if you bring up Ethan and Ingrid . . . you won't get very far. How's Gavin, by the way? I heard he was run off the road."

Now it was Mac's turn to be surprised. She'd just

learned about the white paint on Gavin's car this morning. "Is that what's been determined?"

Tawny shrugged. "I thought that's what I heard."

They were walking into the church together and Tawny's husband, Henry, joined them. He, too, wore cowboy boots, his prominently showing beneath pressed jeans. They could have been brother and sister they looked so much alike, and it didn't surprise her that they owned a farm about an hour south of the urban confluence of River Glen, Laurelton, and Portland.

Mac sat in the pew next to Tawny and Hank and dutifully opened the hymnal to the designated songs, which she knew none of. Her eyes roamed the crowd, but she didn't know what the Stanhopes looked like. When the minister started his sermon, Tawny silently pointed to a couple across the aisle and about five rows ahead of her. Mac could see the woman's upswept blond hair, long neck, teardrop pearl earrings and the man's thinning salt-and-pepper hair, which was barely covering a growing bald spot.

She kept her eyes on them throughout the rest of the service. When it was over, she moved with Tawny and Hank back toward the opened double doors. Rain was now pelting down and the parishioners were waiting for the cloudburst to end. A few did carry umbrellas. In all sorts of colors, they popped open like instantly blooming flowers.

Mac waited in the vestibule, shuffling away as best she could, finally leaning a hand against the wall to keep from being knocked off her precarious feet. When the Stanhopes appeared, Coral Stanhope slid her a cool look. Art Stanhope just brushed forward in front of his wife, frowning up at the sky.

"Mrs. Stanhope?" Mac asked politely.

Coral zeroed in on Mac with laser-like intensity. Her eyes were a cold gray and Mac had a sudden forgotten memory of her from high school. She'd thought she'd never met Coral Stanhope, and though that was true in the main, she remembered seeing her at a football game. It was Homecoming, and Mac had been talked into going by Summer Cochran. "Come on, we gotta do that rah-rah thing our senior year," Summer had encouraged the whole drama class. They'd gone together in a group and Mackenzie had recognized how little she knew about the game, even though her dad used to watch college football and she was aware of a few basics. Ethan was there with Gavin and there was some kind of brouhaha happening between Ethan and his parents with Gavin's eyes ping-ponging back and forth between them. Art Stanhope had been quietly furious, but it was Coral glaring at Ethan with those wintry eyes that stuck in Mac's brain. What had the fight been about? Something to do with church? Maybe? And Ingrid's name was invoked. Ethan hadn't done something right and his parents were furious. Or was it Ingrid they were mad at?

"Hi, I'm Mackenzie Laughlin. I'm a classmate of Ethan's and Gavin Knowles's," she said, her throat dry and her pulse speeding up. "I saw Gavin in the hospital and he—"

"Are you one of them?" she interrupted tensely.

Mac hesitated. "One of . . . ?"

"Are you one of the girls who ruined our son's life?

Brighty said she ran into one of them at the hospital. Was that you?"

"I . . . was at the hospital to see Gavin," she admitted. This was not going to turn out well.

"Coral," Art said, looking back when he realized she'd stopped short. The rest of the congregation was flowing around them, as if they were an island in the stream.

"Go on ahead," she told him. "I have something to say."

Uh-oh . . .

"I've dealt with a lot of speculation over the years, Miss Laughlin. I lost one son and daughter to a terrible car accident, and the only reason I still have my oldest is because he didn't meet any of you."

Mac could feel her face heat.

"So, if there's anything else you want, take it up with our lawyers, Segal & Wexford."

She started to walk away, but Mac called after her, "Gavin Knowles believes someone else is responsible for Ethan's and Ingrid's deaths. He asked me to find out the truth."

Her steps slowed. The blond chignon half turned, the pearl earring faintly swinging as the church vestibule emptied. Coral Stanhope then turned slowly to fully assess Mac.

Might as well burn it all down. "As you know, they didn't die from the accident."

"What are you suggesting?" she asked, but there was a faint quiver in her bottom lip, a crack in her icy facade.

"Do you really want to talk about it here?"

Coral's unflinching gaze slowly turned to pure misery.

Mac felt a pang of guilt for causing her more pain, but if Coral and Art were the ones who'd hidden the tox report, then it was time to come clean.

Coral closed her eyes, drew a breath, and pulled her composure around herself like a cloak. Mac braced herself to be dismissed, but Coral said, "Do you know where we live?"

Mac nodded.

"Can we meet at . . ." She glanced to where her husband was talking to Tawny. Art looked back at her and impatiently motioned for her to get going. "Three p.m. today?"

"Yes."

"I will reserve judgment, Ms. Laughlin. Brighty is grieving and may not be as clearheaded as she could be. I know what that's like." She turned and stepped down the stairs to meet Art.

Mac followed a bit slower, babying her ankle. Tawny waited for her. The rain had momentarily stopped, leaving shallow puddles shining underneath a watery sun. "What happened?" she asked. They both watched as the Stanhopes walked toward a black Mercedes.

"I'm meeting her at three."

"Really?" Her eyes followed the Mercedes as it wheeled out of the lot.

"She jumped to the conclusion that I was one of The Sorority and told me I could talk to their lawyers, but then she changed her mind."

"The Stanhopes vacillate from quoting the Lord to tearing 'lesser' people down. You must have superpowers."

Mac had hinted that she knew about the tox report to

Coral, but she wasn't about to reveal that to Tawny. "I've forgotten their older son's name."

"Sam. He'd been in L.A. for years, but he came back a while ago. He works in television. I don't think he gets along all that well with his parents, but he's living with them now." She lifted her hands in surrender. "I don't really know, I just hear things. You need a hand?" she asked as Mac couldn't quite hide her limp.

"No, I'm good."

A shaft of brighter sunlight fought its way through the cloud cover. She could smell the rain and she inhaled deeply. Tawny said goodbye and that they should really keep in touch and Mac agreed, though she was notoriously poor at staying current with any of her classmates.

Which reminded her that she was going to have to change that situation and start interviewing The Sorority if she wanted to get to the bottom of Gavin's insistence that they were somehow involved in Ethan's death.

She drove back to her apartment, lost in thought. It wasn't all that far from Riversong Church to her place but she surfaced enough to realize a blue car had been behind her all the way. As if recognizing she'd noticed it, the driver fell back and turned off the road into a strip center. Was that the same Accord that had turned around in her apartment parking lot earlier, or was she just on edge? The thrust and feint of conversations with people like Brighty Knowles and Coral Stanhope always tightened her nerves.

* * *

"Say that again," said Cooper, staring at his wife, who was just settling herself back in bed after a trip to the bathroom.

"Mary Jo was nothing but nice, but she sounded like she was reading from a script. Totally monotone. Couldn't scare up an inflection to congratulate me on the baby. I know. It was weird. I don't know what to think."

"Well, let's not borrow trouble . . ."

"I'm not," Jamie assured him. "I just kinda knew she might feel . . . diminished? In some way?"

"We're having two babies instead of one. People do it all the time."

"Not like we are. Not all the time. I'm just saying that her psyche is maybe less solid than ours are. Mary Jo seems great. She really does. I'm just . . ."

"Worrying."

"Worrying," she repeated. "I'm allowed to worry."

"Well, don't worry too much."

"Cooper," she admonished, meeting his gaze. "It's going to be fine. I just want to be prepared if something should go wrong."

"Like what?"

"I don't know. Use your imagination." She was growing testy. "Like maybe she decides to keep the baby when—"

"No. We have a contract. That's your egg and my sperm. It's not hers."

"Yes, yes, I know. And we would probably win any legal fight—"

"We *would* win any legal fight."

"I just don't want it to come to that."

"Well, she knows now. There's nothing hidden."

Jamie nodded. "Good."

"Good," he repeated.

But he didn't feel good after he left her and headed back downstairs. He prowled around the living room and would have gone for a jog if the weather wasn't so unpredictable. He felt . . . uneasy, no matter what he'd told her. He couldn't help himself.

He looked at the sky and thought, *Hell with it*. He headed for the stairs, stripping off his shirt on the way up. He was going for that jog. He almost wished it was Monday already as he wanted to go to work and think about something else.

The Stanhope house was one of the estates at the top of Stillwell Hill. A Tudor in style, cream stucco with dark wooden trim, it was built in a wide arc around an imposing gray, brick-lined drive. Mac parked the RAV to the side of the quadruple car garage and carefully made her way to the portico over the massive mahogany-stained double doors. She rang the bell, hearing it peal within the bowels of the house. Arborvitae ran on either side of the property, marking about an acre of land, but there were no neighbors nearby. She guessed the Stanhopes owned the property that surrounded the house for multiple acres.

She half expected a maid to come to the door, but it was Coral herself. The chignon was still in place but the earrings were gone and she'd changed into a loose silver velour sweater and pants. Her feet were bare and she requested that Mac take off her shoes, then she led the way down a hallway to a room off the kitchen crowded with a small couch and two chairs and a television tuned to a Christian station. Picking up the remote, she cut the picture, then invited Mac to take a chair.

"Art's playing nine holes. I guess he thinks the rain will now hold off for a while." She turned those cold eyes, made more so by the color choice of her upscale sweats, on Mac. "Would you like something to drink? Coffee or tea or something stronger?"

"No, thanks." Mac perched on the edge of an espresso brown leather chair.

"I'm having some J&B." She picked up a glass full of amber liquid and melting ice. "You sure?"

"I'm sure. Thank you."

"What happened to your foot?" She slid a finger toward Mac's bandage.

"Sprained ankle."

"Hazards of the trade? I understand you're a private investigator. Were you chasing a . . . suspect?" She sat down on the couch and tucked her feet underneath her.

The Coral Stanhope who'd seemed to thaw a bit outside the church had disappeared and this version was in complete control. How deep that control went was anyone's guess.

"I was attending Tim Knowles's funeral."

Coral jerked as if stung, but then sipped from her glass. "Life can be so viciously unfair. So, how's Gavin doing? You said you went to see him."

"He asked me to look into Ethan's accident."

"He hired you?"

"Yes."

Neither of them seemed particularly eager to address the elephant in the room, but that's why Mac was here, so... "I'm not sure if Gavin knows about the toxicology results... Or maybe he does and that's why he feels so strongly that there's more to the accident than was reported."

"How do you know about the toxicology? Or maybe I should ask, *what* do you know, as you may be fishing."

"I know it was fentanyl."

She closed her eyes and hugged herself. Mac wondered if she would try to deny it, but she just sighed and opened her eyes again. "I used to smoke. I made a pact with God after they died that I would quit, which I did, on the spot. But they're still dead, aren't they? I guess God doesn't care that I could finally kick the habit. Yes, it was fentanyl. Ethan had it and somehow Ingrid found it. I know he would never have given it to her."

"Do you know how Ethan got it?"

"Some dealer?" She lifted her shoulder. "He bought it from someone. We didn't know for a while that that's what caused the accident. We thought Ethan just lost control. He wasn't drinking... he wasn't... He loved water polo. Loved it. He wouldn't jeopardize that... we thought. But it was graduation and we were here celebrating with family before he went to the Knowleses', and when he came back, yes, he'd clearly imbibed some. I was just happy he was home. But later, he was sober. *Sober*. When they left. We would have never let Ingrid in the car with him otherwise."

"May I ask where were they going?"

She gave a short bark of laughter. "To get ice cream! We didn't have any and there were desserts left over from our graduation party that afternoon, and they both wanted ice cream."

Mac nodded. She felt Coral's pain at the banality, the innocence of their car trip. "How do think Ingrid found the fentanyl?"

"I don't know. They're pills, right? We searched Ethan's room, but never found them, and then we didn't want it to be public."

"Someone helped you quash the tox report."

She glared at Mac. "We have friends in high places who care. Go ahead and make judgments. You don't know what it's like!"

"I'm not making a judgment. I just know fentanyl works pretty fast. Maybe the pills were in the car?"

"That's what we think, but there was no evidence they were there." She heaved a sigh. "I don't want this to be raked up. And I want to know how you found out. If any of this gets in the news, I'll sue."

"Mrs. Stanhope, if you know what you're looking for, it isn't hard to find."

She shook her head, then picked up her glass again and drank the rest of it down, clinking the glass hard against the tabletop. "I wish Gavin would just leave it alone. Brighty thinks one of you is behind everything, I guess."

"I'm not one of The Sorority."

"Have I answered your questions? Have you gotten what you need?" She was beginning to grow belligerent.

Maybe the effects of the alcohol, maybe just a return of her haughty nature.

Footsteps sounded on the stairs. Mac glanced toward the door but Coral stared straight ahead unseeingly, her back toward the kitchen. A man appeared at the end of the hall, looking enough like an older version of Ethan that Mac caught her breath.

"What's going on?" he asked. Unlike Ethan his eyes were gray, like his mother's.

"This is Mackenzie Laughlin, a private investigator."

"I'm actually working to be one," Mac clarified. "Not certified yet."

He stared at her. "Why are you here?"

"I invited her." Coral turned her head slightly, giving him that profile view of her neck and chignon. "She's looking into Ethan's accident."

"*What?*"

She waved an impatient hand at him. "This is my son, Sam."

"Why are you bringing this up? It was a fucking accident!" he sputtered.

"Gavin asked her to," Coral said.

"Gavin's in the hospital." He seemed to be struggling to keep up.

"Yes, well, apparently he wants Mackenzie to prove that those girls from his class killed him. That's what Brighty thinks, too." She folded her arms over her chest.

"The girls from his class . . . The Sorority . . . ?" he asked. "What's he talking about? Why does everything have to be a conspiracy?"

Mac heard an echo of her own skepticism.

Coral added, "She already knows about the toxicology." As Sam took this as another blow, Coral said to Mac, "He thinks he's writing a screenplay about it."

"I *was* writing a screenplay. I'm not anymore."

"Not since we cut off funds," Coral said dryly.

"Oh, shut up, Mother. Can't you see she's taking all this in?"

Coral's lips tightened and angry tears brightened her eyes. High spots of color showed up on her cheeks and she abruptly got up and left the room. Mac got to her feet, too.

"She drinks too much," Sam said, picking up her glass. "Then goes to church and thinks God absolves her."

That wasn't quite the way Coral had depicted her feelings about God. "Do you know how they got the fentanyl?"

"No." His answer was so quick she thought he might be lying. Before she could respond, he added, "I don't think we need to talk to you anymore."

"I'd like to say goodbye to your mother."

"No need."

Mac could feel his tension and her heart began a deep, accelerated beat as she recognized a certain danger. She was about to leave when Coral came down the stairs and met her in the entry hall, carrying a Dell laptop computer. "This is Ethan's. His cell phone got ruined in the accident, but he kept pictures and school assignments and some email on the laptop. Maybe it will help you."

Mac stared at her in surprise. When Coral thrust the computer at her, Sam stepped in front of her.

"What are you doing? That's Ethan's. Don't give it to her!"

"Maybe it will help," said Coral, sweeping the laptop to one side to avoid Sam's grabbing hands. "Maybe Gavin knows something."

"*Gavin*. Not her!"

"I want to know more about what happened, too." Coral stepped around him and placed the laptop in Mac's hands. "Bring it back when you're done. No rush."

"You're not doing this!" declared Sam, which earned him a lethal look from his mother. She glanced back at Mac, who took the hint and quickly headed for the door.

"I don't expect anything," Coral called after her. "But if you do learn something, I want to be the first to know. The password is *waterpolo*."

Mac didn't have a chance to respond as Coral slammed the door shut behind her. She half expected Sam to yank it open again and wrest the laptop from her arms so she trotted toward her SUV, thinking *Ow, ow, ow*, every time she stepped on her left foot. When she backed the RAV around, the front door finally burst open but instead of coming after her, Sam just watched her leave through eyes more worried than angry.

Two hours later, Taft arrived at her apartment with tacos and Coronas from Mexicali Rose. They both had stories to tell but agreed to wait until after they'd downed the food and beer, and then Taft insisted on rewrapping her ankle. Mackenzie braced herself for his touch and managed to make it through without making a fool of herself, though he did mention that she was awfully tense and told her to try and relax.

"Tell me about the Stanhopes," he said, smoothing a hand over the bandage, checking for wrinkles.

"It feels great. Thank you. I'm good." She moved her foot from his hands, but he didn't leave his perch on her ottoman as she launched into her story about Coral, Art, and Sam Stanhope. He listened carefully, his eyes moving to the laptop she'd set on the small table next to her favorite chair as she finished with Sam's reaction.

"So, what do you think?" he asked.

"His reaction was a little over the top, I thought, but maybe not if the laptop's something of his brother's? Or maybe he reacted because there's something on it he doesn't think I should see? Or maybe he's just all-around pissed. It was hard to tell. I'm just still surprised that Coral gave it to me. She's upset with Sam because he was writing a screenplay about the tragedy, although he says that's over now. He's given it up."

"Have you looked at the laptop?"

"Haven't had time. Thought I might start tonight. What about you and the Tim Knowles investigation?" Mac knew he'd gone to see Sally Colville and her boyfriend, William "Ham" Hamilton.

"Sally was nice. Didn't have much in the way of real information that I didn't already know. Ham is a blowhard who thinks he knows everything there is to know about being a cop. When I told him I'd left two different departments he looked at me like I was a degenerate." He smiled. "I asked him if he was thinking of joining the academy and he said it wasn't necessary."

Mac snorted.

"Said he already knew what to do. Apparently he worked security for a downtown Portland financial firm for a while, then got into cryptocurrency, made a bundle."

"Bullshit."

"Sally just stood by while he bragged. I would have liked to have spoken to Sally's daughter, but they didn't want that. Then Gena came out of the bedroom all on her own. She wanted to talk, so she did. She said she was alone in the bedroom, that Kingman entered the house through a back patio window that everyone knows doesn't lock properly. He came into the house and rummaged around in the kitchen and living room looking for items to steal. Gena tiptoed back into her closet and called nine-one-one."

"Kingman didn't really take any valuables, though, right?" asked Mackenzie.

"Just some pocket change, basically."

"So, why did he pick their house?"

"I asked that question. The back patio window that wouldn't close wasn't a secret, but it wasn't something a lot of people knew outside of their family and friends. Maybe he got lucky? Just searching and found an open window?"

"But it wasn't his neighborhood."

He pointed at her. "His mother finally called me back. She said he moved this way a few months ago. There's a group of homeless in tents around the corner from the Presbyterian church where he was shot. I talked to them and they said Kingman was around. Had a small pup tent with a few belongings that were scavenged before the police got there. He had some cognitive issues." He paused, then added, "Something new his mother never mentioned to the police. She thought he moved here for a woman."

"A woman?"

"Maybe she's the one who gave him bad intel," suggested Taft. "Told him how to get into the house and that there would be lots to steal? Something like that. Then Tim showed up and Kingman panicked. He was high or hallucinating and didn't want to get caught and just started shooting. He ran to the church. The officers found him there and he was still waving around his gun and they shot him, and he yelled out, 'Sanctuary' and then died. Body cam shows how it happened. He yelled after he was shot, like he was ready to meet his maker."

"Suicide by cop?" asked Mac.

"I'm sticking with hallucinating and bad intel."

"So, Tim was just unlucky?"

"Looks that way," said Taft.

"End of investigation?" She peered at him. "Or not?"

"I want to find this woman."

Mackenzie recognized that Taft had the bit in his teeth and wasn't going to let go until he'd shaken loose every possible detail. It was both his best and worst investigative trait. He was impossibly dogged and frustratingly bullheaded when after a lead.

"Whatever the case, Tim Knowles was there at the wrong moment and it ended his life," said Mac.

"Yeah . . ." Taft nodded, his blue eyes narrowing at some internal thought.

"What?"

"No, it's exactly as you said."

"But . . ." She could tell he was churning on something that he wasn't saying.

"A detail came out that kind of surprised me and I've been trying to think if it's part of this."

"What is it?"

"Sally Colville is a good friend to your friend, Kristl."

"That *is* a surprise," agreed Mac, jolted.

"The reason Kristl started going to Lacey's was because she would meet Sally there. Then Sally met Ham and they started living together about six months ago, so Kristl kept going alone."

"And she met up with Tim."

He nodded.

"You think she's this woman that Kingman was into?" asked Mac, holding back her incredulity as much as she could. "And just for the record, Kristl is more an acquaintance than a friend. All of The Sorority are, with the possible exception of Leigh, *Elayne* Denning, now Sommers. They're my classmates. That's all."

"Sounds like you want to deny them all," he said with a faint smile.

"Maybe Gavin's infected me. I'm starting to distrust all of them." She added, "By the way, I called the hospital again today. No change."

"Same thing I keep getting about Gavin. I'd better get going. We've both got full days tomorrow." He stood up and Mac's eyes lifted, traveling up his taut torso to focus on his lips and the light scruff of beard that hid his dimples.

"What?" she asked, realizing he'd said something she'd missed while her eyes were devouring him.

"Prudence wants me to come to her house after my meeting with the lawyer tomorrow."

"Don't do it!"

The dimples appeared. "I don't think she'd kill me in cold blood."

"Don't be so sure."

He inclined his head. "Point taken. See you tomorrow."

After he was gone she sank back in her chair, unaware how tense she'd been, even though Taft had said as much. She didn't like hearing about Kristl and she didn't like hearing that Prudence Mangella wanted to meet with Taft. She was dangerous, as was Anna DeMarcos. Taft knew it, but dismissed it at some level.

Damn it. She needed those numbers for The Sorority but Leigh wasn't getting back to her. If worse came to worst she could go find Kristl at her parents' house; it was the same one she'd grown up in. She wasn't as sure about Erin, or even Leigh, but she sure as hell knew where Parker Flooring was.

CHAPTER 14

Monday morning, Mac woke up with a dark cloud of worry hanging over her from a sleepless night. She threw off the covers and checked her ankle, which she'd left unwrapped overnight and was encouraged to see some of the swelling had gone down. Rotating her left foot carefully, she could almost make it full circle without that breath-catching stab of pain. Progress.

She made herself toast for breakfast, thought about the upcoming day. The Beckwiths didn't want her searching for Mia and the Stanhopes were divided on anyone searching into Ethan's fatal accident. Overall, the lot of them appeared to blame The Sorority, at least on some level, and Brighty Knowles also blamed them for Tim's death and Gavin's accident. A lot of finger pointing with no real evidence.

Her cell rang as she was just getting out of the shower and she hurried to answer it where she'd left it on her bed. She tweaked her ankle a bit in the process, stopped, swore, then swept the phone up.

She didn't recognize the number, but it had a local area code. "Mackenzie Laughlin."

"So, you approached the Stanhopes yesterday, at church, no less, and got a taste of Coral's sharp tongue," a male voice drawled. "Thought as a *friend*, you were looking for Mia. You're going pretty far afield, if that's all it is."

"Mason," she said, recognizing the voice and realizing he must be calling her on his personal cell.

"What are you really up to?" he asked curiously.

"How did you know I spoke to Coral?" She set the toast on a plate and put her cell phone on the counter, turning it to speaker, before putting the slices in the toaster and pressing the down button.

"Sam called me. You didn't say you were a private investigator when you were talking to my parents. Tsk. Tsk."

"You know Sam Stanhope?" asked Mac.

"Ethan and Mia dated a while. I know the Stanhopes pretty well. So, what are you after?"

"I barely spoke to Coral."

"Yeah, well, she apparently spoke at length to Brighty Knowles, whom I'm guessing you've met as she had some choice things to say about you."

"Sam relayed all that to you?" Mackenzie was a little taken aback by how swiftly the three households had spread the word about her. She didn't trust Mason much and Sam not at all. She'd looked through the laptop the night before, examining some of Ethan's pictures, and a few class assignments, but hadn't found anything of true interest.

"You're not answering my question. I asked you to be a witness in case my parents killed each other, but maybe I chose poorly. You have your own agenda and

I really don't know what that is, so it would be great if you could tell me."

"How are your parents doing?"

"Madly in love," he said sarcastically. "So, what are you doing?"

She decided to be honest. "I am looking for Mia, but Gavin Knowles also asked me to look into Ethan's accident."

He scoffed. "You'll do anything for money."

What an ass. "Did you call just to malign me?"

"What's Mia got to do with it all?"

"Nothing . . . maybe . . ." She heard the toast pop up in the toaster and smelled the faintly burnt scent that said she'd gotten them too dark. "I just want to talk to her, make sure she's all right. And I'm planning to talk to all of The Sorority."

"You're part of that group."

He wasn't listening and she was getting pissed. "I'm going to have to go, Mason." She plucked the partially charred bread from the toaster and placed it on a plate, opening the refrigerator and pulling out the butter, which she started to spread atop the two slices, silently lamenting the fact she had no jam.

"Level with me and . . . maybe I can help you," he said.

"Yeah? How?" She bit into the piece of toast and started chewing.

"I'll help you find Mia. I have a number for her. Haven't tried it in a while, but I think it's still good."

"Really? So, you've had this number all along?"

He made a sound of frustration. "I wasn't going to

give it to Leigh. I'm not sure I'm giving it to you, but let's talk, then I'll see if I want to get involved in all this."

Mac swallowed her bite and asked, "Do your parents know you have a contact for Mia?"

"What do you think? Of course not. I don't want to be kicked out of the house, or disowned, or any other shit my parents might pull, so, no, they don't know. You want my help? Let's meet somewhere where we can really talk."

Clearly he wasn't going to hand over the number without his pound of flesh. "Okay. Where?"

"I'll ask Sam, and I'll call you back. He'll want to be there, too." And he hung up.

Mac started choking on a second bite. She wanted nothing to do with Sam Stanhope.

She started to phone Taft and then stopped herself. He had that meeting with the lawyers for Mitch Mangella's estate this morning and it would probably be better to leave him alone until it was over.

She waited on pins and needles for Mason's return call, staring out her kitchen window at the parking lot below. No blue car turning around today and the parking lot was fairly empty on a Monday morning. She checked Google on her phone to see how long it took for fentanyl to take effect and realized the poisoning must have happened sometime while Ethan was at home, or maybe right before they drove off.

When her phone rang again and it was Mason, she exhaled.

"Do you know the Waystation?" he asked.

"I've heard of it," Mac said dryly. She suspected Mason thought it was one of those secret places where no one they knew would recognize them, but she'd spent many hours there in the course of work.

"Sam and I will be there tonight. Seven?"

"Okay," she said.

"Haynes."

Cooper looked up from his desk to see Humph standing in the doorway to his office, his long face looking even longer than usual.

Verbena drew a breath from her desk and said softly, "Chief doesn't look happy."

No, he doesn't, thought Cooper as he crossed the room. Humph disappeared back inside the glass-walled office and Cooper followed. All the blinds were already drawn, pretty much the way Humph kept it all the time.

He glanced down at a note he'd scratched on a piece of paper and said, "You ordered tox reports on Ethan and Ingrid Stanhope."

Cooper had known there would be a record of his request and had expected to have to explain. He just hadn't expected it to happen so soon. "I did," he admitted.

"Why?"

"Because the tox report was never made public and I had questions about that accident."

"Why?" Cooper hesitated and Humph stepped in. "This has something to do with Tim Knowles and his brother, Gavin, whose car was driven off the road in Laurelton city limits."

Cooper had no way to explain that he was getting the information for Mackenzie Laughlin so he just nodded.

"I believe I made myself clear about what your role in the Knowles investigation is, but maybe we oughta go over that again."

"A reporter called in about Tim's murder, trying to make it more than it was. I made certain they knew the case was closed," said Cooper.

"Closed with the department. Closed with you?" Humph's bushy gray eyebrows lifted in question. He didn't wait for a response. "There's a flag on the Stanhope file. Still in effect after all these years. The family doesn't want anyone looking into that file and there are some pretty powerful people who helped make that possible."

"They don't want the scandal," suggested Cooper stiffly.

"They don't want the public to know their kids died of fentanyl poisoning."

"You read the reports," said Cooper.

"What's this got to do with Tim Knowles? You're still chewing on that case."

"The two cases are unrelated, as far as I know. But Gavin Knowles was running his mouth a lot before the hit-and-run that put him in the hospital. Talking about Ethan Stanhope's death. Blaming it on some of his classmates."

"It was a one-car accident."

Humph had been doing a lot of reading, Cooper

realized. "If and when we can talk to Gavin, we can ask him if he knew about the fentanyl."

"Not according to the file. It's not for public consumption."

"Do you really think the fact that a nine-year-old girl died from fentanyl should be covered up?" Cooper demanded. He knew he was pushing, but Gavin's insistence that Ethan had been murdered was gaining some traction. Yes, he still wanted to know more about Tim Knowles's death, but with Mackenzie Laughlin's request for toxicology on Ethan and Ingrid Stanhope, a whole new can of worms had been opened. "You'd think the family would want to know. Why are they covering it up?"

"I spoke to the ex-mayor. Told her what I'd learned," said Humph.

"What did she say?" Cooper asked in surprise.

"That the Stanhopes were stunned with grief and didn't want to turn the accident into a circus. That their children were dead. That they didn't want the press all over them."

Cooper chose his words carefully. "Hiding the cause of their deaths is dangerous."

"I'm not saying I agree with those decisions, but if we're going to investigate, we've got to make our case."

"So, you want to go ahead."

He shook his head dolefully. "Yes, and no. Mostly no, right now. Don't talk about the tox report while I work this out on my end."

When Cooper didn't respond, the chief looked up at him, his bushy brows lifting. "Unless it's too late."

Biting the bullet, Cooper said, "I would suggest working this out on your end quickly."

"Shit." Humph waved Cooper out of his office and picked up the desk phone receiver.

Taft sat in the law offices of Tormelle & Quick and again faced Veronica Quick, this time across Martin Calgheny's desk as he was unavailable. Veronica worked for one of the partners, her father, Jonas Quick. Jonas's name was on the door and was in turn the son of one of the now deceased founders, Alexander Quick.

"It's just some paperwork," she assured him, sliding some papers across the wide mahogany desk his way. As he began signing, she said, "I can tell you that Prudence Mangella is contesting the will."

Taft smiled. "And?"

Veronica looked at him as if she were assessing him. She was about five seven with dark brown, shoulder-length hair, and wore a black pinstripe suit jacket over a cream-colored V-neck blouse that emphasized the small bones at the base of her throat.

"We'll keep you informed as we progress," she said. "It's going to take a while."

"Take all the time you need," Taft said with a shrug. "If I win, I'm donating all of it to charity anyway."

"That's admirable, Mr. Taft, but in my experience, people say those kind of things until they actually get the money in hand."

"Are you a lawyer?"

"No, I'm an assistant, sometimes an advisor."

"So, your advice is . . . ?"

"Take care of yourself."

He lifted his brows. "Meaning . . . ?"

"This is a marathon, not a sprint."

He felt a silvery sense of awareness that reminded him of whenever he was visited by his sister's "ghost." He looked around for Helene, but of course she wasn't there. She was his muse, his conscience, a projection that was only in his mind. She'd been gone over a decade and the intense grief and loss he'd felt had faded, but he still saw her occasionally. Seeing her sometimes was a quirk he didn't share with many, though Mac knew.

He heard Veronica suddenly inhale sharply. Her gaze was out the window. He followed her line of sight and saw Helene standing in the lot. The cold wave that swept over him left him momentarily speechless. When he found his voice, he blurted, "Did you see her?"

"Who?" she asked, but her eyes, now trained on him, were wide.

Taft stared at her. He was almost certain she was lying . . . but that would mean . . . he couldn't go there.

His hand was on the door lever. Veronica seemed to be struggling with herself. In the end she said merely, "Sometimes these things get nasty. Be careful."

She'd warned him twice. His heart rate had returned to normal and when he looked out the window Helene was no longer there. In some distant corner of his mind he remembered a conversation with Mitch Mangella where he was saying something about the law firm of Tormelle & Quick. "They keep my affairs in order. Everything legal and tight, just the way it needs to be. They'd bore the shit out of me except for Jonas's daughter. I swear that girl is psychic, the things she seems to know . . ."

"You sound psychic," Taft said to her now and she looked down at the pages he'd signed, her fingers delicately making sure the edges were perfectly even, keeping her expression blank.

He left the offices, feeling on edge. Veronica didn't see Helene, because Helene wasn't there. Maybe her warning was simply because she understood Prudence Mangella's character. Maybe she warned all the firm's clients when an estate was particularly messy.

He'd told Mackenzie that he had no intention of meeting with Prudence, but with Veronica Quick's warning firmly in mind, he decided to face the lioness in her den rather than wait for something to happen.

Mac drove to Parker Flooring, which was located on the south side of town, just on the edge of the commercial district and close to all the construction going on in Staffordshire Estates, a sprawling River Glen development that butted up to the Laurelton city limits and beyond.

The unprepossessing building was tilt-up concrete with a row of large windows street side, a parking lot on one end, and a warehouse that popped up from the back and ran nearly a block behind the business's front offices.

She'd tried to reach Leigh several times and had clicked off when the phone went straight to voice mail. It was damn frustrating not to get through to her. Since Leigh didn't want her husband to know anything about hiring Mac to find Mia, she didn't dare leave a message that he might possibly overhear. She was taking a risk in entering Parker and Leigh's place of business, she supposed, but Parker didn't know her and would have no reason to suspect she was anything but a classmate of Leigh's, and she had a reason to be at the shop anyway.

And the truth was, she kind of wanted to see Leigh in her milieu.

Mac entered the business, which had a short foyer, the floor done in herringbone gray tile that led directly into stacked rows of tile and hardwood and carpet samples with customers desultorily walking through rows of product. She could smell the faint scent of some chemical and decided it was a floor sealant. There was a low hum of voices from the customers and the employees who served them. She could almost taste a woodsy flavor in the air.

An area in front of the windows to the street was set with several large white tables and surrounded by molded plastic white chairs. Offices with curtained windows lined the eastern wall, the doors closed, and two sets of double doors were set into the north wall to what she assumed was the warehouse at the back of the building. An argument was taking place in one of the offices where the door was slightly open. Was that Leigh's voice? She heard "—compete with Marbleworks and we'll go broke. The name's Parker *Flooring*, but do whatever the hell you want, you always do and—"

The door snapped shut and cut off the rest.

"May I help you?" a young man asked her.

Mac put on a smile. "I'm searching for flooring for my mother. She's redoing her kitchen and was thinking about tile, but it might be too hard to stand on all day? What's that sort of fake stuff that looks like hardwood?"

"Like this?" He tapped his foot on the floor beneath him.

"Exactly like that," said Mac. "I thought it was hardwood."

"I'm Ray," he introduced. "We have several brands. Let me show you some samples." He led her down a row and she barely limped as she moved along. She glanced at the line of offices. Leigh burst out of the office door and headed for the double doors to the warehouse. She happened to glance up and spy Mackenzie on her way and her eyes widened. She stutter-stepped and then circled back toward Mackenzie as Ray kept walking, expecting Mac to follow.

"What are you doing here? Parker can't see you!" Leigh hissed in an undertone. She grabbed Mac's arm and dug her fingers into it.

"I'm picking out flooring for my mother's kitchen renovation," Mac responded evenly, pulling her arm free.

Out of the same office came a tall man with sandy-colored hair, a short, trimmed beard, and a supercilious way of looking over the rows of samples. He saw Leigh with Mac and his brow furrowed slightly.

"Leigh?" he asked, with a faint smile.

"I'm . . . with a friend," she said lamely. "Parker, this is Mackenzie."

Leigh might be decent with a script, Mac decided, but she was terrible at ad libbing. "Mackenzie Laughlin," she introduced, speaking loudly so he could hear her across the room. "Leigh and I were River Glen classmates. Feels like a lifetime ago, doesn't it?" she said to Leigh, who stared at her blankly. She turned back to Parker. "My mother's redoing her kitchen, and I was just telling Ray that she likes that faux hardwood. He's just showing me some samples now." Mac smiled and shifted her gaze down the row to Ray, who was silently holding up a square with tan-colored boards. "Oh, I like that color," she told him enthusiastically.

"Ah." Parker lost interest in Mac immediately. He hooked a thumb toward the double doors and said to Leigh, "Thought we were meeting."

"I'll be right there," said Leigh.

He seemed about to argue with her, then pressed his lips together and turned toward the double doors. As soon as he was through them, Leigh released a pent-up breath. "I've got this, Ray," she said, dismissing the employee.

"Sure thing." Ray put the sample back and walked away a little stiffly.

"Can you talk?" asked Mac when they were alone.

"You know I can't," she said peevishly. "Why? Did you find Mia?"

"I think I'm going to get her phone number. Call me tomorrow."

"Oh! Okay," she said. Then, "Sorry I snapped."

"I didn't mean to take you by surprise." Which was something of a lie.

"How're you getting the number?"

"Mason."

"Mason? You said he wouldn't talk to you."

Mac shrugged. "Maybe he's worried about Mia, too."

"Mason wouldn't talk to me. None of them would. I can't talk about this here. I told you that!"

"In the future, can I leave a message on your phone?"

"Um . . . no, just call. If I don't answer I'll see you called and I'll get back to you when I can. I'm sorry you had to see us fighting. This morning I've been . . ." She made a sound of annoyance. "Parker wants to cut employees and have me be here full-time and I've got other things to do. He diminishes what I want, while making sure what he—"

The double doors suddenly slammed open and Parker stood in the aperture, holding both doors so they wouldn't close again. "Leigh?" he called.

"Gotta go," she whispered.

"Can you give me some phone numbers? The Sorority's?"

She blinked at Mackenzie. "Sure . . ." she said, sounding completely unsure.

"I just want to reconnect, you know?" Mac lied, sensing Leigh wasn't going to comply. At this juncture, it wouldn't be wise to admit to Leigh that she planned to look into Gavin's claims that one or all of The Sorority was responsible for Ethan's death. "Text them to me."

She nodded, turning toward her husband, who was still waiting, holding both doors open in an antagonistic stance. She then hesitated, taking her time texting the numbers to Mackenzie before sauntering back toward Parker. She passed through the doors and Parker looked at Mac for a long moment, before turning and following after his wife. The double doors slowly shut behind him with a deep, metallic clang.

No wonder she didn't want him to know anything about her search for Mia. His body language alone said he would be suspicious of anything Leigh might be doing.

"Control freak," she muttered as she headed to her SUV. Parker looked familiar, she thought, but couldn't put her finger on it. She struggled to make the connection but finally had to let it be, counting on her subconscious to work on the problem. Maybe it was just his overbearing attitude.

She got back in her RAV and checked the text from Leigh. She'd given her Natalie's number and Erin's, but there wasn't one for Kristl. Given Kristl's involvement at some level in Taft's investigation into Tim Knowles's death, it was probably better to steer clear of her for the moment anyway. She put in a call to Natalie and reached her voice mail, where she left her own name and number and asked her to call back. She then called Erin and went through the very same routine.

And then she remembered why Parker was so familiar. She'd seen him in a community theater production where'd he'd played the lead in *Sweeney Todd*, the murderous barber who killed his enemies and, with the help of his partner in crime, Mrs. Lovett, turned them into meat pies. She recalled that Leigh had met him at some kind of musical theater camp, though it appeared now that he'd traded the bright lights of the theater for being in charge of a thriving business with his wife, while everything Leigh seemed to care about still echoed back to acting. Huh.

She was driving toward Laurelton, on that same stretch of road where she'd been pushed off, and glanced over as she always did to where her vehicle had slammed down off the road into the grassy area that was outside both River Glen and Laurelton city limits, when she caught movement in her rearview mirror.

"What? Shit!"

A car racing toward her. Accelerating. *Blue? Blue Accord!*

BAM!!!

The vehicle hit the back of her car and Mackenzie was suddenly spinning, trying to hang onto the wheel. Her back tires slid off the road as she whipped the steering wheel. She was suddenly facing backward, tilted skyward, high centered. A truck barreled toward her. She opened her mouth to scream but nothing came out.

CHAPTER 15

She braced herself for impact, aware she was going to be broadsided.

The *screech* of the pickup's brakes blasted her ears. The engine roared. Tires squealed and the truck shimmied wildly under the pressure to stop. Inhaling, she thought of Taft, pierced with regret that she might not see him again.

The dark gray truck stopped inches from her driver's door. A car slowed going the opposite direction, then picked up speed again when they saw that the driver of the truck had put his flashers on and was getting out to help.

Mac was flooded with relief. Damn, though. Who was that? Their car was going to show the effects of the hit, too.

In the next instant she was wary of the man suddenly at her window. The last time she'd been on this stretch, her "savior" had meant her harm. But no . . . this man was older and concern was written all over his lined face.

She lowered her window with a shaking hand.

Adrenaline rush. She was feeling both its impact and slightly sick at the same time.

"You okay, ma'am?" he asked in a gravelly voice, eyeing her beneath bushy gray brows.

"Yeah . . . I . . . dropped my cell phone." It had been in its holder on her dash, but the impact had spun it to the floor. She took several deep breaths and realized the RAV was still running. Switching off the engine, she leaned down to collect the cell, hit by a wave of nausea. She clasped the phone, but it took her a moment to get her stomach under control and straighten up again.

"I'll call nine-one-one," the man said.

"No. No. I'm fine." She tested her limbs and could move them all. "I just need to call a friend."

Traffic was slowly working its way around the stranger's truck, getting into the opposite lane to make their way around his pickup and her SUV.

"You hit your head?" he asked.

"I don't . . . think so." She touched her forehead and came back with blood, then remembered the impact against the steering wheel.

"You sure you're all right?"

"Yes," she said. "Yes. Did you see the car that hit me by any chance?"

"The Accord? Sure did."

"Was it blue? Did you see the license plate?"

"Was no license plate. I looked. Mighta been one on the front. You need a tow truck. Mebbe you should get outta the SUV."

Her heart clutched. The RAV could slip backward, once more off the road on this stretch of county highway, her personal Waterloo, apparently.

"But your vehicle ain't going anywhere," he allayed her fears. "You're high-centered. I'll stick with you till you get through."

She pushed open her door and stepped from the SUV, feeling vulnerable on the side of the road even though the man's truck with its flashing red lights in the gray afternoon was a warning in both directions.

She called for a tow, and after securing that, phoned Taft. He didn't answer and she left a message, explaining what had happened. Now that the initial shock was dissipating she was starting to feel better and the questions were circling. Who was driving the car? Had they targeted her? They'd charged up on her car and hit her on purpose. Dangerous move. To them as well. They were lucky they'd managed to keep going.

She then realized that it was very like a PIT maneuver, Precision Immobilization Technique, used by law enforcement to slow down a car and spin it 180 degrees. Was that purposeful, or had it just happened?

"Thank you so much," she said to her Good Samaritan. "I've got this."

"No, ma'am. I'm not leaving you till the cavalry comes."

"I just called my . . . boss. He'll call back. The tow truck's on its way."

The staccato flickers from his emergency flashers warned the traffic as they stood at the edge of the road, behind the very small space left between his vehicle and hers.

"You left him a message. I'll wait for a while. I'm Marv, by the way." He stuck out a hand and Mackenzie shook it carefully. She was feeling a little lightheaded.

"Mackenzie," she said.

* * *

Prudence Mangella was more than happy to have Taft agree to come to her house to "go over the estate." She invited him into the den/bar area where they'd met with Martin Calgheny and Veronica Quick and she went behind the bar and pulled out the hundred-year-old bottle of Macallan still held by thin leather straps inside its presentation box. Its value was in the hundreds of thousands. Taft looked at it and thought about Mackenzie's urging him to drink it.

"Here," Prudence said, setting the box on the counter and spreading her arms. "It's yours. Take it."

"Okay," he said, but he made no move to even touch the bottle or its wooden case.

"Something wrong?"

"I'm not ceding the proceeds of the estate to you. I'm giving it all to several drug rehabilitation programs around Portland in the name of my sister."

Her eyes widened and her lips parted. "No, you're not. You're giving it back to me. I'm his wife! I'll take you to court!"

"Well aware."

"And I'll win!"

Oregon was not a community property state, but she could end up being right. As far as Taft was concerned, she could do her damnedest. He'd made up his mind and felt the least Mangella could do with his ill-gotten gains was give it back to the people whom his choices had ruined large parts or all of their lives.

"You came out here just to tell me that," she accused, her eyes cold with fury.

"You asked me to meet you," he reminded her.

She suddenly swept her arm across the bar and sent the box and bottle of scotch flying off to Taft's right. Taft leapt sideways and caught the box in his outstretched arms like a football, glad the thin straps held the precious liquid as he stumbled into one of the leather chairs, managing to juggle the box and keep it from crashing to the floor.

By this time Prudence was screaming obscenities and crying. "Get out! Get out!" she shrieked and he tucked the box under his arm and left. Since Mangella's death, Prudence had lost her veneer of cool, calm respectability. Maybe it was because she really missed him, or maybe it was guilt because she'd somehow caused his death.

Either way, he was glad he'd crushed her vain hope that he would give it all back to her. That wasn't what Mangella had asked for.

He'd switched off his cell for his meeting with Prudence and now he saw he had a call from Mackenzie. He listened to the first few sentences and then frantically hit the call button.

"You hit your head. You need that looked at," Marv said for about the fifth time. He'd taken a real interest in Mackenzie's welfare. He wore a gray-and-white flannel shirt over a gray T-shirt, jeans, and work boots and looked like the salt of the earth. Nice as he was, Mackenzie really kind of wished he would just move on.

Her cell rang at that moment. She glanced at the screen and answered with relief, "Hey, Taft." She heard the weakness in her voice. Oh, God, she wasn't going to do something like *cry*, was she? No. *NO*.

"Where are you? Where you had your last accident?" Taft demanded. "Are you okay? Do you need anything? An ambulance?"

Taft's questions came rapid-fire and she could hear the tenseness in his voice.

"No. No." She managed to hold herself together. "I'm fine. A tow truck's coming."

"I'm fifteen, twenty minutes away. Be careful. I'll be there."

Marv insisted on staying. Mac went around to the passenger side of the RAV and pulled out her messenger bag from where it had flown into the footwell. She stood up a bit too quickly and felt dizzy.

"Ma'am, you need to get checked out," Marv said again.

"Maybe so," she finally agreed.

Taft made it in fifteen minutes, parking his Rubicon on the other side of her RAV. He had to wait a moment to open his door as another car was passing them, faces gawking out the window. One look at him and Mac's knees trembled. Oh, shit. Reaction. She leaned against the side of the RAV and he moved quickly to grab her as if expecting her to slide to the ground, though she tried to wave him off.

"I'm fine," she insisted.

"You don't look fine," he stated fiercely. "There's a knot on your head that's bleeding. Maybe a concussion."

He wasn't letting go of her and she had to fight the urge to simply lean into him and stay there. He smelled good, his own faintly spicy scent that she associated with him. Before she completely lost it, she turned to Marv and said firmly, "Thank you, Marv. Really. Thank you."

"You get her looked at," Marv told Taft sternly, clearly reluctant to cede authority over Mac to Taft.

"On it," Taft answered tersely.

Marv nodded and went back to his truck just as the tow truck arrived with its winch. Taft worked out the details with the tow truck driver and Mac eased toward the passenger door of the Rubicon and got herself inside.

"I don't think we need a trip to the hospital," she said. "The auto body shop will be waiting for me."

"I'll call them. We're heading for Laurelton General."

She dropped the argument. It wasn't worth pursuing. She said instead, "It was that blue Accord. It just came at me. I'm pretty sure I saw it, or one like it . . . cruise through my parking lot, and then I thought I saw it again and then this."

"You're saying this was no accident?" he demanded fiercely.

"No accident," she agreed. "I saw a flash of a car coming at me and then I was spinning around."

Taft swore under his breath.

She half laughed. "Guess I can't drive that stretch of road anymore. It's too dangerous."

"When did you first see the Accord?"

"You were at my place, bandaging my foot. Friday? Saturday? I just noticed this blue Accord come in and turn around and leave. And then I thought it was following me Sunday after I went to Riversong Church, but it turned off . . . Marv said it was a blue Accord without back plates. And now it's got damage to the right front side. You know, it was really a PIT maneuver, whether they meant to spin me around or not."

"I'll talk to Haynes. We need to report it."

Mac nodded. "Who would want to deliberately run me off the road?"

"Gavin Knowles was run off the road last weekend." He was grim.

"So you think it's because of my questions on the Ethan Stanhope accident? Someone who doesn't want the fentanyl angle publicized? No," she answered herself. "I was being followed before I even knew about that."

"But you'd been contacted by Knowles," he said. "You were already investigating. Maybe they wanted to stop you. Different car. Same M.O."

She felt cold all over. "I haven't learned anything of import."

"Yet."

He made good points. Whoever had smashed their car into hers couldn't know exactly how much she knew.

"Know anyone with that make and model of car?" he asked.

"Nope."

"They were reckless enough to have made the vehicle too noticeable to use again . . . unless they're crazy."

"That's comforting," she said, trying to scare up a smile, lighten the mood.

It didn't work as Taft was grimly focused on the road to the hospital. After a few moments of silence, and knowing that his phone only went to voice mail when he couldn't talk, she asked, "Where were you when I called?"

"Picking up the scotch from Prudence."

"You said you weren't going to see her."

"I decided it was best to make my intentions clear about the estate." He then tersely explained about his decision to give the money to drug rehabilitation efforts.

"I'm glad to see you're still alive."

That finally earned her a sideways look and faint smile, which dropped off his lips immediately. "We need to figure out who targeted you. It's just as well you'll get a rental car. One no one knows."

"I'm supposed to meet Mason Beckwith and Sam Stanhope tonight at the Waystation, and Mason's giving me Mia's phone number. I haven't had a chance to talk to them yet. I've hardly had a chance to talk in depth to anyone so far."

Taft clenched his jaw. She could tell he wanted to tell her not to go. She also knew he wouldn't dare tell her what to do. He said, "I'll come with you."

"You know that's not going to work."

"You need to be extra careful."

"It's just killing you not to tell me what to do, isn't it?"

"Yes," he admitted.

And then they were circling the lot outside the Emergency. An ambulance had just pulled up so Taft chose to park in the hospital's main lot. "I can walk," she assured him. She was feeling all right, better than all right now that the shock of the accident had passed. Yeah, her head was sore, but if Taft hadn't been with her, with Marv's order still ringing in their ears, she would have skipped the hospital entirely.

She didn't have to lean on him on the way in, but he insisted on holding onto her arm to steady her, and she was past arguing about it with him. They walked in together and ran nearly straight into Brighty and Leland Knowles. Brighty's face was gray and her eyes were wild and Leland looked like the world had caved in.

"Oh, no," said Mac.

Taft tightened his hold on her.

Brighty fixed her eyes on Mac and Mac braced herself for another attack, especially if what she thought was true turned out to be true: Gavin was dead.

"He's gone," Brighty said to her, confirming her fears. Leland reached out a hand as if to stop his wife from whatever she planned, but it was a feeble move that seemed to take the last of his strength. If he didn't get himself into a chair soon, he was going to topple over.

Mac made a move toward him, but Brighty got in her way. "Leland . . ." murmured Mac.

"Gavin's gone," she said. "Both of my boys are gone."

Mac realized she sounded more surprised than horrified, but grief took people in different ways, so there was no way to judge Brighty's feelings. "I'm sorry," she said, meaning it.

Taft suddenly darted toward Leland, catching him as he staggered and leading him to one of the reception area club chairs. Brighty turned to look at them. "They're both gone," she said again.

Mac could tell the news hadn't completely made the circuit into the center of Brighty's brain for processing. She was having a little trouble in that regard herself. Her chest was heavy with sorrow and she felt guilty for all the hard thoughts she'd had about Gavin.

Mac asked, "Brighty, do you want to sit down?"

Taft was back in a flash, grabbing Mac's elbow again. "You okay?"

"Yeah, don't worry about me." She felt fine. Yes, she was still going to have herself checked out, but the cobwebs had cleared. She kept her eyes on Gavin's mother, who apparently hadn't heard her.

Brighty swayed a bit and Taft and Mac both moved forward, but she seemed to come to herself and held up a palm. "Stay back. I don't want to talk to you. I don't want any of you around." Then she moved on shaky legs to where Leland was sitting and sank into the chair next to him.

"Is someone coming to get you?" asked Mac.

"Go. Away." She turned her head from Mac. Brighty blamed The Sorority for all crimes against Gavin and maybe Tim, and lumped Mac in with them.

Mac and Taft left them. She walked down the hall to the ER on her own power, checked in, and waited while others ahead of her were being attended to before she could go behind the counter and through the double doors to be seen by the overworked ER doctors who swooshed in, took a look, ordered tests, and swooshed out. Mac's head and neck were X-rayed but apart from a wrenching of muscles, she was ordered good to go. Her neck muscles were sore, as was her ankle, but all in all she was fairly sound. No concussion. She thanked Taft a bit awkwardly for dropping everything to come help her.

"Not a problem," he told her.

They drove to the auto body lot and Mac checked with her insurance. After that was settled Taft took her to Enterprise for a silver Ford Focus. She hoped she wouldn't have it too long but her poor RAV had now been in two accidents in the last few years.

Neither your fault, she reminded herself.

"I'm going to follow you back to your apartment," Taft told her and though she protested, he did just that. He rolled down his window as she parked and suggested she call Mason and move her meeting. She pretended to acquiesce, but she had other ideas. As much as she appreciated Taft's help, she was going to push forward. The "accident" had made her angry.

She had some time to kill before that meeting and considered calling her mother or her stepsister, but she wasn't ready to reveal what had happened to her. They would just tell her to stay home and rest.

She walked into the bathroom, her ankle faintly twinging, and looked at herself in the mirror. Her face was a tad pale and a knot had formed beneath the skin break on her forehead that had caused the bleeding. No wonder the rental car guy had shot her sideways glances whenever he thought she wasn't looking. Good thing Taft had been with her, otherwise he might not have rented to her. She looked like she'd been in some kind of fight.

As she examined herself, she thought about Gavin and Brighty and Leland, and the solemn people at Tim Knowles's funeral, and the icy and broken Coral Stanhope and the simmering anger beneath Lynda and Charles Beckwith's exteriors and the three members of The Sorority she'd seen on Thursday . . .

She decided to take a bath, something she rarely did as she preferred showers, but as she lowered her body into the steaming water she felt a lot of little bumps and bruises she hadn't first noticed. Closing her eyes, she let her mind wander from point to point, touching on bits of information she'd learned over the last few days: Ethan and Ingrid Stanhope had died of fentanyl poisoning . . . Gavin Knowles had been run off the road, vehicular homicide now . . .

Her heart squeezed painfully. She realized now that she'd believed Gavin would make it. His death had come as a surprise and fueled her growing anger. Whoever had killed him needed to be caught.

Whoever killed him may have just tried to kill you.

She needed to think about that, about all of it. Gavin believed Kristl Cuddahy was responsible for Ethan's death and Kristl was a close friend of Stacey Colville's . . . and Stacey's house was where Gavin's brother, Tim, had died of a gunshot wound after confronting an armed burglar, Dale Kingman, who'd subsequently been killed in a barrage of police gunfire, crying out, "Sanctuary!" inside the church where he'd fled after shooting Tim. Was Kristl somehow involved in Tim's death, at least peripherally? Was Gavin right to finger her for Ethan's death? Mackenzie thought about Kristl and shook her head. She didn't know what that all meant.

Beyond Kristl, Mia Beckwith was presumed missing and was last known to be living with a man named Ben whose family was involved in California's marijuana business. Mia's brother had withheld information about his sister's whereabouts from Mac, but now wanted to meet with her, along with Ethan's brother, Sam Stanhope, to pass on that information. And, come to think of it, it really felt like as soon as Mackenzie began looking into Mia's disappearance, Gavin, his parents, and the

Stanhopes began blaming The Sorority for all the bad things that had ever befallen their two families. The deaths and Mia's disappearance were tied together, and the link was The Sorority . . . and, well . . . Sam Stanhope.

Mac opened her eyes. Her thoughts were a disjointed jumble of pieces of information in somewhat overlapping investigations, but Sam Stanhope's sudden insertion into the equation was new. Was he just using Mason as a means to harass Mac about the laptop?

She stood up in the bath, water falling off her, and grabbed a towel, testing her balance, more determined than ever in meeting with Mason. She dressed in jeans and a black sweater and strapped on the clogs. Lastly, she examined the bandage on her forehead over her right eye. Her bangs partially covered it. Thank God.

Taft tucked the box of Macallan under his arm as he unlocked the door to his condo and let himself inside. He flipped on a lamp to push back the creeping afternoon darkness, then headed into his kitchen. He hadn't wanted to leave Mackenzie alone. Someone had purposely rammed her RAV and spun her off the road, right at the place she'd been pushed out before. Had they known that, or was it just a convenient stretch of highway that could ensure a vehicle would go off the road and away from any chance of caroming across traffic and possibly causing an accident that might harm the perpetrator as well?

He placed the box that held the bottle of Macallan scotch on the counter, thought about it a moment, then opened the cupboard above his refrigerator and placed it inside.

Mackenzie had basically shooed him out, so he'd had nothing to do but acquiesce. He thought about her friend/acquaintance/classmate, Kristl. He'd promised her he would call today. He'd planned to go over a plan with Mackenzie in further detail before that "date" but the day had gotten away from him.

You should have walked her up to her apartment.

Yeah . . . but no. He'd sensed she didn't want him around, which convinced him she was still going to meet up with Mason Beckwith and Sam Stanhope. He wasn't sure what he was going to do about that. She was right that his being there would only complicate the interview, but . . . Pulling his cell phone from his jacket pocket, he walked back toward his front door, which hadn't completely shut. He started texting Mackenzie when the door swung all the way open, revealing a black-cloaked figure. He immediately tensed, ready for an attack.

Anna DeMarcos lifted her manicured hands in defense, then crossed them over her heart and gasped, "It's just me!" her glossy red nails gleaming in the soft lamp light.

"What are you doing here?" Taft asked. He'd lost the ability to be polite with her. She was poisonous and dangerous and responsible for the death of her husband—Carlos DeMarcos, a damn good cop—whether there was enough evidence to prove her guilt or not.

"Well, I came to see you, obviously. See if I could knock some sense into that thick skull of yours." She dropped her defensive posture and smiled. Her red lips matched her nails and her dark eyes looked at him with false innocence.

"You can talk through the lawyers." He didn't invite her in, but she tentatively took a step inside anyway, shifting around his solid form and moving into his living room.

"Has Prudence's money turned you into a mannerless boor? Where's your sense of humor? Your parry-and-thrust of conversation?"

Now Taft was completely on alert. Prudence had a way of teasing and flirting and manipulating, but Anna had never acted that way, at least in his experience. She wasn't known for wordplay; she acted. "I lost it when Mitch was murdered."

"Murdered." Her eyes flashed and he saw the true Anna underneath, angry and resentful. "You're so melodramatic."

"Have you talked to Prudence today?"

"Yes. I know all about your choir boy decision to leave all her money to the druggies."

Taft bristled, even while he told himself not to let her get to him.

"I'm sorry," she said. "I forgot about your sister."

Like hell. His cell silently buzzed in his hand. He hadn't gotten his text out, but the incoming one was from Mackenzie: Will call you after my meeting.

Damn. "What do you want, Anna?" he demanded, clicking off his screen.

She'd flopped herself into a chair beneath his front window and now spread her arms over its back. "Okay, fine. Bring me a glass of that fabulous scotch you were gifted from Mitch and I'll get to the point."

Taft looked at her, then wordlessly turned back to the kitchen, opening the cupboard above the refrigerator and pulling out the bottle of scotch. Did he want to open it? Not really. But somehow it had become the symbol of all that was wrong with his relationship with Mitch Mangella. He was almost sorry he'd been given the bottle.

He cracked it open and poured two fingers of scotch into a glass for each of them, feeling only the smallest twinge of regret. Mac's accident . . . the idea that someone was after her left him cold and hollow inside.

He walked back into the living room. Anna had given up her draped pose on the couch beneath the front window and now was looking pensively through the pane. She turned her head, her eyes widening at sight of the scotch. "Is that really . . . ?"

"Yes."

"My, my," she said, accepting her drink. Her lips quirked and she touched the rim of her glass to his with a soft *clink*. "The last thing Prudence and I want is to fight with you," she said before taking a long sip that must have burned a trail of fire down her throat. She coughed a bit and said, "Whew. That's good."

"What you want is for me to just say it was all a joke and refuse Mitch's gift."

"This should be enough for you." She held up her drink and moved it back and forth in front of him, as if luring him, the amber liquid gently swaying inside.

"It's more than enough."

She narrowed her eyes at him. "But . . . ?"

"But I'm not returning the rest of it."

She looked at the scotch, then tossed the rest back.

Her jaw twitched as she set the empty glass down on the side table with a sharp smack. "That's it? That's all? No further negotiation?"

"That's it."

She got to her feet. "Well, fuck you, Taft. Fuck. You."

She turned and yanked open the door, flinging it behind her as she stormed out. The door banged against the doorstop and shuddered, and he slowly closed it behind her, making sure it was securely shut.

"Well," he muttered with a shake of his head, sipping at his own scotch. He looked at the time, thought about going against his own rules and crashing Mac's meeting at the Waystation, then forced himself to put the rest of the Macallan away and open his phone to text Kristl.

Mac was scrolling through Ethan's laptop, once again having typed in "waterpolo" to gain access to all his information. Last night she'd only glanced through the latest pictures and had read a few of his school assignments and one half-finished attempt at a résumé that played heavily on his sports accomplishments, not so much on academics, though she knew for a fact that he'd gotten pretty good grades throughout the years. He'd been one of those guys who barely cracked open a book and yet managed to do above-average work.

Ethan Stanhope was a contradiction, Mac thought. Whereas Gavin had been the guy who always pushed, Ethan had held back and allowed some mystery. He'd been shallow, swearing he truly cared for Mia while cheating on her with Roxie and maybe others. Still, he'd been likeable, whereas Gavin had been hard to take.

Gavin...

Mac sighed and looked through more of Ethan's pictures, starting with their senior year and scrolling backward. There he was at prom, putting his king crown on Katie Ergon-Smith's head as she gazed up at him adoringly from her wheelchair. Mia was beside him, stiff and unhappy beneath her own crown. Was it in the moment? Ethan showing someone else attention, or stealing the spotlight, like he was wont to do? Or was she unhappy because of her relationship with her parents?

There were a number of pictures of Ethan in his swim gear and goggles. He had a lean swimmer's body with defined abs and wide shoulders.

And, well, what do you know? Here was a picture of Roxie coming out of Gavin's pool house. And then another of Ethan doing the same. And then a third of The Sorority standing in a group and staring to one side of the camera, focused on Ethan, who was lounging in a chair at the side of the pool.

"Who took the pictures from that night and gave them to you?" Mac murmured. Most likely it was Gavin. Or was it someone snapping pictures with Ethan's phone?

She scrolled further back through senior year and was surprised to see a picture of herself and Summer Cochran on stage with the cast of *Oklahoma!* She realized that the camera's focus was on a group of attendees seated in the first row: The Sorority sans Leigh, as she'd been one of the many light-brown heads of the ensemble that all blended into one.

There was nothing in the laptop she could see that offered any clue to how Ethan and Ingrid ended up with fentanyl poisoning—nothing other than the usual photos, papers, and assignments of a high school kid. Maybe Sam Stanhope just wanted the laptop for his own use. She would have to ask him when she saw him.

Holy shit . . . holy shit . . . Natalie could *kill* Leigh for bringing Mackenzie Laughlin into their problems.

She heard her own thoughts as if she'd spoken them out loud and grimaced. This wasn't the day to talk of killing anyone. She'd learned through Kristl, who'd been all over Gavin's accident and Tim's death and all that, that Gavin had died.

But now Mackenzie had left a voice mail, asking to talk to her. What the fuck?

She'd punched in Leigh's number, but Leigh hadn't answered. This was her M.O., apparently. She screened all her fucking calls.

So do you.

She called her again and this time left a terse voice mail. "We need to all get together again, maybe at Kristl's. I'm back. Can we make it tonight? Call me."

She left a similar message on Erin's phone and Kristl's. Jesus. Did no one answer their phones anymore?

It was Leigh who called back first and Natalie launched right in, blaming her for siccing Mackenzie on them. Leigh defended herself by saying that Mac just wanted to reconnect with them.

Natalie snorted. Sure. That's what it was. She just managed not to shriek over the phone at her, and instead ask—rather politely, she felt—that all of The Sorority gather at Kristl's tonight. Leigh squelched that idea right away, saying she was busy and adding that she was pretty sure Kristl wasn't home anyway. "Maybe tomorrow," Leigh bit out, still apparently pissed that Natalie had dressed her down.

Natalie pulled back her anger with an effort and reluctantly agreed to postpone meeting with everyone until Tuesday evening. Maybe she needed a little time to settle herself anyway, as she'd just spent a long weekend trying to convince Beatrix that she could do the series by herself, to minimal success, and trying to talk some sense into Phillip, who had barely listened on the phone to her pleas as he was in Sedona and already wishy-washy and distracted.

"Fucking beige soul," she muttered, heading back to the massive floor-to-ceiling window where she had a nighttime view of Portland's Pearl District with its restaurants and converted warehouses and upscale living spaces. Traffic moved steadily down below and she inhaled deeply, drinking in the urban flavor though she heard very little noise and the only scent she picked up was a light lemony aroma from the set of three candles on the coffee table.

I could live here, she thought, suddenly wanting it very badly. Maybe there was someone in Portland who could share her vision and drive to get *Rose City Ren-o* off the ground.

Her brain twinged her, nagging, always nagging. She couldn't let anyone or anything ruin her future over some silliness from her past. She gazed blindly into the darkness outside, ignoring the bustle on the street below, lost in memories of those last few weeks of high school.

She plucked up her phone from where she'd set it

on the coffee table, held it in front of her, and then scrolled through her contact list. She was kind of mad at her other "sisters" for not being available tonight and for bringing Mackenzie Laughlin into their problems. Sometimes you needed to act on your own.

CHAPTER 16

The Waystation was only about a third full as Mac drifted alongside the counter to where the bar curved inward at the far end. She'd done her share of surveillance seated at the end of this bar and she looked back down its scarred surface to a lone man sitting in the middle, drinking a beer and playing on his phone. Glancing around, she saw most of the patrons were on their phones. It helped avoid eye contact, but at a bar, weren't you supposed to want to meet people?

She ordered a club soda. She might not have a concussion but there was no reason to push the envelope by ordering anything stronger.

Once she had her drink she settled in to wait for Mason and Sam. Little aches and pains had crept up on her throughout the day and she was worried a serious headache could be crouched and waiting to attack. So far so good, but she didn't want to mess with success while she waited for Mason, who struck her as the kind of guy who wouldn't reschedule, maybe out of annoyance, maybe out of loss of interest.

Ten minutes later, the two men walked into the bar,

Mason lean and dark, Sam light-brown-haired and less angular than Mason. Sam's resemblance to Ethan hit her again and she remembered the last time she'd seen Ethan outside Gavin's party, warbling, "*I'm just a girl who can't say no . . .*" The song Mac had sung as Ado Annie in *Oklahoma!*

Her throat tightened at the memory. Ethan was dead mere hours later. And now Gavin.

She rose from her seat to meet them. "Mackenzie, this is Sam Stanhope. Sam, Mackenzie Laughlin," Mason introduced.

"We've met," they both said at the same moment.

"Really?" Mason looked from one to the other. "When?"

"Recently," Mac said.

Mason's dark eyes focused on her bandaged forehead. "What happened to you?"

"Car accident. A lot of that going around."

Sam Stanhope couldn't seem to look her in the eye as Mason said, "You should be more careful."

"Yeah . . ." Mac couldn't help snorting.

Mason asked, "Should we get a table or booth?"

"Table," Sam said promptly. Mac understood. A booth would mean one of them would have to sit beside another, something none of them wanted.

Mason selected a table near the arch that led into the poolroom. Mac sat down with him on her right and Sam across from her. The table backed up to the wall on her left side.

"Okay, I have a confession to make," Mason started right in even before he'd even seated himself. "I texted Mia your number."

"You *what*? You texted her? You said you couldn't contact her!"

"I know. It's a dick move. I didn't know if her number was still good, so I decided to try it and she answered. I told her to leave that fucker for good and come home and I think she is."

"You told her to leave Ben?"

"I sure did." He looked at Sam, who was staring past them toward the bar. Mac couldn't tell if he was tracking the conversation or just waiting to say his piece, which she already guessed would be about the laptop.

The waitress came by, holding a large circular tray at her side. "Want anything?"

Mason ordered a beer and Sam hesitated before asking for a Moscow mule while Mac told her, "No, thanks."

In the momentary silence that followed, Mac addressed Sam, "What do you want?"

He startled. "What do you mean?"

"You want the laptop," she said.

Mason broke in, "What laptop? What are you talking about?"

"My mother gave her Ethan's laptop yesterday," Sam said tensely.

Mason looked blank. "Okay. Why?"

"I'm looking into Ethan's accident," admitted Mac. "Coral thought it might help."

"*Coral* thought it might help you?" asked Mason.

Sam said, "My mother's pissed at me for that screenplay I told you about." To Mac, he said intently, "But she's changed her mind and wants the laptop back."

That sounded like a big, fat lie. "I'll call her and tell her I'll bring it back to her tomorrow. What's her number?"

"I . . . don't know. It just comes up on my phone," Sam stumbled, caught in his machinations.

She gestured to his cell. "Look it up."

"I'm not going to call her. You just need to stay out of our business. My mother said the same thing after you left."

"Whoa, whoa," said Mason.

"She can tell me herself." Mac eyed Sam. It was unlikely Mason knew Ethan and Ingrid had died of a drug overdose as no one apparently did except the Stanhopes. She wondered if Sam had factored that piece in when he decided to confront her in front of him.

Mason asked, "What the hell's really going on here?"

Mac waited for Sam to answer, but when he didn't, she said, "I still want Mia's number."

Sam muttered under his breath, "You threatened my mother."

"*What?* No, I didn't. You saw that she just brought me the laptop. I didn't ask for it."

"Well, give it back. It's not your property."

"What's on the laptop, man?" asked Mason.

Mac could have kissed him for saying what she was thinking herself.

Sam's face reddened. "Mom promised it to me for my work. She should have never given it to you."

"You want a laptop for your work that's *how old*? You don't have anything newer?" asked Mac.

Sam flushed and didn't answer. Mason looked from Sam to Mac and back again, clearly not sure which way to jump.

"You think he was killed," Sam growled. "You listened to those bitches."

It was Gavin who thought The Sorority was responsible. With a heavy heart, she said, "I was at the hospital today and saw Brighty and Leland."

"Gavin's dead," said Sam. "I heard."

"Bro," Mason protested, clearly not in the know.

"What's on the laptop?" repeated Mac.

"It was an accident!" he practically shouted.

For a moment Mac thought he was going to jump at her across the table and even Mason said, "Shit, man. You talking about Gavin? What's going on?"

"I think he's talking about his brother," Mac said carefully.

The waitress appeared with her tray in hand and placed their drinks in front of them, head down as if she didn't want to get involved. Mac didn't blame her. *She* didn't want to get involved.

After the waitress backed away, Sam tossed back half of his drink, slamming the copper mug back down on the table. Then he closed his eyes and his mouth turned down. "Yeah, I'm talking about Ethan," he said, pained.

"It's not your fault," said Mason.

Sam silently laughed and shook his head.

Silence followed.

Mason seemed to shake himself back to the present

and muttered, "Gavin died in a car accident, just like Ethan."

"Not exactly like Ethan," Mac said, trying to meet Sam's eyes, but his gaze was on the scarred tabletop.

"What?" Mason asked. "What aren't you guys telling me?"

Sam glanced up and glared at Mac. "They didn't die from the accident," he admitted in a low voice.

"Who? They . . . Ethan and Ingrid? What did they die of? What do you mean?" Mason looked from Sam to Mac and back again.

"Ethan, he . . . I don't know." Sam's tough demeanor was crumbling.

"Tell me," Mason pressed.

"It was the fentanyl that killed 'em," Sam got out in a rush, his voice so low it could hardly be heard.

Mason jerked back as if burned. "*No.*"

Mac had heard Sam's telltale "the" before fentanyl. "You both knew about it," she realized.

Mason's face paled. "No, no . . . no. It wasn't from that. It couldn't be from that. No, it wasn't from that!"

"You knew about the fentanyl," Mac accused. "Did you supply it?"

"NO!"

"Who'd he get it from?" Mac asked. "How did Ingrid get it?" Sam suddenly stood so fast he knocked the table. His copper cup fell over, spilling ice and cold liquid into Mac's lap and Mason's beer directly into his own lap. Mason didn't even seem to notice as Sam staggered out of the bar. A blast of cold air whisked through the room before the door slammed shut behind him.

Mac shivered and righted the overturned cup. The waitress showed up to the table with a dry bar towel, handing it to Mac. Mason had swooped up his beer bottle too late and now set it back onto the table as Mac in turn handed him the towel. He swiped down the table, then held the wet rag in his hands. He had a sickly smile on his face, the kind that meant he'd just heard something he didn't know how to process.

Mac found herself angry, so angry, even now, over ten years later. "Sam had something to do with the fentanyl. You did, too. Were you dealing?"

"No, no." He snapped back as if she'd slapped him. "It wasn't like that."

"What *was* it like?"

He looked at her set face. "It was a stupid idea. A stupid buy. Sam got it from a friend of a friend of a friend . . . one of those things you suddenly wake up and think, 'Oh, shit, this is dangerous stuff,' and he put the pills away somewhere. Ethan must've found them, or maybe . . . Ingrid . . . I always kinda wondered, but I didn't think so. It couldn't be! It was a bad accident, which was bad enough. Mia was heartbroken and I felt terrible. It was . . . bad," he said again.

"It *was* bad," Mac agreed.

"Ethan coulda got some of his own. Didn't have to be that stuff."

"And Ingrid? Does that really ring true?"

"How . . . how did you know? Did Coral know?"

"I got it from the tox report that the Stanhopes purposely buried."

"Oh . . . shit." He covered his mouth with his hand.

"Gavin wanted to prove that Ethan's accident wasn't an accident. He knew at some level."

"Is this why Gavin's dead? *This?*"

"I don't know," admitted Mac.

"Only Sam and I knew about the fentanyl . . . and Ethan. He wanted some for after graduation but we said no. Shit's dangerous as fuck. Sam threw the pills away."

"Did he?"

"Yes!" he said. "Oh, yeah. He was scared when Ethan said he wanted some. He told me he threw the shit in the East Glen. He wouldn't lie to me."

"Even if he felt responsible?" she tried.

"His family would never forgive him. Never. They would never even let him in the house. They're mad enough at him for the screenplay, which is fiction. Not even close to the truth. If they even thought Sam was involved . . ." He made a sound between a laugh and a sob.

"They wouldn't hide how Ethan and Ingrid died to save Sam from public scrutiny, possible prosecution?"

"Absolutely not." He was positive. "If they hid it, it was to keep from their name being smeared, Ethan's name. They wouldn't save Sam."

"Doesn't it make sense that it was Sam's and your fentanyl that they took?"

"No. *No.* It wasn't *our* fentanyl! It was stupid. It was just stupid!" He violently shook his head. "Look, I'm the fuckup in my family. I know what that's like, but *not like that*! God. My parents think Mia let them down because her grades slipped. They don't even know what bad things happen to people. If Art Stanhope thought Sam was involved, he'd kill him himself."

"Sam's his only surviving child."

"His least favorite," Mason said with an unhappy curl of his lips. "Ingrid was his favorite. If he thought for one second that Sam had *anything* to do with her death . . ."

Mac digested that. Maybe it was just as he said and the reason Art and Coral Stanhope had hidden the real cause of Ethan's and Ingrid's deaths was to save the family from public judgment. "Gavin has always blamed The Sorority," she said. "If he'd known the truth he might have—"

"Oh, he knew. He knew about the fentanyl. He knew that Sam got it and that Ethan kind of wanted it. Ethan told him. Ethan was pissed at both Sam and me. He wanted to strut around with it."

"With *fentanyl*?" Mac asked, disbelieving.

He shifted his jaw back and forth. "Ask Mia. I lied. She knew, too. Here . . ." With that he pulled out his phone and sent her a text. Mac checked her phone. He'd texted a phone number. "That's Mia. She's probably expecting your call anyway."

Mason reached into his pocket, collected some money, and threw it on the table. He got up from his chair, then put his hands on the back of it and stayed there a moment, as if gathering strength.

"You know this is all . . . old information, but be careful," he said, sounding worried. "Sam threw the stuff in the river. No, I didn't see him do it, but I believe him, and Ethan was pissed off about it. Whatever happened, however Ethan got the stuff, he would have never, never, *never* allowed Ingrid to be part of it. It had to be a mistake. Something really wrong. I gotta think about it. If I come up with something, I'll let you know."

She watched him open the door, allowing another eager breath of wind swirling into the bar, causing a couple nearby patrons to shiver. She looked down at the wet crotch of her pants from Sam's drink and felt her niggling headache begin to take center stage.

She called Mia's number and let it ring and ring and ring. No answer and no voice mail.

Kristl checked the time on her phone again. She felt anxious and angry inside and she wanted to have sex with somebody so bad it felt like she would climb the first man who even gave her a look. She really wanted Jesse Taft, but he'd texted that he was busy, but maybe they could meet later in the week. That was not good enough. She'd left Mom in bed after making sure she was asleep, courtesy of a couple of pills, and was looking forward to a full night out. She glanced over at Jerry, who never paid her any attention. She could tell he found her kind of skeevy, but what did he know, the asshole? Rob wasn't on tonight, which was fine, because he got all filled with testosterone and jealousy. Sometimes she liked that. Most times it was just an annoyance.

She'd texted Natalie back. Such a demanding bitch. But she'd agreed to have everyone meet at her house tomorrow night. What the hell was Natalie all worked up about now?

Guilt tweaked her brain, but she pushed it away. It wasn't her fault. Sometimes things just happened.

The door opened and a young couple came in. Kristl sized up the guy but he was too into his date and was a little on the short side. Almost immediately the door opened again and Karl strode in. Karl was tall with dark, thick hair and he was sporting a new mustache that she thought might tickle in all the right places. She didn't want him. She never wanted him. But she seemed to fall back on him more than she really should. He had a streak of meanness that both drew and repelled her at the same time. He'd been dead awful to her when she and Tim were getting together. A jealous goon. She'd only had sex with him the other night just to make herself feel better, but the feeling hadn't lasted and, hell, she wanted Jesse Taft to show up. She was just dying to get in bed with him, but he wasn't here. Her bad luck was holding.

"Hey," Karl said.

"Hey," she said back, looking him over. Was she really going to do this? His place was such a sty. And what if Taft showed up after all?

"Wanna join me in a booth?" he asked, inclining his head toward one of her favorites near the back.

She thought about the roving hand game they could play beneath the table and pushed her disappointment about not meeting Jesse Taft out of her mind. After all, it wasn't like Tim. Losing him . . . especially the way she had. "Yeah, let's go," she said, leading the way to the booth.

***

Mac looked at herself in her bathroom mirror and groaned. She'd thought the bandage she'd put over the knot above her right eye had taken care of things, but the bruising had expanded, sliding down her temple and around the orbital bone. She was definitely beginning to look like she'd been in a prizefight. No wonder Mason had asked her what happened.

She thought about trying Mia again, but she'd already phoned twice to no avail. Mason said he'd told her she wanted to get in touch with her, so she was forcing herself to wait. It could be that Mia was deliberately trying to stay under the radar. The general consensus was that her guy, Ben, was involved in the family marijuana business at some level, so maybe he didn't want his personal association advertised? Or maybe Mia just was taking her time.

Twice, Mac had almost called Leigh to alert her that she had Mia's number, but twice she'd changed her mind. Call it selfish, but after Mason had said, "Ask Mia. I lied. She knew, too . . . ," Mac wanted to talk to Mia herself.

She popped two aspirin and sat down in her chair, leaning back and staring at the ceiling, gently rotating her injured ankle. Her mind immediately went to who'd purposely run her off the road today, which begged the question: Who owned a blue Honda Accord? Whom had she run afoul of? One of The Sorority? Someone else? It wasn't the same vehicle that had pushed Gavin off the road as that one had been white.

Maybe her own car "accident" was something else entirely?

Her thoughts jumped to Ethan Stanhope. Had Sam

Stanhope, with Mason Beckwith's help, unwittingly killed his own brother and sister?

"And why did Gavin keep blaming The Sorority?" she asked herself aloud. Why did he blame Kristl, specifically?

Thinking about Kristl, Mac texted Taft: **How's it going?**

It took a while, but he came back with: *Thought you were going to bed early.*

She smiled faintly. He'd known she was still planning to meet Mason and Sam. She answered: *Not tired. You at Lacey's?*

Her phone rang in her hand. Seeing it was Taft, she clicked on. There was no background music or noise, so she said, "You're not at Lacey's."

"Something else came up. Did you meet with Beckwith and Stanhope?"

"I did," she admitted. "Actually learned a few things."

"How are you feeling?"

"Fine. A little beat up. How come you didn't ask me what I learned?"

"What did you learn?"

She could tell he was faintly distracted. "What are you doing?"

"Putting two and two together. Tell me what you learned."

So much for conversation. Sounded like he was in full-on investigative mode. She brought him up to date on what Sam and Mason had said and though Mason had denied it, her own suspicions that Ethan and his sister were the victims of the fentanyl Sam and Mason had purchased.

"They didn't mention the source?" he questioned when she finished.

"No. It was over ten years ago, and I don't think they'd tell me." As he thought that over, she asked, "What 'two and two' are you putting together?"

For a moment she thought he was going to fob her off, but then he said, "I got a call this evening from Dale Kingman's sister. She told me a little more about him than his mother did. I've been at the church where Kingman was caught and killed. Talked to the minister..."

"And...?" she nudged.

"It's a long story. You up for some company?" he asked abruptly.

She immediately thought about what she looked like. She needed to spiff up a bit. "I'm not doing anything else."

"How well do you know your friend Kristl?"

"Kristl... not well. She's an acquaintance more than a friend. I haven't seen her since high school."

"Want me to pick up anything on the way? I might still go to Lacey's after."

"No, I've eaten, unless you want to get something for yourself."

"I'll wait till Lacey's. See you soon."

She'd changed into her pajamas but now went back to dress in clean jeans and a cozy sweatshirt, then walked back barefoot into the kitchen. She gazed out the window into her parking lot, half expecting to see a blue Accord with a mangled fender cruise through, but there was no movement. The lot was dark except for outdoor lights attached to the building that illuminated the lightly sprinkling rain and glistening blacktop. Apart from bursts of wind blowing leaves and fir needles over the parked cars, it was quiet.

Taft arrived about half an hour later. He had his phone in his hand and clicked it off as he bounded up her stairs. She opened the door and could smell the rain and scent of fir on him.

She stepped back to allow him entry as he said, "Your 'acquaintance' was involved with Dale Kingman."

"What do you mean? How involved? Oh! *She's* the woman he moved for?"

He nodded as they both headed into the living room. Mac eased down into her chair and Taft sat on the edge of her love seat. "According to his sister, Kingman had mental health issues. Burglarizing homes was a teen thrill that carried into his adult life. He would stop for a while, then start up again. Never used a weapon until he purchased the gun that killed Tim Knowles. Apparently Kingman had been passing through the area and started attending service at Welcoming Arms Church. This is part of his M.O. He would commit crimes and then pay penance in church. He crossed paths with Kristl, who occasionally attended service there. Pastor Simons was careful what he said, but it sounds like Kingman fell hard for her. It was obvious. Kingman's sister called Kristl the 'redheaded demon who killed him,' but that's a stretch."

"She knew him, though. You said she was involved with him."

"Welcoming Arms allows tents for the homeless on the far side of the parking lot and Kingman pitched his tent as soon as he met Kristl. He wouldn't come home, according to his sister. In his account to the department, Pastor Simons didn't mention Kristl. He didn't realize Kristl knew Tim Knowles as well. He thought she was just Sally Colville's friend, but then Ham was saying some things and the pastor's been stewing about it. He was almost relieved when I brought it up to him. I think he'll still go to the police now, but it's kind of a moot point. It looks like Kingman insinuated himself into Kristl's life. He knew her friends. Stalked her a bit, maybe. Somehow he figured out about the Colvilles' back window. Maybe just tested all the windows? He sometimes hallucinated. Rarely, but . . . maybe he just saw Tim as a threat. Kristl's pretty up front about how much she cared about Tim. Maybe Kingman was jealous of him. He had the gun and Tim was the guy who came to the house and he knew him and . . . *BAM*."

Mackenzie jumped, enwrapped in the story. "A lot of maybes."

"A lot of maybes," he agreed.

They both thought about that a moment, then Mac asked, "Do you think Kristl knows?"

Taft got to his feet. "I think I might go ask her."

"I'm coming with you." Mac struggled upward.

"That's not—"

"I'm coming with you," she repeated firmly. "I want to see her, anyway. Gavin blamed her for Ethan's death, and I want to know why."

"He blamed all of your friends—acquaintances—in that group."

"Then let's start with Kristl. Let me get some shoes . . ."

She came back in a pair of sneakers that she could leave untied, tucking the laces in on the side of the shoe on her bandaged foot. "I can wear these."

"You sure you're okay?"

"Damn it, Taft."

He held up his hands and they headed down the outdoor stairs to his Rubicon.

As they drove to Lacey's, Mac asked, "Why did Kingman yell 'Sanctuary'?" she asked.

"Relief from the demons that plagued him? Chief among them Kristl, according to the sister."

They headed inside the bar and the noise level hit her, reminding her of the minor headache she'd been actively ignoring. Mac's gaze immediately fell on Kristl, who was snuggled in a booth with a guy sporting a thick, dark mustache. She was sitting so close up against him that two more people could have occupied the seat of the booth beside her. And there was something going on between them under the table that had Kristl's head thrown back and her eyes closed. She was much slimmer than in high school and her hair was a darker red, but Mac had recognized her immediately.

"Fuckin' get a room!" a good-natured yell sounded from a group of guys crowded on some bar stools. They were seated sideways, clearly enjoying the show.

Kristl opened her eyes and slid the crowd a sly smile. The man with her had a different reaction, scowling at the group.

Then he clapped eyes on Taft and he practically

pushed Kristl away from him, his face contorting with fury. He climbed over Kristl to get out of the booth and she shrieked in protest. He stalked forward and said in a menacing voice, "Jesse James Taft."

Taft tensed beside her but said affably enough, "Hi, Karl."

"Who's this you been beatin' up on?" he demanded, jerking his head toward Mac. A frightened gasp sounded from Kristl, who stared openly at Mac and Taft.

"Hi, Kristl," said Mac, which got Karl to give her a long look and swing his head back to Kristl, who was sliding from the booth and adjusting her short skirt and blouse.

"Mackenzie . . . Mac . . . what are you doing here?" Kristl's eyes were all over Taft, definitely in lust, but also in confusion.

"We want to know why you didn't tell the police you knew Dale Kingman," Mac jumped right in. Maybe she should have waited for Taft but he was clearly in some kind war with Karl.

The noise dissipated as the guys around Kristl went silent.

Kristl bit down nervously on her lower lip, then asked, "Who's Dale Kingman?"

"The man who killed Tim Knowles," said Taft, still staring down Karl.

"You all know the name," Mackenzie guessed, looking around at the other men at the bar who were desperately trying to look anywhere but at Mac and Taft.

"Fuckin' Taft. What're you doin'?" Karl demanded.

Kristl looked at Taft in a kind of despair. "You set me up?" she asked, her eyes pained.

Taft spared her a glance. "I want to know the truth about Tim."

"You're hateful," she said, the tears brimming in her eyes.

A rage-filled growl erupted from Karl and he barreled straight into Taft.

Chapter 17

Well, *shit!*

Mackenzie was thrown against the bar as Karl and Taft crashed to the floor. She scrabbled for purchase as she lost her footing. Kristl gasped and her hands flew to her mouth.

Mac hung on and glanced over. Taft was beneath Karl but his hand was at Karl's throat, his expression set and deadly. Karl was trying to pick him up and slam his head into the wooden floorboards. Holy . . . God.

Out of the corner of her eye she saw a beer bottle on a cocktail napkin near her right hand. She grabbed it without looking. Slammed it into the back of Karl's head. Beer sprayed and the bottle bounced out of her hand onto the ground.

Karl yelled and Kristl screamed. The guys at the bar jumped up and the bartender was suddenly blowing a whistle so long and stridently that Mac grimaced, fearing for her hearing. Taft flipped Karl off him, but Karl grabbed him by the left arm. Taft returned a sharp left hook, knocking him hard. Karl's eyes rolled around like billiard balls as Taft jumped atop him, pressing him into the floor. His right hand was cocked.

But Karl went limp. Mackenzie's bottle and Taft's hit caused him to lay on his back, breathing hard, the fight out of him.

Taft slowly got to his feet, keeping his eye on Karl. Then he swept a hard gaze over the other men in the bar. None of them moved. Maybe they were cops, maybe they weren't. This was a cop bar, but whatever the case, they stayed where they were. The bartender came around the car and checked on Karl. "Need an ambulance?"

Karl spit some blood. "Nah," he snapped. "Fuckin Taft."

"You okay?" Mac asked as Taft shook out his left hand.

"Mighta broken the fifth metacarpal. Not the first time." He spread his fingers and almost smiled.

Men. Sheesh.

The bartender turned angrily to Kristl, whose mouth was now open in shock. "Get out and don't come back."

"What did I do?" she cried.

"All you do is cause trouble."

"Can you take her out of here?" Taft asked Mac softly, his eyes on Karl, who was being helped to his feet.

Mac stepped forward and grabbed Kristl's hand. "Come on," she said.

"I'm not going anywhere with you!" she said, snatching her hand back.

The bartender said, "You're eighty-sixed. Go."

"You can't do that!"

Mac was feeling slightly buzzed from the adrenaline rush. She turned to Taft. "Sure you're okay?"

"Never better."

He looked at her in a way that sent something deep and primal sizzling through her veins. Did he feel it, too? His gaze dropped briefly to her lips, but then he pinned his eyes back on Karl, who was on his feet, his head thrust forward. Mac practically hauled Kristl into the misting night as Karl groaned and held up his hands in a classic *No more* signal.

As soon as they were alone, Kristl's shoulders slumped and she started crying in earnest. She leaned into Mac, who staggered a bit, trying to hold her up.

"I still love Tim. You don't know what it's been like," Kristl gurgled. "I love him and Dale killed him. Shot him . . . just shot him and now he's *gone*!"

"You knew Dale Kingman." Mac said it as a statement of fact.

"I was *nice* to Dale. *Just nice*. That's all, and look what it got me. He stole from my friends, broke into their houses, *killed* Tim! He told me he had a gun. He knew Tim broke my heart . . ." Her voice faded into a sob.

"He meant to kill Tim?"

"I don't know. I don't know. Tim went to the door . . . Dale saw him and . . ."

"Took the opportunity?" Mac supplied when she couldn't go on. Kristl nodded her head.

"I didn't want it. I didn't want to lose Tim. If Dale wasn't dead, I'd want to kill him myself!" Her body trembled against Mac's. "It all started with Gavin," she declared in a burst of anger. "He didn't want Tim to fall in love with me. He said I killed Ethan and Tim started to believe him . . . He's such an ass! I hate him!"

Mackenzie realized she didn't know Gavin had died. "Can we drive you home?"

"I've got a car . . ." She looked around the lot. "I don't want to go home." She wrenched herself away from Mac and headed toward a brown Chrysler.

"That your car?" asked Mac.

"My mom's. I don't have one. I don't have anything . . ." She started crying again.

"Let me drive you," Mac suggested as Kristl pulled her keys from the small purse on a thin strap over her shoulders.

Kristl acquiesced and Mac slid behind the wheel of the Chrysler, figuring Taft could pick her up later. All the way to her house, Kristl talked about Tim, how she'd finally found the man of her dreams, how it was like a fairy tale, a prince after a lot of ogres, how she was aware she had a sex addiction, how the rest of The Sorority would make fun of her if they knew, how taking care of her mother was harder than anyone gave her credit for, how her life was just a pile of shit.

Mac parked the Chrysler in the driveway and then walked Kristl to the front door, handing her her keys.

"Are you coming in?" Kristl looked at her almost hopefully.

"I think I'll wait out here. Taft's picking me up."

"Is he your boyfriend?" she asked sadly. "He pretended he was single."

"He's my business partner . . . kind of a boss/mentor."

She tilted her head and sighed. "I saw the way he looked at you. It kind of pissed me off that he lied to me, but whatever." She turned toward the door and as Mac headed down the driveway, she asked suddenly, "Can you come tomorrow night? The Sorority's meeting at my house. I want you to come. Please come."

"Um . . ." Mac stopped and turned back.

"Say yes!"

Mac had never been all that close to Kristl. They hadn't really run in the same circle in high school. But Natalie hadn't called her back, and neither had Erin or Leigh.

This was an unexpected and golden opportunity to meet with all of The Sorority at once.

Kristl added, "Natalie arranged it all. She's still as bossy as ever, but I . . . there are some things . . . I don't know. I just think I would feel better if you were there."

"What time?" asked Mac.

"Seven thirty. Okay?"

"Okay," said Mac and Kristl smiled as she closed the door behind her.

Mac was shivering with cold by the time Taft arrived. She jumped into his car as soon as it stopped. "Brrrr," she murmured, rubbing her elbows and hugging herself.

He'd opened his own door to help her in, but she'd been too fast. Now he closed the door, then shrugged out of his coat and handed it to her. "Took longer than I thought. You okay?"

"Fine." She didn't mention the headache that was almost full blown, which was just as well because it quelled those feelings for him that had sparked at Lacey's. "Wow. What an evening."

"I don't know the last time I was in a bar fight," admitted Taft.

"How's your hand?"

"Not bad. How's your head . . . and your ankle?"

"A-okay." She leaned back into the headrest. "Kristl invited me to her house tomorrow to meet with The Sorority."

"How did that happen?"

Mac proceeded to tell him what Kristl had revealed as he drove her back to her apartment. He listened carefully and when she was finished, he asked, "Do you believe her?"

"Well, I don't think Tim's death was premeditated. I mean, yes, it sounds like Kingman got the gun with that in mind, or something like it, to win Kristl's heart, and it all tumbled together. A lot of bad decisions that culminated in a shoot-out. I don't think it was really her fault even if she was the cause. Tim was incredibly unlucky."

He humphed in agreement. "All right. I'll tell Haynes."

At her apartment, he insisted on walking her up the stairs. "Think we'll be in trouble for brawling at a bar?" she asked.

"Only if Karl complains. I don't think anyone else in there will."

"He attacked *you*," she reminded.

"He doesn't like me much."

"Yeah, really?" she said wryly. "How do you know him?"

"We worked together at Portland P.D. He didn't like that I was on a faster track up the ladder than he was."

"You?" She lifted her brows.

He grinned. "Don't believe all the bad reports you hear."

"I don't," she admitted. Then, as they looked at each other, she cleared her throat and glanced down at his swelling left hand. "You should probably ice it."

"Planning on it. Thanks for the help in taking down Karl."

"Anytime."

"See you tomorrow."

She watched him head down the stairs, then closed the door and leaned against it for a moment. She inhaled and slowly exhaled, then headed for aspirin and bed.

Tuesday morning, Mia Beckwith felt her cell phone silently buzz against her skin from inside her pocket. There was no way to answer it without being seen and Mia didn't feel like having to explain herself to Ben, which was all she'd been doing these days.

She was seated on the front porch in a rocker, looking down the dusty strip of asphalt that led to the cabin and this outpost of Ben's family's legal marijuana operation. But the business's legality didn't mean their fields were immune to poachers, so the security forces the Cabreras employed were downright lethal. One trespasser had been killed the previous summer and the mood was always tense. What Mia had found exciting, dangerous, and romantic in the beginning had devolved into being a prisoner in her own home.

She'd made a big mistake. She'd been led into a cultlike relationship with Ben, whom she'd believed in totally. It had taken years for her to see that most of what he said and did was utter bullshit. She'd dropped her friends for him . . . her family . . . everyone. And she had no one to blame but herself. Shame filled her with how she'd treated her parents. It was . . . reprehensible.

Her only defense was that she was scared—deep-down scared to the core of her being, and she'd lived all the years since graduation wanting to not be scared anymore. Ben had seemed to offer her that security, that protection, that love . . . but in the end it had come with too steep a price.

It isn't just since graduation, she reminded herself, feeling a shiver start in her gut and spread to her extremities. *It's since Ethan's death. And Ingrid's.*

She sucked in the sharp, cool morning air and looked up at the cloud-scudded sky. She tried so hard not to let those thoughts, those memories, escape the locked box inside her head where she put all the terrible issues she didn't want to look at.

When did you become such a coward?

She swallowed and answered herself:

When I discovered those innocuous-looking pills . . .

Her first instinct had been to ask Ethan about them. How naive she'd been! Her second had been how to get rid of them . . . but they weren't hers to destroy. He told her they wouldn't be used. She was chastised for even believing they would be, but everyone knew how dangerous fentanyl was. She even convinced herself the pills weren't used . . . half-convinced herself, anyway. Losing control of his car could be from any number of factors, she inwardly argued. Nothing ever came out that Ethan and his sister had overdosed, so she'd left River

Glen believing their deaths had been an unfortunate driving accident . . . though she'd wondered.

Ben had helped her forget River Glen. She'd run to him and his wealthy and protective family. The tonic to cure her from all the ills she left behind in River Glen, and that's the way it had been in the beginning.

But now . . . not so much. Truthfully, the rest of Ben's family didn't really care about her one way or another, but Ben had grown possessive. He sometimes talked marriage and she sometimes thought she wanted that, but she sometimes thought not. She'd run to him when everything else had been coming down on her. Those terrible grades, the repressed memories Ben's guru friend had pulled from her about how her parents had treated her so badly, which now she wondered if they might have been planted memories instead. Mason sure thought she'd been programmed. "You're brainwashed, Mia," he'd said enough times that she'd cut him off. For a while she would only allow Leigh's calls, and then she quit her, too, though she'd texted Mason again. He was currently her only connection to her old life, a life that didn't look so bad in retrospect, and last night he'd sent her a text that made her catch her breath:

I gave your number to Mackenzie Laughlin.

And then Mackenzie had called and left a message, asking Mia to call her. Mia had not been able to listen to that message till this morning when she had a moment alone from Ben in the bathroom. She hadn't dared call back because he would ask too many questions and she didn't have any idea what Mackenzie wanted, unless . . .

She shook her head. No . . . no . . . she wasn't going to go there. She knew from Leigh that Mackenzie had gone into law enforcement and then private investigation. But that couldn't be why she was trying to get in touch at this late date, could it?

Her heart beat deep and heavy, so deep and heavy she could practically see it through her nightgown. She thought about pulling out her phone but then she heard the screen door open and slam shut behind her, and she was glad her phone was in her pocket. It was growing cooler, almost cold, and she felt Ben place a jacket over her shoulders. She turned to smile up at him.

"What are you drinking, babe?" he asked, looking at the amber fluid in her glass.

"Iced tea."

"You can't lie to me," he said, wagging a finger in front of her nose.

Did he really think she would imbibe so early in the day? Yes, she answered herself, because that's what he would do. "Taste it." Her smile grew fixed as she watched him pick up her glass and take a big swallow.

"Iced tea," he pronounced.

He dropped into the chair next to her and reached for her hand. They sat there quietly, holding hands.

Ben was sandy-haired and blue-eyed and took after his mother, who'd been swept off her feet by the handsome and suave Miguel Cabrera. Mia could still see it in Ben's good-looking father. She'd fallen a little in love with the idea of the whole family. In the beginning there'd been fabulous trips and expensive cars and an avalanche of presents while Ben was wooing her. Maybe she'd grown too used to the extravagance. She certainly let Ben take over her life and make all her decisions. After years of getting the grades and trying to please her exacting mother, she'd just let go. She'd just . . . stopped.

But over the years Ben had tightened his grip and slowly she'd lost her liberties. Hell, she'd thrown them away. Now he gave her the third degree about any and all phone calls, any kind of connection to her old life. When she visited her parents they berated her for leaving school, and then came the time she'd accused them of abuse. Ugly, ugly words that she didn't even mean! She'd just been so mad at them. She could not admit that she was struggling in school, drowning in work, on the verge of going under. They wouldn't understand. They couldn't. Not their Mia. Good, good Mia.

So, she'd just plain freaked out. Gone mental. Ended up in *jail* for resisting arrest at a protest she didn't even care about, for God's sake! Mia had never really failed at anything before but she was failing, failing, failing . . . she couldn't get past Ethan's death and that night when they'd all vowed to kill him in a car accident—which is how he'd died a few weeks later!

And there was Ben, ready to make it all better. His therapist friend helping her with her "memories." She'd believed it at the time because she wanted to believe it. She didn't believe any of that shit now.

Leigh had tried to tell her that maybe the abuse wasn't real. So had Mason. She hadn't listened to either one of them. She'd been pissed at them. Now, she suspected they were right all along and all she wanted to do was go home again. To that time before Ethan's and Ingrid's deaths. To when life was simple. Good was good and bad was bad and it all made sense.

But it didn't make sense, did it? That's why you ran to Ben in the first place.

Ben's cell buzzed and Mia startled. He dropped her hand and pulled the phone from his pocket. He then put the cell to his ear and answered with a friendly "Hello, there." He always seemed to be friendly until he wasn't. She watched him take the two steps down to the ground and walk away from her.

Wiping her now sweaty palm on her pants, Mia kept an eye on him as he stepped out of earshot, strolling down the asphalt drive. She glanced upward to the towering firs and pines that surrounded their compound in this fertile Northern California valley—a valley not all that far from the Oregon border.

Ben walked farther and farther down the road. When, from her perspective, he appeared to be about a half inch tall, she slid her cell phone from her pocket and looked at Mason's message again: **I gave your number to Mackenzie Laughlin.**

She was slightly afraid of calling Mackenzie back, but it was a moot point anyway. She couldn't explain it to Ben. She slid the phone back into her pocket just as surreptitiously and got up and went into the cabin. The main house was more lavish than their little bungalow, but she had insisted on her own place, one of the few times she'd asserted herself. The cabin was rustic in design, modern in practicality with a spa bath that would rival anything she'd seen on television. It certainly was better than anything she'd seen on Natalie's program. Such a bitch. Did Natalie realize how that came through to the viewers? Probably not.

Mia had an emergency go-bag packed. They all did.

There were unpredictable criminal organizations that tried to raid their lands and it was good to be prepared. She pulled hers out from the closet and did a cursory examination of its contents. Then she examined her stash of cash, collected over the past few years from leftover grocery money, enough to get home and then some.

And it wasn't like she was a true prisoner, she reminded herself. Ben's brother would just as soon she disappeared forever because he believed, wrongly, that she had her eye on the family business and fortune. She couldn't care less about it. Sure, it had had its allure in the beginning, but she'd been confused and delirious and generally messed up. Those sinking grades . . . She'd been so mortified it had nearly killed her.

Why was Mackenzie calling her? Mackenzie had been Leigh's drama friend in high school. The rest of The Sorority hadn't known her all that well.

The Sorority.

She felt herself shiver. Was it something to do with Ethan?

Did Mackenzie know what Mia suspected?

She shook her head and tucked the envelope of cash that she'd kept hidden behind feminine supplies in the closet into her go-bag. She slung the bag over her shoulder and hurried out the back door and toward the massive garage attached to the main house, a rambling mansion of redwood and bullet proof soaring windows. She saw Jim as she slipped in the side door of the garage and she smiled at him. "Going to town," she told the workman as she passed an array of vehicles that could rival a dealer's showroom. She slipped her bag into the passenger seat of a black Landrover, hoping Jim didn't wonder why her "purse" was so much bigger than usual. But he just nodded at her. Maybe he found her as uninteresting as Ben's parents apparently did.

She smiled and waved at Jimmy as she left, but he barely looked at her. In the beginning she'd wanted to prove how worthy she was. She'd damn near groveled in front of Ben's family, seeking approval they were never going to give. They didn't care what Ben did or with whom. She was simply that pretty, broken-down, part-Asian girl who occupied some of his time.

It had really fucked with her mind over time, she'd finally realized. From being the brightest star of her class, she'd become a failure at Stanford and her confidence sank to the bottom. Her professors had tried to help her, but her mortification wouldn't allow their aid. At that critical moment Ben had swept her into his world and she'd been so grateful.

The last time she'd visited her parents had been an unmitigated disaster. Ben was with her, of course, but he hadn't been the biggest problem. The biggest problem was her own brain. She'd had one of those triggering moments that confirmed her parents' belief that she was crazy, though they would never admit it, and resulted in her being more dependent on Ben.

It happened every time she went home. Those memories . . . *graduation day*.

Mia shut her mind down. She could excise those memories when they seeped in, which they did when she was stressed. They'd overwhelmed her back in the day, but she wouldn't let them anymore.

She swallowed as she drove down the asphalt lane,

waving at Ben as she passed. He would think she was just getting groceries. She did it all the time . . . well, once in a while, rarely by herself. He looked alarmed, but she didn't care. She dropped her hand out of sight behind the dashboard and her happy wave turned into a jutting middle finger that he couldn't see. As soon as she was out of sight she plucked her cell phone from her pocket.

Mac awoke late and had just gotten through the shower and dressed, feeling every ache and pain from her brutal past week, when her cell buzzed. She picked it up from her dresser and looked at the screen, feeling a jolt as she recognized the number: *Mia*.

"Mia?" Mackenzie answered. Every nerve on alert.

"Hi, um, you called me?" she said slowly.

"I did." Mac was enthusiastic. "Thanks for calling back." She could hear noise in the background and thought Mia was in a vehicle. "Leigh was worried about you and couldn't get hold of you, so she asked me to try."

"That's it?"

She sounded careful, maybe slightly disappointed. "Are you all right? Leigh was worried about you . . . and so was Mason."

"Mason gave you my number."

She seemed to be picking her words, almost accusingly careful. "That's right."

"I'm fine. I'm . . . actually coming your way."

"To River Glen?"

"That's right."

Mackenzie's brows knit. It felt like Mia was saying something without saying it. "Are you coming . . . alone?"

"If you mean Ben, he's not joining me on this trip."

"Did you leave a Post-it type note on Leigh's car?"

"What?" The question was edged with emotion. Fear, maybe?

"Leigh got a note that said 'Help me,' and she was convinced it was your writing."

Mia made a sound low in her throat. "I see I need to talk to Leigh. I'll call her."

"Good. That's what she wants. But as long as I have you, can I ask you a question? Mason said something about you knowing the real cause of Ethan and Ingrid Stanhope's deaths."

Mac heard her sharp intake of breath. "Mason told you that? I don't know anything! They died in a car accident. That's it. Mason knows that."

"He said he and Sam Stanhope bought fentanyl, Ethan wanted some of the pills, and that you knew about it."

"I don't want to talk about this." This time Mac was certain it was fear in her voice.

"Mia, fentanyl was found in both Ethan's and Ingrid's systems. The toxicology report was shelved, but it's come to light now."

"I don't know why Mason would tell you that. Ethan had . . . I mean, I saw at the party . . ."

"What party? Graduation night?"

"There were pills . . . maybe . . . I saw them. I didn't know what they were. I didn't want to think about it. I still don't."

"You saw pills at the graduation party at Gavin's house?"

"No. Before . . . when he was with Roxie. I didn't know! I—I blocked it. I ran away. I thought it was Mason who made the deal because Ethan had told me his brother and Mason had the stuff . . . I didn't think it killed Ethan. *I didn't know.* And then Ingrid . . . I was a mess . . ." She drew a breath, the words tumbling over each other. "But Mason insisted that he and Sam had gotten rid of the pills long before that party. But . . . maybe Ethan got some of them . . . ?"

"It's possible that—"

"I'm going to call Leigh. I need to talk to her."

"Mia, maybe it wasn't Mason and Sam's—"

Click.

Mac was cut off before she could finish her thought, which was that maybe Ethan got the pills from another source. Mac tried to call Mia back but the line went directly to voice mail.

She blew out her breath. Had Mason lied to her? To protect Sam and himself? Mia clearly had all kinds of guilt and emotion over worrying that her brother was at least partially responsible for Ethan's and Ingrid's deaths, but Mason had sounded convinced he and Sam were not Ethan's source of fentanyl.

Her cell phone buzzed again. She saw it was Leigh and grimaced. Mia had said she was going to call her, and Mac figured Leigh would not be thrilled that Mac hadn't immediately let her know Mason had given her Mia's number.

Not that Leigh was great about calling her back after the messages she'd left on her voice mail. "Hi, Leigh,"

Mac answered lightly. "Glad you could return my call." Might as well go on the offensive a little.

"*You didn't let me know you had Mia's number!*" Leigh shouted into the phone.

There it was. "Well, I just learned last night."

"And you didn't think to let me know?"

"You told me not to leave a message on your phone," Mac reminded levelly.

Leigh caught her breath, slowed down for the moment, but she recovered quickly. "Well, you could have told me. Found me. Or something."

"Yeah?"

"Yeah!" She clearly believed Mac had betrayed her somehow. She had to take several deep breaths to get herself under control. "I just thought maybe you could try a little harder."

"It was too late to go back to Parker Flooring last night," Mac drawled.

"Okay, fine. Enough said. I don't want to be mad."

"I don't, either. So, you talked to Mia?"

"She called me after she called you, apparently. She said she was leaving Ben. I told her to come home. I begged her! I don't know if she will, though, because she and her parents are still estranged."

"She told me she was coming back to River Glen."

"She told you that? Well good. I'm glad."

She didn't *sound* glad. She sounded like she was clearly still irked that Mac had contacted Mia first, but it was kind of a moot point at this juncture.

"Did she say she left you the 'Help me' message?" asked Mac.

"We didn't talk about it. I was off the phone too fast," Leigh said tightly. "I told her that I was upset she cut me off and that no one in her family would help me, so I hired you. And then Mason just handed you her number? Thanks a whole helluva lot. I'm really pissed off at him for holding out."

"You didn't ask her about the note?"

"I just told you no! Why are you so on this?"

"I just wanted to know how she physically got away from Ben to leave that message on your car, but then didn't call you."

"I don't know."

Mac let it go. "I'll write up a bill and return what you overpaid me."

"No, keep the rest. It's fine. We're good." Leigh was suddenly magnanimous.

"I feel I should pay you back for a good chunk of it."

"No, no, no. Just leave it. Please."

"Okay." There was a long moment where neither of them spoke. It didn't seem like Mia had discussed the fentanyl with Leigh so Mac let it lie herself. "Are you going to Kristl's tonight?" she asked instead.

"You know about The Sorority meeting?" Leigh was clearly surprised.

"Kristl invited me."

"She did? . . . Well, good. I always said you should be part of our group." She sounded nonplused. "Does Natalie know?"

"I don't know."

"I gave Natalie a 'maybe' when she said she wanted us to meet. If Mia's showing up in River Glen . . . maybe she'll go to the meeting, too. She said she was going to call the sisters, so who knows?"

"She sounded like she was driving when I talked to her. Unless she catches a flight from California, I don't see how she'll be here in time," said Mac.

"Okay, maybe not. But you'll be there tonight? You're coming?"

"Planning on it," said Mac.

"Okay. And . . . I'm sorry. I don't mean to be a bitch. You got Mason to give you Mia's number and that's kind of amazing, but it all worked out. See you tonight, then."

Mac clicked off and let out a pent-up breath. Leigh could be a workout.

She picked up Ethan's laptop again, her mind on what Gavin had said about all members of The Sorority being involved with Ethan before narrowing in on Kristl as responsible for Ethan's death. That certainly seemed to have ramped up after Kristl had grown close to his brother . . . so maybe he blamed Kristl unfairly? Because he didn't want Tim to be with her?

But someone had run Gavin off the road . . . in a vehicle with white paint. Not the blue Accord that had come after Mac, and not Kristl's mom's brown Chrysler.

Maybe one of the other "sisters"?

Her cell buzzed and she saw it was Taft, which gave her heart a jolt in a way that really pissed her off. She had to get over this and fast. "Hey," she answered.

"How're you doing today?"

"Still okay. I got rid of the bandage on my head. Thought it would cover up the worst of the knot, but it's too late. What about your hand?"

"It's fine," he dismissed. "I think maybe you should tell Haynes about the blue Accord, if you haven't already."

They'd discussed this and Mac had determined she didn't want to report the accident yet. "I don't want the police getting in my way. I want to keep digging into Ethan's and Ingrid's deaths. I know I'm not getting paid. Don't say it. I don't care. I just want to do it for Gavin."

"You didn't like him, and now you feel guilty that he's dead."

"Yes. Probably," she said testily. "All I know is that I want to see this through, so don't say anything. And Mia Beckwith has been found." She quickly brought him up to date about her conversations with Leigh and Mia.

"I'm talking to Haynes today. We're meeting this afternoon."

"Well, keep the blue Accord out of it. You think Kristl's confession will put suspicions about Tim Knowles's death to bed?"

"I think so. We feel that way, so Haynes probably will, too. Though none of it explains what happened to Gavin or you."

"Don't bring me into it," she warned again, and Taft reluctantly promised to keep her accident out of it.

They discussed a few more of the ins and outs of the events of the last few days, then he exhaled and said, "I have a couple of things to tell you . . ."

Those couple of things were that Anna DeMarcos had dropped by his condo and that he was meeting Prudence and her at the Mangella home this afternoon.

"You're going to see that lethal woman *again*?"

"Prudence apologized and said she wants to accept the terms of the will."

"Bullshit."

He laughed. "I know it's bullshit, but she's got my curiosity stirred up."

"Well, great. That makes me feel better. She and Anna DeMarcos are probably lying in wait for you. You should tell Haynes where you're going, so he'll know who to blame after they throw you off the roof, too."

"I'll make sure I don't go upstairs."

"Ha-ha."

"I'll call you later," he said, a smile in his voice.

She went back to the laptop, trying hard to forget the amused timbre of his voice, gave it up and decided it was time to visit her mother, Stephanie and the baby, or something, anything, to clear her head.

CHAPTER 18

Mac sat in Stephanie's family room, holding baby Jessica, staring at her little pink lips and tiny soft lashes. She'd never been one who felt the tug of maternal need, but Jessica was just so perfect. "It kills me how cute she is," Mac said with feeling.

Her stepsister smiled. "You haven't told me what happened to you. You look like you've been in a bar fight. What?" she added, when Mac started laughing.

She lifted a hand to her forehead. The knot was stubbornly persistent and though Mac had tried to cover up the worst of the bruising that ran down her temple with makeup, she'd clearly been only partially successful. "I was actually in a car accident," she explained, relating a truncated version of events. "Oh, my God." Stephanie was horrified. "And they didn't stop? Did you go to the police? That's hit-and-run."

"I'm trying not to involve them. Maybe the driver didn't mean to hit me."

Stephanie narrowed her eyes. "You don't believe that. I can tell."

"Doesn't matter. I just want to figure it out on my own."

"You're scaring me a little. Is Jesse helping you?"

Stephanie felt that Mac and Taft should be together and to that end, she called him by his first name and felt Mac should, too. Maybe she should, but that would add an awkward intimacy between them after years of their current status quo, which she didn't think she wanted.

Mac left Stephanie's and started to drive to her mother's, then thought better of it. She didn't want another go-round about her looks.

Am I that bad?

She chanced a peek in the rearview mirror. She looked okay . . . sort of . . . as long as you didn't count the somewhat swollen and purple lid above her right eye that she'd covered with brown eye shadow. Well, maybe there was a little purple peeking through. She carefully touched the knot on her forehead.

"Ouch." Tender.

Sighing, she set her jaw. No more fooling around. She wanted to know how Ethan, and especially Ingrid, had ingested the fentanyl that had killed them. She wanted to know if the person driving the blue Accord had targeted her because of her digging into their deaths. Could it possibly be because of her search for Mia Beckwith? She couldn't see why that would spark someone enough to try to kill her. Was it something else entirely? Were there toes she'd stepped on that she didn't even know about?

She was glad she was going to Kristl's tonight to meet with The Sorority. She had a lot of questions.

Might as well get them all in one place, maybe even Mia, if she arrived in time. In any case, Mac was sick of being half laid up and lost in what-ifs. She wanted answers.

Taft sat at a table at a diner near Cooper Haynes's home. Haynes was leaving for a late lunch, though Taft had eaten and just wanted to exchange some information. Haynes was home today. Something about taking his wife for a doctor's visit after this upcoming meeting.

Before long Taft saw the detective striding up the street outside the restaurant's front windows. He entered, spied Taft seated at a booth, and slid in across from him. The look on his face was tense.

"Your wife okay?" Taft asked.

"Yep. That's not the problem." He eyed Taft's coffee in its thick white diner mug and swivelled in his seat, looking for the waitress.

"What is the problem?"

The waitress lifted her coffee carafe in recognition that she'd seen him and went to get an empty mug from the stack behind the counter.

"Art Stanhope has lodged an official complaint that we leaked the information about the actual cause of his son's and daughter's deaths. The chief's in the hot seat and I put him there." Taft grimaced, but Haynes shrugged and went on, "No one's fault but my own. I made the choice to act on Laughlin's request. The truth shouldn't be covered up."

"Mangella always accused me of being a boy scout. I pass that mantle to you."

Haynes's smile was tight. "Thanks to Art Stanhope, the fentanyl trail is a decade old."

Mac's warning not to get Cooper Haynes fired swept through Taft's mind. "Watch your back on Stanhope. Only know the man by reputation, which is that he's humorless and vindictive."

"That's what I've heard, too."

Taft thought of telling Haynes about the blue Accord. He'd promised Mackenzie he wouldn't say anything to Haynes but wondered if he was making the same mistake Art Stanhope had made ten years earlier.

"So, you've got something on the Tim Knowles shooting?" Haynes said and Taft launched into the Kristl Cuddahy/Dale Kingman/Tim Knowles connection and his and Mac's feeling that it was a set of unfortunate events that had snowballed into a huge tragedy. He finished with, "You'll hear how Karl Bradley and I got in a fight, if you haven't already."

Haynes looked down at his swollen left hand. "Fifth metacarpal?"

"You know it."

"Bradley is not well liked."

"No one jumped in to help him although Laughlin hit him with a beer bottle."

"Laughlin?" For the first time since they'd sat down Taft felt like he'd gotten Haynes's full attention.

"He launched at me and we went down and she grabbed the bottle and cracked him over the head. Gave me a chance to get the upper hand. It was all over pretty fast."

"Not a word's hit the department yet." There was a smile on his face.

"Maybe it won't. Like you said, he's not well liked."

"Tell Laughlin to take care."

They wrapped up and left the diner together. Taft checked the time. He had a meeting with a potential client in North Portland and should have just enough time to make it back to see Prudence by four p.m. when they'd scheduled their meeting.

His cell buzzed and he saw it was his neighbor, Tommy Carnahan, and he suddenly remembered Tommy had asked him to walk and feed the pugs because he was already on another trip to Vegas.

Mac's cell rang as she was pulling into her apartment parking lot. By habit now she checked the area for the blue Accord or really any vehicle that seemed to be occupied by someone who was just waiting around. She'd kept an eye on her rearview on her trip to Stephanie's and then to the sandwich shop not far from Steph's house where she picked up a BLT.

"Hi," she said to Taft.

"I have a request," he said. "I've got some appointments, but Tommy is heading to Vegas today and I said I'd take out the pugs this afternoon. Can I ask you to—"

"Yes."

"—take over for me? Okay. Great. You're feeling okay?"

"I'm on it."

"The key to Tommy's place is in the kitchen junk drawer on the dog key chain."

"I know. I've got this."

"The ankle's okay?"

"Yep. Lots better."

Like Taft, Mac almost felt like she was a part-time owner of Blackie and Plaid. More than a few times she'd hugged the dogs close in a need to express pent-up emotion she didn't feel like sharing with anyone else.

"Tommy fed them before he left so don't let them fool you into giving them more than they deserve."

"I won't." She smiled. The pugs were literal chowhounds.

Discriminating, they were not. "You going to Prudence's?"

"After my appointment. I won't let her kill me."

"Good plan."

She clicked off a few moments later and headed into her apartment. It was a complete waste of energy and time to spend even one more minute with Prudence Mangella, no matter how amenable the woman had suddenly decided to be, in Mac's biased opinion. Maybe it was jealousy, but she didn't trust the woman at all. Prudence's husband was dead under questionable circumstances, and though Taft suspected there was more to Mitch Mangella's fall from the roof than had been reported, he seemed way too cavalier about his own safety.

Checking the time, she saw she had a couple hours before she needed to take out the pugs. She thought over Mia's tortured comments about the fentanyl and Leigh's pique over Mac's delay in revealing when she'd gotten Mia's number. Mac had second-guessed herself over discussing the fentanyl with Leigh and now wondered if she should have brought it up. Mia had tacitly explained the reason she'd dropped out of sight was because she couldn't face the possibility that Ethan and Ingrid had died of a drug overdose and that her brother could have some responsibility for their death.

Did Leigh know? Did *The Sorority* know?

Mac picked up her cell and called Leigh. She expected to get her voice mail again. It was hell not being able to get through to her, but then Leigh answered in a soft hiss, "What?"

"Did you know Mia suspected fentanyl killed Ethan and Ingrid?"

"Uh . . . y . . . yeah. I'm at work. I can't talk."

"You *did* know."

"She told me and Erin a while ago. I gotta go." She abruptly clicked off.

Huh.

"Woulda been nice to know," Mac muttered. At least Leigh had answered. Still, she could have been a little more forthcoming rather than force Mac to pull the information out of her. But then, of course, Leigh had only wanted her to find Mia, not honor Gavin's request to look into Ethan's accident.

She told me and Erin a while ago . . .

So, Erin knew, too?

Mac scrolled through the contacts on her phone. She'd tried calling Erin a few times, had left several messages, but like Natalie, Erin hadn't responded.

Now, she clicked on Erin's number and waited, but once again, the message went to voice mail.

"Hi, it's Mackenzie Laughlin. Just talked to Leigh and she said you and she learned the real cause of Ethan and Ingrid Stanhopes' deaths from Mia."

That oughta get an answer.

Grabbing the keys to the rental car, she then headed outside and down the stairs. Once again she eyed the parking lot closely. She didn't really expect to see a blue Accord with maybe a broken headlight cruising the lot, but she couldn't afford not to be vigilant.

She drove to Taft's condo, still getting used to the Focus, flipping on the lights as it was dark and threatening more rain.

Pulling into his lot, she was planning to park in her usual spot, but movement caught her eye outside Taft's condo, so instead she chose a visitor's slot in front of the manager's unit at the far end of the row from Taft's. Was it Tommy? Had he not left yet?

She'd pulled in between two vehicles, so it was hard to see. She wondered if she was overreacting, but she pushed the button to lay her seat back, her nape against the headrest, and slid her eyes to the left, looking through the windows of the vehicle next to her while trying to appear like she was just waiting in the car for someone.

The figure she'd seen was suddenly hurrying across the lot, tugging her black coat around her and belting it tight.

"Holy shit," she whispered.

Anna DeMarcos.

What was she doing here? Where was she going?

Carefully, Mac backed the Focus out of the spot and turned it around. Her headlights just caught Anna crossing a brief swath of field grass that had sprouted between Taft's condominium lot and the apartment complex on the other side.

So, not parked in Taft's lot.

What the hell was she up to?

Mac turned the car around, nosing carefully to the entrance of Taft's parking lot and pausing at the main road. There was a short row of emerald arborvitae that bordered the entrance and gave her some cover. It took a few minutes but then a black Mercedes flashed out of the apartment complex and turned right, and Mac edged out behind it. The Mercedes moved smoothly forward, its sleek body washed by a streetlight.

The pugs would have to wait, Mac thought with a jolt of conscience. She'd get back to them as soon as possible, but she wanted to know where Anna was going. She was glad to be in an unrecognizable rental just in case Anna knew what she drove.

It didn't take long before she realized Anna was heading toward the Mangella house. Did she know Prudence was meeting with Taft?

What were you doing at his place, Anna?

"Oh . . . hell." Taft's Rubicon was parked right in front.

She watched Anna drive around the thick, laurel hedge on the side of the house that accessed the four-car garage. As Mac drove by, she watched in her rearview as one of the garage doors slid upward and the light turned on to admit her. It appeared Anna had her own garage door opener.

Mac picked up her cell and called Taft's . . . and it went straight to voice mail.

She swore a blue streak. He always turned off the ringer when he was in a meeting.

Should she burst in, guns blazing, so to speak? Was she being crazy? She texted him: Anna was just at your place.

Should she wait outside Mangella's?

What. The. Hell.

She pulled over to the side and hung around for ten minutes, her fingernails forming half moons in her palms.

Then Taft texted her: She didn't know I was meeting Prudence.

What did that mean? She was looking for you? Mac asked. After a while: Yes.

Okay . . . he clearly wasn't alarmed by Anna's appearance at his complex so maybe she shouldn't be, either. Still . . . it felt . . .

"Evil."

She heard herself and shook her head. She wasn't known for flights of fancy, but geez Louise.

She circled back to Taft's condo and this time took her usual parking spot. It was just starting to get dark, a deeper gray than the cloud cover, the rain a fine mist. She had a key to Taft's condo and let herself inside, turning on the overhead light and inhaling deeply. She was used to his scent, the familiar musky spiciness that was uniquely him, but there was something else in the air. Perfume. *Shit*. Anna DeMarcos had been inside!

How?

Did she have a key? Taft had certainly handed over

his key to Mac without much fanfare, but then they worked together. Could he have done the same with Mitch Mangella? And Prudence had it, and then gave it to Anna? That made no sense at all. She was just making up stories, trying to explain the unexplainable.

She checked the front door. It was solid core with a Mortise lock, automatically clicking into place after the last person who left. Either she had a key or she didn't enter that way.

Mac prowled around the apartment, checking the windows in the kitchen, the bathroom, and both bedrooms, her eyes cataloguing Taft's rooms and possessions. She examined his wall safe, which she did not have the combination to, but it appeared untouched as well.

She strode back into the living room. The large living-room window that looked onto the parking lot had smaller panes on either side that could slide open. She examined both of the screenless windows, which appeared shut, though the one closest to the door gave a little. She pulled with her fingernails against the metal frame and the window slid back, leaving a space wide enough for a small woman to enter.

And was that a smudged palm print on the pane?

"You sneaky . . ." Mac ground her teeth together.

She would bet money Anna DeMarcos let herself in that window and walked out the front door.

Quickly she went into Taft's kitchen, throwing open his junk drawer where she not only found the key to Tommy's condo but a flashlight as well. She grabbed it up and let herself back outside. The ragged bushes beneath his front window spilled over onto the sidewalk.

No mud. No footprints. But was that a tiny bit of black thread caught in one of the twigs?

Oh, man. Mac left the thread in place and texted Taft again: **She was inside your unit.**

She waited tensely for an answer.

Finally it came: **She says she left me a note in my bedroom.**

So, he called her on it? And she had an answer?

And there was a note?

She stalked back into his bedroom and glanced around. She'd been in here looking at the windows, but hadn't looked closely at his belongings. Though she'd stayed at Taft's place during her earlier physical recovery, it felt way too intimate to wander around and seriously examine his belongings when he wasn't here.

Wait . . . was his pillow disturbed?

Heart in her throat, she yanked back the pillow and saw the white, hand-printed card beneath.

Anytime, anyplace. A.

Mackenzie saw red. Was that a threat, an invitation, or *both*? She couldn't tell whether she was feeling rage or jealousy or even if there was a clear and definite threat. In any case, she forced her emotions into a box. It was hell not knowing.

Pushing it all aside with an effort, she left his apartment, stalked next door, collected the pugs, and took them out for a brisk walk.

* * *

THE SORORITY

Mia stood at the Budget Car Rental counter on the ground floor of the parking garage at Portland Airport. She kept feeling the hairs on the back of her neck rise and had whipped around numerous times but only saw other people standing in line, waiting for cars.

She had her go-bag over her arm, a rucksack with a strap that she held in a death grip. She hesitated on putting down the credit card for her car, but they wouldn't rent her the vehicle without it. *Ben will find me.* But he would know she would likely go home first anyway. She needed to get right with her parents, so she was taking the chance.

She knew he was going to be following her. He was probably furious, so she needed to be quick . . . and then she wasn't sure where she would go next, but she wasn't going back to him. She recognized she might need help and she'd called members of The Sorority, who had mentioned the meeting tonight. She yearned to go, but she had to keep moving, had to put things right.

Her phone rang almost as soon as she got behind the wheel of the gray Nissan Sentra, pulling out of the lot and aiming south toward River Glen. She glanced at the screen with trepidation, expecting another call from Ben, but then frowned when she saw the caller.

"Hi, I'm in River Glen, but I'm heading straight to my parents," she said by way of answering." She listened for a moment, then said, "I really wish I could stop for coffee, but I just can't. I—" She paused again. Truthfully, she half wanted to be talked out of facing Mom and Dad . . . maybe just a few minutes' reprieve before she had to face the music. A wave of emotion swept over her. She'd been so messed up and unfair and wrapped up in herself and if she could just rewind the past . . . take those pills and flush them down the toilet, throw them into the East Glen River, crush them under her heel, then Ethan and *Ingrid* . . .

"Okay, fine. But I don't have a lot of time. Where do you want to go?"

An hour later, Mia drove slowly along once familiar roads. She felt weird and sluggish. Confused. The tarmac was like black ribbon candy, buckling and folding in on itself, up and down, up and down, only she knew this road was straight. It was her . . . her perception was off . . .

Oh . . . no . . . oh . . . fuck . . . no . . . What am I on?

She could hear her heart pounding. How fast was she going? The speedometer was a big, bright 17 blasting her eyeballs. Seventeen? Seventeen miles per hour? She needed help. Had to pull over. Her parents' house was right up the street, but she needed help now. She turned the wheel and rammed her tires into the curb, half jumping it. She reached into her purse for her phone, couldn't feel it.

The coffee . . . in the coffee . . . something . . .
Why? Why? Because of the pills.

Mia's head whirled and her hand stilled. She stopped searching through her purse.

NARCAN, she thought. *I need NARCAN.*

And then her breathing slowed . . . and stopped.

Chapter 19

Erin listened to the message from Mackenzie Laughlin with growing dismay. She'd talked to Leigh about what Mia had said? About the *pills*?

Erin stood at the hub inside Pickwick Lighting, barely noticing the overhead displays of light fixtures that winked and sparkled across the broad showroom, the bulbs like a thousand tiny suns trapped inside astral cages. She loved it here. Still so grateful for Leigh's help in getting her the job.

But she was currently blind to everything around her. And Mac's call wasn't the only surprise today! Mia herself had texted Erin, saying she was coming back to River Glen, that she was leaving Ben. That message had thrown Erin back to that time before Mia disappeared completely from their lives, back when she was still making trips to River Glen, back before she'd gone so completely weird.

Back when she told them about seeing the pills.

Erin could still remember what she was wearing that day that she and Leigh had met Mia for lunch. She'd worn that new sky blue blouse she'd paid a fortune for, a fortune she didn't have, but she'd charged it and figured somehow she would pay for it later. Her mind had been on her appearance and it wasn't until Leigh had gasped, "What?" that she'd really picked up that Mia was hinting that Ethan and Ingrid had died because of those pills . . .

Erin had gone immediately cold inside, like her insides were hit with a freeze ray. She'd looked at Leigh, whose face seemed to reflect exactly what Erin was feeling.

"Are you sure?" Erin had managed to choke out.

Mia had closed her eyes and swayed a bit. Leigh, seated beside her in the booth, had put out a hand to steady her. It was . . . weird and scary. Mia had always been so focused and driven and full of plans. She'd made it into Stanford—no easy feat!—and she'd gone through rush and maybe joined a sorority, like she'd planned; Erin wasn't sure about that. But then she started unraveling under the stress and the Mia from high school was gone. At least that's what Erin had thought, although Leigh, as Mia's best friend, had seemed to want to ignore the changes and pretend everything was still okay. She had kept in contact with Mia long after that meeting, though that was the last time Erin saw her.

Now Erin swallowed and tried to bring herself back to the moment. Seth Halliday, one of the Pickwick salespeople, was listening politely to a woman in a red coat explain what she wanted for an entryway light. "Nothing with glass that I have to dust. Just a cage. Wrought iron. You know what I mean?" Seth nodded his understanding. "Good choice," he said, making her smile with pride as he added that he would be right back with a book to show her what was available.

Seth was a master. He was also Erin's immediate boss at Pickwick Lighting and he was good-looking and nice. Really *nice*. It was a downright shame he was married, but all the good ones were. It was a sad fact of life.

The front door opened and a woman walked up to the hub. "Do you sell light bulbs here? Specialty ones?"

"We sure do," Erin told her.

The customer pulled out a used bulb from her purse and handed it to her. Erin looked up the number and ordered a half dozen at the woman's request, taking her credit card. Once she was gone, Erin looked back at Seth, who was still smiling at the woman in the red coat. She was thanking him profusely and jutted out her hand, which Seth warmly clasped. Erin knew he treated every woman the same, including herself. *Makes us all feel special*, she thought.

Erin sighed as Seth showed the customer out. It was close to six o'clock and Erin went to the door, waiting for the last few minutes before she locked up. She left Pickwick ten minutes later and drove back to her apartment and Chili, sweeping the cat into her arms, burying her face in its fur. She was never going to get a Seth Halliday.

Her mind moved on to the topic she never wanted to think about: *Pills . . . a smattering of them . . . on a counter in the pool house . . .*

Mia wasn't the only one who knew about them.

Chili *meowed* in protest and scrambled wildly

from Erin's tight grasp. Her back claws scraped deep into Erin's arm.

"Ouch!" Blood filled the scratches in the flayed skin on the back of her wrist as Chili ran off and hid under the couch.

Erin went to the bathroom, found some antibiotic cream and Band-Aids in the medicine cabinet, and doctored the scratch. "I'm sorry, Chili," she said, following the cat into her bedroom.

She walked straight to her nightstand and opened the drawer. She'd kept a Hello Kitty diary in grade school and had long ago listed a time line for the important future events in her life: when she would be married, when she would have her first child and her second and maybe a third, how she and her husband would go on a round-the-world trip for their tenth anniversary, how years later, as empty nesters, they would move to a small cottage overlooking the sea, or maybe a mountain retreat . . . And they would have cats, maybe a litter of kittens or two, and he would tell her how much he loved her every day, and how beautiful she was, and how his life wouldn't have been the same without her.

Now her eye traveled over that rounded cursive with its pink hearts dotting the *I*s. Once again she felt the melancholy that had been her companion for so long. Her thoughts turned to Leigh and Parker and she felt a tightness in her chest. She certainly didn't want that kind of a marriage. Then she thought about Natalie, who'd said she'd basically split from her husband when she'd called and told Erin about tonight's meeting. Erin hadn't asked, but Natalie had told her that her husband, Phillip, had left for Arizona to "find his fucking self," which apparently was a joke because "he can't even find his own asshole." Erin had winced a little at Natalie's crudeness. You just didn't need to be that way, in her opinion. But then Nat had gone on about Phillip's "beige soul" and Erin hadn't known what that meant, but she didn't really want to ask because it was just hard to talk to Natalie.

Still, she was going to Kristl's to meet her and her other "sisters" tonight. Apparently Natalie was thinking of buying a condo in the Pearl District, and she wanted it to be the first project that she was independently videotaping for a new show she wanted to launch on HGTV. Well, good for her.

Leigh had called to make sure Erin would be there, too. She'd asked her if she'd heard from Mia, which of course she had, but she just pretended she hadn't because she didn't want to really talk about it, to Leigh or anyone else. Leigh had said that she had talked to Mia, that Mackenzie had gotten her number, and that she hoped Mia would show up tonight, which had increased Erin's unease. Leigh had sounded pretty uptight herself and when Erin said as much, Leigh had tersely admitted that she and Parker had had another fight.

Parker Sommers . . . Erin wanted to like him better than she did.

Was it wrong to think he'd only married Leigh for her money? Was that being a complete bitch? Well, she wasn't going to tell Leigh what she really thought, so it probably didn't matter. Parker kind of reminded her of Gavin Knowles; they shared the same sort of egotistical nastiness. She'd dated Gavin briefly in high school, but neither of them had been into it. Gavin wanted Mia or Roxie or whoever Ethan wanted and Erin had wanted . . . well . . . Ethan.

She briefly closed her eyes, hating herself a little, shivering at the memory. She'd had that one night with Ethan before dating Gavin when she'd simply grabbed him and pulled him atop her after everyone had gone home at one of Gavin's parties. It was the only time Erin had smoked dope and she'd been reckless and wanton and *glad* she had an excuse to explain away her behavior later . . . if anyone had known.

Gavin had given Ethan the joint, and it was late in the evening and Ethan was sitting on a hilly slope of grass, away from the pool area, twiddling the rolled joint between his fingers. At that point Erin had been sober and had purposely stayed behind after her friends left by telling them her mom was picking her up. But really she'd seen Ethan wander off and wanted to be with him. *Just as a friend*, she told herself though she knew deep down that was a lie.

She followed after him and sat down on the lawn beside him, ignoring the dampness of the grass, ready to be that all-important sympathetic ear to listen to his woes over his relationship with Mia. And that's what she got, pretty much, as Ethan did talk a lot about Mia and how things had grown difficult between them because Mia was a perfectionist and he could never live up to her exacting standards, or maybe her parents were forcing her to be a perfectionist, which was the same thing, really, and it didn't matter anyway because she'd accused him of being unfocused, which apparently was a mortal sin in Mia's world. Erin had nodded and said she loved Mia, but she knew how hard it was to live up to her standards. She let her soulful eyes—her best feature—stare at him understandingly.

And when Ethan sighed and said, "Fuck it," and lit the joint, Erin imbibed with him, though she damn near coughed up a lung at the harsh burn down her throat. Woowee . . . it was awful. . . . but she wasn't going to back down. Her senses swam and she had to lie on the moist ground and let the dark sky fly overhead, distorted in a kind of wonderful way. She felt a little sick, not bad, just weird, but she didn't let that stop her. She wanted to kiss Ethan so she simply pulled him over on top of her. He was slow to react at first—the weed, she realized later—but then he'd done more than kiss her. Pretty soon they were naked and then he was pushing into her and it was kind of hurting and she was half laughing and thinking, *Wow. I'm having sex with Ethan Stanhope,* and then he groaned and it was over and he rolled away and started pulling on his clothes, muttering, "God. Oh, my God . . . oh, shit . . . ," which had penetrated her blissful consciousness, and she'd recognized she should feel the same but didn't.

She tried to talk to him the next Monday at school after a long weekend of thinking about him and having sex and wanting to try again when she was completely sober and generally thinking about *him*—*Him!*—and not wanting to remember that he was her friend's boyfriend. But Ethan wouldn't even look her in the eye.

He practically threw her at Gavin, or Gavin toward her, or both, and Erin finally realized he wanted to wash his hands of her. Though she and Gavin were both reluctant, it was almost like they started seeing each other by order of the king. Of course it didn't work. They tried kissing but it just wasn't there. All Erin could think about was Ethan, and Gavin seemed to know it, and he was really mean about it afterward.

She'd wondered if she could be pregnant. Lived in a kind of contained excitement at the thought, but then she got her period, so that was over. After she and Gavin gave up trying to like each other, she started seeing Ethan a little more clearly. He didn't want her. He'd never wanted her. And though she should have felt badly for what she did to Mia, it was just so . . . *nothing* . . . that it didn't even feel like it counted.

And then Ethan went into the pool house with Roxie and Erin's dreams—the ones she'd tried to pretend didn't exist— just crashed. She was almost glad when Natalie had called for them to kill him.

Now she glanced at the clock. Closing in on seven. Erin sighed. She loved her friends, loved to be with them, but it sure took a lot of energy and she wasn't certain she was up to it tonight. The last time she'd been with them, she'd come away with armpit sweat ruining her clothing.

But . . . they were all she really had. Without them, what was she? She didn't have boyfriends like Kristl, or a husband like Natalie and Leigh, though those relationships sounded toxic, and she certainly wasn't Mia, who was living with a guy who was smothering her, according to Leigh, and maybe hadn't ever really gotten over Ethan, no matter what she said . . .

And she sure as hell wasn't Roxie, who treated men like toys. Erin thought about the sick yearning she'd seen on Ethan's face as he'd trailed after the blond bitch. She could just imagine what had gone on in that pool house.

The pool house.

She shook her head and walked into the bathroom, giving herself a good, hard look.

Her cell phone rang as she was changing out of her work clothes into jeans that were a little too tight for her these days. She gazed at it with trepidation, checking the screen, not recognizing the number. "Hello?" she answered.

She thought she could hear someone breathing on the other end and she listened for a moment, the hair rising on her arms. A wrong number? "Hello," she said again and when there was no answer she hung up.

Chili had jumped up on the bed and was walking around, purring, having forgiven her. It took all her willpower not to snatch the cat close again because she couldn't shake the feeling that whoever was on the other end of the line was sending her a force field of evil intent.

Mac stared at Taft in disbelief while the pugs snuffled around her feet, uncertain about the tension emanating from her. "She told you she broke into your place and just acted like it was nothing, and you just . . . what? Laughed it off?"

"I told her she was playing a dangerous game."

They were standing in the middle of his living room. Mac had gotten her tangled emotions under control and still had been so relieved to see that he was all right, she'd felt tears prick the back of her eyes.

And then she'd wanted to throttle him. "That was it? That's all you did?"

"Should I have called the police?"

He was regarding her soberly, but she heard her own voice warning him not to tell Haynes about being run off the road. Neither of them wanted the authorities involved.

"She broke in," Mac said again.

"And left me a message. Do you have that?"

"It's on your bed."

He lifted his brows at her and she stepped out of the way so he could go into his bedroom. He returned a few moments later with the white card in hand. She could see Anna's distinctive printing. "It might be hard to get her arrested for this."

He was right. Of course he was right. Anna told him what she'd done. Whatever her intention, it would look to the police like a prank by a woman who wanted to be with him. Stalking . . . maybe . . . but . . .

"She's doing it on purpose. Making it hard for you to strike back," said Mac.

"Yep."

"What did Prudence say? Was she in on this?"

"She tried to deny it, but they're in on it together. Whatever they hope to accomplish isn't going to work."

Mac realized that Anna's ploy had backfired. Taft was becoming more and more set in his decision to give Mangella's money away. Even though she'd told him to spend some of it, Mac had changed her mind and now agreed with him. Get rid of the blood money, because that's what it felt like it was.

"I'm just glad you're okay," Mac admitted.

He shot her a smile and then got a pensive look on his face.

"What?" she asked, leaning down to pet the dogs and make sure they understood that all was well.

"I didn't tell you about my meeting with Veronica Quick at the law firm."

"This doesn't sound good."

"It's not about the inheritance," he assured her. "Not directly, at least. You know how I told you Helene is a symbol of my subconscious."

Mackenzie nodded. "You see her sometimes."

"In my mind," he reminded firmly.

"Well . . . yeah . . ." Where was this going?

"I was with Veronica and she warned me about Prudence, twice. And then I saw Helene outside the window, and she told me to be careful, too, which is normal. The way I remind myself to pay attention because whatever is going on is important." He drew a breath. "And then, I swear . . . Veronica looked out the window and saw my sister, too. I know what that sounds like, believe me. But her face went white . . . I called her on it, but she wouldn't answer me."

Mac stared at him. The Jesse James Taft she knew was totally grounded in reality. Yes, he saw Helene's "ghost" from time to time, but he was the first to admit it was a trick of his own subconscious, that he used his sister's image and guidance as internal checks and balances. She, too, drew a breath and asked, "So, what are you saying?"

"I don't know," he freely admitted. "This 'seeing' quirk of Veronica's is known within business circles. She's good at her job, maybe excellent, but her father's a partner in the law firm. Without him, I don't think she'd be there. They downplay that she's . . ."

"A psychic?"

He half laughed and shook his head. "Forget it. She spooked me. It was a strange moment. Nevertheless, I've taken her advice to be careful around Prudence Mangella to heart . . . and Anna DeMarcos."

Blackie stood on his hind legs and scratched at Taft's. Taft leaned down. "So, how did you do with these guys?"

"Fine." She looked around. "What time is it?"

"Six thirty? No seven."

"I gotta go." She quickly tried to brush the dog hair off her jeans. "Tommy's keys are on the counter. I didn't feed them."

"I'll give 'em something." She slipped her arms through her black jacket and as she drew the strap of her crossbody purse over her shoulder, he suddenly grabbed her elbow, startling her. "Be careful," he said firmly.

She nodded and stepped out into the cool, cloudy November night. This time she couldn't help looking around his parking lot for Helene even though she'd personally never seen her and knew, as well as Taft, that she didn't really exist.

Kristl opened the door to Natalie, who blew in with a glance over her shoulder, as if expecting someone behind her. Kristl looked, but there was no one there. Natalie was the first one to arrive, so it appeared that everyone, Natalie included, was going to be late.

She carried in a large grocery bag and dropped it on the counter, pulling out two bottles of red and two bottles of white wine. "Here," she said, pushing the white wine toward Kristl. "Put it in the refrigerator."

Kristl should have felt annoyance at the high-handed way Nat was taking over again, but she was emotionally drained over the night before's antics at Lacey's. Her stomach was tight as she wondered whether Mackenzie was going to make it tonight, or if she'd just given her lip service. She didn't know what she wanted from Mackenzie. Support that she was unlikely to get.

She's an investigator. You shouldn't have invited her.

But she still wanted her to come.

"I thought I'd be the last one," Nat complained. "What the hell's going on? Gavin's dead, killed in a *car accident*. What's happening?"

"I don't know."

"Well, I want to get to the bottom of it, so I've made some . . .

I've set some things in motion."

"What?" Kristl asked, surfacing a bit to regard her with trepidation.

"You'll see. Where the hell is Leigh, and Erin, and *Mia?* I told her to come. She said she'd talked to you, too. She should be in River Glen by now."

"How do you know?"

"She was flying. She had to get away from that Ben guy, so she flew out. That's what she said she was doing."

"She didn't say that much to me."

"Maybe you didn't ask her the right questions." Natalie briskly opened a bottle of Merlot. "I brought some crackers and Brie. Give me one of your cheese spreaders."

"Cheese spreaders?"

"The little knives for appetizers?" Natalie peered at her closely. "What's wrong with you?"

"I don't know. Maybe I think you just run over me all the time."

Natalie tucked in her chin and frowned at her. "Are you grieving about Gavin?"

Kristl looked at her as if she'd never seen her before. "Gavin," she repeated disdainfully. "If he hadn't interfered . . ."

"Never mind."

Natalie poured each of them a glass and slid one in Kristl's direction. "You didn't say anything about you and Tim at the funeral. We all thought you were still involved with those other guys."

Kristl wondered what it would be like to smash the glass on the end of the counter and charge Natalie with the jagged remains. They all thought she couldn't keep a man. They all dismissed her.

"I have a surprise later, if everyone would just fucking get here." Natalie lifted her glass and then glanced pointedly down at the wedge of Brie.

Kristl had wrapped her fingers around the stem of her own glass but she carefully unwound them and went to look for a plate for the Brie and to find her mother's "cheese spreaders." She set the plate down with a sharp clunk, then plucked the knife with its rounded blade from the drawer.

Natalie had problems of her own, so Kristl tried to shake off her mad funk. Nat's husband had left her and though she acted like it was good riddance to bad rubbish, she was hurting. Kristl understood that.

The doorbell rang and Nat swept past her to answer. Kristl was irked anew but then she heard, "Krissy? Krissy . . . ?" and went to find her mom, heaving a sigh.

Natalie opened the front door and looked past Leigh. "Are you the only one?"

"You waiting for someone better?" asked Leigh, piqued.

"Don't get pissy. It's just everybody's late. Me, too," she admitted. "And I want to make sure everything's in place."

"For what?" asked Leigh, shrugging out of her long black coat. She wore a white silk blouse and black slacks beneath it, and Natalie caught the designer initials on her handbag and knew it had cost Leigh over a thousand dollars. She felt a twinge of envy for Leigh's money. It was solid. Nothing she had to work for. Sure, she had that business but it was more entertainment for her husband, whereas Natalie was on her own, no family money to fall back on, and the ground beneath her feet had grown slippery, especially now that Phillip had abandoned her. She needed to keep moving forward.

"For my surprise." Natalie lifted her glass and smiled cheekily.

Leigh didn't respond. Instead, she said, "Well . . . it's almost seven thirty and I haven't gotten a callback yet."

"Oh, yeah? What play?"

"*Chicago.*"

"I never liked that one that well. You're still doing that acting thing, huh?" Leigh bristled, so Natalie raised her hands. "Sorry, sorry. We've all gotta follow our dreams."

"I know I had a good audition for Roxie."

Natalie choked a little on her wine and spilled some on her black cashmere sweater. "Shit."

"You don't think I can win a major role?"

"I'm sure you can. Jesus, Leigh, don't be so touchy. I just forgot one of the leads is Roxie something."

"Roxie Hart," Leigh clarified.

The doorbell rang and Natalie glanced down the hall to where Kristl was apparently still dealing with her mother. Good. She hustled to answer the door. But it was Erin with those big mouse eyes that just *bugged* Natalie. And right behind her, just getting out of a Ford compact, was Mackenzie Laughlin. Natalie's pulse jumped. *What?*

Natalie threw a fulminating look at Leigh. "*Mackenzie Laughlin?*" she hissed.

"Don't look at me," Leigh hissed back, hooking a thumb in the direction Kristl had taken.

Erin stepped around Natalie and said, "I almost didn't come. I got a call—"

"Goddammit," Natalie whispered, cutting her off, practically pushing her into the room. She then pinned on a smile and turned to face Mackenzie, who was striding toward the bottom concrete step of the porch.

"I didn't know Mac was coming," Erin said behind her, sounding worried.

Natalie held the door open with one hand and greeted Mackenzie, "This is a definite surprise. Kristl didn't tell us you were invited."

"It kind of just happened," said Mac with a cool smile that made Natalie's blood freeze in her veins.

Mac was in jeans and a black turtleneck topped with a black jacket. She wore black Sketchers and looked surprisingly fit in a way that made Natalie a bit envious. There was very little sign of the ankle injury she'd sustained at the funeral, but there were bruises down the side of her face and a knot on her forehead. "What happened to you?" asked Nat.

"Someone tried to run me off the road."

"Shit. Really?" Natalie peered at her. Couldn't tell if she was kidding.

"Really," Mac assured her as Natalie stepped back and allowed her entry into the house.

"Like Gavin? God, it's an epidemic," she murmured.

Leigh and Erin greeted Mackenzie like the long-lost

friend she was, but inside Natalie's mind the words PRIVATE INVESTIGATOR seemed to flash over and over again in neon. She took a last glance toward the street before she closed the door.

"Who are you waiting for?" Leigh wanted to know.

"Mia," she said in a tone that suggested, *Duh*. "You said she might come," she reminded her.

"I said I didn't know if she would make it in time," Leigh snapped.

Natalie held up a hand. "Okay. Whatever. Who wants a glass of wine?" She spread her hands to indicate the stemmed glasses, open bottle of red, and cheese board.

Mac sipped her wine, her head full of Taft, Anna DeMarcos, and Prudence, and the blue Honda Accord that had run her off the road . . . and now that psychic person, Veronica Quick. She needed her full attention on what was happening in front of her and had to push everything aside. This was an opportunity to learn about all of The Sorority's relationship to Ethan.

Get in the game, she warned herself.

Natalie was pacing back and forth from the door to the kitchen and her tension had infected Leigh and Erin, both of whose eyes kept turning toward the door as well. Mac hoped they were right. She would like to see Mia herself, though she fought an urge to check the time on her phone.

Kristl appeared from down the hallway, looking a little wild-eyed. She said, "Hi," to Mac and seemed to want to come over and talk to her, but then thought better of it, apparently, as she turned away and picked up a glass of wine that she'd had tucked at the back of the kitchen counter. She took a deep swallow, then began searching through one of the cabinets, pulling out a small saucepan and mumbling something about oatmeal for her mother.

Natalie rubbed her hands together as if she were cold. She was in all black, but it wasn't nearly as Goth-like as high school. Tight black jeans and boots and her hair pulled back and tied at her nape.

Erin broke away from talking to Leigh and said to Mac, "You must have really interesting cases."

"Sometimes."

"What are you working on now?"

"Don't ask her that," Natalie cut her off.

"Is it a secret?" asked Erin, quelling a bit in the face of Natalie's brusque order.

"No, it's—" Mac started.

"I told you all I hired her to find Mia," Leigh interrupted. "And she found her. Job well done."

Mac smiled and inclined her head in acknowledgment. She wondered if the others heard how snippy Leigh sounded.

"Let's call Mia," urged Natalie. "Find out where she is.

Leigh, you call her."

Leigh gave Natalie a look, but she obediently clicked through to her saved numbers, punched a button, then held the phone to her ear. They all went quiet and after a long moment, Leigh said, "It's going to voice mail. You want to leave a message?"

"No." Natalie was firm.

Leigh clicked off. "She'll call me when she's here," she said with confidence.

"So, what are we doing besides waiting for Mia?" asked Kristl, pouring boiling water over quick-cooking oats in a bowl.

"We're getting together," Natalie said tightly. Kristl snorted.

"What's that mean?" Natalie demanded.

"Nothing." She slid her gaze over the group and then said, "So . . . Mac's here. Let's tell her about it."

"About what?" Erin asked before Mac could.

"About Ethan. And our pledge to kill him in a car accident." Kristl spread her hands and smiled. "How we all freaked out after that very thing happened."

Natalie, Leigh and Erin froze. Mac looked from one to the other of them. Kristl turned to Mac and added, "A few weeks before graduation we all pledged to kill Ethan because he slept with Roxie in the pool house. Even Roxie pledged."

"It was a FUCKING JOKE!" Natalie screamed. "How many times do I have to say it?" She turned to Mac, too. "We said we were going to kill him. We all . . . hated him. I said we should do it by a car accident and it was . . . I was joking and everyone was joking. We just were mad at him. We didn't plan it. We *couldn't*."

"I wasn't really joking," Erin said, as if the words were torn from her throat. Everyone whipped their heads her way. She shrank a bit under that hard appraisal. "Okay, I was sort of joking, but I really wanted him dead. *Not Ingrid!*" she added immediately. "But

Ethan was a *prick*. I thought he wasn't. I thought he was better." Her eyes filled with sudden tears.

Leigh said, "Oh, my God. You wanted to be with him."

Nat chuckled. "Did you get with him? Have sex with him?" she teased.

Erin's mouth opened but no words came out.

"Holy mother of God," Natalie exhaled. "You did. You did!" Leigh gasped.

Kristl didn't try to hide her surprise. "You had sex with Ethan Stanhope? When? How?"

"It wasn't like that. I didn't mean . . . Oh, please don't tell Mia!"

"At Gavin's," said Natalie, blinking, processing. "The night we left you there. I thought it was weird you were waiting for your mom to pick you up. You stayed behind to be with him. You'd been following him around all night with those big eyes. Oh, my God, I can't believe it."

"It wasn't like that!" Erin fought back tears.

"Yes, it was," Natalie insisted.

"I loved him! I thought I loved him, okay? I made a mistake, but I wasn't the only one. You all were with him, too!" Erin glared at her friends as if they'd all betrayed her.

"Why would you say that?" Natalie demanded.

"But *you* slept with him," Leigh stressed.

"Oh, Christ. Holy mother . . ." muttered Kristl, looking from one friend to the next.

Mac just stayed silent, watching how the reveal played out.

"Ethan and I did not have sex," Leigh said. "We just . . . fooled around a bit, but it was nothing."

"Seriously?" Natalie started laughing, so hard she bent over. "Oh, my God."

"You were with him, too," accused Erin. "He told me."

"He told you? What? That we kissed in his backyard once?" She glared at her.

"He told Gavin and I overheard."

"Jesus," muttered Kristl.

Natalie immediately switched her ire to her. "Okay, let's hear what you did."

"Me? I didn't do anything."

"You've slept with everybody," Leigh jumped in as if she'd just been waiting for the opportunity.

"I did not sleep with Ethan." Kristl looked thunderous, then retorted, "What does 'fooled around a bit' mean?"

Leigh just shook her head.

"So, Gavin was right?" Natalie looked faintly horrified. "We all cheated with Ethan and betrayed our friend." She turned to Mac. "What do you think of our dirty little secret?"

"Which one? The one where you all pledged to kill Ethan?"

Natalie's mouth twisted into a sour smile. "Look what you made us confess to. Betcha didn't count on that." She chuckled, but her amusement had a hysterical edge.

"Nice to know I'm not the only one with a sex problem," Kristl muttered as she spooned cinnamon and sugar over the top of the oatmeal, then headed with a tray toward the hallway.

"You have a sex problem?" Erin asked in a small voice. She almost sounded hopeful.

"I have a relationship problem," she shot back as she stalked down the hall.

Another silence fell and then Natalie looked at Erin. "Did you kill him?"

Erin reared back as if she'd been slapped. "He was driving and didn't make the turn. He killed himself." Under Natalie's dark stare, she blurted, "I didn't give him the pills."

"What pills?" Leigh asked on a sharp intake of breath.

"The pills that Mia told us about," Erin reminded her.

"What pills?" Natalie repeated, but something in her eyes told Mac that she knew where this was going already, too.

"The fentanyl," said Mac, as if it were understood by all already. "You saw the pills?" she asked Erin.

Erin's wide eyes grew even wider. "Mia didn't say it was fentanyl!"

"What *did* Mia say?" Mac asked as Natalie and Leigh looked stunned.

"She said Ethan had pills. That he was a stupid fool. That she was pretty sure he'd taken some before he left Gavin's graduation night, but that can't be true because it took too long to have any effect. The pills were in the pool house, so maybe he just took them with him, but he didn't *take* them at Gavin's."

"The pills were in the pool house?" asked Mac.

"I saw them there. We all went in and out of the pool house, before and after Roxie got with him there."

"Maybe Roxie gave them to him," suggested Leigh.

"He didn't swallow them *there*," Erin repeated.

"He took them home and saved them for graduation," said Natalie.

The doorbell rang and Natalie jumped. Everyone turned and Leigh said, "Mia!"

But it wasn't Mia.

It was Roxie Vernon.

CHAPTER 20

Natalie hurried to open the door and admit her, while the rest of them stared at Roxie in shock.

"Surprise!" Natalie called to everyone in the room, grinning like a pumpkin. "Roxie and I have become friends again!"

Roxie stepped inside but her look said maybe "friends" was a little overstating her relationship with Natalie. "Hello, *I Eta Pi*," she greeted them. "Looks like we have a new member." She lifted elegant brows at Mac, who, like everyone else, was a bit bowled over at the sight of their long-lost classmate.

Roxie's hair was still blondish and artfully shaggy. She wore black Lululemon pants that hugged her slim figure and flared at the ankle, and a matching black top with a cream-colored fake fur jacket.

"You weren't waiting for Mia," Erin accused Natalie, unable to take her eyes off Roxie.

"I wanted to surprise you all!" declared Natalie.

"Natalie told me she was going to be here and I was coming through Portland so I thought, okay, I'll drop in." Roxie's lips lifted in a half smile. "You were expecting Mia?"

"She said she was coming," Leigh murmured.

"Who knows?" said Natalie.

"We were talking about the pledge to kill Ethan," explained Mac.

Roxie turned her clear blue eyes on Mac. "Really. So, you know."

"Just learned," Mac admitted. Her pulse had jumped when she'd heard about the pledge, but now she was trying to assess if it had propelled someone to actually kill Ethan or if it was just as Natalie claimed, a terribly prophetic joke.

Roxie drew her gaze over the rest of them. "And what about Gavin? And his *little brother*?"

"None of this has to do with Ethan." Leigh's lips were tight. She looked at Mac. "It just doesn't."

"How do you know?" asked Roxie.

No one had an answer for that.

"Did you see the pills . . . when you were in Gavin's pool house?" questioned Erin. She hadn't looked away from Roxie since the moment she'd walked in.

"What are we talking about?" A slight frown marred her brow.

"Why don't you tell her, Kristl, since you brought Mac here? Or, Mackenzie, step right up." Natalie waved a hand at her.

Kristl looked at Mac and she looked back, but when Kristl shook her head, Mac took the opportunity. "Ethan and Ingrid died of fentanyl poisoning. Erin said she saw pills in the pool house on graduation night.

Maybe they were fentanyl. Maybe Ethan took the fentanyl himself. But somewhere along the line he and Ingrid were overdosed."

Roxie listened with ever-growing seriousness. "My God, was it in Ethan's food?"

Erin blinked. "What makes you say that?"

"I don't know. I wasn't there graduation night. But before that . . . Erin, you were hanging by Ethan at the party where I got in so much trouble with Mia."

"When you slept with Ethan," Leigh reminded.

"I didn't sleep with him," Roxie shot back tersely. "Erin, you saw. He was getting that sandwich and someone . . . Gavin . . . was saying be careful because it could be poisoned."

"Because of you!" declared Erin. "He was joking because *you* were with Ethan that night and he said Mia might poison his food."

"Where *is* Mia?" Kristl demanded.

"We don't know if she'll even make it!" Leigh snapped. To Roxie, she said, "Well, he was joking, then. Mia didn't poison his food."

"Maybe she did," said Roxie.

Erin said, "I think someone took something out to his car . . . maybe . . . I thought I saw his overhead car light come on."

Roxie's hand flew to her mouth and she looked both horrified and scandalized. "Oh, my God, was it *pie*? I joked to him about 'I ate a pie'! And he said cherry pie was his absolute favorite." She pulled herself up straight. "Whether you believe it or not, I hardly spoke to him after seeing him in the pool house. He wanted sex and I wasn't going there. I didn't like him. I didn't like anyone."

"You liked *everyone*," Leigh countered.

"Stop being such a bitch, Leigh," Roxie snapped back, narrowing her blue eyes. "I knew that's what you all thought. My mom was in a 'relationship' with our landlord, who was butt ugly and coercing her to have sex to help pay our rent. Made me sick, even though I understood it. I didn't think I'd ever like a guy again, but . . . Jeremy asked me to marry him and I said yes."

There was a pause, then Leigh said, "Jeremy *Orsini*?"

Kristl gasped and Natalie looked poleaxed as Roxie said, "Yessiree. We both live in L.A. now. Just ran into each other and one thing led to another." Her smile was tender. "Never thought I'd feel this way, but here I am."

Natalie stared at her. "You didn't tell me it was Jeremy."

"You didn't ask," Roxie responded.

Leigh's phone blurped and she had to pull herself back to the present and finger-scramble through her purse to find it. She collected her phone, glanced at the screen, and took in a breath. "I got a call back!" she said in relief.

Mac's cell phone rang at the same moment and she pulled it from her purse. She recognized Mason's number. "Excuse me," she said and let herself out the front door and away from the house before answering. She didn't need The Sorority peppering her with questions she didn't want to answer.

She clicked on. "Hi, Mason."

"She's DEAD! Mia's DEAD! Someone killed her. Who did you talk to? Who knew where she was? It's your fault and that fucking psycho, Ben! I'm going to kill him. I'm going to KILL HIM!"

Her arms rose in gooseflesh. "Mason. Wait. Where are you?" she asked tersely. "What happened?"

"Her car's down the street. She just pulled off and died! Someone gave her something. They took her away in an ambulance but she was already DEAD!" He clicked off.

Mac looked back at the house, then stalked straight to her car. She put in a quick call to Kristl as she switched on the engine. "I've got to go. Sorry. Thank you," she apologized.

"What happened?" Kristl's voice was anxious. "Something's happened."

"I'll call you later," Mac promised, fairly certain she was lying, uncaring that she was.

"What did she say?" demanded Natalie as soon as Kristl was off the phone with Mac. She looked out the window toward the road, watching Mackenzie's car drive off.

"She just said she'd call later," said Kristl, following Nat's gaze.

"Something bad's happened to Mia!" Erin declared on a little gasp.

Leigh snapped her head around. "You don't know that." She'd put her phone back inside her purse and was waiting for Natalie and Kristl to make room at the front doorway so she could pass by them.

"Leaving so soon?" drawled Roxie.

Leigh shot her a fulminating glance. "I need to call Mia, make sure she's all right."

"And check in on your callback." Roxie smiled.

"Is that a crime?"

"No."

But the smile on her face irritated Leigh. "You are still such a bitch," she muttered as she stalked through the now open door that Natalie was holding for her.

"Back at 'cha," said Roxie.

Erin gazed after Leigh. "She's worried about Mia."

"We don't know anything happened to her," reminded Natalie.

"I need to go, too," Erin said.

"Didn't mean to ruin the party," drawled Roxie.

"Krissy?"

The sound wavered from the hallway. Kristl swore under her breath and glanced impatiently in that direction but didn't move.

"What do *you* have to do?" Natalie asked Erin.

"I have a life, Nat. And I need to get home to my cat."

"Your cat. Well, don't let us hold you back." Natalie rolled her eyes. She looked at Kristl, who'd turned in the direction of her mother's voice even though her feet were still planted, and then at Roxie, who'd pulled out her phone to check the time. "Don't tell me you have somewhere to go, too."

"You asked me to stop by. I did. Looks to me like the party's breaking up."

Natalie glared at her.

"I don't know what you want out of us." Erin picked up her coat from where she'd thrown it over a chair. "Now Mackenzie knows about what we said about Ethan . . . and now we know he was killed with those pills."

"He killed himself," Roxie reminded her. "By accident."

Erin looked troubled.

"Krissy!"

"Shit," muttered Kristl, heading in the direction of her mother's room.

"Sorry, Nat," she heard Roxie say. "Not the reunion you'd hoped for."

By the time Mackenzie got to the Beckwiths' street there were two patrol cars on site along with the crime team. Mac's heart was beating fast. Mia was dead. Dead.

She saw what was likely Mia's car parked at the side of the road, driver's door open, the tech team already taking pictures. Mason was talking to a woman whose hair was scraped into a tight, black bun, her back to Mackenzie. She parked her own car a block down the street and jogged back to find the dark-haired woman in the long camel-colored coat was Detective Elena Verbena, Cooper Haynes's partner at RGPD.

Lynda and Charles Beckwith were standing to one side, clinging to one another, maybe holding each other up, both pale as death themselves.

Mason saw Mac and she braced herself for another onslaught but his eyes were dull, his movements slow. It looked like all the fight had leached out of him.

Detective Verbena stepped back and let Mac approach. They knew each other from previous cases, but their relationship wasn't as warm as hers with Haynes, whom she'd been on the force with before Verbena was part of the team.

"I'm going to kill Ben," snarled Mason. In that, he hadn't changed, but his energy was down. He walked over to his parents and put his arms around them. They stood in a group of three, sobbing, shoulders shaking, heads bent together.

You were wrong, Taft. They turned to each other instead of ripping each other apart.

"Who's Ben?" asked Verbena.

Mac dragged her attention back to the detective, fighting a sense of depression at the loss of another high school classmate. "Mia's boyfriend."

"I got that. What else?"

Mackenzie filled her in tersely on what she knew about Ben, also explaining how she'd become involved in the Beckwiths' tragedy.

"We'll get the local police looking for him," she said grimly.

"Mia's death was definitely homicide?" Mac asked, looking back at Mia's car and watching the bright *flash, flash* of the tech's camera in the night.

"Overdose. Tried to give her NARCAN but it was too

late. She was slumped up against the steering wheel. Looks like she just managed to pull over."

Overdose.

"Where's Detective Haynes?"

Verbena regarded her with dark, glittering eyes. Mac didn't understand why she was looking at her so intently until she said, "He's on administrative leave."

Mac stared back at her and instantly knew it was because Haynes had slipped the information about the cause of Ethan and Ingrid Stanhope's deaths to Taft at her request. "Art Stanhope complained?" she asked, her throat tight.

Verbena didn't answer but she didn't have to. Mac felt both guilty and angry. No wonder Verbena was so careful and cold. She probably blamed her, too.

Mac thought of Cooper and Jamie, pregnant and bedbound, and Emma, and the rest of their family. At least Cooper would still be paid, but . . . shit.

She wrenched her gaze to Mason and she thought about Sam Stanhope and how they'd scored fentanyl on a stupid teenage lark and Ethan had wanted some. Though they swore they never gave him any, Ethan had gotten hold of some. The pills had been in the pool house, according to Erin. Who was the dealer? Same person? Someone they'd all been connected to?

Mason was trying to herd his parents back into their house. His mother looked ready to collapse and his father wasn't far behind. No sniping now. Mac excused herself from Verbena and followed after them. She knew Verbena wouldn't be far behind but she wanted a moment alone with Mason.

"Mason," she said at the door. He didn't respond and

she followed him inside without being asked. Both Lynda and Charles collapsed in the same chairs they'd been sitting in when she'd been here the first time.

He came back to where she was standing near the front door. He glanced over her shoulder and said, "The detective's coming."

"Who was your dealer? Who got you the fentanyl?"

His mouth tightened but his lips were trembling. "I don't fucking know. That was all Sam. Who cares? Mia's dead, Ethan's dead, Ingrid's dead . . . Gavin's dead . . ."

"Mr. Beckwith," Verbena said coolly behind Mac. "I would like to talk to you. Excuse me, Mackenzie, this is police business."

Mac didn't stick around to argue.

She walked back to her car, reaching for her cell in her back pocket. She put in a call to Taft but it went to voice mail.

Taft was walking the pugs when his cell rang. He looked at the number, expecting Mac, but it wasn't one he knew. Thought about letting it go to voice mail but clicked on. "Taft."

"Mr. Taft, it's Veronica Quick."

He unconsciously straightened. Anything to do with the Mangella estate put him on high alert, and then there was her strange gift of "sight."

"You're working late," he said.

"I've already left the office." She exhaled carefully, as if she were dreading what she had to say next.

"You're going to tell me you saw her," he guessed.

"I wanted to talk to you . . ." she said uncertainly. "I don't normally involve myself personally in the firm's cases. I don't want to be misunderstood."

"You can cut to the chase, Ms. Quick. You saw my sister outside the window, like I did. My sister's been dead over ten years, so I'm still trying to figure out how that's possible."

"Call me Veronica, or Ronnie, please. I know you'll think I'm a crackpot, but I have to warn you. You're in danger from those women. One or both, I don't know. I just know you are."

"You already warned me."

"I don't feel you're taking it seriously."

"They're dangerous women . . . Ronnie. I'm in complete agreement with you on that. But I'm more interested in how you saw Helene. Have you been doing research on me? If it's a little trick, it's a good one."

"I understand your skepticism. I'm taking a real risk here. I think they're plotting against you."

"I'm the epitome of careful."

"Don't go there tonight. Please."

He had no intention of going anywhere. "To the Mangellas'?"

"I don't want to read about you in the papers tomorrow. That's an experience I only want to live through once." And then she clicked off.

Tree limbs shivered above him and a cold drop of rain ran down the back of his neck. He corralled the pugs on their leashes and hurried them back to his condo. He looked at the time. Ten p.m.

He wasn't going to Mangella's. Had no intention to.

He looked down into the pugs' masked faces. "But what the hell is she talking about?" he asked them.

His phone dinged. Oh, right. A message. He'd heard Mac's message come in while he was talking.

Mia Beckwith is dead. Leaving Beckwiths now.

"What the hell?" he gritted out and was just starting to dial her back when the phone rang in his hand. Mac. "What happened?" he demanded. When she started to tell him, he interrupted and said, "Hold it. Come to the condo. Give me the whole story then."

Natalie waved to Roxie, who drove off with scarcely a lift of her hand. So much for her big reveal. Like everything else in her life, it was just a joke.

You're the joke, she told herself and she set her jaw.

She walked to her rental car and sat with her hands on the wheel for a long time. She wasn't interested in going back to the townhouse. The whole Portland idea felt like a mess. In her bones she could feel that things were going to blow up. She wouldn't get her new show off the ground because all the shit about pledging to kill Ethan was going to kill her career.

You can do something about it, that voice in her head reminded.

She switched on the ignition.

"Krissy?" her mother's voice wavered, though there was a thread of steel in it, too. It was maddening. Kristl felt the anger and despair and misery of all the broken relationships, of all the time taking care of her feeble yet demanding mother, of all the bad choices that had led to Tim's death and the likewise death of her dreams.

"Krissy!"

She was glad everyone was gone. Glad to drop the mask of friendship, wondering what the hell she'd been thinking by inviting Mackenzie Laughlin to the house. She barked out a short laugh. Well, she'd wanted a surprise, hadn't she? And it had fallen as flat as Nat's had when Roxie strolled in. No one really cared. Everyone was locked in their own private hells. Just like she was.

She stalked into the bedroom and gazed down at Mom, who was lying flat in the bed instead of sitting up in it. She looked pathetic.

"I can't get back up," she whined.

"You're too heavy for me to keep lifting you," Kristl told her.

"No, I'm not. You just don't want to."

Kristl inhaled a deep breath, letting it out slowly. Almost of their own accord, her eyes moved to the top drawer of her mother's dresser where deep behind the socks and old lady undergarments lay a small metal box full of pills.

Are they still potent after ten years? she wondered.

"Okay. I'll wrestle you up. Then I'll get you a glass of water."

"I don't need water."

"Then tea." She smiled and her mother regarded her a bit warily. A cup of tea and then Kristl would go for a nice long ride in her mother's car. It was a cold, crisp, dark night.

* * *

Leigh dug her fingernails into her palms. Parker had laughed when she'd told him about tomorrow's callback. Laughed! She'd tried to hide her enthusiasm a bit because he was such a downer about anything good that came her way. "How were the murdering bitches?" he'd asked her as soon as she returned. He, like Gavin, firmly believed The Sorority had taken Ethan out, and Leigh, in that first blush of love, had foolishly admitted to Natalie's pledge, thinking Parker could be trusted with their secret. He'd promised to keep it to himself, and so far she guessed he had, as it hadn't come back to bite her in the ass yet—though that cat was out of the bag now, thanks to Kristl— but he was untrustworthy and getting more so every day.

"You think you're going to get a big part?" His smile was wicked. "What about when they find out you and your friends knocked off the stud you all slept with?"

"We didn't all sleep with him," she hissed.

"Oho. Somebody did, didn't they? Which one? How many?" He leaned in close to her face. "Was it you?"

Leigh shook her head.

"Screwing around on your best friend?"

"Shut up, Parker."

"Hit a nerve, did I?" He stood back again with that smirking smile. "You know they already cast the main parts. You might get something else but Roxie and Velma are out of reach."

"You don't know that," she ground out. She might

get one of the two female leads. They hadn't said she wouldn't.

"You don't have the voice for it." He shrugged and walked away.

They'd been standing in the foyer, but now Leigh stalked back to the garage and her Tesla. Parker liked to torture her. That was the truth of it. He knew her weaknesses, her fears and insecurities. His words about Ethan made her feel ice cold with fear and red hot with fury at him.

Erin petted Chili so vigorously the cat *meow*ed in protest and slunk away. She almost grabbed for her, but held herself back. She still had the battle scars from the last time she'd tried that.

She had a lot to think about. A *lot* to think about.

She didn't like that Mackenzie had been there. She didn't understand why Kristl had invited her. Mac was fine, but she was an investigator and Erin really didn't want to be investigated. She had this picture of herself in a courtroom, on the stand, pointing fingers at everyone, herself included. They were all at fault for Ethan's and Ingrid's deaths. They'd wished it on Ethan, and Ingrid had gotten ensnared by default.

She choked on a sob and got her Hello Kitty diary out, flipping back to those last days of high school. She'd quit writing in it after she graduated, but she'd been fairly religious about keeping things in order before that.

I love Ethan. She looked at her scrawl with the little

hearts around it. She'd wanted to have sex with him some more. But then he'd *died* and she'd never had sex again. She almost envied Kristl who was able to sleep with lots of guys, apparently. She tried to imagine that for herself and couldn't, so she'd purchased a vibrator but still hadn't had the courage to use it.

She thought back to what she'd said at The Sorority meeting . . . about the pills. She thought Roxie had remembered them, too. Erin had always suspected they were Ethan's, but she hadn't really wanted to know.

And Roxie . . . Ugh. She was still so pretty. And slim. And toned. And uncaring what other people thought. That was her superpower: aloofness. Erin couldn't manage that and neither could the rest of them. Natalie was too bullish and intense, Kristl was too dark and needy, Leigh was a pretty close second to Roxie, but she could get mad and stay that way, and Mia . . . Erin could hardly remember her.

When the knock came on her door, Erin started. It was late. Nobody stopped by at this time of night. She walked to her front door and looked through the peephole. Her brows lifted and she opened the door.

"What are you—"

That's as far as she got. The hypodermic hit her in the neck and she stared in utter shock as her attacker plunged whatever was in the vial into her system. She screamed and staggered toward the kitchen cabinets, holding her neck, eyes wide.

"Wh . . . why . . . ?" she cried.

"You talk too much," she heard.

What had she said? When had she said it? "I didn't say anything. I don't know anything!"

Her attacker remained silent and Erin began to feel numbness stealing through her body like a thief. She gripped onto the counter but her knees were growing weak and she slid down the bank of cabinets to the floor.

"Why?" she asked again on a sob, but there was no answer. She heard the door close behind her attacker. She tried to think, to remember. It didn't make sense.

Her mind focused on Roxie . . . her voice . . . I Eta Pi. Pie . . .

Erin thought back to the moment she'd seen the pie, put in the back seat of Ethan's car.

She choked on another sob, tried to fight the numbness, vaguely remembered her phone was in her back pocket. She managed to pull it out. Saw the dial. Pressed the numbers. Nine . . . one . . . Her heart was beating in her ears. She could see her finger hover over the number. With her remaining strength she pushed ONE and sank back.

"Nine-one-one, what is the nature of your emergency?"

"Erin . . . Erin Humbolt . . . I'm dying . . ." she whispered.

The last thing she remembered was Chili stepping carefully past the phone as she gave it a hard look out of one golden eye, and then strolling away.

I drive the van back to its parking spot. Don't want to risk taking a car that might be recognized even though this van's a risk, too. But it had to be done. Erin is too unstable.

I'd practiced with the hypodermic. Thought to use it on Mia, but didn't need to.

Maybe I'm done now. Maybe the others will stay out of my way. I need to shut down this investigation.

Mackenzie Laughlin . . . private investigator . . . wily and persistent.

I hope she's as inept as I think she is, otherwise she may turn out to be the biggest problem.

CHAPTER 21

By the time Mac arrived at Taft's place, it was closing on eleven. She could see moving light beneath the window curtain—the television—as she knocked lightly. Almost immediately Taft pulled open the door, standing in the aperture half a heartbeat before the pugs scrambled up from wherever they'd been lolling and charged toward Mackenzie, curly tails whipping, their welcoming snorts bringing a smile to her face, lifting her spirits. She bent down to them, closed her eyes, and let them eagerly lick her face. She knew she wasn't responsible for her classmates' deaths, but it felt like she kind of was.

Standing again, she stepped inside and Taft closed the door behind her. He was in light denim jeans and a thin camel sweater that hugged his upper arms. He'd pushed the sleeves up and she could see his taut forearms. She wanted to wrap her arms around him and bury her face in his chest.

"Hey, sit down," he said, pointing to the couch. There was real concern on his face.

"Do I look that bad?" Mac asked, but damn near collapsed onto the cushions. The pugs immediately swarmed her and she closed her eyes again, leaning her head back.

"You look like you're spent."

"That's a good way to put it."

"Have you eaten?"

"Yes. Sometime in my life. I can't remember when. Oh, right. Cheese and cracker at Kristl's."

"Cracker? Singular?" She opened her eyes and he was staring down at her. "Burger, pizza, DoorDash . . . I'm good with ordering, if you're interested. I always have crackers. Plural."

"Crackers would be good."

"Wine? Beer? Scotch?"

"Water is fine."

As he headed for the kitchen her mind circled back to Mia's death. Drugs suspected enough for NARCAN to be employed. The Sorority . . . words tumbling out of their mouths . . . fear and lies and deceptions, mostly for show . . . the blue Accord that was nowhere to be seen amongst the cars they'd driven to Kristl's . . . Kristl herself and her part in Tim Knowles's death . . . bossy Natalie . . . self-absorbed Leigh . . . Roxie Vernon . . . *I Eta Pi* . . . and Erin, who admitted sleeping with Ethan and was the only one who seemed to truly rue his death.

Taft came back with a plate of water crackers, sliced cheddar, and plump green grapes and placed it on a side table along with a glass of ice water. Then he shooed off the pugs, who'd come to attention at the sight of food.

"The grapes are a nice touch," she said thankfully, holding a small sprig and popping several into her mouth.

"Occasionally I pick something up at the store," he admitted as if it were a deeply held secret. He mock frowned at the pugs, who looked for all the world like they were going to launch themselves back onto the couch. "Be good or it's a trip to behind the bedroom door."

He then went back to the kitchen with Blackie and Plaid eagerly trotting behind him as he poured some more kibbles into their bowls.

When he returned he sat on the couch on the side next to her. She tried to pick up the half-finished plate and hand it to him but he waved it away and she set it back down. "That's for you. When you're ready, keep going about tonight."

She nibbled some more but finally shook her head and Taft took the plate to the kitchen. He came back and then fought the pugs for his spot on the couch and Mac just started in, beginning with the meeting with The Sorority and ending with the call from Mason, learning about Mia's death, seeing the shattered parents, and her conversation with Detective Verbena.

Taft listened throughout, his frown deepening. "Haynes is on administrative leave?" he asked at the end.

"Because of me. Because Art Stanhope has connections and is mad that I got the tox report."

Taft swore softly. "And Mia died of an overdose."

She nodded.

"From this boyfriend who followed her from California?" He sounded doubtful.

"Mason thinks so, but . . ." Mac thought through the evening. "I don't have the time of her death, exactly, but it could have been someone she knew here. They were all waiting for her at Kristl's. Someone told her about the meeting."

"You gave Leigh her number."

Mac was half turned toward him with Plaid sprawled on her lap and Blackie on his. "But she called them all apparently." She gently pushed Plaid off her legs. "I gotta see what I look like," she said, easing away from the dog and heading into Taft's bathroom.

The sight of her wan pallor and bluish-green bruising made her suck in her breath. The makeup she'd applied before her meeting with The Sorority was all but gone and her lips were bloodless. She pinched her cheeks to throw some color in. No wonder Taft had told her to sit down.

"I look like hell," she said as she came out of the bathroom.

Taft had moved to the kitchen and was pulling down the prized bottle of scotch.

She remembered he'd shared some with Anna De-Marcos and a cold feeling settled in her stomach.

"You look fine to me," he said. "I've had a few long weeks like the one you're having." He pointed to his chest in the approximate area where a bullet had nearly sent him to his maker.

He poured two fingers of scotch into both glasses and handed her one, lifting his to his mouth.

"Don't drink it!" she ordered.

Taft stopped with the rim of the glass at his lips. He slowly set the glass back down, taking hers from her nerveless fingers.

"Anna DeMarcos left you a note to cover up her real reason for being here."

"Damn," Taft said softly.

"Maybe I'm wrong, I don't know. But something's off about that—"

"I don't think you're wrong," he cut in.

They looked at each other. Mac asked herself: Would Anna spike his bottle of Macallan? Oh, yes. No question.

Taft said tautly, "I've been . . . dismissing them. And I've been warned enough times that I should listen. I got a call from Veronica Quick, who told me not to go over to Mangella's tonight."

"The psychic?"

"She also admitted to seeing Helene, in a way."

"You're kidding."

"Bullshit."

"I know."

"So, you're a believer?" That was so un-Taft-like she wanted to laugh.

"She believes it. Enough to call me, even though she knew I'd scoff."

"Were you thinking about going to Mangella's?"

"Not consciously, but yes. I don't believe he fell off that roof. I'd like to prowl around that house sometime. See if I can find something."

"That is a bad idea."

He smiled faintly. "Wouldn't be my first." He carefully pushed both glasses of scotch to the far back of the counter, placing the fancy bottle beside them. "She came back to poison the one thing I wanted, the one thing Mangella knew I cared about."

Blackie yipped at him as if in agreement. He and Plaid had settled into their beds but were watching Mac and Taft with bright, brown eyes.

"She came back to kill you," Mac murmured.

They both moved toward the living room at the same time and she stumbled and he shot out an arm to steady her and said. "And maybe you."

"I'm not on her radar like you are."

"Yes, but you're my partner and I . . ." She saw his eyes widen.

"What?"

"Oh . . ." he growled softly.

"What?" she repeated impatiently, but then she picked up his thoughts almost by telepathy. "You think she's the one who ran me off the road!"

"You matter to me."

"We don't know—"

"That fucking car is in the Mangella garage."

He moved purposely away from her and she grabbed his arm. "Don't go there tonight. Veronica warned you."

"Now *you're* the believer?" His eyes were bright with repressed rage.

She grabbed his other arm as well, holding tight. "Don't do anything to get yourself killed. You'll play right into her hands."

"I'm not going to get myself killed."

"I don't have to be psychic to know that you might."

She rarely touched Taft. They weren't physically demonstrative in day-to-day life, only in extreme circumstances. And this was one of those extreme circumstances. She could feel it in her bones.

"Mackenzie . . ." He tried to pull away from her grip.

"Jesse," she responded.

The intimacy of their first names stopped him. He regarded her stonily, his thoughts clearly full of Anna DeMarcos's treachery, not on the tense moment between them. "She's systematically attacking what matters to me. She did this. She hurt you on purpose."

"Maybe . . . yes . . . but—"

He yanked an arm free of her grip, but didn't move away. His gaze was on her face, focused on her bruises. "That's because of me."

"It's because of *her*." His eyes moved to the knot on her forehead. "I know," Mac said quickly. "I know you want to kill her. I can feel it. But I'm okay and now we know."

"Now we know."

The muscles in his arm bunched as he turned away, and Mac instinctively moved into him, pressed herself against him to keep him from leaving. At least that's what she told herself. Her breasts crushed into his chest.

"I'm not going to—"

"Yes, you are. You're going straight into danger. I don't want you to. I want you to stay here with me."

"Mackenzie—"

"Don't leave me. Don't." She was gripped onto him, nearly embracing him.

He carefully turned his head and looked into her upturned face. His eyes slowly focused on her mouth. He was tense as a coiled spring. So was she.

Mackenzie's lips parted in anticipation and his gaze suddenly slammed directly into hers.

"Don't think too much," she breathed.

"You're trying to *seduce* me into staying?"

"Is it working?"

His brows lifted in surprise at her candor. His eyes moved back to the bruising, then to her mouth, then up to meet her steady gaze.

"Yes," he whispered.

He pulled back and regarded her steadily. She slowly unclenched her fingers from her grip on his arm. Mackenzie's heart was beating so hard she could feel it pulsing at the base of her throat.

He said unevenly, "You're my . . . partner . . . and that matters to me more than anything."

"Same." She couldn't find the breath for more.

"This could ruin . . ."

Everything. He didn't have to say the word. He was right. It could ruin everything. She'd been fighting this war within herself for ages, hanging onto their friendship, their partnership, by her fingernails. But she *wanted* this.

It must have shown on her face because he expelled a pent-up breath and his swollen left hand moved to her neck, sliding around to the nape, easing her toward him until his mouth was less than an inch from hers. She wanted to reach up and capture his lips. Her heart was thundering in her ears. It was madness, but she didn't damn well care.

"Are you going to kiss me or not?" she whispered.

He groaned and pressed his lips to hers, hot and hard and lovely.

She felt herself melt. Her knees wobbled. Oh, God, it was good. She'd known it would be. She'd thought about this for so long.

She kissed him back carefully. She wanted to ravage

his mouth but held onto the moment, stretching it out. Her lips parted of their own free will and his grip tightened around her as his tongue slipped in to taste her.

They were standing in the kitchen aperture but he suddenly moved her back against the wall. Thank God. She needed the support! Her own arms were around his waist and she wanted to pull him as close as possible, press his hips to hers, hold him in place. Her blood sang in her veins, pounded through her body. One kiss . . . one long, wonderfully exquisite . . .

He pulled back long enough to say, "If you—"

"Don't stop," she cut him off.

He swore softly and kissed her even harder. His hand slid to the small of her back, increasing the contact between them. She rejoiced in the feel of his hardness. Man, she didn't want to wait. She sensed this could be it. Her one and only chance. Maybe. Maybe not. She didn't care, she just wanted.

And Taft was into it now. His one hand slipped beneath her sweater and slid up to her breast. The other held her hips in place as he pushed her against the wall. The sweet pressure was *killing* her.

Blackie suddenly howled, a keening wail that broke their kiss as if he'd sliced between them. Her chest was heaving and Taft was catching his breath the moment before Plaid squeezed between them, too, on her hind feet, paws scratching at Mackenzie's jeans.

Taft let out another groan and pulled back to stare down at the dogs. Blackie was attacking his jeans in the same way Plaid was attacking hers.

Taft looked at her and Mackenzie looked back. "Damn dogs," he said.

"Damn dogs," she agreed and then they both started grinning. She saw the dimples hovering inside his three-day growth of beard and wanted to drag his mouth back to hers, his body pressed against her. She restrained herself with an effort as he took a step back, but she didn't have the strength to push herself away from the wall.

"Don't look at me like that," he warned, but the smile still played on his lips and she sucked in a breath when he leaned forward and lightly cupped her chin, tilting her head upward until her eyes met his. "I'm going to tell you something. Don't let it piss you off."

Oh, great. What did that mean?

"I would love nothing better than to spend the rest of the night, all night, right here, with you." The intensity of his gaze said he was telling the truth.

"But . . ." She also heard the unspoken caveat and was flooded with disappointment.

"I'm going to take that bitch down tonight. Stay here. Sleep. Rest. Get your strength back. I'll be back as soon as I have proof and we can . . . pick up where we left off . . ."

"I'm coming with you."

"No. You're beat and I—"

"I'm coming with you!" she insisted. "—don't want you to—"

"I'M COMING WITH YOU, TAFT. Get that through your thick skull!"

"—be caught up in it, in case Ronnie's right."

"Ronnie?"

"Veronica Quick. She told me to call her Veronica or Ronnie, and I—"

"You chose Ronnie?"

"—want you to be safe. Jesus, Laughlin, let me finish!" He was torn between frustration and laughter.

"All I'm hearing is NO. But if you're going, I'm going. That's all. We're partners. You just said so. So treat me like one."

He drew a breath and said slowly, "What we just did wasn't treating you like a partner."

"Partners with benefits, then."

Something flickered in his eyes, but he just shook his head and turned to the pugs. "Be good," he advised them and they grinned and wagged their tails. To Mac, he said, "I don't want you to go because I'm going to break into the Mangella garage."

She felt a little thrill. "B and E. You could lose your license.

I'm still going."

He shook his head and went into his bedroom. He returned a few moments later, tucking his Glock into the back of his jeans and grabbing up the black jacket that lay across the back of a dining chair. She owned a Glock as well, leftover behavior from her time on the force, one that she used to stash under the seat of her car but had resorted to keeping in a drawer in her bedroom as she rarely used it. He surveyed her own black jacket and sweater, which was hiked up a bit in the front. His eyes darkened for a moment, then he turned away as he said, "You're lookout."

"I think—"

"You're lookout," he said again, stronger, shooting her a glance that said there was no further argument if she wanted to go.

She snorted but nodded. Fine. This was his show. Her job, from her point of view, was making sure they both got out unscathed. A shiver of cold fear ran down her spine.

"You're not listening to Ronnie," she said.

"I listened. I'm just not following her advice."

"Semantics."

He opened the door and stepped back. Mackenzie moved forward but his arm blocked her at the threshold. She turned and shot him a warning look, until he said, "For luck," and kissed her hard and fast before she could step into the cold, black night.

Damn, it was good.

Cooper lay in bed next to his wife and listened to her even breathing. It had taken Jamie a long time to fall asleep but now she was dead to the world and it gave him time to think. Humph had buckled to the pressure exerted by Art Stanhope and the mayor and all Stanhope's other wealthy cronies who silently ran the government behind the elected officials. He'd thought things would get better, that the department would stand tough after Chief Bennihof's departure. Humph had seemed like the guy to do it. But his "fight for right" had eroded with all the subversive politics and now Cooper was at a crossroads. *Should I stay or should I go?* It was a crazy question to be asking himself in light of the fact he was soon going to become a father for the first time—twice.

But he'd been burned. Same old political shit.

He wasn't sorry he'd given Taft the results of the

tox screens on Ethan and Ingrid Stanhope. Hiding the information had only muddied the truth. It was just disheartening that the department was back to square one per accountability.

He hadn't told Jamie about his leave-taking thus far. He knew she would be supportive, but he didn't want to worry her unduly. And she'd already dealt with a surprise visit from Mary Jo, whose girth had grown wide as her pregnancy progressed.

Mary Jo had wanted to see Jamie for herself; it was the first time she'd witnessed the evidence of Jamie's own pregnancy. Cooper hadn't been able to tell what the surrogate thought of the situation. She'd actually seemed a bit boggled, but had gotten over it and then acted like she was delighted that "her" child and Jamie's would be almost like twins.

Something a bit odd about Mary Jo, though. Jamie had always felt it, but he had dismissed her fears as this wasn't Mary Jo's first rodeo. She'd been a surrogate before and all had been well. Now, he wondered if he'd been too eager to get started. Mary Jo had been vetted, but . . .

Don't borrow trouble.

He snuggled in closer and Jamie murmured in her sleep.

Bzzz . . . bzzz . . . bzzz . . .

His phone was on the dresser, quietly humming. Gently he eased himself away and walked barefoot to where the cell was charging.

Verbena.

He glanced at the clock. Midnight. Sweeping up the phone, he headed into the upper hallway, quietly snicking the door closed. "Haynes," he answered in a sober voice. She wouldn't be calling if it wasn't important.

"Sorry," she said. "A classmate of Mackenzie Laughlin's, Mia Beckwith, is dead, probably overdosed. And Erin Humbolt, another classmate, was brought in unconscious to Glen Gen. Also an overdose."

He sucked in a breath and moved as quietly as possible down the steps to the first floor.

"I knew you'd want to know."

"These aren't accidental overdoses."

"Doesn't look like it," said Verbena. "I think someone's trying to kill them."

His blood ran cold. "Does Mac know? She could be in danger."

"I've tried to reach her. Phone's off. Left a voice mail."

"Erin Humbolt's still alive?"

"So far. Still unconscious. If she makes it to morning, she's got a good chance, but it's iffy. Front door wasn't properly locked and a cat was roaming around. Neighbor knew it was Erin's and found Erin on the floor as the paramedics arrived. Humbolt had called nine-one-one, but couldn't make herself clear." A pause. "I didn't call you earlier about Mia Beckwith as her family's convinced a boyfriend involved in the marijuana trade treated her like a prisoner and that she slipped the leash whereupon he found her and killed her."

"But you don't think so."

"It looks like something's going on right here in River Glen."

Cooper thought about Gavin Knowles, his death only

a few days ago. And Ethan and Ingrid Stanhope, whose own deaths' cause was hushed up by their father.

And then he thought about Mackenzie, what she'd said about a particular clique calling themselves The Sorority. "There are other classmates who could be in danger. Mac knows them. I don't. Except Kristl Cuddahy. She's a regular at Lacey's and was involved with Tim Knowles."

"On it," said Verbena grimly. "I'll keep trying Mackenzie."

He hung up and phoned Mackenzie. Got the voice mail.

Clicked off and called Taft, got his voice mail as well.

Maybe they were together. He needed to know who the other classmates were, fast.

The Mangellas' quadruple car garage looked vaguely threatening under a row of black barn lights washing the exposed aggregate that served as the wide curving driveway. Or maybe that was just her imagination as they moved silently and quickly, past the obscuring laurel hedge and across the side yard. They'd parked up the street, far enough to be outside of any camera range, though Taft said Mangella was less concerned with security than he ought to have been, something Taft had warned him about more than once back when they were "friends," so working cameras were unlikely anyway.

Taft stopped with Mackenzie behind a tree in the backyard and pressed the Glock into her hands. He'd loaded it in the Rubicon before they'd taken off. Now he handed it to her and Mackenzie felt the cold metal and her heart started a slow, worried cadence.

"Be careful," she mouthed.

He nodded and skulked quickly to the door on the garage's northernmost side. Mac moved around the tree to get a better view. He was bent down in the dark, working the lock, a penlight held in his teeth. She gripped the gun loosely by her side. He was just going to find the Accord, that was all. See if it was there. They would figure out the rest later. Have the scotch tested. Explain about both Prudence and Anna's threats. Find a way to get them arrested.

She shivered, not because it was cold, though the temperature was definitely dipping. She didn't want to think about it, but there was "Ronnie's" warning to consider. Mac didn't believe she was psychic. She didn't believe there even were true psychics. Those who proclaimed they had "powers" were all charlatans and grifters or misguided fools who believed they were tuned into the universe, in her opinion.

She realized she was trembling from head to toe and had to move her shoulders up and down to release tension. There was a soft wind blowing but not enough for her to miss the light snick of the lock opening.

Penlight off . . . and Taft was in.

Hurry, hurry. See if the car's there. Get out.

Nothing happened for a moment and then a strip of light shot out from the door Taft had left cracked open. Someone had flipped on the lights.

And then a voice . . . "I wondered when you'd figure it out."

Anna DeMarcos.

All the hairs on Mac's arms lifted and she was already moving stealthily forward as Taft drawled, "You should have gotten rid of the Accord . . ."

"You're the only one who knows it's here and you're not going to tell."

Bitch. Fucking bitch.

The Glock was ready to fire. Mac held it in front of her with both hands and gently, quietly, carefully moved up to the partially opened door.

"All you had to do was sign off on the will and none of this would have happened," Anna said on a dramatic sigh.

"You rammed Mackenzie's car with a PIT maneuver."

"Well, I don't remember what that is, though Carlos taught me a lot of things, so it's probably true."

Carlos. Her deceased husband. A cop. The one she'd helped murder.

"You also poisoned the scotch and left your calling card," he went on conversationally.

Keep it up, Taft. Buy time. Mac's pulse beat deep and hard.

"What are you talking about? I just left you a love note."

Her voice was cool and amused. "Try proving that one."

Mac took a breath, held it, dared a quick glimpse inside before darting back. Taft was being held at gunpoint, his arms up, his back against the opposite wall, forcing Anna to face him, which kept her back toward Mackenzie.

Mac looked again. Anna was holding the gun like a pro.

Mac started to ease the door open when the door from the house suddenly flew open, freezing Mackenzie where she stood.

Prudence Mangella stood in the door's aperture, but her gaze was on Anna. "What the hell are you doing?" she demanded.

Prudence was in Mac's line of sight. Mac carefully aimed her gun at her, pulse rocketing. If she looked this way . . .

"Saving your fortune," Anna snarled, not in the least intimidated by her friend.

"Well, don't kill him here!"

"You killed Mitch," Taft said to her, but his eyes were on Anna and the gun she held so steadily.

"I only asked him to go up on the roof," Prudence denied. "I didn't know what was going to happen. I heard something. That's all. And he went up and slipped and just slid right off. It was terrible." Her words sounded rehearsed.

"You pushed him," accused Taft.

"I did not!" Prudence turned hard eyes on Anna.

"Or you let Anna do it . . ."

How could he sound so calm? As if being held at gunpoint was something he took in stride. Mac was about out of her mind, counting the seconds. What was her next move? He wouldn't be able to keep them talking forever. Something was going to snap.

Anna said, bored, "Too bad your scruffy little friend survived. I thought she might go over the edge of that ravine. That's where her poor driving got her sent to the hospital last time, right? I pay attention to these things."

Taft's face hardened. "You made a mistake going after Mackenzie."

"Touched a nerve, did I?"

"Anna, stop," Prudence warned and at that moment she glanced toward the door and her eyes widened. "Oh, shit."

Anna jerked her head toward Prudence and Mackenzie threw open the door. In that moment, Taft made a flying tackle at Anna, who yelled and squeezed the trigger.

BLAM!

Taft connected with her the same moment her gun flew from her hand, landing on the step below Prudence's feet. Prudence stared at it and scooped it up.

"STOP!" Mac yelled, aiming at Prudence.

Anna was shrieking and hitting at Taft, who'd pinned her to the cement floor.

Prudence leveled the gun at Anna and pulled the trigger.

BLAM!

The sound deafened in the hollow environs of the garage. Taft jerked his head toward Prudence, who was shaking, her eyes wide as if she couldn't believe what she'd just done. She lifted the gun toward Taft. "Are you going to give me back my money?" she demanded.

Mac's eyes followed the barrel of Prudence's gun as she pointed it at Taft. Mac didn't hesitate. She pulled the trigger.

BLAM! BLAM!

Sheetrock exploded as the bullets ripped into it next to Prudence's head. She screamed and squeezed the trigger. *BLAM!* But Taft had already dived away from Anna. He rolled forward and yanked Prudence by her ankles, hard.

BLAM!

Another bullet sang through the garage, hitting one of the vehicles, but Prudence lost her balance, arms pinwheeling as she toppled off the step, pitched forward, her head smacking into the concrete with a loud *crack*. She lay still but her gun skidded beneath the nearest vehicle to Mackenzie. The one whose protective tarp had been yanked back revealing the blue, smashed right fender of a Honda Accord.

Mac had no time to process that as she flew forward to where Taft was just getting himself into a sitting position. She saw the blood, then, splattered on the right side of his face. Anna's blood? But no, his jacket had pulled back and she could see the spreading carmine stain across his upper chest.

"You're hit." She tried to keep her voice calm, sought to rely on her training, but this was *Taft*.

"My shoulder. It's okay." He looked at the prone bodies.

Neither Anna nor Prudence was moving, though they were both still breathing. Prudence had shot Anna in the head and blood was pooling rapidly beneath her dark hair.

"Call nine-one-one," said Taft.

Mackenzie's fingers were trembling as she pulled her cell from her pocket. They'd left Taft's in the Rubicon. She saw she had several messages but ignored them to punch in the emergency numbers.

"Thank you," he said, indicating where her bullets had ripped into the Sheetrock and scared Prudence into missing a straight shot at him.

"If I were a better shot, I woulda killed her."

"You're a good shot. You missed on purpose."

"If she hadn't shot Anna first . . ." *I would've blasted her to kingdom come.*

"Nine-one-one. What is the nature of your emergency?"

Mac gave her name then quickly listed the particulars about Taft's, Prudence's, and Anna's gunshot wounds and the Mangella address. She left her phone on, but set it aside.

"Let me see that wound," she ordered as Taft had reached inside his coat and come back with a bloody hand.

"Bullet went through under my arm."

She saw how tight-lipped he was, the loss of color in his face. "Shit, Taft. Let me see!" She wanted to cut the jacket off him. "Lean forward."

He obeyed and she gently pulled on the jacket's arm, aching as she saw how he gritted his teeth as his arm slid from the jacket. She paled at the sight of so much blood.

"I've had worse," he said to whatever he could see on her face.

"I know."

He reached up and touched her chin with his good hand, smiling faintly. "I'll live." He then glanced down at the two prone women. Prudence was starting to stir, but Anna was immobile.

"Keep the gun handy," he said grimly.

CHAPTER 22

Taft was sent directly to surgery at River Glen General Hospital—Glen Gen to the locals—as was Anna DeMarcos. Prudence had suffered a concussion and was being monitored at the hospital to make sure there weren't further complications. Mackenzie had told the police that Prudence had shot Anna point blank, so there was an officer stationed outside the door to Emergency's inner sanctum.

Mac had met the EMTs and ambulances at the Mangellas', along with two officers from River Glen P.D., and then had driven Taft's Rubicon to the hospital where she'd anxiously waited outside of surgery for the results on Taft. Detective Verbena was called and she came to interview Mac—twice in one day—clearly roused from sleep and not happy about it. Mac related the sequence of events that had led to the shootings. She'd been tested for gunshot residue on site; Taft's gun was taken from her. She knew the evidence would prove that Prudence had fired the bullet that had hit Anna, and that Anna had been the one to shoot Taft from the same gun, but in the meantime she was peppered long and hard with questions that ran over the same information again and again. Verbena was clearly suspicious over the fact that Taft had inherited the bulk of the Mangella estate, and she wanted to interview Taft as soon as possible. Mac tried to keep from telling exactly how Taft had gotten access to the garage, but Verbena was not the kind of person who overlooked those kinds of details. Because Taft had broken into the garage, it could be construed that Anna had every right to protect herself from an intruder, and therefore every reason to shoot at Taft. But with Mac a witness to what had actually occurred, that would be harder to swallow. In the end it was for a court of law to decide.

Now, Verbena said, "Did Haynes get hold of you?"

Mac was practically pacing in the small waiting room outside the OR, her mind on Taft. "Was he trying to?"

"He wanted to warn you about Erin Humbolt among other things."

Mac stopped short, so sure Verbena had been going to say Mia Beckwith that she'd almost said her name first. "What about Erin?"

"She's a patient here, too." Verbena's brows rose. Clearly she'd expected Mac to know.

Mac gaped. "What happened?"

At that moment the doors to the elevator at the end of the waiting room opened and Cooper Haynes himself stepped out. Relief made Mac's bones damn near liquefy. She hadn't realized how much she'd been holding on by a thread till she saw him. In her mind, he was almost as much a mentor as Taft.

"I'll let Haynes fill you in," Verbena said dryly, clearly seeing Mac's reaction.

Verbena reminded Haynes, "You're on leave," as he strode forward.

"Right. I forgot," he told her, to which she threw him a mock glare and moved away from them.

"She called you?" Mac asked, as Haynes gestured for her to step to the side of the room closer to the elevators.

"She knows I was trying to get hold of you."

Mac felt a warmth for the prickly Verbena who, whether Haynes was on administrative leave or not, was still keeping her partner well informed. "You didn't have to come in the middle of the night."

"It's morning," he pointed out with a faint smile. "When I heard about Erin Humbolt I tried to call both you and Taft."

"We were busy."

"This is totally unofficial. I'm on leave, but I'd like you to give me what you gave Verbena."

"I'm sorry about Art Stanhope."

"Forget it."

"Can you tell me about Erin first?"

"Verbena didn't fill you in?" He didn't wait for a response. "It was a drug overdose. She managed to call nine-one-one."

Mac could feel the blood drain from her face as he explained the circumstances of Erin's call for help and the fact that she was unconscious and still when the paramedics found her. First Mia, then Erin . . . *all just hours ago.*

He finished with, "She may not make it."

Mac nodded grimly. They were saying the same thing about Anna DeMarcos, but she didn't feel any kind of empathy for her. "Mason thinks Mia was followed to River Glen by her boyfriend and that he killed her. Your partner doesn't really think so, and neither do I. Now with Erin . . . it's something closer to home."

He mulled that over and asked, "Can you tell me what you told Verbena?"

So, Mac slowly launched into her tale again, but she also added a brief recap of her meeting with The Sorority. Someone had run Gavin Knowles off the road, someone in a white vehicle. Mac now knew the blue Accord was from the Anna/Prudence camp, and she hadn't seen any white cars outside Kristl's house in the cursory look she'd given the street, but that didn't mean one of them didn't own one.

And what about Roxie? Was it coincidence that she had shown up last night? Natalie said she'd invited her, but when had that invitation been given?

And Kristl . . . who'd genuinely seemed to want Mac at the Sorority meeting. Did she suspect something, or was that giving her too much credit?

Mac was beyond tired. It had been a very long night and she needed sleep, but she wasn't willing to leave the hospital until she knew Taft was all right.

She wrapped up with Haynes, then went to one of the couches and collapsed as Haynes walked over to

THE SORORITY

his partner. She was glad to have a few moments to herself. She knew Taft was going to fully recover, but she wanted to get her eyes on him, wanted to be *sure*.

She could hear a little bit of Haynes's conversation with Verbena. They were treating Erin's overdose as attempted homicide, though there was an outside chance she'd tried to commit suicide, then had changed her mind in the eleventh hour. Everyone was hoping she would wake up soon and be able to tell them what exactly had happened.

Finally, the doctor came out and approached Verbena and Haynes. Mac jumped up, aware they were discussing Taft's injury. She heard enough to learn that he was in recovery and would be transferred to a room soon. He'd sustained enough damage to require a more serious surgery than originally expected.

Anna DeMarcos was still in the operating room.

"You need a ride home?" Haynes asked her as she sighed with relief that Taft was through surgery.

"No, I've got Taft's car. Oh, my God. The *pugs*! What time is it?" She searched in her purse for her phone.

"Six a.m."

"I've gotta go. I think Taft's neighbor's coming today to pick up his dogs, but they've been alone since last night."

She would come right back. Take care of the dogs and return. She hurried out but it took her over an hour to drive Taft's Rubicon back to his place, feed and walk the dogs, then return to the hospital in her rental car. She stalked straight to the OR waiting room again, only to find that no one was there. It took her frustratingly long minutes to learn which room was Taft's and when she finally had the floor and number, she practically burst through the door to find him awake and sitting up, but hazy, his right arm wrapped from shoulder to elbow.

"Hi," he said with a dopey grin.

Mac laughed, then felt tears burn her eyes. She quickly blinked them away. "You look terrible."

"Yeah?"

"I took care of the pugs."

His eyes widened. "Oh, good. God."

"They were pretty glad to see me. I think you said Tommy was coming back today?"

"Yeah . . . he'll let himself in . . ." He shook his head, as if trying to displace the brain fog. Making a face, he asked about Anna and Prudence, so she brought him up to date with what she knew. She also told him about Erin, but wasn't sure he was taking it all in. He needed time to fully come back.

His eyes were closed when she finished and she whispered, "I'll be back later," slipping out before she could disturb him further.

On the drive to her apartment she ran out of energy completely. No sleep and, as Taft had reminded her, she'd been half done in when she got to his place last night. She barely made it up the stairs and through the unit to the bathroom where she stood under the shower till the water ran cold, then stumbled into bed, naked. She fell asleep thinking of being pressed warmly up against Taft.

She awoke hours later, shocked to see the long shadows creeping in through her window. It was a dark day and growing darker. Sweeping up her cell from where she'd left it on her nightstand, she saw it was past four o'clock.

And there was a text from Taft: How're you? I am leaving this hospital if I have to break out.

She grinned and checked the time on the message. An hour ago. She wrote back: Want me to come get you?

Yes.

On my way.

She climbed out of bed, took a look at herself in the mirror, and inwardly groaned. "Scruffy," she muttered aloud. She looked pale and drawn. Well, hell. She hurriedly added some makeup, then put on clean jeans, a dark blue sweater, her black Nikes and jacket. She had a slight headache and wouldn't you know, her ankle, which she'd all but forgotten about, had somehow gotten tweaked in the melee at the Mangella garage and now jabbed her if she moved too fast.

At the hospital, she ran into Taft's surgeon, who very clearly and plainly told Mackenzie that it would be much better if he spent the night at the hospital. The doctor had said the same to Taft, who had not taken it well.

Mackenzie steeled herself to run up against serious resistance when she had to renege on springing him, but when she entered his room his head was sunk into the pillow.

"You're not ready to leave," she said.

He pulled himself upright and sent her a baleful glance. "Yes, I am. Where're my clothes?"

"Your doctor wants you to stay."

"Yeah, well . . ." He didn't finish the thought but his tight lips declared his feelings on his doctor's orders. He tried to lift his bandaged shoulder and said, "It isn't that bad," but the effort clearly cost him.

"Oh, your wound? The one where the bullet ripped through your shoulder and caused a lot of damage?"

"Laughlin, get me out of here."

"I'll see you tomorrow."

"Where are you going?" he snapped.

"Home. To give us both some more rest. I could sleep for a week."

He muttered something beneath his breath, but she ignored him. Cranky was good. Cranky meant the patient was getting better.

Back at her apartment, she beelined for the kitchen and made herself a tuna and pickle sandwich, cutting it into quarters. She sat down to eat it and had to push Ethan Stanhope's laptop to the side of her kitchen table. Holding a piece of the sandwich in one hand, she scrolled aimlessly through Ethan's pictures again with the other. When she finished the sandwich, she got up and grabbed an apple, then returned to the laptop. As she bit into the apple, she thought about The Sorority . . . forcing her mind not to circle back to Taft.

Why had Sam wanted this laptop so badly? she asked herself. Though he'd apparently given up the idea after she and Mason had met him at the Waystation.

Had he been afraid she would find something about the fentanyl, then when she admitted she already knew about it, it hadn't mattered to him any longer?

She moved from the pictures to his documents. She realized with a start that Sam's screenplay was one of the more recent files and when she clicked on the icon it opened to page one. Maybe this was the reason Sam wanted the laptop so badly? Because he'd moved his screenplay to it? He'd been promised the computer and it looked like he'd actually started using it before Coral handed it over to Mac.

She started reading the screenplay, only half paying attention to the words as her mind still kept wandering. Forcing herself to concentrate, she learned that Sam's story was more of a complaint about his main character Stu's life within a wealthy family who didn't understand his fervent desire to play water polo in college and maybe professionally and how he resented being pushed into business classes by his overbearing father. Well, that rang true, she thought with an inward snort.

Mac hadn't read any other screenplays but she could tell this one was all over the place, continually cutting into the narrative by flipping back and forth to flashbacks of high school water polo games that Stu had played against opponents. There were so many characters listed who didn't seem to have any point in the present day, where Stu was slaving away as a middle manager in an insurance company with minimal chance of moving up, all the while dreaming about his past and what could have been if only he'd followed his heart. In the end he improbably finally got placed on an underdog team that had no chance of winning, except Stu nearly single-handedly led the team to victory. End of story. Stu never had any breakthrough moment with his overbearing father, nor did he come to grips with the accident that killed his two siblings even though that was a big part of the screenplay's first scenes. So much of the story was taken up with high school water polo game after high school water polo game, that it felt like Stu was still living in the past.

Mac figured Coral and Art Stanhope had never read the screenplay. If they had, they probably wouldn't have been so concerned about it as it didn't really explore their family tragedy.

She sat back and closed her eyes. Something was tickling her brain. All those games felt like real memories and probably were.

She looked at the screen again and slid her finger across it, backing up a number of pages, settling on one of the games where Stu's team had lost. One of the players on the opposing team was named Sumner Parker. It had caught Mac's attention, she realized, as she breezed through the first read, but she hadn't made the connection till now. The name was almost the reversal of Parker Sommers, Leigh's husband. Was that just a coincidence? Or did Sam know Parker? Was he from the area? Leigh had said she met Parker at musical theater camp, but that didn't preclude Parker and Sam from crossing paths.

Mac exited the screenplay and clicked back onto

Ethan's pictures. She scrolled through them again, concentrating harder on the ones from water polo games. There was Ethan . . . and there was Sam in several pictures. Though the brothers were two years apart, they'd both made the varsity team Sam's senior year and Ethan's sophomore. She slowly checked out other photos, examining the members of the visiting teams . . . and stopped short at one photo in particular. The guy was wearing swim goggles and his hair was covered beneath a tight rubber cap as he was caught half leaping from the water to catch a ball. Could that be Parker? Something about his mouth made her think it was.

What school was River Glen playing? It was impossible to tell from the picture.

Would Parker have also been in drama at his school, or possibly community theater? Maybe that's why he seemed so familiar? Maybe she, Mac, had seen him in a production?

She picked up her phone and called Leigh, whose cell went straight to voice mail. Mac clicked off. Well, okay. Leigh was probably still ignoring her calls if she was anywhere near Parker.

She glanced at the time. Parker Flooring would still be open and Leigh would likely be there. Was it worth going to talk to Parker about his possible friendship with Sam Stanhope?

She settled for calling Sam himself, even though he'd made it pretty clear he wanted nothing to do with Mackenzie. But he did pick up the cell and answer with, "Who is this?"

"Hi, Sam, it's Mackenzie Laughlin. I wanted to let you know you can have Ethan's laptop back."

"Okay . . ." He was surprised by her call and sounded like he was looking for the catch.

"I noticed you have your screenplay on it."

"Yeah, I was working on it. But I've got it on a flash drive, too," he let her know, as if he thought Mac was criticizing him.

"Okay. Well. It's here if you want it, or I can drop it by."

"No . . . I'll pick it up. Maybe tomorrow."

"I also saw that you were on the water polo team with Ethan. And I recognized Parker Sommers in one of the photos."

"Okay."

"He was at Glenview?"

"No, Laurelton. Valley Sunset High."

"Laurelton. Leigh said she met him at musical theater camp. I thought he was from farther away. I didn't realize he was so multitalented."

"Yeah, well, Parker was an all-around guy. What time should I pick up the laptop?" he asked hurriedly.

The thread of tension in his voice came through over the phone. If it wasn't the screenplay that made him so desperate to have the laptop back, then what was it?

His anxiety had really ramped up when she'd mentioned Parker.

She could hear him breathing hard on the other end of the line and decided to take a wild guess. "Parker was your dealer, wasn't he? Ethan knew it and when you and Mason wouldn't give him the fentanyl, he went right to the source."

"*What?* Fuck, no! I didn't have a dealer. We didn't . . . have one. You don't know what you're talking about. It wasn't like that with Parker or anyone . . . it wasn't that way."

It really sounded like it was.

"Ethan didn't know about the fentanyl," he went on without waiting for her to say anything. "You're trying to make this something it's not. You're trying to pin the blame on us when it was just an accident!"

"Maybe I was wrong," Mac allowed, trying to ease off the topic with him, though she was pretty sure she'd landed on the truth. She'd gotten what she needed and now just wanted off the phone.

"You're such a fucking bitch," he snarled but there was fear in his voice as he clicked off.

"You're going to have to try a lot harder than that," she muttered. She'd been called names from about everyone she'd questioned, a sign she was on the right track.

Mac wondered if Leigh knew that Parker had likely been Mason and Sam's dealer ten years earlier. Was Parker still involved with the drug trade? How strong were the tentacles into that world?

She got into her Focus and cruised to Parker Flooring. Thought about alerting Taft, but then diverted to Cooper Haynes as a backup. Since he'd left her messages on her phone she had his number, so she redialed his cell. He answered almost immediately with a worried "Mackenzie?"

"I just was going to call Taft and let him know where I was going in case something happened. Like you and I talked about earlier, there've been a lot of deaths, but I didn't want to worry him and—"

"Where *are* you going?" he interrupted.

"Parker Flooring, to talk to Leigh Sommers. I don't really expect anything to happen." She was debating whether to reveal her feelings on Parker, but heard the voices of his family members and realized they might be preparing dinner. "I'll call you when I leave, all right?"

"Yeah, don't forget or I'll be calling you."

She drove to Parker Flooring under leaden skies that opened up just as she pulled into the lot. She saw Leigh's Tesla and several other vehicles, a Humvee and some vans, parked toward the back of the lot. So, Leigh was here, and Parker as well.

She didn't have a rain hat and hurried through the sudden spate, shaking water from her hair beneath the awning over the front door. She twisted the knob and let herself inside and waited for one of the salespeople to approach her as they did last time. After five minutes she stepped farther into the room, peering around the rows of flooring samples, but the place was deserted. Pulling out her phone, she checked the time. Straight up six. Maybe they'd all gone home and someone had forgotten to lock the door.

So, where were Leigh and Parker? She cruised by the offices at the back of the room but the doors were closed, curtains drawn, lights out. She listened at the door to the warehouse and heard the faint beeping from what sounded like the warning of a vehicle backing up. She tried the door and found it unlocked. Opening it, she listened and heard the light grumble of an engine and saw the strobing yellow flashes of light from whatever vehicle was moving behind the row upon row of marble, granite, and quartzite slabs.

She cautiously stepped forward just as said vehicle rounded the corner to where she was walking. It was moving slowly, holding a huge slab of gray-veined marble in its front claws. Leigh was in front of it, moving quickly down the row toward Mackenzie. Mac opened her mouth to greet her when the vehicle suddenly sped up, coming straight at Leigh, the enormous slab practically at Leigh's heels. Jesus!

"Look out!" Mac yelled.

Parker's head snapped out of the vehicle's cab and he glared at her. "Get out of the way!" he roared at her.

Panicked, Leigh ran toward Mac, who'd stopped short when the vehicle picked up speed. Now she grabbed for Leigh, pulling her toward her, and both of them started racing away from Parker. Mac turned onto a row perpendicular to where she was running, and Leigh skidded and grabbed at her and made the turn, too.

Parker slammed on the brakes and the slab of marble crashed to the ground.

Mac didn't know whether he'd lost it or dropped it on purpose. She hung onto Leigh. They were both breathing hard. Then Leigh was barreling ahead with Mac on her heels. Behind them, she heard Parker shift gears to turn their way.

"He's trying to kill me!" Leigh sobbed. Her makeup was running in rivulets down her face and there was a rip in the sleeve of her green blouse.

"We gotta get out of here!" Mac yelled. "Call the police!"

"He's crazy! He knows I know about Ethan."

Parker was having trouble getting the machine to squeeze through the smaller side rows. "Here!" Leigh ran to a door against the far wall, yanked it open, and then she and Mac were running down a concrete corridor that ended back near the offices.

"What does he know about Ethan?" Mac asked, panting, looking behind them as they careered into the main showroom. "That Ethan stole the drugs. Had 'em in the pool house. Mia knew and Erin saw 'em. I didn't know that till yesterday. And then . . . and then . . ." She fumbled with keys for one of the offices.

Hurry . . . but no . . . "We need to leave, Leigh. We need to leave. He can't trap us in the office."

"We're safe here!" She pushed Mac inside and Mac fell against a desk as Leigh locked the door from the inside. Her ankle throbbed and it was dark as pitch till Leigh switched on the light. Mac blinked in the sudden blast.

"And then fucking Roxie had to remind them all . . . *I Eta Pi*. And Erin looked at me and knew. Just like Mia knew. Parker's had his thumb on me all these years because he's blamed me for what happened, which is so unfair, because he's the one who got the pills in the first place. I just used some of them."

Mac stared at Leigh, her chest heaving as she caught

her breath. She gazed at the twin black streaks running over the hill of her cheeks. "What?"

"You were right. Mia never wrote that note to me. I was just trying to push you to find her. She stopped talking to me and started blaming me, too. I had to find her!"

"For what?" Mac held her gaze but in her peripheral vision she was looking behind Leigh to the door. She needed to twist open the lock and get out but Parker was likely somewhere outside this room, off the machine but still in pursuit.

"For giving Ethan the pie. I didn't know about Ingrid. I just wanted him to die, like we'd all pledged. I never expected him to actually crash the car. That was . . . *Karma*! But Ingrid wasn't supposed to be part of it."

"Leigh, I don't know what you did, but we need to get away from Parker."

"I was just doing what we all agreed on. I didn't know about Ingrid! All of a sudden I'm the bad guy. But Parker was the one who sold Ethan the drugs! I just put them in the pie."

"You doctored a *pie*?" Mac saw again the strange look on Erin's face at the moment Roxie declared, "*I Eta Pi.*"

"I put it on the back seat of his car, watched him drive away, the asshole. I brought the pie to grad night. I'd crushed the pills. People ate off it before I added the powder under the crust. I could tell Ethan was leaving, so I wrapped it up and put it in his car."

Mac blinked at her, just as Parker roared again and

slammed his fists against the window to the showroom. Both Mac and Leigh jumped, but Leigh just yanked open a drawer and grabbed a wicked-looking knife, one used for cutting carpet.

"Holy shit. Leigh, don't use that. We need—"

"It's Elayne," she snarled. "Elayne Denning. I'm not staying married to that fucking leech." Her blue eyes were lit by a flame of fury. "He blackmailed me into marriage. I've been acting for years . . . the loving, dutiful wife. He told me I wouldn't get the part. He cursed me. You know what I ended up getting in Chicago? One of the jailbirds. That's it. That's all!"

Mac was beginning to see that Leigh—Elayne— was teetering on the edge of crazy. No arguing with her, so she changed tactics. "Those are good parts, too."

"It was a mistake to hire you. I should've just pushed on Mason. He would've given her up."

Parker howled with frustration and then there was silence. What was he doing? Mac couldn't trust either of them. "Did you . . . see Mia yesterday?" she asked cautiously.

"You mean, did I kill her?" She struggled to answer. "I met her for coffee and she was all upset about Ben, but then she said we couldn't be friends because she knew I'd killed Ethan! But she was done with him. She said so. I knew it, she knew it! She pledged with the rest of us. Erin got it wrong, but then Erin . . ." She clenched her fists. "She knew . . . when Roxie cackled, 'I ate a pie,' she knew. She always knew but pushed it down. She was so grateful to me. But I saw that she remembered . . ." Leigh cocked an ear to the sample room. "What's he doing? Don't trust him. *What's he doing?*"

"Leigh—Elayne—what about Gavin?"

"Asshole!" she snarled. "Blaming us all . . . but they aren't my friends anyway. You saw them. They're all a mess and they think I'm the one with problems!"

"I didn't hear that, I thought—"

"I should have never hired you! And then Kristl invited you! You know why, don't you? She wants to be *friends*." She said it like it was a dirty word. "Because The Sorority isn't about friendship. It's about power and popularity. That's what we had, but Ethan . . ." She gritted her teeth. "Erin had sex with him. Can you believe it? The worst of us and he fucked *her*?"

She was jumping all over the place. Mac said carefully, "Is that why you gave Ethan the pie?"

"You're not listening! I just found that out *yesterday*!"

"I'm sorry." Where was Parker? Mac glanced at the door.

"Open your eyes, Mackenzie. They were all backstabbing me: Parker, Mia, Erin, Natalie, Kristl, *Roxie*." She spat the last name out. "None of them cared about Ethan like I did and I would have done anything for him after . . . how nice he was to me!" Her voice broke and her hand shook. Mac looked down at the wicked, curved blade of the carpet cutter.

Mac was counting the seconds, expecting something

from Parker. She wasn't certain Leigh would actually use the knife, but she was volatile and emotional and unpredictable. It appeared she'd killed Ethan and Ingrid, and Gavin and Mia . . . because she was *jealous*?

"I loved him and he failed me," said Leigh. A declaration. "He was a cheater," Mac suggested carefully.

"He *was* a cheater," she agreed. "But I knew he was a cheater."

"That's why you gave him the pie."

"NO! He told me I was a shit actor! He laughed at me. Said Summer Cochran was terrific and that I was *third string*. He was drunk, but he meant it. I thought he cared but it was all a lie!"

"What happened with Parker?" she asked. "Are you taking his side?" Leigh demanded. "No, I just don't know—"

"ELAYNE!" Parker suddenly screamed.

Leigh's face went blank. She suddenly jumped forward, slashing. She caught the arm of Mac's coat, slicing through, scratching her skin. Mac grabbed her arm as the office window suddenly burst apart, glass spraying everywhere. Leigh screamed and whipped around as Parker took the chair he'd broken the window with and threw it at her. It knocked her sideways, and Mac leapt for the door, fingers fumbling on the lock.

She yanked the door open but Parker bowled into her, throwing her into the desk again. Leigh leapt forward with a war shriek and ripped the carpet cutter across Parker's face.

He howled in fury and grabbed for her.

Mac jumped forward, seeking freedom. Leigh grabbed her by the hair, jerking her head back. "Don't leave!" Leigh snarled.

Mac saw the curving blade above her eyes. Oh, God . . . ! *Holy God . . . !*

Parker yanked Leigh by the neck, spinning her around. Mac stumbled forward, through the door, and crashed into one of the rows of samples, tiles flying all around her. She covered her head, tried to get her feet under her. Looked back. Saw Parker wrest the blade from Leigh's hands. Toss it aside. Leigh clawed his face with her nails. Broke free. Staggered forward. Reached for the knife again, holding it, twisting her hand.

Parker jumped on her and she collapsed with a scream that sent cold shivers down Mac's back. He banged her head against the floor as Mac scrabbled for her phone, staggering forward.

She ran for the front door and the outside and ran and ran, sloshing through the mud puddles to her rental, skidding to a stop. She'd left it unlocked and threw herself inside.

Parker came screaming out of the door but Mac was already reversing, spraying water, her tires shrieking. He snatched for her driver's door, hooked his hand. She slammed the Focus into drive and the car leapt forward, dragging him a few feet before he wrenched his hand free.

She barreled out of the lot, nearly smashing into rush-hour traffic. She dared a glance back. Parker was standing in the rain, clutching his hand as dark, bloody streaks ran down his ravaged face. As soon as she was far enough away to feel safe, she dialed 911 with one hand.

Epilogue

Three days later, Natalie stared out the window of her Pearl District condo, her cell phone pressed to her ear as she listened to Beatrix tell her all the reasons why they wouldn't be producing *Rose City Ren-O*. Phillip had come back from Sedona and he and Beatrix were working out a deal between them with that shit piece of property he'd bought against her wishes. Surprise, surprise, saving his beige soul hadn't been as important as cold, hard cash. They wanted to cut her out but Phillip had forced her into ownership of half that property, so she was now going to require an epic ransom from them if they wanted her share. Maybe with the money she would receive she could get her Portland show off the ground on her own. Maybe not. With all the bad press that had been coming out the past few days about how The Sorority had pledged to kill Ethan Stanhope, catching Ingrid in the trap, she didn't think she'd be hosting anything anytime soon.

And Leigh . . . Elayne . . . Natalie was infuriated with her for turning the joke into a reality, killing not only

Ethan and Ingrid, but more recently Gavin—with a white van—and Mia, by hypodermic. She'd apparently confronted Erin with a hypodermic, too, and the little bug-eyed squirrel was lucky to be alive.

Kristl had called and said she'd spoken to Mackenzie, who had revealed that Leigh—*Elayne*—had admitted to lacing a cherry pie with fentanyl and putting it in Ethan's car. Somewhere during the night, Ethan and Ingrid must have both eaten the pie.

Leigh was in the hospital with a twelve-inch gash in her stomach from some carpet-cutting tool, and her husband, Parker, had been treated as well. They'd been in some kind of horrific fight, which Mackenzie had stumbled into, and there were criminal charges now leveled at both of them. There were rumors that Parker was, or had been, a drug dealer, and that the fentanyl that killed the Stanhopes was purchased from him by Mason Beckwith and Sam Stanhope, both of whom denied they gave it to Ethan. The media was trying to contact Mason and Sam about Parker, but neither of them was talking. Leigh, apparently, had a lot to say, as long as you addressed her as Elayne Denning, as she was now insistent that was her name. Natalie had assumed Leigh killed Ethan out of jealousy, but there was another rumor that she'd gone pure psycho because Ethan had dissed her acting skills.

Natalie snorted. "They're all psychos," she muttered as soon as she was off the phone with Beatrix. And that included Phillip. Leigh/Elayne wasn't the only one heading for divorce.

Natalie wasn't quite sure what had happened to cause

Leigh to go after Gavin and Mia. Fear of discovery? Revenge? Maybe some jealousy, whether she was admitting it or not. Or maybe it was just that Gavin was an ass and Mia was Ethan's ex. There was a theory that Mia had been chased down by her jealous lover, but that had proved untrue. Kristl had said that she talked to Erin, who was out of the hospital now, and that Erin had seen Leigh putting the tainted pie in Ethan's car. Roxie's "*I Eta Pi*" reminded Erin of the pie Leigh had put in Ethan's car, so that's why she was targeted.

The whole thing was a Greek tragedy, or maybe a farce. She was just glad that Leigh had left her alone.

Her cell buzzed again and Natalie's brows lifted when she saw it was Roxie. She hadn't completely forgiven her for whisking away with hardly a word, but whatever. "Well, hello," she answered. "Where are you these days?"

"L.A. Jeremy's got some interesting friends in the film business. I told you about them, didn't I?"

"I don't think so."

"Well, I told them about what's happening in River Glen and his friend's production company is really interested."

For a moment, Natalie's hopes had soared, thinking it was going to be something to do with her condo renovation idea, but then she realized Roxie meant the Leigh debacle. "Seriously." She snorted.

"Yes. And I told them about you, and they saw some of your shows and think you'd be right for the narrator of the whole story. I mean, who better than the person who started the pledge?"

"It was a joke," Natalie said automatically.

"And that's a great title: *It Was a Joke*. Why don't you come back to sunny SoCal and meet with them. We can work out some stuff."

"You're involved in this project?"

"Well, maybe. Jeremy thinks I have what it takes to coproduce with him."

Natalie blinked several times. She'd only really searched out and befriended Roxie to deliver the big surprise to the rest of The Sorority. She'd never thought of her as anything but a silly, slutty girl-next-door type. She'd never considered she might actually have some brains.

"I could fly to L.A.," she said.

"Do it," Roxie urged her and Natalie clicked off and gazed out at the skyline one more time, a bemused smile on her lips.

Maybe Portland could be her bread and butter after all. Portland and River Glen. She was just going to have to go to Hollywood to make it happen.

Kristl flushed her treasure trove of pills down the toilet. The ones that she hadn't dissolved in her mother's oatmeal. She'd fixed up that oatmeal and then stared at it a long, long time before she'd dumped it down the disposal. She'd almost given it to Mom because she never wanted to hear "Krissy!" as long as she lived. But she'd waited, trying to work out just what her life would be like with her mother off to the great beyond and her the ungrateful daughter who'd murdered her. She'd wanted to be free. More than that, she wanted to be loved. She'd wanted Tim, yes, but maybe he was just a symbol of that love, not the real thing.

She hadn't really understood why she'd invited Mackenzie to the meeting with the other members of The Sorority. Leigh had always been the one to cheerlead about how Mackenzie should be a part of their group, which Kristl had always thought was a no-go because Mac just wasn't like the rest of them. Mac just didn't care about the same things they did.

But Mac had driven her home after the bar fight, making sure she was okay. It had just been so *selfless* compared to her other friends that Kristl had wanted to see more of her. She'd been seduced by Mac's sanity. And then after The Sorority got together the other night and Kristl knew they'd all seen the pills, like her, but they didn't know she'd taken some for herself, and then Mac had informed them that Ethan died of an overdose . . . it just felt like it was time to DO something. Like tell Mac about the pledge . . . and finally give herself permission to use the pills . . . on Mom. She'd gone so far as to wear a mask and smash them up and put them in her oatmeal.

And then Mackenzie had called. Like she was an old friend. Like *she* was worth something. And she'd told her about Leigh and Parker and Erin. Had actually thought to inform her. *And* had apologized for leaving the meeting *early*. Wow. "Krissy? Krissy, come here."

Kristl walked down the hallway to the bedroom and looked down at her mother, really looked at her. Mom stared back at her, her already lined face creasing with worry.

"I think we need to have a talk," Kristl said.

"I want something other than oatmeal."

"I'm calling for in-home services. I've got some brochures on assisted living places. You need more care than I can give you. I'm going to get a job and figure out the rest of my life and make it so we're both happier."

"I want mashed potatoes and gravy. I like those little red potatoes, too."

Kristl smiled and patted her mother's shoulder, then walked out of the room and began scrolling through her cell phone.

Mac sat beside Taft on the couch. She'd collected him from the hospital two days earlier and had offered to play nursemaid, saying, "You took care of my ankle, I can take care of you."

Taft had wanted her to take his bedroom while he slept on the couch, just like the last time she'd stayed at his place while he'd recovered, and just like that last time, she'd refused. In truth, he was doing fine and probably didn't need her attention, but neither of them had wanted to change the status quo as yet.

"How's Erin?" he asked now, as she'd checked in with her.

"Home. Glad to be back with her cat, who's been staying at the neighbors."

"Good."

Silence fell between them, the same unspoken awkwardness that had developed since the shooting in Mangella's garage. Gone was the flirtatious edge and promise of intimacy to come. A wall had formed between them. The damn wall that she'd worried about from the moment she'd acted on her impulses that prompted the kiss. And they hadn't even had real sex!

It was a pisser, and she wasn't entirely sure if the wall had been erected by him, or by herself.

"Sorry about the Macallan," she said, not for the first time. She'd turned the bottle of scotch over to the police crime lab where it was being tested.

"Anna," he said, grimacing.

Anna DeMarcos had died shortly after surgery and Prudence Mangella was in custody for homicide.

It was late in the afternoon on a surprisingly sunny November day. Thanksgiving was around the corner and Stephanie was already making plans to have dinner at her place. Mackenzie had mentioned the meal to Taft, who generally eschewed holiday functions, had since he'd lost his sister. He hadn't committed to joining her but Stephanie needed an answer, so she brought it up again.

To her surprise, Taft reached over and clasped her hand, threading his fingers through hers. She stared at him.

Glad you called Haynes before you went to Parker Flooring. You always need backup."

She peered at him. He was saying that now but she knew he hadn't felt the same way when he'd first heard. Instead he'd gone ultra quiet. Unusual for him.

"But . . . ?" She could tell he was heading somewhere, somewhere she was pretty sure she didn't want to go.

"I wasn't there for you."

"Well, yeah, but we know why. That's not unexpected," she said dismissively.

"I was powerless to help you. I don't want to feel that way again."

"What does that mean?"

"I need to rethink this partnership." He'd been staring straight ahead, his eyes narrowed, but now he turned to her, giving her the full blast of those blue eyes. "I don't like the danger this job puts you in."

"Come on, Taft. I was a cop before. I know what the risks are."

"I can't do both, Laughlin. Partner and lover. I know it. And I think you know it, too."

"Well, we haven't been lovers, yet," Mac pointed out, her throat dry.

"But we're going to be." His gaze dropped to her mouth and stayed there for a long moment, causing Mac's pulse to rocket. Then he drew a breath and lifted his eyes to hers again, arching one brow. "Or we're going to be partners."

"We can't try to do both?"

"Go home. Think about it. I can get along fine tonight. We need to figure this out because whatever happens, I'm not losing you."

He could have added "too" onto that statement because she knew he was also thinking about Helene. He was basically saying he considered her family, which was what she now understood she yearned for. But it also put a pretty clear point on the fact he believed it was one or the other, lover or partner/friend/family.

Well, hell.

She remembered that kiss he gave her for luck. How breathless she'd felt.

And then watching Anna hold him at gunpoint, hearing the shot, seeing the red, red blood stain his sweater.

"Ronnie was right," she said hoarsely. "You shouldn't have gone to Mangella's that night."

"The danger was there, whenever I decided to go."

"You believe her more than you're saying."

"That she's a psychic?" He shook his head.

Mac let it go. Taft slowly unclasped his hand from hers and she got to her feet. "I don't like making this choice."

"I don't either."

Then don't, she thought, heart squeezing painfully, but the truth was he had a valid point. A very valid point. Because she didn't want to ever see him a hairsbreadth from death again like she had in Mangella's garage.

"Emma!" Harley said, staring at her as she bit into the sandwich Harley had called a yee-ro.

Emma chewed carefully and looked around the dinner table. Harley and Cooper were watching her closely. Marissa, too. They'd all gone to a food cart that specialized in Greek food and brought home yee-ros and salads with lots of cucumbers and onions and round pita bread and hummus and something with yogurt. Marissa had flown home from college for the weekend because Cooper had lost his job for telling on someone who'd hidden the truth, which was a bad idea.

"What do you think?" asked Harley. She had a sandwich she called a chicken shawarma.

"I like it," Emma said.

Harley held up her hands. "Okay. Full disclosure. I've got to tell you something. It's lamb. I don't think you've had lamb before. You okay with that? There's another chicken shawarma if you're not."

Emma thought about lambs. They were cute. And she was eating one. But she ate cows and chickens all the time. "I'm okay with it."

Marissa was looking at Cooper. She wasn't really his daughter. She had a different father, but she called him Dad. She'd been looking at him a lot since she got home. "So, when do you find out?" she asked.

"It's a process," Cooper said in that way that meant he didn't want to talk about it.

"Is Jamie eating the lambs?" Emma asked.

"Doubtful," said Harley. "I'll take her the shawarma." She pushed back her chair even though she hadn't finished her own shawarma.

Harley headed up the stairs and Duchess leapt to her feet and followed after her. Twink was in with Jamie and Emma thought Duchess being there was a bad idea. She knew how that went.

"Everything's okay with Jamie, right?" Marissa sounded worried.

"Yes. Everything's fine," said Cooper. "Except the job thing."

"Except the job thing," he repeated.

"He doesn't want to talk about it," Emma informed Marissa.

Marissa made a face. "I know."

Cooper's cell phone buzzed and he plucked it from his pocket. Normally he switched it off at the dinner table, but this time he frowned at the screen and then said, "Hello," in that way that sounded like he was worried, and then he got up from his chair and walked down the hall to the back door. Emma heard him open the door, walk outside, then close it behind him.

"He doesn't want us to hear," she said.

"I guess he needs privacy," Marissa agreed.

"He feels bad about not having a job."

"I know, Emma."

Marissa got up quickly and took her plate to the sink. Emma thought maybe she should stop asking Cooper all those questions if she already knew he felt bad.

The back door opened again and a swirl of cold air came in, then Cooper was back. He had his "cop face" on. The one where Jamie always said, "Uh-oh," when she saw it.

"What happened?" Marissa demanded.

"I need to talk to Jamie," he said.

He headed upstairs, taking them two at a time. Marissa looked at Emma and Emma looked back at her. Emma heard Cooper ask Harley to leave the bedroom. He needed some private time with her mom.

Harley stepped into the hallway and Cooper shut the door. But Harley stayed on the landing. Marissa made hand gestures at Harley that meant she wanted to know what was going on. Harley put her finger to her lips and leaned in close to the door. Duchess gave a few barks and Harley flapped her hand at the dog, shooing her downstairs.

"Duchess!" Emma yelled and Duchess reluctantly bent her head and slowly came down the stairs. She wanted to stay up and listen at the door like Harley. Emma grabbed her by the collar as soon as she was near to keep her from going back up.

A few minutes later, Harley suddenly hurried away from the door and sneaked back down the stairs to them. Her eyes were really big.

"*What?*" demanded Marissa.

Harley drew a shaky breath. "Mary Jo's husband called. She's missing. She's been gone for a few days. Mom's trying not to freak out, but she's barely holding it together. Cooper's trying to assure her that they'll find her, but I don't know. God, Mom was so right about Mary Jo!"

Marissa just stared with her mouth open.

"Uh-oh," said Emma.

Visit our website at
KensingtonBooks.com
to sign up for our newsletters, read more from your favorite authors, see books by series, view reading group guides, and more!

Become a Part of Our
Between the Chapters Book Club
Community and Join the Conversation

Submit your book review for a chance to win exclusive Between the Chapters swag you can't get anywhere else!
https://www.kensingtonbooks.com/pages/review/